D1349071

DAMASCUS
CHRISTOS TSIOLKAS

atlantic·*fiction*

First published in Australia in 2019 by Allen & Unwin.

Published in hardback in Great Britain in 2020 by Atlantic Books,
an imprint of Atlantic Books Ltd.

Map by Wayne van der Stelt.

10 9 8 7 6 5 4 3 2 1

A CIP catalogue record for this book is available from the British Library.

Hardback ISBN: 978 1 83895 021 7
E-book ISBN: 978 1 83895 023 1

Atlantic Books
An imprint of Atlantic Books Ltd
Ormond House
26–27 Boswell Street
London
WC1N 3JZ

www.atlantic-books.co.uk

Printed and bound by CPI Group (UK) Ltd, Croydon, CR0 4YY

For Malcolm Knox, with gratitude

'. . . for he who always hopes for the best becomes old, deceived by life, and he who is always prepared for the worst becomes old prematurely; but he who has faith, retains eternal youth.'

Fear and Trembling, Søren Kierkegaard

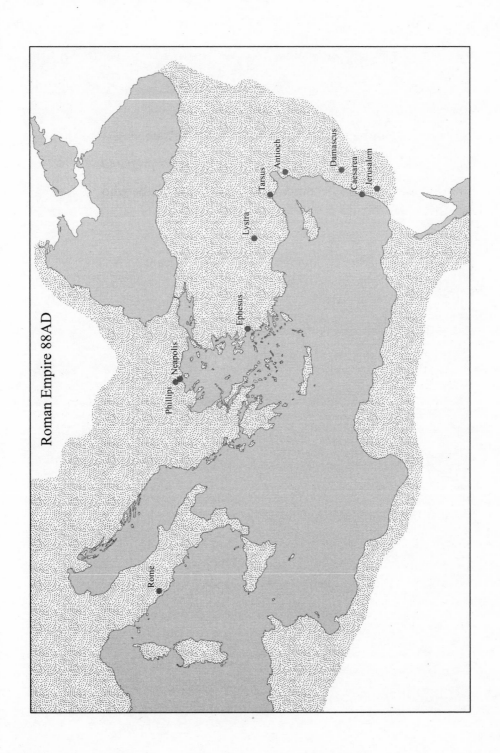

Roman Empire 88AD

Saul I

35 ANNO DOMINI

'Where were you when I laid the foundation of the earth? Tell me, if you have understanding.'

—THE BOOK OF JOB

The world is in darkness. The hood the guards have placed over her head scratches at her cheeks and neck. She takes fleeting comfort from the smell of the greasy fibre, the odours of sheep and goat. From her first memory their bleating was part of her life. They were her companions during the day and over countless nights, when she'd join them in their rough stable to escape the drunken violence of her father and her brothers, and then that of her husband. The warm bodies of the goats had been her solace and her bed; they had been her work and her friends.

She also recognises another smell, far more noxious. Fear. How many others has this hood covered? The stink of their terror is soaked through the fibres. With every hoarse breath she too releases the acrid taint of fear. She must not let them know her dread. She prays. *Our Lord is a shepherd, He is not a king or a priest or a master, our Lord is a shepherd.* With every silent repetition of that prayer, the demon that is fear subsides. She falls into calmness.

The rope that binds the caul is loosened and a tremor of light battles with the darkness. The hood is snatched off her and the overwhelming sunlight burns her eyes. The world is white: blinding, terrifying white. At first there is only that brilliance of light. Then she discerns the shadows. And as those shadows take form she sees that she is in the centre of a circle. Surrounding her are bearded men, each one holding a rock. As her eyes adjust to the day, she can see the sun flaring off the wall of the Sacred City in the distance. Then she sees crows and vultures wheeling above her. They are in a gully—it is accursed ground. And with that thought, fear reclaims her. On this ground she will die. Piss runs down her legs, darkens her smock, streams onto the stony ground. Her hands are still tied behind her back so she cannot cover her shame. She drops to a crouch.

One of the men marches up to her and roughly grabs her shoulder, forcing her to stand. His nails dig through the cloth and bite into her flesh. But this pain she can endure. She stares at the man; he's a youth, not much older than she is. His eyes are dark and pitiless. She knows those eyes, knows such contempt. He wants her to scream, to curse, he wants her to hate him. And she wishes she could curse, could strike him dead with her words. Then she remembers the shocking and unbearable commandment of the prophet. Love him. Love him as if he were of your blood. She shudders, she leans forward, her lips graze his cheek.

'Whore!' He strikes her with such force that she sprawls across the dusty ground. She sees him marching towards her, she sees his foot lift. She closes her eyes, bracing for the kick.

'Enough.' The priest's command is sharp. She dares open her eyes. The man has returned to his place.

She struggles, falters, wavers to her feet. This time she sees an old man and a boy standing beyond the circle in the shade of a laurel. From the splashes of dye across their cheeks she recognises them as deathworkers. They will return her body to the earth when her soul ascends to the Lord. A little beyond them stands the man who tricked her. How gentle his questions had been; his sympathy almost womanly. She fixes her gaze on him, his broad forehead, the receding coils of his black hair. He looks away as soon as her eyes meet his. Fear. She sees that he too is filled with fear.

The young man who struck her has raised his arm, stone held high above his head.

'Adulteress!' he roars. 'Ask the Lord to pardon your wicked sins!'

The circle of men rumble assent. At the meanness of that charge, she begins to weep. Her eyes turn again to the man who'd seduced her with his false kindness. She had believed him to be as she was, bonded to the Saviour, trusting in the marriage of their fellowship, understanding that she was now married to her brothers and sisters. He had nodded in fierce agreement, as if he too comprehended that real marriage wasn't the ugly, forced rutting she had experienced with her husband. After discovering friendship, knowing kindness, awaking for the first time to a world in which men need not be cruel, how could she return to that vileness? And he had nodded and agreed. She had been drawn to his sympathy. Yet it had been his testimony which had condemned her.

Her innocence and anger fortify her. She is no whore and she has not betrayed the Lord. She faces her accuser. He will not look at her. Her mouth is dry but she must speak. She doesn't care about the other men in the circle. She wants that coward to hear her words.

'If you are without sin, then cast your stone.'

One of the men steps forward. 'Shut your ungodly mouth!'

She spins to face the speaker and as she does the first rock smashes her shoulder. She stumbles and falls. A rock slams into her neck, it steals her breath. Another rips open her brow. And then she hears the crack of the world splitting, as if the heavens above are tearing. There is darkness. There is blood in her mouth. There is a pain so terrible that she knows it is not the world that is breaking but her own body.

And then the darkness lifts and there is light.

The men keep hurling the rocks but the girl is dead and so justice is done.

———

The priest hurries through the prayers, conscious of the pulsating heat of the rising sun and the black swarm of flies already descending on the pariah's body. The white prison shawl is dark with blood. As he intones the last word, the men quickly bend to drag their hands along the ground, rubbing the grit across knuckles, fingers, palm and wrist, beginning their purification.

The priest turns towards the south gate of the city and the men follow him. Not one of them looks at the bowed man, hunched on his knees, his head and body twitching in furious prayer.

Saul looks up only when he can no longer hear their footsteps. He calls a final invocation to the righteous Lord. He forces himself to look at the body of the dead girl. The old deathworker has dragged his cart up to the corpse, calling for his apprentice.

The boy jumps to attention, peels off his tunic and skirt, then wraps the cloth around his mouth and nostrils. Naked, he rolls the girl over. A splinter of shattered jawbone has pierced her chin and the split gash is the pink of meat laid on a butcher's trestle. Saul leans forward and retches.

The old man looks at him, then strips. Every bone is visible through the scarred membrane of his aged skin. Years of poverty have sculpted him into the very form of hunger. He too bends over the body.

Saul wipes the bile from his lips and chin. 'Don't bother searching her,' he calls out. 'She had nothing.'

The old man pokes at the body, not in the habit of believing anyone. Then, with a shrug, he nods to the boy. The boy stands and turns to Saul.

'Uncle, what was her crime?' He is Arab, both in tongue and in the shock of the hood of flesh that collects and covers the head of his sex.

'She denied the Lord,' Saul answers in Syrian, 'the Lord of her people. She abandoned her family. She had to be punished for her blasphemy.'

At this, the old man snorts. 'She was just a chick of a girl— what does she know of blasphemy?'

He wipes his nose and rubs his hand across his straggle of chest hairs. His next words are a sneer: 'Did you hunt her down? Was she one of yours?'

As if Saul were a filthy mercenary, a slave trader, a collector of tax for the dirty Romans.

A thousand curses are on his lips. *Shut your foul mouth, you Arab piece of shit. Child of a whore.* But no sound comes forth. His head is heavy, the light is banished and the curses are snatched from his lips. The din is a madness in his head, and he has to cover his mouth to keep the words from escaping: *If you are without sin, then cast your stone.* Brazen, unholy words; the devil's words. He knew those words were for him, that she was judging him. As if he were the one who stood condemned.

'Are you ill, uncle?' The naked boy is before him, his hand raised, seemingly about to touch Saul.

He jerks away from the filthy deathworker. 'Do your foul work,' he spits at him. 'You've been paid.'

Saul turns from them, abandons the judgement ground, and climbs up the hill, thistles scratching across his calves. He can hear the vile old Stranger laughing; he hears the thud as the girl's corpse is thrown onto the cart.

Someone calls out after him; the torrent of violence in his head is such he can't discern if it is the apprentice or the old man.

'Do we bury her or do we burn the cunt?'

To earth or to fire, the girl is lost to the Lord. He does not reply.

———

Death's breath is on his skin; he can smell it. The blood and meat and sin and poison of the girl. He wants to be careful not to touch anyone, lest he stain them with his pollution, but the market-sellers have set up their tables and the streets are full of people and slaves, beggars and labourers, scavenging dogs and bleating goats. Saul keeps close to the walls, ducks into narrow passages to avoid contact. In this way, slowly, he weaves through the back streets and manages to avoid the crowds. He breathes deeply with relief. He has reached the wide marble steps leading to the Temple. The mansion of the Lord reaches up to the heavens, the smooth face of the rock glistens from the touch of the sun. He smells incense and burning wood; wisps of smoke curl around him. He unties his sandals, delivers his prayer and enters the bathing pool.

He washes death off himself.

Finally, rocking back and forth on his knees, he begs the Lord, the One, the only One, to cleanse him and forgive him.

I am not a filthy child killer.

———

Cleansed, he passes through the first gate of the Temple and enters the courtyard. They have sent Ethan, a novice priest, to pay him. And even that young cur won't look at him—there's disdain in the way he drops the coins into Saul's palm. As if to touch Saul were an abomination. *I am not a filthy child killer.* He wishes he could grab the young man's throat, slam him against the walls, deliver blow after blow until the supercilious fool pled for mercy. He has heard the little shit take classes in the Temple, stumbling over the words of the prophets, forgetting the sacred text. It is he, Saul, who should be teaching the young men, it should be Saul promised to priesthood. Every sacred word is carved across Saul's heart. Every single word of the Lord. But Saul was born to toil, unlike this pampered and sneering child.

He needs the four meagre coins in his curled fist. The skinning season has not yet begun and there is a cycle of the moon to be completed before he can return to Tarsus, to his brother's farm, and begin his work of preparing hides to stitch into tents and canvases. This is the life Saul was born to.

'Sir,' and the word fills Saul's mouth with bitterness, 'do you need any tutors?'

Ethan has turned away. 'No. We don't need you this season.'

Saul groans as he descends the Temple's steps. How dare he believe himself worthy of priesthood? Though silently, he cursed in the Lord's house. He could wash and scrub at his skin for years and he would never be washed clean.

———

As soon as he enters his sister's house, Saul intuits danger. He stoops through the doorway and an ill-feeling knocks against his chest and heart, as if a malevolent force were in the room. He brings a prayer to his lips but even before he can recite the words, his sister rushes at him out of the darkness, her fists banging against his chest. He knows that not even prayer will still Channah when she's in such fury. Her curses are not words, they are the shrieks and wails of the monster that has possessed her. Her fingers claw his cheek and the violence brings him to his senses. He hits her.

He sees his brother-in-law, Ebron, rise from his seat by the hearth and go over to his fallen wife. 'You deserve that.'

Channah curls her veil over her face but the cloth cannot mask her sobbing.

Saul nods at Ebron and goes to where his nephew, Gabriel, is sitting. The youth jumps to his feet, embraces his uncle. The boy's arms are as steadying and peace-giving as a prayer. Saul inhales the youth's scent: toil and strength, salt and earth.

He turns to his sister. 'Forgive me, Channi.'

Even muffled, her words can be heard. 'May the Lord grant me death.'

Ebron, furious at her for inviting evil into his home with those words, slaps at her head.

Saul turns to his nephew. 'What has happened?'

'They have arrested Jacob.'

At this Channah stirs, unwinding her veil. 'And now they will arrest you,' she seethes. From the ground, her burning eyes then fix on Saul. 'All this begins with you, brother. You are the oldest—you are our father, and you have abandoned all responsibility. That's the root of all this evil.'

She spits on the ground. 'Unmarried, unfertile. You are no man.'

A great weariness falls on Saul. It is the cloak of iron that he must wear, the heaviness that cannot be shed. Ebron has raised his arm again but Saul clicks his tongue—an almost imperceptible sound, but it is enough to stay Ebron's hand.

'What have they arrested your friend for?'

Gabriel shrugs, makes no answer.

'It will be for sedition,' says Ebron quietly.

At the word, Channah starts moaning.

Turning his back to his sister, Saul beckons the men to come close. 'Tell me what you know.'

The boy lifts his shoulders, his eyes returning to the flickering embers of the hearth. 'I know he had with him a message from our brothers in the Stranger's city.'

At this his father snorts. 'May the Lord shit on Caesarea. Nothing but evil comes out of that stench-hole.'

Saul takes his nephew's chin, forces the boy to face him. 'Please tell me that there was no letter. Tell me that he had memorised the message from your comrades.'

Gabriel does not answer.

His father strikes at his son. 'You play at being warriors,' he snarls. 'You emulate and crawl after those arse-fucked Zealots but you are not men, you are just boys. And ignorant children at that. It's no wonder that the Romans eat us alive.' He spits into the fire. 'Your friend has probably already betrayed you.'

Channah wails.

Saul turns to his nephew. 'Tomorrow we will have to leave for Tarsus. You will stay at your uncle Samuel's house and he'll find you work as a labourer until the skinning season starts. Then we can work together. In Tarsus you'll be safe.'

Gabriel begins to protest but Saul cuts him off. He knows what he has to do. He is not the helpless eunuch his sister believes him to be. He will save this boy; he will not allow the Romans to take him.

'You have no choice in this matter, son,' says Saul. 'You will stay with your uncle and I will ask him to find you a bride.' He grabs the boy by his nape, brings his face close. 'Your father is right; you are no warrior.'

It is a mistake. The boy struggles, breaks free and leaps to his feet. 'How dare you speak of right and wrong? You who do the Council's bidding, who hunts fellow Jews for those depraved priests? They're not our rightful priests—they're lackeys of the false king and of the Strangers.'

The youth's eyes burn with his mother's lethal fire. And like hers, his voice is filled with scorn. 'You hunted a girl for them, didn't you? We've heard. She was a child and still they stoned her. How do *you* know what makes a warrior? You're a lackey to lackeys. My mother is right: you are not a man. We don't need your counsel and we don't need your filthy blood money.'

Saul can't answer. His nephew's words have wound tight around his heart. Shame is burning into him. He loves this boy as a son. How often has he dreamed of Ebron's death, so he could truly be father to Gabriel? Reprehensible thoughts, but he cannot stop dreaming them: this is how much he loves the boy. But the boy detests him, as does their world; can think of him only with revulsion.

Saul cannot move, he cannot speak. But Ebron is on his feet and has grabbed his son by the hair, cuffed him and thrown him against the wall. The dazed boy drops to the ground and his father stands over him.

Ebron's voice is cold, sure, allowing no dissent. 'You little turds think you're better Jews than we are because you've been schooled in words. I may be an ignorant worker but I know that one of the eternal commandments is to obey your parents and elders.'

He shoots a look at Saul. 'Isn't that right, brother?'

He doesn't wait for Saul's answer. And Saul has no spirit with which to answer.

The father, shaking, drops to his knees beside his son.

'Boy, my boy, I am sorry to have hurt you. But you don't have the ruthlessness to be a fighter. I know you. I've raised you. That little whore they stoned, she insulted the Lord—she left her husband and her children. Your uncle did her a mercy to denounce her.'

Ebron strokes his son's face. 'You say you hate the Strangers, that you want to expunge them from our lands. Have you got your uncle's courage? Can you put a knife to the throats of the bastards the Roman soldiers are breeding in the whorehouses behind their camp? Can you hold a blade to an infant's neck and cut it?' He kisses his son. 'That is the kind of warrior we need, my son, my sweet boy. Can you do that?'

The boy coughs, spits blood. But his hand tightens around his father's arm. Trying to steady his breathing, struggling to form words, he finally says, 'I will do as you say.'

Not as I say, thinks Saul, never as I say. I will never be his true father. *You are not a man.* The truth of these words slam into him. They are right: he has no son, he has no home; as he is constantly travelling between Jerusalem and Tarsus, he is always in the keep of his sister and his brothers. He is pitiful; he creates nothing. What an absurd vanity to hope that he could ever earn Gabriel's respect.

Saul gets to his feet, a storm in his head and a violent trembling in his body. He must flee this house. He stumbles to the door but his sister grabs at him. She kisses his hands, thanking him, praising him, forgiving him. The four winds roar in his head as he searches his tunic, finds the coins, lets them fall to the dirt where they belong—the evidence of his sin and his unmanning. But even as he does so he knows he has kept back two pieces of the thin metal, cold against his heart. The darkness has been expelled from the house but as he pushes through the door, he understands that the darkness is in him, that it comes from deep within himself.

The wine is new in the barrel, sweet, thin and potent. Between his second and third drink the tavern fills with market workers. He finds himself sitting with Barak, a fellow tentmaker. The man is a bore, always whining about being cheated. But coddled by the warmth of the tavern and the heat of the wine, Saul is content to listen to the man's complaints.

He feels a breeze as the thick hide over the doorway is pulled aside and another trader enters. It is dark outside. When did it become night? In the courtyard, servants and labourers are squatting on the ground, drunk and squabbling.

'We must eat.' Saul goes to get up, to shout to the tavern owner, but he cannot stand and falls back onto the bench. Barak laughs out of his toothless black mouth and calls out for olives, for chickpeas and pickled figs, for oil and bread.

A young servant boy, half his face carved away by pox, brings the dishes.

Saul grabs at the figs in vinegar, stuffs the soft fruits into his mouth; they ooze over his chin and fingers. He uses a piece of bread to wipe off the sticky juice and burps in satisfaction. 'Another wine?'

Barak's eyes narrow. 'Are you buying?'

You cheap goat. Saul fingers the two coins underneath his tunic. One coin will pay for two more drinks. He will not waste the second. He gets to his feet and this time he remains upright.

'More wine,' he calls out.

The boy comes and pours the wine, then stands back as the

two men raise their cups. There is something in the servant lad's scowl: disdain, almost judgement.

'Do I know you?'

The boy starts and moves away.

Barak blinks, snorts, and leans into Saul. 'He belongs to the Nazarene's sect.' He winks. 'He's probably terrified that you'll have him be stoned.'

'If I could,' Saul growls, 'I'd stone the whole diseased mob of them.'

Barak gently taps his knuckles against Saul's temple. 'All that learning of yours is useless, Saul. Your parents were under a wicked curse when they were convinced to send you to school.'

He gestures towards the boy, who is serving another table. 'That one believes that the Lord sent us a saviour who got arse-fucked by the Romans before they nailed him to a crucifix.' He spits after that accursed word. 'Concentrate on your work. Why waste your time on such madness?'

Saul straightens, not wanting to slur his next words. 'I do it for the Lord, I do it for our people. The madness of that sect undermines us—their madness is what keeps us slaves to Rome.'

Barak grabs Saul around the neck, holding him close, glancing quickly around the room. He whispers, his breath hot in Saul's ear, 'You do it for the coin, friend. And you should learn to keep your mouth shut in a public place.'

Saul pulls away. But he is chastened. The room is crowded, ringing with noise. Even so, he knows he shouldn't have spoken so loudly or so recklessly.

'You are right,' he confesses to his friend. 'I've drunk too much—I've got to go.'

Barak has a grip on his arm. 'Marry, friend, raise a son. That is the first and the wisest law of the Lord. Mind your trade and forget the nonsense the priests have infected you with.'

Saul pulls away. He stumbles, knocking against a bench. One of the men seated there shoves him hard and Saul lands face first on the dirt floor. He clambers to his feet. The whole tavern is laughing at him. It burns. He finds his way to the door and as he pulls back the hide, the servant boy is there, returning from feeding the louts outside. The man and the boy stare at each other.

'Who's your father?'

The boy, shocked, frightened, does not open his mouth.

'Who's your father, boy?'

One of the drunks in the alley calls out, 'He wouldn't know.'

The laughter, now louder, is a roar.

And Saul laughs too. 'A bastard, hey? Just like your Yeshua of Nazareth. They say his father was a Roman soldier. Is that right?'

Fury, hatred and loathing flash in the boy's round dark eyes. And danger. But then, as if those evils have been lifted from him, the boy's eyes are smiling. He slides his fingers down one cheek, as if removing phlegm from it.

'Sir,' he says humbly, 'I need to work.'

Pushing the boy aside, Saul steps out into night, the rage collected in his fists. First, to snap that boy's spine; and then to shatter the whole world.

———

Marry, raise a son; his words to his nephew have returned as a curse. The wine swills in his body, poisoning his thoughts and his stride as he bashes through shrub and thickets of nettles. *Marry, raise a son*. It is a new, weak moon, and there is no light, only darting and disquieting shadows. He is not carried by will, his feet are leading him; he has no thought except to stay upright, to not slip and break his neck as he makes his way into the steep valley. *Marry, raise a son*. Will he never escape those words? He is nothing but shame, lower than a beast. That whining fool Barak was right: he isn't even capable of fulfilling the Lord's first and greatest commandment. He has no son, no heir and no purpose. He kicks at stones on the path, feels the warm wind against his cheek and naked chest; his smock has fallen off one shoulder. He clutches at the cloth, feels for the coin.

None of them, not his family, his friends—none of them know the depravity of his yearnings. He has no will, all is simply movement, leading him inexorably to corruption. How can anything that comes from him not be poisoned? How can any issue of his not be damned? He has no will, he is only the sum of his lusts. At a bend he trips and falls flat on the ground. The pain brings tears. He twists, tests his foot. Nothing is broken, he can stand. He looks up to the sky and a black cloud glides over the heavens, revealing the slender curved slice of the moon. The Strangers bow and beg to her, believing that she is a goddess who can illuminate their souls. They make offerings to her and they claim she answers their prayers. What if he were to drop back to his knees, what if he were to offer himself to her? Here, on this very spot, outside the Lord's city itself, the silhouette of the Lord's house clearly evident? Would the goddess rid him of the fear that winds its coils around him whenever he is near a woman? Would she make him whole, give him a wife and a son? He spits to the moon; he spits at her—at the idiocy of the Strangers.

Pray to the moon, pray to the hearth, pray to the eagle, pray to the goat, pray to the fire, pray to the wind, pray to the sea, pray to the sun. A thousand gods, a thousand dumb and blind idols. He is as broken as Job, but yet his Lord loves him. A thousand idols and a thousand kingdoms have come and gone, only Israel stands immortal.

Love for the Lord has conquered time. He has climbed to the top of the ridge; he is descending into the second valley. Before him are the fires of the Roman camp. He can smell the wine and he can smell their sins. He can smell the lust. That is why his feet have brought him here. Saul raises a hand, claws at his cheek, is satisfied only when he senses the warm blood. He is no Job, he is not a good man, he is vileness and sin, his will is lust.

———

Guarding the wooden gate that opens to the brothel tents, two young Roman soldiers are flicking pebbles into the air, seeing which can send theirs the highest. Saul, his head clear now, marvels again at the Strangers' fascination with games, with the foolish trickery of sorcerers. This is a new people, thinks Saul, a young people, and they have the manners and pursuits of children. And the cruelty of children. They crush kingdoms as if they were insects.

At his approach the soldiers stand alert.

He bows. 'May I pass?'

The younger soldier, long-jawed and thick-lipped, points the hilt of his sword to a mound of rocks by the gate. Ash from incense covers the flat headstone. There are offerings before the idol—twigs and torn cloth, petals and a broken reed flute.

'Do what you must do,' the soldier orders.

The young idiot speaks a terrible Greek.

Saul answers clearly. 'I am a Judean, sir.'

The youth's eyes glare.

They hate us as much as we hate them, thinks Saul.

But the soldiers move aside and let him pass.

He hears their laughter, he hears one say to the other, deliberately in Greek so Saul will understand, 'I pity the poor whore who has to suck on his ugly cut cock.'

Saul's cheeks burn with disgust and shame. And from hate; the hate outweighs the shame and makes him forget his disgust. May he live to see the day that the Strangers are routed, the heads of the soldiers lopped, but not before they suffer violation, skull crushed against skull and bowels slit open.

Saul stamps on the heads and hearts and loins of Strangers as he weaves down the path to the fires, the illicit camp, where men sit on their haunches, waiting, peering into the darkness of the tents. The sputtering lamplight within casts grotesque shadows against the canvas, spectres that writhe and twist. They reach out for him, serpents from the depths of Hades seeking to possess him. His righteous hatred is gone, strangled by the shadow hands and ghost vipers that graze his skin, coil around his head and whisper in his ears, a cold reptilian hand that has slid between the folds of his robe and settled on his sex. And he is possessed by the loathsome beast, inflamed by it: his putrid sex is hard. He squats in the line, covering his depravity.

All around him, he sees his fellow sinners in the ravenous queue seeking the oblivion of fornication, the stench so palpable that it releases fumes: he can see the smoky vapours wisping off his skin and twisting up into the hideous night. He more than any of them, he stinks of lust. And yet knowing all this, he is too fearful to raise a prayer. He must not foul the words of the Lord by uttering them in such a place; and even though he knows the depths of his disgrace, he cannot rise and run, cannot leave these abominations behind: his betraying flesh will not let him.

Saul peers over the heads of the men in front of him to look into the tent. A hairy arse, more goat than man, rises and falls in thrusting convulsions. The whore beneath him is hidden by the vileness of the exertion; whether a boy or a girl or a boy-girl, it is not possible to tell. The thrusting beast moans and collapses with a final stab. The whore rolls out from under him; she grabs a cloth, wipes feverishly at her naked flesh. The man stumbles through the flap of the tent, wiping at his wet loins, covering his shame. Already another has approached from the front of the line. A naked boy leaps from the shadows holding a copper dish. The wind rises in the valley, intensifying the flickering light coming from a lantern in the tent and revealing the boy's heavily kohled eyelids. Near the bed a clay idol is suddenly visible: a squat, ugly form with seven flopping teats. The new man drops a coin into the dish, already pulling back his robe and dropping to his knees before the woman. In Greek she tells him to wait. She intones a prayer in Syrian and waves her hand over the idol, then lies back, opens her legs, and lets the man fall into her.

The rancid smell of sweat and corruption has the thickness of blood on Saul's tongue and mouth. He is no longer of the Lord, no longer of Israel, no longer of his people or the world. He is bloodless, a demon. He is death. The boy whore is walking along the queue of customers. Hands reach out to grope his stubby sex, clutch at his thighs and buttocks. One of the hands presents a coin and the boy snatches it, pulls the bearded man from the line and takes him by the hand into the tent. The boy also stoops and rushes through a prayer to the idol; and then they fall back into the black depths of the tent, behind the fornicating couple. Again the shadows leap and dance, they torment and goad.

The line of men stir, impatient, their complaints indistinguishable from the moans of the rutters. The man sitting in front of Saul turns and offers him a wan smile. His face is boyish, his black beard still thin, yet corruption has begun its relentless desecration—Saul sees it in those sad hollow eyes. The lad is rubbing himself. Saul leans forward. To embrace him? To urge him to leave? To flee; to regain youth? Saul cannot move. The youth's other hand has climbed Saul's thigh, is scratching at Saul's loins. Only then, his fingers tightening around Saul's sex, does the youth look up again, a smile touching his lips.

Saul closes his eyes. The evil is within him and he is possessed; succumbing is a glorious release. That flare of pleasure is worth death, worth the everlasting silence of his Lord.

The youth has turned his back to the line, for discretion, and as skin brushes skin, the wicked odour of flesh, putrefying and decaying, fills Saul's nostrils.

He comes to at the sound of anguished howling. The youth is lying kicking in the dirt—every time he tries to clutch his hand, the base hand that reached for Saul, he screams louder: one long finger dangles, broken at the joint. The men have abandoned the order of the queue and form a ring around the writhing boy. Saul finds himself standing over the screaming youth, his wrist throbbing with pain, such was the force with which he snapped the other's fingers. One man pushes Saul, another yells, 'Go on, finish off the dirty man-cunt.' From her bed, and over the back of the sweating beast still thrusting into her, the whore unleashes furious oaths in Greek and Syrian. From the distant camp, a soldier yells out for silence, threatening slaughter to the filthy Judeans and Arabs.

Saul slips in the mud, so eager is he to flee.

A spirit emerges from the night. It reaches out to him. 'Coin,' it cries, in scavenger Greek. 'Coin!'

He blinks and sees the condemned girl before him, unbroken, naked, the tiny mounds of her breasts, the puff of her emerging nipples. Her words in death split open his brow, storm into his head: *If you are without sin, then cast your stone.*

He cannot move. He is not in his body. He is with her, they are both soaring in their abandonment to death.

Again the squeal: 'Coin, coin.' Her small hands, the sharp blades of her long dirty fingernails, feed into his flesh. For the second time in this evil hour, he awakens. This girl is younger, darker, a Stranger. He fumbles under his tunic, finds the remaining coin, throws it to the ground. The girl falls upon it, a ravenous hound seeking meat. She grabs it and rushes to embrace Saul. He allows his arms to drop around her bony shoulders. Her hand reaches under the robes, finds him. He shudders, thrusts once, releases. The girl stoops and wipes him off her palm and into the dirt. Night then swallows her. Swallows him.

———

The sun slices his eyes. He blinks. His lips are toughened hide, his neck cannot support his head.

Channah is pouring water into a pot. 'Wash,' she orders. 'Gabriel has already packed the mule.'

She comes and sits beside her brother. And then shocks him; she kisses him on the brow. 'Oof,' she cries, flapping her hand, 'you still stink of wine.'

As he washes, he listens to her relating gossip shared at the well. He washes hands, feet and, turning from her so she can't see, carefully washes his loins. He could wash for eternity and he would not be clean.

'I thought you were the foul Strangers,' she laughs. 'When you smashed into the house in the middle of the night, I thought they had come to take our Gabriel.'

She raises his hand and kisses it. 'Thank you, brother, thank you for saving him.'

As she prepares a breakfast of rye and milk, she continues her tales. 'A group of Zealots attacked the Strangers' camp last night,' she whispers, so the children can't overhear. 'They went rampaging through the brothels, slitting the throats of the whores and their clients.'

Saul has no words.

'The soldiers retaliated. They murdered those poor boys.' She thumps a fist against her breastbone. 'Those young rebels are deluded but the Lord is just and they died righteous getting rid of that Greek filth. Their descendants will be proud for generations. They will live forever.'

And I will expire with my last breath, thinks Saul. I have no heirs and I will not live. I don't deserve to.

———

Saul is waiting patiently with the mule when his nephew returns from his ablutions at the sacred pool.

Gabriel kisses him on each cheek, a roguish grin on his face. 'Are you suffering this morning, Uncle? Has the wine turned sour?'

'Wine always turns sour,' Saul answers gruffly.

The youth goes to take the reins but Saul won't let him.

'I can wait, Uncle, go and wash. I'll wait till you return from the Temple.'

The older man shakes his head. 'No, I have wasted enough time.'

Gabriel, shocked, begins to protest.

His uncle pulls tighter on the rein and the mule brays in protest. 'Come on, let's go. We're not wasting any more of this morning.'

As Ebron kisses and farewells Gabriel, Saul hears him say in a hushed tone, 'You must learn, son, to be cautious around a man being punished by wine.'

Channah is weeping, and cannot let go of Gabriel. The children too begin to wail.

'Don't cry,' Gabriel says gently. 'I'll be back for Passover.'

Channah has taken her son's hand and places in it a tiny, knotted garland of hyssop. Saul pretends not to see the unholy trinket.

His mother releases Gabriel. 'Of course he'll be back for Passover,' she tells her younger children.

She kisses her son one last time. 'With a wife,' she adds, 'the Lord be willing.'

———

As they begin the descent into the first valley, Gabriel keeps turning to look back at Jerusalem, at the glorious and commanding edifice of the magnificent Temple. Saul refuses to do so. He has no right. As they march past the judgement ground, he shudders, recalling the bloodied body of the stoned girl. Further on, they walk along the back wall of the Romans' garrison, the brothel tents now collapsed and lying limp on the ground, spent grey ash all that remains of the fires.

Saul steps on a patch of darkened soil. Is it the wind? Is it the wind in the valley calling: *Coin, coin*? He sees a blade carve the night, sees the knife slash the throat of the beggar girl, sees her blood weeping into the earth. His nephew keeps looking back, mouthing prayers until the city of David disappears in the brilliant haze of the defiant sun. Not once does Saul turn. He knows it was not the Lord who'd saved him last night. The Lord had intended him to be there, to face the Zealot's blade, to suffer the Lord's justice. Those demons that have tainted his blood—the Greek spirits, the temptations of the Romans, the evil music of the Strangers—the demons gloat. They want to keep playing with him, because they know they own him. He is their servant. The Sacred City, his world, all that is wondrous and true and pure, it is forbidden to an accursed man such as Saul.

Hope

LYDIA, ANTIOCH
57 A.D.

'Do you believe in God, Momma?'
'I don't know—why doesn't He help me?'
'You're supposed to praise Him whether you're in
    pain or not.'
'That's unfair.'
'Well, we're not supposed to judge Him.'
'I don't want a God like that,' she said.
'If you believed what the Catholics believed, you
    could pray to the Virgin Mary.'
'No woman made this world. I couldn't pray to
    a woman.'

—Harold Brodkey, 'A Story in an Almost Classical Mode'

I know what they call me. Witch. Sorceress. Hag. They fling their shit and they throw their stones and words.

But they cannot hurt me. My son, my brother, my Jesus, he is always with me, he is always beside me. The boys and the old shepherds, the slaves who collect firewood from this hilltop, they curse me, condemn me to Hades and to the obscene tortures of their callous gods. I wipe their shit from my cheeks, brush their dirt off my rags. Nothing they do can hurt me.

None of them dare to touch me, nor even to come close. The degradation of my work takes care of that. Their gods would demand a year-long ablution, their fathers would throw them out of their homes, their spouses banish them from their beds. The city gates would be closed to any who dared touch me. My corruption is absolute.

I need neither house nor company. On this dark side of the mountain, these bleak crags and desolate caves are the rooms I dwell in, and the sparse cypress canopies are all the shelter

I need. In the storm seasons I have seen lightning dislodge a tree, cleave it from its roots and shoot it far into distant thickets. The noise is the thunder of the earth splitting. But no lightning has ever touched me. I have no fear. I gave up the world and in that surrender I was made brave. I was released from servitude and I was released from being a woman. The rocks and the trees are my home now. Beyond is the desert and behind me is the world. I have no need for it. I am no longer part of it.

'Witch, witch!' they scream, thinking the word will hurt me. I smile and I say, 'Thank you.' A stone grazes my cheek. I repeat, 'Thank you.' Shit spatters my lips. I wipe them, and again say, 'Thank you.'

To this mountain they bring their children. On these ledges and in these caves they lay their newly born. Here they leave the blind child, the crippled child, the child born with a purple mark across its face. And here they abandon their girls. They light their offerings if they can afford them, and they chant their prayers to the Mother. Demeter, Isis, Al-at. *We have virgins promised to you, Mother, may the next child born be a son.* If they see me, they shriek and hiss. *Witch. Sorceress. Hag.* But they do not dare to come close. They abandon their infants and they flee.

I wait. Till their chanting can no longer be heard. Till their scents have been banished by the wind. Till I can no longer hear their footsteps. Then, only then, do I go to them. To the children they've abandoned.

This one has been born with no eyes. I kiss his brow. 'Child, child,' I whisper, 'you I will name Fortitude.' I tell him of a God who knows mercy and who loves justice. I tell him of a world to come that has a place for him. 'It could even be tomorrow, child,' I whisper. 'Soon, very soon, he is returning.' I go to the next infant. I kiss her belly, I lay my ear against her still-beating chest. I ask the wind and the birds to stop their songs. Faint is the beat of her heart but I can hear it. 'You, child,' I say softly, not to frighten her, 'you, I will name Devotion. There is a God, child, who will make the last first and the first last. I promise you this, Devotion.'

Night. Dangerous night. I could choose to leave, I could choose to turn my eyes away, flee to the other side of the mountain, where the cypress trees grow taller, where shepherds have seeded bushes of thyme and a wild yellow garden of chamomile. I could sit there, look down at Antioch. If there is a ripe moon I could raise my finger and trace the shadow outline of the city's walls. Or I could look beyond to the river, winding silver in the moonlight. I could cover my ears, make myself deaf to the wretched cries.

But I don't. I stay to look. I stay to hear. As the wolf circles the crying infant, as it bares its teeth, growls and bites, as the infant offers one last cry, as the body becomes blood and meat. I crouch in the cave, hearing the slither of the snake, hearing the crunch of bone as the serpent's jaws engulf the child. I do not look away; I stay, to be witness, to know what it is we do when we forsake our children, when we leave them on the mountainside. How can I bear witness to all of that and not be deranged? Because my son, my brother, my Jesus, he is with me, he is beside me. These are not my sobs, not my lamentations. They are his cries. This is his suffering.

In the mornings I build a fire. The meat that remains, the bones, the hair, the torn clothes that swaddled the infant, I gather and place in the fire. I watch them burn. I recite his words as I watch the fire grow and feed. I recite the words my teacher Paul first taught me. In the kingdom to come, the last will be first and the first will be last. All that remains is burned. But to the charred bones and ash I whisper, 'This I promise you: the last will be first and the first will be last.'

———

I was not born a witch. I was born a woman. I was raised a Greek. When I first came to Antioch I said that I was born in Philippi, but my village lies over a day's journey from there. My father's blood is Macedonian and it is those mountains and those springs of pure water that are my true home.

My father was a brickmaker and it was to that trade that our family was bonded. All my brothers bake the clay. Of my mother's clan I know nothing. My father's first loyalty was to his ancestors and to his gods. Once she was married my mother forsook her allegiance to the spirits of her home and she never saw her family again.

'You are my oldest daughter,' she would whisper to me, cradling me so I might fall to sleep, 'and it is you who are now my family and my life.' She would quietly sing songs from her mountain home, her fingers weaving through my locks, her kiss on my brow. When she thought me asleep, she would gently unwrap her arms. 'Don't leave me!' I would cry—I was terrified of the dark. 'Don't be silly, Lydia,' she would say. 'I will never leave you.' With that promise I could sleep.

We all worked. I was the elder sister and as such the responsibility for my younger siblings fell to me. My father was stern and distant. He barely spoke to me. But he was generous to his two daughters and refused to have us work at the kilns. He was a hard worker, as was my oldest brother, Hercules—well named, for he was strong and fierce. All my brothers had to work. Every day was spent digging and then on the moulding of the clay: hard work—but the worst ordeal by far was working in the kilns. The ferocious heat that burst from them had scorched and prematurely lined their faces. In time my father's dedication was rewarded by the gods, and he was able to hire two labourers to assist him and also to purchase three slaves. Two of them were men, who worked in the clay quarries and in the kilns. The third, Goodness, was a young maiden who helped us with the chores of the household.

Of all my tasks, the one I enjoyed most was attending to the altars. There were three of them in the house. The first and the grandest was the altar to the Mother just inside the gate that opened to our courtyard. It stood on a dais that my father had built from the first batch of bricks he had ever fired. He had kept them with him through his apprenticeship and into his marriage, through the building of our home, in order to make this dedication to the Goddess. Her form had been sculpted in clay by an artisan priestess bonded to the Great Mother's temple. The second altar lay just before the hallway to the night chambers, and was dedicated to Hermes, to ensure that He would bring us dreams of peace and dreams of providence in the night, and not punish us with visions of furies and monsters. And the third altar was within my parent's chamber, in honour of the god Priapus, a likeness of His sex, erect and thick, carved from wood that came from an ancient pine tree on my father's home mountains.

Every morning, on rising, it was my duty to prepare a meal for each of the deities. The first offering was always to the Mother. Under instructions from the priestesses, my father had planted a pomegranate tree to shade the Goddess. And every morning I would stand under the tree and curse it on behalf of the Mother. The tree that had enslaved Her daughter was now slave to the Goddess. With the end of the winter, and with it the resolution of Her lamentations, I would take a budding fruit from the gnarled branches and bite into it. That hard, shiny skin was often resistant, but there was a blade by the altar that I could use to slice it open. I preferred, however, to bite into the pomegranate if I could, so that the scarlet juice would spurt over my chin and neck. 'The red juice of the fruit is a blood offering,' my mother instructed. 'The Goddess is a woman and Her due is blood. Give the Goddess Her due and She will never abandon you.' I would smear the pulp across my mouth and lips, and then I'd bow and kiss the brick on which She sat. Once that was done, I'd carefully scoop out six seeds and place them in front of Her. Then I would offer the meal and make my prayers. For Father, for Mother, for my brothers, for my sister, for our household, for our good fortune.

Then I would take what remained of the food I had prepared and share it amongst Hermes and Priapus. Of the first I asked that He chase misery and sadness from our house. Of the second I asked that He protect us from the evil eye. It was drummed into me from my mother's first instructions that I was never to touch the sex of the God. That honour, of polishing His splendour with a salve of myrtle oil, the perfume sacred to His mother, Aphrodite, was only to be performed by my father, each morning on awakening and each evening on retiring to the marital bed. If he was called away, that duty fell to Hercules. 'Never, my child, never touch the sex of the God,' my mother warned repeatedly. 'For a woman to do so is to bring great misfortune into our home.'

It is strange to think how diligent I was once about those rituals. But as an ignorant child I was bonded in servitude to those idols. They were gods and they had the power to call forth death and poverty, malice and pain. Though I feared rousing their anger, I was also proud that my mother entrusted me with their care.

My sister, Penelope, was jealous that I was the only child allowed this honour. She'd follow behind me, demanding, 'Why aren't I allowed to feed them? It isn't fair.' One morning, tired of her persistent whining, I let her serve them. Our Goodness was there and reported this to our mother. I received a whipping that drew blood from my back. 'How dare you insult the gods?' my mother hissed at me as she brought down the lash. 'Do you want to bring calamity to our home?' I was distraught. I had not meant to upset the one I loved most in the world. 'No, Mother, I promise, Mother. I will always honour the gods.'

And this is how I came to break that promise.

My mother was with child. And so was Goodness. My mother grew increasingly cold and aloof towards her, and though it was never spoken about, I realised that her bastard child was my father's. I bore Goodness no ill will. I gave no thought to the child she was carrying. I was excited about the child that my mother would soon bring into the world. I knew that she and my father wanted another son but secretly I implored the Mother that it be a daughter. I wanted another sister, a little girl I could look after, that I could dress and play with, to whom I would teach the skills of housecraft and order about as I did Penelope.

As the day of the birth came closer, my mother took me aside and told me that I was to be present at her labour.

'You are nearly a woman, my sweetness,' she said, stroking my hair, 'and soon you too will know what it is to give birth to a child. You will do all that the midwife demands of you?'

'I promise, Mother.'

I was delirious with pride.

Goodness shook me from my sleep. I followed her to the outhouse, the small room we used to store food and wine. All the provisions had been cleared away and a bed of straw had been prepared in the middle of the room. My mother was lying on it. The bedding was already sodden from her waters. The midwife was an ugly crone whose face was etched with the tattoos of her trade. Rosemary was burning on a makeshift altar to the Mother and the air was thick with its pungent smoke. I rushed to my mother. In one hand she clutched a clay figure of the Goddess. Her face and hair were drenched with sweat, her eyes searched the room as though she was looking for sanctuary but could not find it—it was as though she could not see me. I kneeled by the bed and took her hand. Though terrified, I was determined not to cry. I don't remember what I said to her. She turned at the sound of my voice and for one moment it was as though she recognised me and was back in the world. Then she jerked in the bed, threw back her head and screamed.

'Hold her down,' ordered the midwife.

Goodness came behind my mother and took hold of her

shoulders. I still recall the shock of that outrage. And my furious outburst: 'You filthy beast—how dare you touch my mother?'

I was on my feet, ready to slap her, when the midwife hissed, 'Offerings have been made to the Goddess, child—the slave can hold her.'

For hours, my mother did not cease her spasms. Scream followed howl followed scream: abominable cries, animal cries. I would do anything, fulfil any desire of the gods, if only I could have stopped my mother's suffering.

The crone's hands searched deep within my mother. 'Hold her legs,' she ordered. 'Hold them apart.'

Blood was everywhere. I prayed incessantly to the Mother. *Save her, please save her.* After a while my mother's shuddering and screaming lessened, but the listlessness and moaning that replaced them were even more terrifying. I saw the anxious glances exchanged between the slave and the midwife and felt pure terror. 'Save her,' I urged the Goddess. 'Please, save her.'

The midwife let out a jubilant yell. 'The child is coming! Quickly,' she commanded Goodness, 'raise her, raise her!'

And here I betrayed my mother. The sharp odour of the incense, the virulent smoke, the lateness of the hour—all overcame me. I fell into darkness.

I woke to find myself slouched against the wall. Goodness, strain contorting her, was holding my mother upright while the midwife crouched, one arm lodged deep inside my mother. It was as if Goodness were holding up a doll. The crone was still pleading with the Goddess, her chants unceasing, even as she was lost in the exertion of her work. And then there was a final dreadful bawling. My mother's face was fixed in a cast of a howl, her jaw stretched in agony. The idol she was clutching shattered as the midwife pulled out her hand and brought forth the child, along with gouts of blood. A hideous black cord connected the infant to my mother. The crone bit into the cord and released the child into the world. With one hand she held the blood-soaked infant and with the other she wiped the blood from her mouth. At that moment the child kicked and released a cry. I cared nothing for that. I was praying to the Mother. *Save her, save her.* My mother was slumped, she did not move.

The midwife examined the infant. And then, her voice weary, she announced, 'It's a girl.'

She turned to me. 'Go tell your father, child: that he has a daughter and that his wife is dead.' She banged her breastbone to ward off the evil. 'May the gods have mercy on her spirit.'

Goodness, her exhaustion terrible, had dropped my mother onto the blood-soaked bed. I rushed to her broken body but the midwife stopped me. 'Go,' she said, quietly now, even kindly. 'Do your duty, child.'

How did I leave that room? How did I find my way down the corridor? I don't know, but there I was standing in front of the screen to my parents' chamber. I called out to my father.

'Lydia,' he returned in warning, 'don't come in. You are in pollution, do not dare come in.'

Then his voice softened. 'What news do you have, child?'

Despite his warning, I dared peek through the gap between the curtain and the doorframe. He was kneeling in front of his god.

Somehow I said the words. 'Mother is dead.'

A long silence.

'And the infant?'

'It's a girl. She lives.'

Only then, with that news, did he release a groan.

I waited. I did not know what to do. I wanted only to return to my mother—I could not believe she was dead. But I knew I had to have his word. I needed his permission.

I heard him rise, I heard his steps come towards me.

'Step away, daughter,' he commanded.

He would not look at me. I bowed my head.

'Lydia,' he said, coldly and swiftly, 'you are the mistress of the house now. Goodness knows the instructions for the preparations of the dead. You will ensure that they are followed.'

I glanced up at him. He was so very old. His labour at the furnaces had singed the youth from him.

'I will wake your brothers and we will go to the temple and find a priest. You will raise your sister. You will ensure she does as Goodness commands. You have permission to punish her if she does not obey.'

He started walking towards my brothers' chamber.

'And the infant?' I blurted. 'What should I do with her?'

His body slumped, as if the weight of the question was an impossible burden.

His back straightened. 'We have no use for another daughter. Tell the midwife to have her taken to the mountain.'

Only then did he turn to me. 'And, child, you will never mention her again. She was not born and she did not live.'

My first defiance. Not out loud—I was not then brave enough for that. But silently, inside me, I called out, 'Mother, may the gods have mercy on your spirit.' And then, 'You were born, sister, you lived.'

———

As always I rise before the sun. The fire has died and there is only the ash remaining, black remnants of logs and grey scorched bones.

I'd slept under the trees. It is summer in Antioch, and this far east the heat does not submit to night. I rise and find the surging brook that runs down the mountain. The water is refreshing, and wakes me up.

'Salvation,' I call, 'where are you, child?'

She has slept under the night sky. Even on the iciest winter nights, Salvation prefers to sleep outdoors. She will find the hollow trunk of a toppled tree and watch the stars and the milky shadows of the heavens from her bed. She does not fear night. 'The one God created it,' I tell her. 'He made the stars and all of the heavens.'

They also call my child a witch. And worse. They are ferocious in their abuse. Monster. Dog. Medusa. Even the charitable say it were better she had been abandoned, better she had died in the womb.

She cannot answer me in words. She comes up to me, brushes her fist against mine, coos and rubs the top of her head against my chin. It was in this brook that runs down our mountain, in this sparkling water that I baptised her, and brought her to our son, our brother, our Jesus. Always with us, always beside us.

On seeing her I only see light; I see the true brilliance that the ignorant claim for the gods of the sun and the goddesses of the moon. I do not see the misshapen eyes, the stump that is her right arm, the scaly skin that covers her neck and her shoulders. I see light. I see radiance.

She tugs at my rags. Urging me. Butting me with her head like a lamb.

I take her hand. 'Show me, Salvation.'

The sun is stretching, rising, and the newborn light casts a golden splendour across the mountain. She takes me on a path that our feet have worn through the cedar forest. Here the trees grow so large that the sun's light is a faint glow in the darkness. At the edge of the forest we see the city down below, the gleam of the river, the plains that stretch into Syria.

On a boulder they have left us a bowl of food and a small flagon of wine.

My brethren, my true brothers and sisters in the Saviour, they have not forgotten me and they have not abandoned my child. She and I crouch in front of the boulder. I am ravenous with hunger's fire, greedy with its calling, and my hand reaches for a loaf of bread, ready to tear it, ready to stuff as much of it as I can into my mouth. But my child is more devout than I am. She stops my hand. She pats her chest.

I understand her. She cannot form words, but I understand her. Her light makes whole her meaning.

I take the bread and as I break it the odour of the sesame grain almost makes me faint. My stomach growls so loud that Salvation laughs.

I say, 'And on the night he was betrayed, our Jesus took bread and, when he had given thanks to the Lord, he broke it and said,

This is my body, which is my sacrifice for you. When you break bread, remember me.'

I place bread on her tongue.

And I say, 'And then Jesus our Redeemer took his wine after the meal and said, *This cup is a new understanding between God and Creation. This wine is the blood that I spilled to seal this promise.'*

I make a cup of my palm, I pour the wine, I offer it to my daughter. She laps at it eagerly.

After I have also taken the bread and wine, I lift her chin and I say, 'Salvation, he has risen from the dead.'

And every time this small miracle. No grunts, no spitting, I hear her clearly. She says the words. 'Truly, he has risen.'

'He is coming,' I say.

And she sings her answer in a voice that must come from heaven. 'Soon, soon, any day now he will return.'

As always, she looks up at the sky, and then over her shoulder, down the mountain. Expecting him and not knowing from where he will come.

We share our feast of love, this blessed thanksgiving. Down below, in the far city, I know that there will be crowds in the market, sacrifices in the temples, drunks in the taverns and fornication in the brothels. There will be the children begging, slaves bowing to their masters, there will be violence and death and misery and suffering. I am with my child, on our mountain. The forest is full of birdsong, the sun is ascendant. Our good brethren have left us bread and wine, but also date cakes and olives. We share our seat on the boulder, looking around us, from the world to the heavens and from the heavens to the world.

We witches, we dogs, we madwomen. And our Jesus is always with us, always beside us.

———

My mother was dead. I diligently performed the sacrifices and rituals for her passage to the underworld. I instructed my sister on the herbs for incense she should gather and the prayers she had to chant. We washed and dressed our mother's body, and after her cremation, during which the smoke and ash from her funeral pyre dusted our skins and mourning dresses, we attended the temple of the Virgin to be cleansed in the baths. The next day we scrubbed the walls of the outhouse, burning myrrh and chanting prayers to banish death. On finishing we trudged back and forth from the sheds, returning the harvest stores. I did it all in strict obedience to custom and to the will of my father and the rites of our ancestors. But I was halfway between this world and the underworld and in a daze. I longed to be with my mother. Her guidance, her care and her love had been my only pleasures. I wanted no part of the world of the living.

The rites of my father's clan required a full cycle of the moon to pass before we could abandon our fasting and our silence. Once the journey of the Goddess had been completed, meat was permitted to us again and wine could be drunk. And with the shedding of the white mourning clothes, I had to return to the world.

All through my period of mourning I had kept faith with the deities. I had fed them and offered them my prayers. My mother's safe passage to the underworld should not be denied because of her daughter's wickedness. So capricious were the gods to whom I was once bonded.

On that first morning, knowing that my mother had safely crossed, I prepared the morning meals as usual. I lay the dish before the Mother, I snatched a pomegranate from the tree and bit into it. I extracted the seeds. And then, sitting before the idol, looking at Her ugly pebble head, I placed the seeds in my mouth. I chewed and swallowed them.

'You did not save her,' I hissed. 'I owe you nothing.'

I expected the world to shake, I expected Hades to erupt from the earth and seize me.

Nothing happened. There was the mild summer breeze. The chirping of a swallow.

Next I took the dish to Hermes. And in front of that God I ate it all, every last crumb. I left nothing for Him. Then I went into my father's chamber. There I did the same with the dish for this God. I wiped the oil from my lips. And then I reached out my hand and touched the sacred wooden phallus.

'You did not save her,' I cursed. 'I was dutiful and reverent and you betrayed us!'

Nothing happened. I could hear my sister at work in the kitchen. I heard one of our labourers call out a morning greeting.

I shuddered. I could not rid myself of my mother's twisted and anguished face, the howls of her pain, the bed drenched with all that blood. She was gone—it would bring misfortune even to say her name.

With the long nail of my little finger I picked at a swirl of grain on the deity; I scratched the wooden cock. So He too could feel pain, so He too could suffer. Now, surely, the spirits must burst forth from Hades and drag me down below to face punishment and torture. In terror, I shut my eyes.

And opened them again. I was alone in the room.

I sprung to my feet. 'Goodness,' I demanded, 'where are you?'

I had to search for her. She was in the outhouse, nursing her bastard. It had been born alive. A son. I looked at her plump breast, the engorged nipple that the brat was loudly sucking on. The sly, proud smile on her face.

'I need you to go to the markets.'

'Darling Lydia,' she said, 'I'm feeding the boy. Can't you ask Penelope instead?'

I struck her face with the back of my hand so hard that I too flinched in pain. The force of the blow unglued the bastard from her tit. He started to wail. I forced my hand to my side so as not to strike him as well.

'I am the mistress of this house.'

She bowed her shaved head.

That noon, taking the meals down to the brickworks, I asked my father for permission to talk with him. He grunted in annoyance. But I had been careful to be respectful and decorous in my request, so as not to shame him in front of his sons, his workers and his slaves. With a nod he agreed and I followed him out of the fiery chamber.

He took an old urn that lay against the wall and poured water over himself. 'What is it?'

The tears came easily. 'Goodness insulted me, Father. I gave her a task to do and she refused. She said, "Your mother is dead, I'm the mistress of this house now."'

My father recoiled. In his proud eyes I saw first confusion, then distaste. 'Is this true?'

I banged my chest five times. 'I swear it on the great Mother, I swear it by all the gods.'

I could only see his rage now.

'I will punish her.'

'And the bastard?'

He clicked his tongue in annoyance. 'What of him?'

'It is he that gives her the confidence to speak such outrage.'

He looked down at me. 'This is not your business, daughter.'

'Sell him.'

'He's just born, girl—we don't yet know if the gods will take him from us. Let him grow, let him live out his first year, and then we can fetch a good price for him.'

I shamed myself. I fell to my knees, gripped his legs. I smelled the wood that fired the kilns, the pungent scent of man and work.

'She insulted our mother. May the gods have mercy on her spirit.' I kissed his foot. 'Sell him, Father.'

That very night he beat Goodness; he thrashed her so hard that she limped for a full cycle of the Goddess, her left eye black and closed. Within days of her punishment, the bastard was sold. And for the first time since my mother's death, I felt joy.

But I was not destined for happiness. With the approaching winter I had my first blood. My mother had prepared me for it, had told me of how proud she would be to sing the prayers to the great Mother as I offered Her my blood to drink. But my mother was gone. It was Goodness whose sullen voice implored me to sing to the Mother as she forced my hand across my wet sex, shoving it deep into the soil so the earth could be sated. Let my blood be poison, I cursed silently. Let nothing fertile grow from this ground. My rage stemmed my tears.

After I had submitted to the rites of cleansing and purification, my father gave me a shawl of azure blue to wear as my head cover and veil. It had belonged to my mother and I wore it with pride. Soon after, my breasts grew and I lost my childhood slimness. I didn't like what was happening to my body, I hated the restrictions placed on me. I could no longer walk through the villages or into the woods without one of my brothers coming with me. Even my duties with the deities now had to be shared with Penelope. It was forbidden for me to perform the rites when I was bleeding.

Once winter made way for the reborn sun, my father declared that it was time for me to marry. I knew that such a day had to come, but the shock of it was overwhelming. I barely listened as my father explained the good fortune of the match, how the youth was the son of a canvas and leathermaker, that the family owned a small tannery near Philippi, that they too had come from Macedon, that they had not been greedy in the dowry that they had asked for—all of that bode well for my future. To every jubilant utterance I replied obediently, 'Yes, Father'. But a fear had bored into my body. I was to leave my family, my home. I was to lie with a man.

It was true, my father had indeed made a good match. My husband, Theodorus, was a mere lad. But he had been made strong by work. Penelope was envious the first time she met him.

'He's got a lovely face,' she whispered as she pinched me. 'You're lucky, sister. I hope my husband will be as handsome as he is.'

Penelope and I cried for hours on the eve and the day of my wedding. When we were ready to leave for Philippi, I could not bring myself to break from her desperate embrace. My brothers too were weeping. Even Goodness dropped to her knees and kissed the ground in front of me. She was heavy with child again and I am ashamed that I did not bid her farewell—my last cruelty to her.

My father didn't hug me. He took my shoulders and he looked down at me. 'Be honourable and do your ancestors proud, girl,' he said. 'Be a good wife and raise many sons.'

And then my new husband helped me onto the mule.

Heaving with sobs, I turned to wave at my family as the beasts started their way down into the valley. I never saw any of them again.

As we approached Philippi, I was awed by the immensity of its fortified walls, the vast spread of hamlets and villages that lay outside it. I was dazed by the shining acropolis, the grandeur of the marble palaces and temples. We continued our trek past the city walls, and descended into Neapolis, the port town that was to be my home.

Neapolis was perched on the edge of the Salonikan Gulf and my first sight of the sea made me gasp. It was more dazzling than the city, it outshone even the canopy of the heavens.

My husband turned and smiled. 'The Aegean,' he called back to me. 'Witness the birthplace of gods.'

I could not answer. I was struck dumb by its beauty. And by

its power. Then and there I made a vow: if my new life were to prove unbearable, I would go to the water and disappear into its waves; I would seek the release that must surely exist beneath that luminous surface.

'It's calling you, isn't it, wife?'

Shocked, I looked at Theodorus. Had he guessed at my defiance? But it wasn't that: he was gladdened to see my wonderment. He thought I was grateful to be brought to his city and to be his wife. And for the first time since our betrothal, I smiled at him. I allowed him to think it so.

And so I was married. I knew I was lucky. It wasn't just that Theodorus was handsome and kind—all his family were welcoming. Dion, my father-in-law, had been a boy when his own parents were freed by the nobleman who had owned them, and their former master's generosity and benevolence had become a guide to how he and his family were to treat their own slaves and labourers. Not that they were a rich family. My husband's mother had died in labour like my own, giving birth to his younger brother. His father had then remarried, a young woman named Calliope, who was not much older than me. She was now carrying their first child together, and worked in the tannery alongside her stepchildren and husband. There were two slaves in the household, Psyche and Fortitude, as well as three bonded men. There was also a skilled leatherworker, a labourer called Daniel, whom the family trusted to trade their tents and canvases all along the Thermaic coast and across the Aegean into Anatolia.

My son, my brother, my Jesus, you were there, beside me.

This Daniel was the first Jew I had ever met. You sent him to me, you placed him on my path.

My husband was kind and strong and handsome, but he was a man. On the first night in my new home he turned me over, lifted my dress and entered me. I was consumed by the wildness of the furies. I bucked and screamed for him to release me. I had never experienced such pain. I knew that my cries would awaken the household but I was convinced that it wasn't a man inside me but a malevolent creature sent by the most cruel of the gods. Theodorus kept whispering, 'Hush, child, hush, this is what it is to be a couple,' as I struggled to escape from him. In the end, angered by my disobedience, he forced me onto my back, hit me across the face, lifted my legs and pushed into me again. Shocked by the blow, this time I was quiet and compliant. It was blessedly quick and it lasted an eternity. He released himself in me and even in my stupor, with the pain and blood, I was stunned that I could feel his seed slither inside me. From that night on I didn't cry out, and didn't refuse him. I remained still and silent. But whenever he was inside me I no longer thought him kind and strong and handsome. I thought him foul, ugly, monstrous. I hated that bestial act. It was sacred to the uncaring gods. It had taken my mother.

Soon I was with child. And knowing this, he no longer came for me. He now took his pleasures with Psyche, and sometimes with Fortitude, though she was old and not at all good-looking. He also made use of the youngest of the slaves, a boy called Salonikos. Calliope was always jealous of her husband's carnal use of the slaves and apprentices, and often treated them spitefully because of it. I was grateful. To begin with, Salonikos averted his eyes out of shame when passing me. But I would greet him cheerfully and soon he came to trust me. He would drop everything to do what I asked of him, risking the opprobrium and the beatings of my husband.

'He's in love with you,' whispered Calliope once as we worked side by side.

'Please, Mother, hush,' I replied.

I was annoyed at her reminder that the boy too would grow up to be a man.

In work, I discovered freedom. Our job was to strip the skins that were purchased from the priests after the sacrifices, or from the butchers that serviced the nobility and the rich of the city. The skins were first boiled in a giant vat. Once they had cooled it was my and Calliope's task, along with our slave girls, to strip the boiled skins of sinew and gristle, of clotted blood and hair. We did this by tightly gripping a blade and scraping it back and forth across the skin to make it clean. The first days were agony. My wrists cramped at night and the throbbing pain made sleep impossible. But soon I became accustomed to the labour and found peace in the monotony of the work. I became quick and efficient with my blade, and took pride in my efforts. The stink was abominable, from both the boiled skins and also from the guts and boiled meat we were scraping away. We kept our mouths and nostrils covered, but even so the foul odours would rise and sting our eyes. It was only with time and greater skill that I would end the day without bleeding from a slip of the blade. The calluses, the blisters, they have never left.

And there was always the sharp, intoxicating perfume of the sea air. No matter how difficult our work and no matter the jealousies and grievances within our home, I would smell that potent salt spray and I'd return to peace.

As the time of my labour approached, my husband ordered me to abandon my work and retire to seclusion. Though we were not sharing a bedchamber, I knew that every morning and every evening Theodorus prayed to Priapus, pleading that his firstborn be a son. Though I had lost any belief in the efficacy of the gods, I took up silently chanting incantations to appease the Mother. A tremendous fear, childlike in its ferocity, had overtaken me. The terrifying visions of my mother's final hours returned, and I was convinced that the same fate awaited me. Now, surely, the gods would take their vengeance. Calliope, who had given birth to a son and had completed her moon cycle of isolation, tried to allay my fears. 'You will bear the pain, daughter,' she promised me. 'You will give your husband a son.' She would bring me grains sanctified at the temples of Isis and of Demeter in Philippi. She would light the incense and make offerings to the gods on my behalf. I was not soothed. I was certain that the world of shadows awaited me.

The labours came. In the vicious racking of my body I was transformed. No longer a child. My first scream pierced the dawn. My final spasms took place at night. So much blood. So much torment, and so much exhaustion. Finally, the midwife pulled the infant free. As she murmured a prayer to the Mother, she cut the cord between my child and myself.

Her voice was dull. 'It's a girl.'

Psyche, who had been with me through day and through night, muttered, 'May the gods have mercy on her spirit.'

I did not have the power to speak. It was all I could do to breathe.

A wail filled the tiny chamber. At the sound, I found my voice. 'Give her to me.'

The midwife laid the child across my breasts. The infant was sheathed in blood. I did not care. Calliope was kneeling next to me. She took the child, wiped it with a cloth and carefully laid her on me again.

'Put her on the nipple,' the midwife ordered. 'It will help flush the afterbirth.' Calliope pushed the infant's mouth towards my nipple. Another jolt of pain.

But the child sucked. Even though my milk was not yet ready, my child knew I was her mother.

My hands were scrabbling in the soiled blanket on which we lay. I had been given a likeness of the Mother but had dropped Her in my struggles. Now I needed Her—I had to beg for Her mercy.

Calliope found the idol and placed it in my hand.

My fingers curled around it.

'Thank you, Mother, I am returned to you.'

The sharp odour of the burning rosemary, the final prayers of the midwife, the contented suckling of my child. I collapsed into blessed sleep.

I was alone in the chamber. My hands searched the blanket. It was dry; it had been changed in my unmooring from wakefulness. I could not locate my child.

'Where is she?'

My cry woke the slave sleeping in the corridor and she came in.

'Where is my child?'

Psyche wouldn't speak.

I struggled to rise and a blade tore through me, from my sex to my chest, as if I were being filleted.

Psyche ran out of the room.

In my sleep I had lost my grip on the deity and it had fallen to the dirt floor. I groped for it and found Her. I kissed Her, I promised eternal fealty, told Her that I would crawl on my knees to Her great altar in Arcadia, if only She would return the child to me.

Calliope came in and took my hand. 'Daughter,' she whispered, 'you will have another child. You will have a son—you will have many sons.'

Her hands were stroking my hair, her lips were on mine. 'My husband has struggled many years to make a success of our business and our home. We're nearly there, my love. In a little time we will be wealthy and we can indulge in daughters.'

My love? How I hated her for such false words. She was not my mother.

'Where is she?'

But I knew where she was. Already in those icy shadows.

'Sleep,' she counselled. 'Sleep, little Lydia.'

I shut my eyes. I obeyed. I heard her leaving the room.

I opened my eyes. Twice now the Goddess had betrayed me. Every day without fail I had taken Her our offerings; daily, I had bitten into the bitter fruit to give Her the seeds She needed to bring Her daughter back from Hades. I clasped Her in my palm. My son, my brother, my Jesus, you must have been there with me, you who also died in blood, you who understands our suffering: that is how I must have found the strength. I twisted my body, I endured the agony, as I tightened my grip around the Mother, until my whole body shook from the pain. The clay form shattered. She was nothing, she was dust.

My child was still here. In the empty chamber drenched in death, I could feel her. I slipped into ill-omened dreams. Whether I was awake or asleep, she was there. Her tiny hands touched my sides, reached for my breasts. I turned to hold her. I called for her.

She was gone. I heard her cries as she descended into Hades. *I will follow you there*, I promised her. *I will climb down after you*. She was my child and she was my mother, returned to me and then maliciously stolen back by the gods. Death would not mean forgetting for me: I would avenge my mother and I would avenge my child. I hurled insults at the gods. At the edge of my vision and at the borders of my hearing, I knew that the slave girls and Calliope were shuddering at my words. I saw Calliope's mouth hover above me, I saw her lips move, but I was deaf to her pleading. I refused all food and water. How else would I follow my child into the afterlife? But I was broken by the weakness of my body. One morning the heady odour of the freshly risen bread that Psyche was offering me proved my undoing. Like a dog, like the dog I was, I grabbed it from her hands. I mashed it into my mouth.

I had betrayed my child. I had returned to life. The gods had taken their revenge. This life was my punishment, this world my torture.

The moon completed its cycle and I was released from the birth chamber. My husband was waiting for me. I was frail and unsteady on my feet. He rushed to hold me.

'Husband,' I whimpered, 'our child.'

I did not finish my sentence. He raised his palm and slapped me. For mentioning the dead, for naming that which never was, for tempting the cruelty of the gods.

I did not cry. I bowed my head. 'I am sorry, husband.'

I devoted myself to work. My fingers curled in pain, my palm blistered and aching from clutching the blade, from ripping through sinew and bone fragments. In that punishing and unforgiving work I lost memory and feeling. I could forget. Pelt after pelt I scraped and made clean. In the strain of that work I could forget her face, the sensation of her tiny fingers locking with mine, the sight of those curious eyes that first opened to look at me. But when our day's work was done, when we retired to our bed after supper, as I lay there listening to Theodorus's coarse snores, she returned to me. Her perfume, her milky smell, I breathed it in. I could hear her defiant crying. My child was calling me. It was impossible to sleep.

'Where are you going, Mistress?'

It was noonday and Psyche and I were returning from the markets. As we pushed through the crowd, I chanced to look down a winding narrow lane and there lay the sea, that dazzling cloak worn by the God, Poseidon. Theodorus and Calliope had warned me of the dangers of the wharves, of the licentious drunkenness of the sailors and dockworkers. We women and our slaves were forbidden to go there. But the abrasive smell of brine acted as a drug on me, and I turned down the lane to make my way to the water.

Psyche was calling after me. I furiously demanded that she leave me. The foolish girl was petrified—to abandon me was to risk the wrath of my husband, and to defy my orders was also unthinkable. I heard her crying as I left her.

I was scared of getting lost in the confusing maze of alleys, also terrified of the crowds; beggars were thronging around me with piteous demands for coin and food. I had enough sense to turn back to the market square, and from there I walked towards the southern gate of the city consecrated to the first Emperor. I ignored the outraged looks of the men who were scandalised to see an unescorted free woman there. I didn't care—all I knew was that I had to reach the sea. I marched to the Augustan gate. I showed the seal of our tanners' guild to the young guards there and they let me pass. Did they think me a madwoman, a whore? I didn't care.

And there I was, for the first time in my life, at the edge of the world.

A stretch of boulders formed a bulwark between the shore and the hungry sea. I stood there, looking out to where dolphins leaped out of the water. On the rocks a colony of cats screeched for fish from boats moored nearby. The sea spray dampened my tunic and skirts but I was oblivious to it. I searched the churning water. Under the blue-green blanket of the sea the black shadows of the depths seemed to reach to the very centre of Hades. My child was there. I could hear her calling me from the deep. If I jumped from the rocks I would join her. I stepped to the very edge of the quay.

'Lady, be careful, the tides are wicked here.' An old man was casting a net over the water.

I stepped back. I had lost her; I could no longer hear my daughter. The waves gently broke and withdrew, broke and withdrew. I could not hear her but I wanted to believe that she could hear me.

'I will come back for you,' I whispered to the sea.

Of course my husband whipped me on my return. I accepted his punishment. My taking off had frightened him and the household, and my beating was nothing compared to the lashing he gave the slave. That evening, I kissed him and cajoled him. With artful tenderness I dared to ask if I might go back to the ocean again. I told him it calmed me and banished the furies.

He relented. Theodorus was kind, and had been troubled by my descent into melancholy and grief. As long as I took a slave with me, I was allowed to go to the waterfront. 'On the Sabbath,' he stipulated, as my kisses rained down on him. 'You can go there on the Sabbath.'

My husband's grandfather had been born in bondage to a nobleman in the city who had Jews counted amongst his slaves. This ancient people, as venerable as the Greeks, as eternal as the
· Egyptians, kept a day of the working week sacred to the worship of their god. The gentleman who had freed my husband's grandfather and thus liberated all his descendants excused the Jewish slaves and workers of his household from labour on this one day sacred to them. In time he did the same for all his slaves and labourers, be they Jews or not. When Theodorus's grandfather was freed, he upheld this obligation in his household, and so did his son, our father Dion. My husband swore that we would do the same when we had a household of our own.

When I had first heard about this indulgence, I'd been scornful. I had been pleased to work and serve my father and my mother. Our only days of rest occurred when we celebrated the harvests and the feast days of the gods.

'This is madness,' I'd said to my husband early in our marriage. 'It will lead to laziness and waste.'

'It is a promise my grandfather made to his master. I will not dishonour that vow.'

I'd shaken my head in bewilderment. 'Do I let Psyche and Fortitude laze around in a torpor all of that strange day?' I demanded. 'That will only breed insolence and disrespect.'

He'd laughed. 'The slave girls are not Jews. They won't abandon you—they'll still prepare the meals, they will collect our water.' He'd added, 'The only Jew who works for us is Daniel. But such compensation is a boon for the other labourers as well.'

His eyes were distant, as if he had forgotten I was there and was convincing himself of the righteousness of his grandfather's promise. 'They are an old race and sacred to the gods, Lydia, and as is true for all ancient peoples, their traditions contain great wisdom. There is justice in the observation of the Sabbath, you will see.'

Two words that had given me pause. One strange and unfamiliar, yet timeless, as though I had always known it. *Sabbath*. The other, known to me, but rarely associated with worship. *Justice*.

And so that became my custom. Once every seven days, I could journey to the port. I was always accompanied by Salonikos, as well as one of my slave girls. Once we got to the seawall, the slave would sit herself as far as possible from the treacherous water, for she knew Poseidon to be wild and intemperate, and would sew and sing while I stared into the depths. Salonikos would lie down beside her and sleep. I had no notion of time passing. I had found myself a home here. On these rocks, between earth and water. In the sea's song, the lapping of the waves, I believed that I could hear my daughter; and I could also hear my mother singing the songs I'd loved as a child.

'Sir, sir, greetings, how are you this fine morning?'

On one visit I was awoken from the spell of the sea by Fortitude, who had risen and was calling and waving to someone. The endless blue of the sea and sky had blinded me; I had to squint to see that she was greeting our workman, Daniel.

The spit we were on shot straight out into Poseidon's lair, but after a length it twisted and formed a further rampart that stretched westwards towards the port. The sea there had been dredged to create a shallow channel where the fishing boats could gently cast themselves into the further waters. Between the straight spit where I found my comfort and the entry to the city's grand port, there was a rise dotted with small hovels and cramped dwellings. I had barely paid it any attention; I thought it the miserable abode of beggars and day labourers. It was this hilltop that Daniel was ascending.

He had his honour and he knew his duty. Daniel turned around and bowed and made his way down the hill towards us. He was barefoot but his steps were sure as he navigated the rock-strewn path. He nodded to Fortitude but for me he struck his chest and bowed once again. Salonikos was still curled in sleep. I went to kick him awake but, with a quiet gesture, Daniel indicated that I should let the slave sleep.

'My lady, I greet you.' A rough voice.

'Greetings,' I answered. 'I hope the gods find you well.'

I immediately realised my mistake. His god forbade loyalty to any other.

But Daniel's response was gracious, if his tone was still gruff. 'My Lord is benevolent,' he replied.

And then came an uncomfortable silence. He was looking out at the sea, not wishing to embarrass me with his gaze. He was dressed in a coarse flax tunic that fell to his knees. And his smell was potent: sweat and salt and man. I wanted to move away from him, to return to the sweet breath of the sea.

I found courage. I indicated the hilltop beyond. 'Is your home there, sir?'

'No, my lady, our meeting house is there.'

As honour demanded, we were not looking at each other. But he sensed my confusion.

'It is a meeting house of we Jews. It is my duty to attend on this day.'

I dared to turn. His head was still bowed, and I looked beyond him to the cluster of huts and outhouses that sprawled across the higher part of the hill.

'May I come with you, sir?'

My boldness surprised us both, and for the first time his eyes met mine. They were the colour of chestnuts, paler than his skin. We both swiftly averted our faces.

'If my lady wants.' His voice gruffer now, suspicious.

This courage to be so shameless, where had it come from? I knew that Theodorus and his father had great respect for the Jews. It was said their mysteries were so profound that they had adherents amongst the noblest of families in Thrace and Macedonia. But this was not what provoked my impudence in demanding what I did of Daniel. What fired my curiosity was the desire to know about a god who disavowed all other gods, who claimed enmity between Himself and those gods who had betrayed my mother and my daughter—who had betrayed me.

I nodded to Daniel. 'Thank you, sir. I will follow you.'

Fortitude and Salonikos walked two steps behind Daniel and I walked two steps behind them. In this procession we scaled the hill.

The slope was crowded with camps and beggars, mired in squalor and filth. I covered my head and raised my shawl to my nose and mouth to keep out the stench. We approached a high wall of roughly laid stones. Daniel led us to the pine gate, opened it, and politely ushered us into a courtyard.

It was chaos: people, noise, the yelling of children. Chickens darted and pecked amongst the seated crowd, mothers took their children to squat by the wall to relieve themselves in a small grove of olive trees. The yard was not paved and my sandals sank into the mud. The noise was matched by the clamour from the dwellings and hovels all around us, now hidden from view. I could hear the obscene yelling of a drunk from over the walls. The sputtering and sizzling of food cooking over fires. The sounds and stink of poverty.

Fortitude, looking dazed and horrified, stood as close to me as she dared without touching me. She was gripping tightly to the basket on her head with one hand, scared that someone was going to snatch it.

I looked ahead. A long and tattered screen made from goats'

hides stitched together was hung over thin reed rods that divided the width of the yard. A two-storey wooden building rose behind it.

I pointed to the dwelling, thinking it might offer some respite from the crowd. 'Sir,' I said to Daniel, 'could we go there for some shelter?'

Regretfully, he shook his head. 'I'm afraid it is not possible, my lady. Only Jews can enter.'

I was outraged. After such a brazen insult I was ready to go. But just then the screen was drawn and an old woman emerged, her head shrouded, her thin hands clutching a basket laden with dried fruits, breads and pickled nuts. The crowd rose as one and rushed to her. As the very young and the very old lunged towards her, as tiny hands and aged curled fingers pulled food from the basket, it was as if the world consisted only of the cries and calls of birds, and that the birds spoke every language known to man. Stunned, I watched. In an instant, the basket had been emptied. And then, in another instant, the yard was deserted.

Except for my slaves and I. Except for the wary Daniel, and a handful of women nursing their infants. From within the ramshackle wooden dwelling hidden behind the screen, for the first time I could hear chanting. I became aware of prayers being spoken and sung. A youth pulled back the screen. He stepped out into the yard and with a haughty air he surveyed the few who remained. And then, I was dumbstruck. He spoke in Greek but his words made no sense to me. What appalled me was that his gaze fell indiscriminately across us all.

Daniel's eyes were still respectfully lowered from mine, but he came as close to me as he dared. 'My lady, it is best you leave,' he said quietly.

'What is he doing?'

'He is teaching the stories of our people.'

One of the young mothers, a tiny infant suckling, interrupted the youth's incantations. 'Sir, sir,' she gasped, shocked by her own daring, 'I have done as your god demands: I have saved my child; I have not allowed her to be abandoned.'

The youth was clearly affected by the young woman's words.

'I am hungry, sir, my family have deserted me. Please, I need food.'

The youth now looked like a scared and foolish boy. He looked plaintively towards Daniel. The women too were looking at him as though only he could answer the mother's desperate plea.

Behind me I heard Fortitude say quietly but with spite, 'Beg in the street, that's what the rest of us have to do.'

But Daniel went to the suffering woman. 'We will feed you as best we can,' he said to her. 'Keep coming here to our yard and we will help you.'

He squatted next to the mother. And then he did something that won him my favour for eternity. He loosened the rags around the child and gently tickled the sparse down on its head. The infant cooed with pleasure.

'If she survives we will sell her in the markets. We will find her a home.'

Behind me, Salonikos snorted, his contempt clear. I too gasped at these words. She was a girl infant; there was no good price they could get for her at the markets: to feed her, to raise her—there was no way that such costs could be recouped.

Daniel was again at my side. The youth had returned to his recitation of his people's ancient lore.

Our labourer's next words were full of trembling. I sensed his great embarrassment. 'Our Lord considers it a great disgrace to abandon an infant. Once He has breathed life into a soul, only He has the right to reclaim that life.' He said it almost apologetically, anticipating my indignation and scorn. 'That is what is written,' he mumbled. 'That is what we must obey.'

He thought I would be repelled, insulted by such words.

I made my way to where the women were sitting. I adjusted the shield of my veil across my hair. I sat down with them and I looked up at the awkward youth, nodding that he might continue. I had found a god I could serve.

———

She is dying, my Salvation is dying. She knows it as well as I do. The winter encroaches, the trees are losing their leaves and the winds that come ripping up our mountain are now made heavy with ice. The birds have gone. We are enveloped in silence, save for the wind thundering through the trees. There are days when my Salvation cannot get up off the blanket of twigs and crushed bones that is our bed. I stoke and replenish the fire with foraged kindling and dried branches. And, as always, I remind her about you: our son, our brother, our Jesus. Our hope.

On entering the cave after my morning's scavenging—I had collected some roots and mushrooms—I find her in agony. Her body is convulsing, her eyes swollen red from crying and filled with despair. I drop the fruit and am at her side. 'Where is the pain, my daughter?'

She cannot hear my words; all that she can communicate is pain and distress.

I collect her in my arms, I kiss her all over, I murmur words of comfort and devotion. And slowly my endearments and my love calm her.

I dutifully recite to her the prayer that our teacher Paul taught me. Even as I begin, on those first words—'It is better to find refuge in the Lord than it is to trust in humans'—I sense her pain receding. The malevolent spirits that devour her are cowed by the prayer and so I continue. 'It is better to find refuge in the Lord, child, than it is to trust in kings. All the kingdoms of the world surround us, child, but I call out the Lord's name and I defeat them. They surround us on every side, but we call out His name and the evil gods flee.' I know that the whimpers and the groans she makes are her accompaniment to the prayer. 'The Strangers swarm around as bees,' I chant, 'but they are destroyed as quickly as a bush is consumed by fire. We call out the name of the Lord and they are destroyed. We are attacked and we stumble but the Lord hears our call and He lifts us up. The Lord is our strength and our song. He is our Salvation.'

I kiss her lips, her eyes, her stump, I kiss the fingers on her good hand. My tears fall, they cannot stop falling. 'This is why I named you so, my daughter: you are promised to the Lord.'

I feed her. She shakes her head, indignant and stubborn, and I have to force the gruel down her throat. I will not let her starve. She spits, she chokes, but I hold her mouth closed until I see her throat swallow. She is furious, but I pray she knows that I wish her only good. Once she is fed, her hand finds mine and wraps itself tight around it. That trust breaks me. I have to flee our cave, run as far from there as I can so I might release my despair without her knowing. I howl into the night. Like a witch. Like a dog.

'When is he coming? When is he returning?'

I asked that once of my teacher, and Paul replied, 'He'll come when we are not expecting him. He'll come as a thief in the night. We must be ready, Lydia. Every moment of our waking and every moment of our sleep, we must be prepared for him.'

The air is biting but the wind has abated. Down below the city is in darkness. The moon is new, and even the glow of the winding river is faint as it is swallowed by black night and disappears. I have no strength left for lamentation. I dry my eyes.

Jesus, if I could ask you anything it is to come now, to come today.

I look up to the night sky, to the fiery glow of the stars. An owl hoots. A sudden sharp awakening. I have not fallen asleep; my eyes haven't been shut, but I have been lost in reverie. The fire will be spent. My child will be cold. My naked feet trample stone and branch, dirt and thistle to get back to our cave.

The embers smoulder. The fire is not dead. And my daughter isn't in pain. She is sleeping peacefully. Carefully, as quietly as I can, I lay more kindling on the fire; I watch the wood spark, the blaze take and the flames rise. I rest a thick branch across it.

You returned, my Jesus. Not in fire, not with a battle cry, not in splendour. You returned for this child.

———

I bore my husband two sons. The first, on surviving his first year, my husband named Fidelus, an Italian name that honoured the nobleman who had freed his kin. The foreign name proved

difficult for our Greek tongues and the boy was soon nicknamed
Philos. Our second was named Leonidas.

This should have been the period of my greatest happiness.
I was a mother to two sturdy sons who had survived the demonic
illnesses of infancy. I was the wife of a prospering artisan, a kind
and hardworking man, and my children were the first generation
born to full liberty and citizenship. Calliope was all graciousness
and benevolence and our father, Dion, pledged to grant most of
his fortune to his beloved and honoured firstborn son. And yet
this was the period of my deepest melancholy.

My boys did not bring me peace. With each birth, with each
confinement, when it was just myself and the child in the world,
I found myself puzzled and then distraught by the estrangement I
felt. I could see nothing of me in them; they were only their
father's sons.

I could not forget her. She who had been taken from me. We'd
had only the merest sliver of time together. But I could not forget
the ease with which her tiny mouth had found and seized my
nipple. Philos and Leon had bit as they drank from me, as if to
rip into my flesh. When I was left blessedly alone, I would allow
my grief and wretchedness to show. My tears were never-ending.

As if sensing my estrangement, my boys grew detached from
me. They were obedient and respectful children, and grew to
be resolute and admirable young boys. But it was no secret
that they preferred the company of Fortitude and Psyche. The
slave girls admired and praised them for their boyishness and
mischievousness. 'Look at your long prick, Philos,' they would
tease the eldest, tugging at his sex. 'You will have a hundred
sons.' That would make little Leon complain. 'And what of

mine? Isn't mine big enough?' Fortitude would cup his pebble testes in her hand, kiss his tiny sex. 'Yours will grow to be huge,' she would chuckle. 'It will be enormous, I pity your wife.' The slave girls would fall into merriment, and the boys, not under-standing, would erupt into joyous laughter as well. I found such revelry noxious; my head felt as if a score of furies had alighted within it, pecking at my sanity.

The shaving and the scraping of the hides, the work that exhausted me and granted me sleep, this work saved me. And the stories I heard at the Jewish meeting house, they also saved me. Though Theodorus had initially been suspicious of my attendance there, Philos's birth confirmed the benevolence of their deity. Without these visits I would not have endured, I would have thrown myself into the sea. There I learned about the only god who was enraged by the abduction and sacrifice of *my* firstborn. It was this knowledge that saved me.

Not long after Leon was born, there came a time of plenty. The city prospered, our work increased and we too grew wealthier. My husband purchased another slave, Rectitude, for our household, and two more men for the tannery. Demand was so great that he hired more labourers. I saw them as I worked at shaving the skins. In the distance I could see our new labourers and slaves at their toil. I saw them yet I did not pay them any attention.

My teacher, my guide to the Lord and to His son, my Paul: you were there and I did not know.

'Two of the men I hired are Jews, Lydia. They were vouched for by Daniel. Are you pleased?'

.

I was crouched in front of my husband, washing his feet. He had grown stout. He now indulged himself completely.

I said nothing. I washed his feet, his calves, his thighs.

'You must have noticed the old ugly one.'

I had noticed him. A beaten and bent-over body. The gods hadn't been kind to him from birth, but time and the world had been crueller.

'Is he blind?'

My husband shook his head. 'He has only one good eye. But he's a hard worker. Daniel was right about that. But by the gods he is ugly.'

His fingers stroked my braided hair.

'But the boy with him,' my husband sighed, 'he is as beautiful as Apollo.'

With those words his grip on my hair tightened and one hand reached for my breasts.

'Husband,' I said warily, 'I have my monthly blood.'

He jolted back then as if I had struck him, then kicked me hard. I sprawled across the floor.

His voice was a snarl. 'How dare you touch me then.'

I smiled as he sullenly ordered me to my bedchamber. I could hear him calling out for Rectitude. Let her have him, let her give him bastard sons.

I was standing on the edge of the world, looking out to the churning sea. The water was grey and black. Winter had come.

'The sea is calming, isn't it, my lady? Even in its most savage aspect it cannot help but soothe.'

Behind me Salonikos released an incensed gasp at his temerity in addressing me.

Our labourer, the half-blind easterner, was also looking out to sea.

Insulted, I did not deign to speak.

'Our Lord's Creation,' he continued. 'All one has to do is look into it and thereby come to know His truth and His power and His grace.'

I knew that he had turned to face me. A further outrage.

'You know this. You have found peace that way.'

My slave stirred, as if preparing to strike him on my behalf.

I lifted my hand and Salonikos drew back.

My eyes were locked on the sea, my palm out to indicate my disdain for the man's impudence. 'I will have my husband whip you for your insolence. If I could I would lash you myself.'

He inclined his head slightly. 'Forgive me, my lady. I saw you at our meeting house and thought you were a believer in the Lord, in the one God. I apologise a thousand times for my disrespect.'

I had noticed him there as well, and realised he was the old man my husband had hired on Daniel's advice. I had also observed that he and his younger companion often argued with their fellow Jews. The nature of their disagreements remained unknown to me as they occurred behind the screen. Only the previous Sabbath, this one-eyed fool had interrupted a young boy reciting his people's odes and started haranguing us with absurd stories. Something loathsome about a slave or a criminal nailed to a cross. The man's voice was high-pitched and grating— I had hardly listened. And not long after, a group of men had pushed back the goat hides and demanded that he stop his raving. Daniel had been amongst them. He might have vouched for the quality of the man's work, but Daniel's anger that day revealed his hatred and suspicion of the man's stupid stories.

I kept my eyes fixed firmly on the sea. If he had any sense of decency he would take his leave.

He didn't, he stayed there right beside me.

'Forgive me,' he said. 'I thought you were a friend.'

'Shame on you, shame on you,' Psyche hissed.

The spray off the water was cooling. Was that why my fury abated so suddenly? Was that why I turned to him?

'I am not a Jew.'

'Do you believe in the one Lord, the Creator of all?'

He had a squeak of a voice, a careful command of Greek, but an accent that marked him as foreign.

The waves rose then withdrew.

'I do believe.'

'There is a world coming, Lydia, a kingdom of the Lord where there will be no cruelty, no injustice. That world is coming soon.'

And in that instant his voice no longer seemed thin and effete but strong and stirring. I understood that an offering had been made, one so strange and unexpected, one so astonishing and world-shattering, that I was afraid to move, to breathe, to utter a word. No man had ever before spoken to me so directly: not my father, my brothers or my husband. It was if the veil separating men and women had been torn away; as if we were man and man and not man and woman. His familiarity, his use of my name, his disregard for the boundaries of caste and honour, all of that should have made me turn away from him, should have brought a thousand curses to my lips. But I was transfixed. When I had first come to this seawall, when I had first stood there and looked out to the water, I had known that I could have leaped from a world I despised into an oblivion I wanted but did not have the courage to submit to. That moment of life or death had returned. Such was the momentous offering being made to me.

'How do I enter that kingdom, sir?' I asked, shaking.

He took a step and was beside me. 'Courage, sister; you will need courage.'

I was looking straight into his one good eye. He dared to look at me and I dared to look at him. And in that eye, I saw light, kindness, understanding.

'Sir,' I answered, 'I am ready.'

He had been watching me. He had seen that my shoulders were bowed, that I was without joy. He'd seen my suffering and distress.

He spoke gently. 'You know that the Lord is just, Lydia. Let me show you that He is also loving. Will you allow me to bring you to His love?'

Behind us, outraged gasps from the slaves.

'Shut your mouth,' I snapped at Psyche.

And then another obscenity, a further shattering of the world and its laws. He turned to her, a slave, as though she was his equal. 'The Lord created you as well, sister, and He loves you too.'

Psyche made no answer. She had turned away to face the sea. But I sensed her distress. Her hands, folded together and clasped against her belly, were trembling. From the shame and the rage. Was he touched, was he mad? Since friendship between a slave and a freeman was impossible, she thought he was mocking her.

He turned back to me, suddenly seeming weary. 'You must tell your husband about our conversation. He has to know we've spoken. If he wants to punish me, then so be it. But you must speak to him and ask his permission. If he grants it, we can meet on the next Sabbath, and I will lead you to the Lord of justice and love.'

For a staggering moment I thought he was going to touch me. 'Can you do that?'

I was stone. With great effort, I forced a word from my mouth. 'Yes.'

I watched him walk back along the bulwark, back to the world. And still I could not move.

'Are you alright, my lady?'

I did not answer my slave, I did not hear her as she spat curses and insults about the Jew. I was struck senseless by an astonishment as great as any I had experienced in my life. When I thought he was leaning in to me, when I believed our very skin would touch, when I was sure that he was to enact the greatest of dishonours, I was not afraid.

My husband had grown soft and fat. He indulged my wishes.

The Sabbath arrived. I decided I would take only Psyche with me; Salonikos was headstrong and unable to hide his contempt for the Jews.

The old man and his young friend were waiting on the stone wall.

That morning, I was so keen to get to the meeting house, I hardly glanced at the sea.

'Shall we go?'

He turned, bowed, and said in that weak stuttering voice, 'I am Paul and this is my brother, my friend in the Saviour, my most beloved Timothy.'

'Are you only known by your Greek name?'

He smiled at this. 'In my tongue I am called Saul.'

Sa-aul. Something ancient and indeed god-fearing trembled through such a name. I tried it on my lips, silently recited it. *Sa-aul.*

'And I, my Lady, I am born Greek. I have no other name but Timothy.'

As he spoke I felt a stirring of something long gone, from when my mother would tend to Penelope and ignore me. I recognised it as jealousy. I wanted to be instructed by Paul alone. This youth was comely, polite and respectful, but why did he have to be here?

I ignored him, turned to the old man. 'Shall we go?'

We walked alongside the seawall, passing the fishermen and the cats waiting for the catch, turned towards the port, and began our walk up the hill. To my surprise we didn't turn into the narrow street that led to the Judeans' meeting house but instead continued up the rise. The higher we climbed the less huts we saw. We passed a tiny field, overgrown with weeds, bordered by rough ditches overflowing with animal and human shit and rotting food. The stink was such that I covered my face with my shawl.

The old man turned. 'I apologise, Lydia, it's not far now.'

Again, I felt divided within myself. Curious to continue. Mortified by his familiar use of my name.

We came to three makeshift cottages. The walls had only recently been rendered and their roofs consisted of bound sheaves of the lowest-grade rye grass. The occupants were so poor there were no gates or fences. Their animals—a few sickly-looking dogs and skeletal sheep and goats—roamed freely across the hillside.

We stopped in front of one of the cottages, and the old man bowed and gestured for me to enter.

Even though she remained behind me I could sense Psyche's disdain. So these were the followers of the Judean god? She would be scornful at the paucity and weakness of such a deity.

I pushed aside the hide over the door and entered.

There were five of them, three of them women, and of them one a slave with shaven head. There was also a slave youth and an older man, dark-skinned but with a thick tawny beard. I was shocked anew to see that the freeman had his hand on the boy's shoulder, a gesture that I immediately perceived as being gentle and paternal, as though they were father and son, not man and slave.

The eldest of the women bowed. 'Welcome, sister,' she said. 'Welcome to our home.'

I could not contain my anger. 'I am not your sister!'

The woman recoiled. I was glad she could see my fury.

Paul was beside me. 'We are all believers here, Lydia. We are all brethren together.'

I sniffed, looked over my shoulder. Psyche had not dared enter unbidden.

And then the man spoke. 'Child,' he called out, 'you may enter.'

Psyche drew the curtain. Shyly she came inside, keeping her back to the wall. She gazed around in mistrust.

The first woman smiled at me. 'He is returning.' Her gaze was direct, as though she expected me to reply.

Paul stepped forward. 'Lydia is vouched to the Lord,' he said, 'but she doesn't yet know the Saviour.'

The other man lifted his hand from the slave's shoulder and turned to me. 'The Anointed One is returning.'

Were they talking about a high priest? Or a king?

Paul shook his head, as if warning the other man. 'The Saviour,' Paul almost growled. 'The Saviour is returning.' He turned to me.

I realised that if Paul looked directly at you as he spoke, the blank orb of his damaged eye, the ridiculous pitch of his voice, his stutter, all were forgotten. Returning his unwavering gaze, I understood his power. Looking into that eye was like staring into the sea.

I glanced around the pitiful dwelling. There was a table, a blackened hearth; a narrow alcove that served as a bedchamber. Two openings in the roof, one above the hearth and one opposite, were the only source of illumination. It struck me that there were no deities to be seen. No altars. No clay Mother. No wooden phallus. Nothing of the gods. I thought how this absence must be filling Psyche with terror. But for the first time since entering this pauper's hut, I felt calm.

'Are you all Jews?' My voice was hoarse.

The young slave girl spoke for the first time. 'My lady,' she said timidly, 'we are like you. We fear and worship the god of Israel but we are . . .' She hesitated over a word and then blurted, 'But we are Strangers.'

My excursions to the Jewish meeting house had taught me what she meant. That Israel was the kingdom that the Judean god had bequeathed to His people. That everyone else who was not of that kingdom were Strangers.

Paul beckoned to the slave girl. 'Daphne, daughter, will you take Psyche with you to collect some water?' He pointed to some cheap stone jars against the hearth. 'I fear we are nearly empty.'

My slave was reluctant to leave me but I commanded her to.

Once they were gone Paul brought me a stool and sat himself, facing me again.

'Lydia,' he said firmly, 'all that are in this room with you are of Israel. They have become so through their faith in the Son of the Lord. His name is Jesus the Saviour. Have you heard of him?'

I shook my head.

'Do you believe as we do that there is only one God, the Lord of Israel? Do you believe that He created all that is visible and all that is invisible? Do you renounce your belief in all other gods?'

I knew now why he had banished Psyche. This was a wickedness beyond all wickedness: to insult the gods by denying them. But even though I was shocked by such sacrilege, I was aware of a delicious warmth filling me. I didn't know what Paul meant by that word, *belief.* The gods were as real as demons and nymphs, as attested to as ghosts and shades. But I had no trust in them. They had stolen my daughter.

'I don't believe in any god but the god of the Jews,' I answered.

He was beaming with the satisfaction of a father witnessing a child rising and taking his first steps.

'There was a veil across the world, Lydia,' he went on, 'a veil that kept us from the light of the Lord. All of us fell into evil and a great darkness. My people, the most beloved of the Lord, they too have fallen into the shadows. They sin and they are greedy and cruel. I have travelled from the east to the west, from Syria to Greece, and all I have witnessed is that darkness. Rome too, great Rome, is the most wicked and the most blind to the light.'

At this, I could not help but gasp. My hand leaped to my chest and I beat it repeatedly to ward off the evil his words had conjured. If Psyche had heard him, if she had seen that I did not protest, did not rise and flee on hearing those traitorous words, I would be dead. One word to my husband and I would be dead.

Paul grabbed my arm. 'There is no need for that. Those silly rituals won't save you.'

His eye was as mesmerising as that of a serpent. I was numb; unable to protest the obscenity of his touching me.

'A momentous event took place, Lydia, when you were a child and I was still a young man. An event of such magnitude that it tore apart the earth.'

He was trembling; he let go of my arm. 'How did we not feel it? How did we not realise that the very ground beneath our feet was splitting open?'

His voice firmed, and he continued, 'The Lord had fulfilled an ancient promise. A man came out of Judea, the man we call Jesus. He was not of high caste, nor was he wealthy. But he was the one sent by the Lord to be the light for the whole world. To be the Messiah, in my tongue, and in yours, Saviour.'

He scratched his beard. 'A saviour,' he repeated, as if nourished by the word. 'The Saviour.'

I felt light-headed. All these words were meaningless. Was this Saviour a god?

'She doesn't understand,' the red-bearded man barked.

Paul held up his hand. 'She will.'

I found my voice. 'What is it that I have to understand?'

'That the Lord is done with His Creation. The coming of the Saviour brings a new kingdom where sin is defeated. And where death, that comes from sin, is also defeated.'

The eldest of the women stepped forward. I was still looking at Paul and at first I didn't fully take in her words. She realised this and repeated them. 'Sister,' she said, 'that coming kingdom—we will all live to see it, and there we will be reunited with our departed sons and our daughters.'

She uttered the only thing that I had desired since my daughter was taken from me, the only thing that had meaning for me: to hold her in my arms and undo my betrayal of her.

'Where is this kingdom?' I demanded. 'Is it Hades?'

Paul laughed. 'No, Lydia, it is not our world of shadows. It is a new Creation that is as real as the world we live in now. But it will last forever and means that we will finally be able to walk again with the Lord in His garden.'

I forced my gaze from his to address the woman. 'Are all our children there? Is everyone who has died to be found there?'

'No,' answered the bearded man. 'In this new world the last will be first and the first will be last. This is what Jesus has sworn.' He was almost animal in his passion. 'Only those who've suffered will be there—those who've been enslaved, those who've endured cruelty and evil. Only they are promised to the kingdom to come.'

My daughter suffered. She endured cruelty and evil.

I turned back to Paul. 'Is my daughter with this God, is she with this Jesus?'

A spasmed racked his body, his jaw clenched, his eye rolled back. Was he possessed? Timothy placed a hand on Paul's

shoulder and the old man grasped at it. And through the touch
he was released. He must be a seer, I thought, he has been granted
visions into the worlds beyond this one.

'Do you see her?' I pleaded. 'Is she with Jesus?'

His voice trembled with pity. 'She is lost. But the Saviour
mourns her loss.'

And of what use is that mourning to me? I wanted my will
to be a force that destroyed this hovel, this city, this world.
But the sorrow that came from that piercing eye, that sorrow
sucked my rage from me. He had not lied. His God grieved for
my daughter and I was suddenly stunned by the enormity of
such unthinkable compassion. And with that understanding I
realised that I had been in shadow, that since she had been taken
from me I had been in league with death. My gods deceived and
tormented and abandoned us, but this God mourned the loss
of a child.

'Will your God avenge her death?'

The bearded man stepped forward. 'Yes,' he answered. 'That
is the kingdom we seek.'

In the vehemence of his wrath he became my ally.

'I will follow this Jesus,' I declared. 'I will worship this God.'

Paul shook his head. 'He is not a god, Lydia. He came to fulfil
the promise of the Lord.'

'Where is he now? Where is this Jesus?'

The younger girl spoke up. 'He is returning.'

And as though in prayer, all answered, 'Truly, this season or
the one next, he is returning to us.'

'From where?'

Paul hesitated. He was looking at his young companion. And

for the first time, Timothy spoke. 'He died, sister. He was killed, but on the third day of his interment he rose from the dead.'

My head ached. None of it made sense. I tried to understand. 'How did he die?'

I waited. And I waited. Would no one answer?

Paul's voice, for once, was deep and clear. 'He was crucified by the Romans.'

And then I laughed. I laughed so hard I nearly fell off my stool. The old man attempted to fix my gaze once more with his serpent stare, but all I saw before me was a deluded and ridiculous old fool.

'I saw him, Lydia, he came to me after he died. I've been sent by him to bring you Strangers to the Lord. He was crucified, he suffered the most vile and obscene of deaths, and he was resurrected three days later. I saw him with my own eyes. He died but he came back.'

That strange word, *resurrected*, replaced my levity with hostility. I felt fury for how they'd mocked and deceived me.

'What nonsense,' I spat out. 'What idiocy is all of this? Men who die on the cross are criminals and bandits. They are filthy slaves. How can such a man be a god? How can such a man avenge the death of my daughter?'

'How did she die?'

I whirled around to face the older woman. 'You have no right to ask me that question.'

Her eyes narrowed. 'Yet I did. And I'll ask it again. How did she die?'

I could not answer. I was afraid that if I did the truth would rent me apart. I would not reveal my anguish to this deluded and treasonous mob.

'You abandoned her. You killed her.'

The levee that had for so long held back my grief, that impenetrable wall, suddenly cracked and shuddered and was destroyed. I fell to bawling.

But the bearded man's words broke through my grief.

'You abandoned her to the wolves and the vultures, didn't you? You weren't there to hear her screams as they tore at her body, feasted on her bones. But that is how she would have suffered. Wasn't that a vile and obscene death?'

I didn't want to hear but I heard. His words, the tearing of flesh, the howls of my child. Her last scream before death and Hades and darkness.

Paul dared to insult me once more. With both hands he grabbed my face, and held it until I could not help but look at him.

'Our brother Perseverance is harsh, I know, but his truth is a way towards understanding. Perseverance too has abandoned a child—he knows your shame. Don't you understand, Lydia? This Jesus whom you believe scandalous and base, he knows what your daughter suffered. He knows because he understands what it is to be the most despised. Don't you see, sister? Our Lord is not only the Lord of justice, He is also the Lord of love.'

My revulsion and anger calmed. But I still couldn't understand. The cross, that shameful weapon of torture and death—how could a god rise out of such debasement?

Paul was stroking my cheek. 'Don't try to make sense of it all now, Lydia. It will come. But ask yourself: what other gods would weep for your child?'

Paul, that is the moment you became my teacher, my guide to the Lord and to His son. I did not understand then. But those words entered my heart. I knew the other gods. They had forsaken me; they cared nothing for my daughter. They taunted us, abandoned us. Was I to believe in a god nailed to a cross? Maybe such an impossible reconciliation would never come. But I also knew what to abandon and forsake. I knew what I despised. I carefully moved his hands away from my face. I looked around the decrepit hut. No incense, no altars, no idols. I did not understand, but at that moment I pledged myself to their world and not the world of the gods. I dried my eyes, and I said, 'I believe.'

Paul leaned forward. 'You believe that there is one God, the Lord of Israel?'

I nodded.

'And that Jesus, a son of man, is the Saviour promised to Israel?'

'Yes.'

'That he was crucified on the Roman cross, buried and rose to the Lord on the third day?'

I couldn't reveal my doubt. 'I believe.'

'And do you believe that he will return to us any day now?'

'Yes.'

The man, Perseverance, the older woman, the girl, Timothy and Paul, they rushed to embrace me. They called me sister and for the first time Perseverance smiled. And though their faith was strange and their mysteries yet unknown, I was calm and content. In the hovel that only an hour before I had abhorred, in that sanctuary, I was at peace.

*

Paul was a seer; he had no doubt that I would accept their fellowship, so he had already prepared a thanksgiving for me that afternoon. Psyche returned with the slave, Daphne, except I was not to call them slaves. Within that wretched dwelling we were sisters. This commandment, I learned, had been given to us by the Saviour himself. There would be no master and no slave in the promised kingdom. No castes. And there was a greater gift: no women and no men in the coming kingdom. We would all be equal. As we prepared the dishes and the wine for the feast—bread and the most basic gruel, wild herbs, honeycomb, a plate of wood-smoked nuts—Clemency revealed that she and Perseverance were married, but in preparation for the returning Jesus they lived now as brother and sister not as husband and wife. She no longer had to endure the humiliations of rutting; she was freed from that curse. She'd had two daughters taken from her when she was a slave. This was how she knew the ordeal of abandonment. Yet she had the fortune to be bonded to a household where her mistress, though a Stranger, had come to hear of and to respect the god of the Judeans. This noblewoman had pleaded for her husband to free Clemency. And he had done so. I asked if she and Perseverance had any children. Her eyes clouded with tears and she said simply, 'Our son died not long after he was born.'

And I was amazed by the sensation that overtook me. Clemency's face was turned away from mine; I sensed her struggle to contain her suffering. It was as if her grief was mine and my grief was hers and she was not a freed slave and I was not the wife of a landowner. Suddenly I was next to her, I was holding her. Her deep sigh was a warm breath across my neck.

'He is coming,' I said. 'Truly, the Saviour is returning.'

Not long after the dishes were ready for the meal, there was a greeting at the door and three more people arrived. The first, Temperance, was a slave. With him was his master, an ironmonger named Apollonius. The greater shock came with the entry of the third. This was a woman adorned in silk, her veil shimmering with gilded thread. This was Clemency's former owner, Heraclea, a woman of the highest caste. I went to bow but Clemency stopped me. I was astonished to see the noblewoman kiss and embrace us all, even the slaves. This was a miracle, a scandal, more unthinkable and perverse than any nightmare. Psyche's mouth hung open, her eyes were as wide as those of a terrified child.

When the noblewoman went to hug her, the foolish girl burst into tears.

'You cannot touch me, my lady, you must not touch me.' Her sobs were such we could only just make out the words.

'She is not yet one of us,' explained Clemency.

The noblewoman moved away and, bizarrely, apologised. To a slave. Psyche dropped to her knees, offering thanks for her mercy.

Next to me Clemency whispered, 'I was like that girl once.'

Her husband snapped back at her, 'Yes, we were all like her once—we were forced to be.'

Then, in a loud voice, he called out those dangerous and seditious words. 'In the kingdom to come the last will be first and the first will be last.'

And the noblewoman nodded.

Then came the feast. Temperance had a sistrum that he shook as Paul sang prayers that he declared were of the heroic age, when a king named David ruled the world. 'These are his songs, dear Lydia,' he called to me between chants. 'These are the songs that Jesus our Saviour sang.' And there in a circle, a slave on one side of me and a noblewoman on the other, I glimpsed the kingdom to come. This was the music of the kingdom, this was the fellowship of the kingdom, these were its citizens and its laws. The merciless and mocking gods had no place here. 'Teach me these songs,' I called out joyously as we whirled and danced. 'Let me learn these songs.'

We will teach you, dear sister, you will learn them, and you will speak in tongues of a thousand peoples. You will see the face of God. Take this bread, sister, swallow your portion, pass it along to Temperance, who is neither slave nor man but brother. Pass it to Heraclea, who is neither lady nor woman but sister. Pass it along, and as you swallow this bread, remember the sacrifice of the Saviour. Take this wine, sister, sip this delicious warm wine, pass the cup to your brother and your sister. As the wine flows from tongue to throat, remember that this is the blood the Saviour spilled for us. You are one of us now, Lydia.

As Psyche—not my slave, my sister—led me down the rocky path, past the stinking field, past the hovels, through the markets and temple squares of the city, up the rise to our home, as my husband and sons greeted me, embraced me, as my husband took me to our bedchamber, as he pushed apart my legs and entered me, I was in a dream. I was still lost in the songs and in the dance, and the body and the blood of my new god was in me and there was no stench from Theodorus, no weight pinning me down. I wasn't there. I was in another kingdom. Another world.

*

As my husband's belly spread so did our home. While our labourers and slaves worked at the dye sheds and stoked the furnaces, our father added rooms to our house and purchased the land alongside his property to build us a home of our own. Tutors were hired for our sons. Theodorus was puffed with pride. 'Our sons will read and write,' he crowed. 'They will marry rich girls and they will father gentlemen.'

I now lived for the Sabbath, when I would enter a world that was invisible to all but those in our secret devotion. I lived for the world that Paul had created for me. I felt unshackled from the chains that had bound me my whole life. All Theodorus saw was that now I laughed, that I was gentle with my sons, that I indulged him. And so he spoiled me, believing that my interest in the Jewish God was benign. He had no idea that the Lord and the Saviour were gods who shattered worlds.

One more ritual awaited me before I could claim complete fellowship. I was to be bathed in running water. It was this ritual that breached the division between the two worlds, and I would emerge from that baptism cleansed and ready for the kingdom to come. I knew who had to baptise me; there could be no other. But I was afraid to ask. How I loved Paul: for the way he sought my counsel, for his chaste affection for me, for how patient he was with his teaching; love of neighbours and meeting spite with forgiveness—so much of the Saviour's words were impossible to comprehend. 'I am uneducated and a woman,' I'd complain. 'I can't understand it!' Paul would laugh and reject such petulance. 'Lydia,' he'd answer, 'our Saviour said that a woman must become as a man to enter the kingdom. She must not doubt herself. One of his most cherished and honoured disciples is a woman.' He would grow stern. 'Such excuses will no longer do. We are all capable of understanding, slave as much as master, ruled as much as ruler, woman as much as man, and son as much as father.' I loved Paul. This was not the love demanded by the Greek gods, this was not the love of the hunt and violation. Paul had to be the one to baptise me, so that in the new Creation, it would be him to whom I was bonded.

I awoke to a crisp and clear morning, promising cloudless skies and sunshine, but the return of winter was on its breath. On awakening, I knew that I was with child.

I rushed through my duties, I was impatient. All I knew was that I had to see Paul, I had to ask him what to do.

I waited for them at our gate. As soon as I saw them approaching, I knew that something was amiss. Paul's gait was heavy and he looked troubled. I rushed to him, resisting my impulse to embrace him. Words of greeting were on my tongue, but he was the one who spoke first.

'Lydia,' he said softly but firmly, 'Timothy and I have to leave Greece.'

It was as if a cold hand was at my throat. The vengeful gods had prepared this final, lacerating punishment for me. I heard their mocking laughter: *Did you really think that we were finished with you?*

'Why must you go?' I implored.

'We are needed. I must return to Jerusalem.'

'I will come with you.'

'No, you can't.'

'Why not?'

With a sternness he had never shown me before he said, 'Because you are married to our master. That bond cannot be broken.'

I understood. His teaching had been clear. This faith we followed, this Saviour we believed in, they both renounced divorce.

His tone softened. 'We will meet again, Lydia. In the coming kingdom.'

I ignored Timothy. I dared an outrage. Visible to anyone who might be working nearby, I touched my Paul's face. 'I am with child.'

His sombre expression lifted, a wide smile transforming his face. 'This son,' he said, 'you will raise him for Israel.'

My voice was peevish. 'What if it is a girl?'

He dared outrage as well then. He took my hands, I felt his gnarled rough fingers.

He leaned in towards me. 'I know your sadness, sister,' he whispered in my ear. 'But Theodorus is not cruel and his home is secure and his trade is flourishing. He will not abandon this child.'

'What if he insists?'

There was a noise from within the house. We sprang apart.

'That will not happen,' he answered.

'What if he demands it?'

A great tiredness came over him. He looked like an old and beaten man. 'You must not abandon this child.'

My fate, ordained at the beginning of Creation, had been sealed.

My voice was now confident. 'Baptise me?'

Age and suffering were lifted from him and his eyes were as

luminous as those of a child. He could not speak, he clutched my hand. Quickly, recognising the danger, he dropped it but his eyes glistened with joyous tears.

The next sacred day, with my brothers and sisters as witnesses, we walked through the Augustan gate of the city, singing the songs of the Judean king as we followed the path that led to Apollo's stream. There my teacher, my guide to the Lord and to His son, my Paul, took me by the hand and we waded into the rushing silver water and I fell into his arms and the water was dancing over my body and my face. When I emerged, spluttering and shivering, I was promised to the kingdom.

After our thanksgiving and the joy of our celebrations, I could not stop weeping as I walked back through the city. My beloved teacher was leaving Philippi the following morning. I was inconsolable, more desolate than when I left home as a young woman.

When we got home and Theodorus saw my red and tearstained face, he came running towards me.

He turned to Psyche, he raised his hand. 'What have they done to her?'

'Leave her alone,' I demanded.

I bowed to my husband. 'Theodorus, I am with child.'

———

The wind has roared all night long. The fire affords us little warmth, but I don't care. For the last three nights my Salvation has slept. Those malign spirits that torment her and contort her body have departed. I know that they will return. They have had their sights set on her since she was born; they watch us both.

But for three nights she has slept and for three days she has been calm. She has sipped water from my cupped hands and she has swallowed some broth. Her body is at rest, but I fear it's because she doesn't have the strength to move. I braved the storms and found wood for the fire, collected chicory for the broth. Apart from that I have not left her side.

I awake with a start before dawn. Looking wildly around the dark cave, I search for the cause of my unrest. Then it comes to me. The world outside is quiet. The storm has abated. And as I have every morning since Paul brought me into the new world, I prayed. My son, my brother, my Jesus, is this the day you will return?

Salvation is still asleep. Quietly I leave our rough bed and crawl to the entrance of the cave. In the dull light of the fading moon the forest floor is silver. A blanket of ice and dew covers the earth. Deep in the black horizon there is a faintly pulsing glow from the awakening sun. I sit there, watching the sun gather strength, until the white light is climbing the mountain. I look back into the cavern. Salvation has not stirred. I leap to my feet. The storm is over but winter is still here. We need more kindling, we need more fuel.

The Lord provides. Near the gushing stream, full from the rains that have battered our mountain overnight, mushrooms have bloomed under a moss-covered rock. They are liver-brown, their curved heads spotted with white flecks as if marked by the hard rain. I know them to be safe to eat. They will be a feast. Thank you, Lord.

That's when I hear footsteps. I look around in panic, grab my knife. The steps are human, not animal.

A scrawny, terrified girl emerges from the glade of cypress trees. She has a bundle in her arms. My fear vanishes. Another infant to be abandoned.

On seeing me the girl stops. I crouch there, blade in hand. Neither of us speaks.

Tentatively, timidly, she approaches.

I hear the growl. It comes from me. I am now a creature of this forest. I have become what they claim me to be. A witch. A hag. An animal.

Then she astonishes me.

She kneels before me as if I were a noblewoman. 'Lady,' she says in a trembling stutter, 'is your god the one they call Jesus the Saviour?'

'Get up, girl. Get off your knees.'

My instruction scares her; she turns to flee.

I had not intended to frighten her. I make my voice gentle. 'What is it you want? Are you abandoning your child?'

She shakes her head. 'Does—does . . .' And then she speaks in a rush, though her voice is still soft. 'Does your god raise the dead?'

I make no answer. She dares come closer until we are an arm's length from one another. She unwraps the bundle.

The child is dead. Its tiny limbs are bloated. Already the stench of rot is upon it. The dull blankness of its soulless eyes. A tiny bump dangling from its grey corpse. A boy. A son.

She offers him to me. 'Please. Raise him.'

I don't understand. I wonder if she wants me to burn the body, to take it away from her. But the feverish demand of her eyes gives me pause.

My voice is hushed. 'What is it you want?'

'Raise him from the dead. Ask your god to make my child live again.'

I know if I move closer I will scare her. I want to hold this girl. To make her understand that I know her grief.

All I can do is shake my head.

With extreme care, she places the infant on the ground and then falls again to her knees. She coils her arms around my feet.

'Lady,' she is moaning, 'I'm sorry, but I am poor. I can't give you anything but my pledge that if you raise my child I will follow your god. They say he's a god for the poor. They say he hates the rich and that he cares about those of us most wretched.'

Her tears fall on my feet.

'That's a god I can worship,' she continues. 'That's a god for me. This is the first son born living to me, my lady, all the others were born dead. My husband will beat me—he'll throw me out.'

Her voice rises to a scream. 'I need a son! Bring him back, make my son live again.'

I crouch, I pull her arms away from around my feet.

'Sister,' I say, 'I cannot.'

Still on her knees, she stiffens. 'What does your god want of me?'

To cherish your neighbour with a love equal to that you feel for your mother, your husband, your child. To abandon all possessions. To turn your cheek and offer love to cruelty.

I do not say any of this. I remember how absurd these commandments sounded when I first heard them.

She picks up the child, lays him at my feet.

It is the way she looks up at me, the trust I see in her eyes, that reminds me of Salvation. And though I know it is futile, I pick up the body and cradle it in my arms. The stench of death. I swallow, refuse the bile, I look down at the child.

She is expecting spells cast from a trance. Rituals and narcotics and invocations. All I have are words.

'My redeemer, my master, my lord, my son, my brother, my hope, my Jesus, you who are always with the last, you who will make them first, raise this child.'

The dead infant in my arms. The soft wind rising, the branches cracking and swaying. The rushing stream. All of this, and the cold child in my arms.

She looks at me expectantly. 'Is he coming back to life?'

I pass him back to her. 'I'm sorry. Your son is dead. May the Lord have mercy on his soul.'

The sighing wind, the coursing of the water. And her weeping, tears without end. And then the rage, also without end.

'Witch. Dog. Hag.'

This time there is no timidity. This time there is only hatred.

'Witch. Dog. Hag.' She spits on the ground. 'Mother of an abomination.' She takes a breath, laughs bitterly. 'You know what I hear about your god? That he was born to a whore, that his father was a drunk, a coward, the lowest of Roman soldiers. That's what they say about your god.'

She spits once again. 'And he was hung on the cross.' Her tears have ceased. 'Your god was hung on a fucking cross. That isn't a god. That's just some poor cunt of a slave.'

The hand not holding the infant is a fist that is pounding at me, her nails are clawing at my face. I do not resist. I do not try to escape her fury. I offer her my cheek. She gouges at it. She punches me, she spits at me, she curses at me till her fury is gone. Then she is empty. She drops and lies whimpering on the ground, curled around the bundle of her child.

I take my blade and start stabbing at the hard ground, preparing for the burial of the child. She is huddled, shivering, watching me. I dig and I dig till it seems I have gone all the way to Hades. I will not place this babe on a fire. I will not turn it to ash. This child, this mother, they are the last who will be first. I will not burn this child. I take him from her and lay him in the grave.

The mother does not move. It is only when I begin to pray that she struggles to her feet.

'Not in the name of that god of yours,' she snarls. 'Never in his name. I won't let you bury him in that god's name.'

I am without tongue. I dare not move.

She looks down at her child in the freshly dug hole. She spits one final time, she spits on her son. 'You have brought me shame. May only evil meet you in the afterlife.'

She turns and runs back down the mountain. I cover the body of the child, push in the earth and press it over him. I kneel and say, 'May the Lord have mercy on your soul.'

I clean my hands in the thundering stream, I take my horde of wild mushrooms in one hand, and under the other arm I take my wood.

I return to my Salvation.

———

There had been a time of plenty and then came a time of want. At first there were the great floods, when the heavens were torn and the rain poured unceasingly onto the earth. And then I learned what it was to go hungry in a city. At first the prices in the markets doubled. Then they tripled. In the end all that remained were scant provisions. Rotting vegetables, maggot-infested meat. Guards were stationed at every market square to beat back desperate thieves.

Our stores of food were gone within a season. We released one labourer and then another. We sold Fortitude. She was far from young and the price we received for her was paltry. We got a better price for Salonikos but he was still sold at a loss. We were reduced to Psyche and Rectitude and one skinny youth, Atticus. Theodorus could not bear to part with him. He was a hard worker, and devoted as a hound to his master. That was all that remained of our household.

We all returned to work, scouring and drying the hides, sewing the canvases together. It was our labour that made the tents. Philos was no longer tutored. He was apprenticed to the craft of his father and grandfather. His muscles thickened, his body became leaner and stronger. Every day his speech grew coarser and he had no time for games with his little brother, no patience for conversation and gossip. He was becoming a man.

The floods had swept away the most ramshackle buildings and made homeless half our city. When the deluge ended and the skies cleared, the temples were full of people rejoicing. But the respite was fleeting, for then came the plague. They dug pits outside the city walls and filled them with the bodies of the dead, covering them with lime. The stench of death permeated everything.

We lost Psyche. We came close to losing our Leonidas. I sat beside his bed, I put heated cloths on his chest, I gave him purgatives, I washed him twice a day. My husband prayed to his gods and I prayed to my Lord. I slipped into his bed and took my son in my arms, whispering to him, 'Leon, my dearest son, please know that our son, our brother, our Jesus is always with us, always beside us. He will not let you die. If you pledge your honour to his Father, He will not only heal you in this life but He will welcome you into eternity.' In the delirium of his fever I had no idea how much he understood, or even if he had truly heard me. But one morning I awoke beside him, and when I opened my eyes he was looking back at me. My heart refused to beat. I thought I was looking into the eyes of my dead child. Then I saw his chest rise, so very gently, and I knew that he had been saved.

'Mama,' he whimpered, 'I am so hungry.'

I clambered out of bed, I rushed to our hearth where Rectitude was already kneading the yeast for the bread. 'Hurry, hurry,' I ordered. 'Your young lord is hungry!'

The slave searched our paltry larder and quickly prepared a gruel of soaked barley and buttermilk. I fed my child. He gorged the soup like a beast of the forests, his hunger insatiable. When the bowl was emptied, Leon fell back into his bed, exhausted.

'Mother,' he said, 'Jesus the Saviour made me well, didn't he?'

'Yes, my child.'

He fell to sleep in my arms.

It was a time of want but I felt only bliss. I was bringing my child to the Lord. And in my belly, another child of the Lord was growing. As soon as I was sure that Leon had conquered the disease, I returned to my work. I was in a fever myself, impatient with the slowness of time, longing for the day of rest. When that blessed day arrived I awoke before dawn, wrenching Rectitude from her bed and demanding that she follow me. The silly child wanted to make prayers to her useless gods. I was on fire with impatience as she kneeled before the altar and bleated her incantations over the sacred flame.

We rushed through the town as first light glimmered. The streets were already full of the din of slaves and labourers at work, rebuilding dwellings destroyed in the floods. We ran until we reached the top of the hill. Only then did we draw breath.

Clemency welcomed us to the hut, drawing the screen and standing back so I might enter. We fell into each other's embrace as I joyously proclaimed, 'Sister, my son lives!'

She covered me with kisses. 'He is returning, sister.'

'Truly,' I answered, 'he is returning.'

And then I added breathlessly, 'My son is coming to the Lord.'

She whooped in jubilation, clapping with her hands held high. We were both cheering and crying. Perseverance came to see the reason for so much racket. I repeated my news and soon we were locked in one embrace, one celebration. Out of the corner of my eye I saw my slave. Her eyes were lowered but her pursed lips and stiff back conveyed her disapproval and revulsion.

Finally, we released each other. Perseverance playfully grabbed my hands. 'Can you bring him to the next thanksgiving? Can we welcome him into our way at the next Sabbath?' His smile was radiant.

I kissed his cheeks. 'I promise you, brother, he will be here for our next feast of love.'

I was bringing a son to the just god and I would be avenging the daughter that the unjust gods stole from me. My God was stronger. My God was Lord.

I could sense trouble as soon as we got home. As we passed the kilns, Atticus was there on the path, a load of heavy timber across his narrow shoulders. He bowed to me, careful not to upturn his load, and then he beckoned Rectitude. They moved away, whispering. I ignored them and immediately went to see my son. His bed was empty. I heard voices from our chamber. I could smell the cloying odour of myrrh. I drew aside the curtain.

Leon was kneeling with his father, their palms upturned. They were wreathed in smoke from the incense. I heard the drone of their prayers to that impacable deity, to that wooden fraud sitting on the altar.

Leon turned on hearing me but his father sternly commanded him to continue his prayers. The boy did as as he was ordered. Once they were finished, Leon jumped to his feet and rushed to me.

'Go, son,' ordered his father. 'Leave us.'

Leon bowed and ran out of the room, calling out for the slaves. As if he had never been ill, as if he had never felt the tender caress of our Saviour who had spared him from death.

My husband was silent. I did as I had to, I waited for him to speak.

'Lydia,' he said finally, 'I will not let you make my son a Jew.'

I had to assure him, had to make peace.

'He was saved by my God, husband. I prayed day and night for the Lord of the Jews to save him and it was done.' I placed my hand over my heart. 'I made a vow to that God, husband.'

'I will not have my son castrated.'

At first I was stunned by the madness of his words. Why would he dare think I would make a eunuch of my child? And then I understood.

I went to him then. He was still at the altar. Averting my gaze from the hideous god, I kneeled before my husband, taking his face in my hands. How rough the skin, how he had aged.

'No, my husband, this is mistaken. My god does not demand such a barbarity.'

He grasped my hands, hurting me with his force. His eyes were wary and suspicious. 'We all know that the Jews demand this violence. I will not have my son's manhood disfigured.'

'We don't do that! My teacher, Paul, was definite. We don't do it.'

The mention of my teacher conjured a vision. He was before me, the crooked one-eyed smile, his reedy voice saying, 'Our Saviour said that a woman must become as a man to enter the kingdom.'

I knew what to say. 'Husband, my god is a god of justice and a god of love. He is not a barbarous god. I give you my word: our son will not be harmed.'

I was on all fours, I was kissing his feet. 'I promise you this. Not one hair of his will be touched. Our mysteries are not violent.'

My husband was a good man, a kind man. 'If you promise this, then you can honour your vow to your god.'

I bowed, rocking back and forth at his feet. 'Thank you, husband, thank you.'

'Stand.' His voice was still unyielding.

I rose, not daring to look at him.

'Leon can worship your god but he cannot abandon his worship of our gods. Do you agree?'

'Yes, husband.'

'And you will not take him with you on the Sabbath and you will not initiate him into your cult.'

I was silent. Broken.

'Lydia, your girls have told me what goes on there. That slaves mingle with freemen, that women and men pray together, that beggars and orphans stand side by side with merchants and with traders.'

His voice was hoarse from disgust at such shamelessness, such madness.

'I have been too lenient with you, wife, too soft. You can worship your god but you are never to join with others from this accursed cult again. I forbid it. You can pray to your god as we pray to ours. In your home. Only in our home.'

It was as if the walls had collapsed and the roof fallen upon me. I stumbled, I fell. The earth opened up and darkness, death, the shades of Hades fell upon me. The cruel gods had conquered. Jesus was not beside me, I could not feel him there.

I knew that I was in my husband's arms, knew that he was carrying me to bed, calling to the slaves to come immediately. I was lost to love. I was lost to my Lord. All I could think of was death. And that I wanted them all gone. Husband, sons, slaves, the world. I wanted it all gone. The cruel gods had been triumphant.

The agonies began. Calliope and Rectitude had hold of me, the midwife was before me, squatting and intoning the prayers to her goddess. I crouched, I pushed, I held my screams. I was no longer a young girl; I knew what to expect and what to do. The sun had just lowered and night was beckoning when the infant came. It emerged covered by a caul, and even in the torment of labour the sight choked my heart. Had I given birth to both child and tomb? But then the slick membrane ruptured and I heard my child's cry. I held my breath and awaited the midwife's pronunciation. Nothing came. All I could hear was the infant's crying. I heard Rectitude gasp.

Only then did the midwife speak. 'She's an affront to men and to gods.'

In my stupor, all I could see was the blood. And then my hand flew to my chest, as if I had been returned to the old world and must bang my breastbone to ask mercy from the gods. The tiny creature only had one arm. I dropped back into the bed.

The midwife had her hand over the atrocity's face, her fingers like talons.

'I will destroy it now.'

But the infant was wailing. She was searching for me.

And it was then that I knew my Saviour had not abandoned me. His arms were around me, offering me strength. I heard him whisper to me: 'My father is the only god who will love this child.'

I lifted my head. Thunder cracked as I did it—was I the only one to hear it? I was reeling from my efforts to rise from the bed. I could not fail.

'Let me keep her for one night.'

Rectitude threw a frightened glance to her mistress.

'Mother.' I forced the words through cracked and burning lips. 'My dearest mother, let me keep her this one night.'

Calliope had borne children, she had raised sons. She understood what I was asking but she was unmoved. 'It will do no good to keep this thing alive, daughter, she is an outrage. A creature reviled by the Mother and by all our gods.'

I sensed the rebuke in her tone. That it was *my* god who had brought this pollution upon our house. This was the Mother's revenge.

And even in my exhaustion and pain, in my bed sodden from my labours and my blood, I knew what I had to do. Was it the breath of the Lord giving me the voice I needed?

'Dear mother,' I said to Calliope, my voice contrite, 'let me take her on my breast. So I can look on this creature and understand my great transgression. Just for tonight. So I can truly know how deeply I have insulted the great Mother and all the gods. So I can prepare for my dishonour.'

Calliope leaned over and, even though I was unclean, she came so close I thought she might kiss me.

'One night, child,' she whispered kindly. 'I will speak to my son, I will intercede for you, daughter, and explain your shame. You can have her tonight.'

With disdain and revulsion, the midwife lay the child on my chest. My first glance and I was also horrified. My urge was to hurl this insult across the room. But Jesus was there; he was with the child. I forced myself to look at those eerie eyes, the eyes of a crone in the face of an infant. I saw the purple stain desecrating her neck and shoulders. Finally, I was brave enough to touch the tiny nub where the arm should have been. As I held it, the child stopped its mournful cries and gave a slight gurgle.

I heard the midwife whispering to Calliope. 'Such an

abomination should be destroyed immediately. It is an insult to the Mother to let it live even for a day.'

The hag rapped repeatedly across her chest and spat to make her disgust known to her gods.

My hand formed a fist around the nub. The child stirred. I lay my palm on her chest and felt her tiny heart beating. I searched, found her good hand. Instantly her fingers curled into mine and her whimpering calmed. She made small noises of contentment. I heard again my first daughter's voice.

The infant remained quiet on my breast. There was no kicking from her as there had been with my sons. At the thought of my boys, I shuddered. I could not abandon them, I did not possess such strength. I dropped my head on the soiled bedding, knowing defeat. But it wasn't the foul excretions of the birth that I could smell. It was her infant's scent, the milky fragrance that was stronger than the reek of blood, of man. That scent was fortifying. I placed my hand on my child and I made my vow. I must not be mother and I must not be woman. I must be as a man not to be defeated by this world of men.

Though I was exhausted, I did not sleep. I waited. I closed my eyes until I was sure that Rectitude was asleep. I had to reject the pity I felt for her. They would lash her a thousand times; the scars from the whip would never be erased. But I could not save her. I had to save my child.

I prayed. This was the moment of danger. As I rose gingerly from my bed, I squeezed shut my lips and bit back on my tongue to stop myself from screaming. A burning erupted from my womb, searing my entire being, as the afterbirth ran down my legs. I made no noise. I conquered all pain. My arms cradled my daughter, and I prayed that she wouldn't cry. And, yes, she stayed quiet. You who are always with us, you who are always beside us. There was no time to find my sandals. I crept naked down the dark corridor, hearing my husband's snores, Philos muttering in his sleep and a whimper from my Leon. Harden your heart, Lydia, I commanded myself. I didn't pull back the curtains to their chambers to see their faces one last time. I had become as ruthless as a man. I crossed the hearth and was in the yard. Our dog woke and started wagging his tail. My heart froze. But you were with us. The dog shuffled towards me and licked my free hand. It was a warm night, and the plump moon had bathed the world in light. Rectitude had draped clothes on the fig tree to dry. I grabbed a long shawl and wound it around my body and that of my daughter. I opened the gate and stepped into the night.

I followed the path that winds down towards the distant port and was soon in the street that led to the market square. I was taking a terrible risk. The city was teeming with beggars and thieves, with the hungry and the enraged. Drunks leered at me, beggars sleeping in the alleys awoke and saw me, but thinking me a ghost or a fury dared not call out. And though it was night and all was unfamiliar, I had no fear. I could smell the brine stench of the harbour, I could hear the drumming of the distant waves.

Two seasons had passed since I had been allowed to visit my brethren, but my feet knew the path, and soon I was at the door of the cottage. I pulled back the curtain and only then did the child in my arms begin to cry.

'Are you hungry?' came a frightened voice, for we knew how much the ignorant world hated our poverty and our faith.

That was what we were taught. Not to challenge in fear or anger, but to welcome strangers with love. The timid voice belonged to my sister.

'Clemency, it's me, it's Lydia.'

She came out of the shadows, her arms held out. 'Is this your child?'

'Yes,' I answered, and as I offered my daughter to her, I said, 'Her name is Salvation.'

I had always known, from when you were a child in my belly, daughter, that I would name you hope.

If we weren't with the Lord, if we didn't know about the coming kingdom, such a thing would have shattered the order of the world: no one was allowed to name a newly born child—no one could dare such presumption. The Mother was an arrogant god, She was cruel. People thought She would answer such impudence by claiming the child. But my sister lived in knowledge not ignorance, my sister came with love and not with fear. She took the infant and held her. She did not recoil. What she saw wasn't evil; she saw a child.

She smiled at my daughter, gently stroking the nub of her failed arm. 'Welcome, Salvation,' she said. 'Welcome to the Lord.'

———

Overnight the first flowers of spring have emerged. The sun is regaining its power and the days are lengthening. The larks have returned and birdsong fills the forest. They are building their nests; soon their chicks will be born.

Here, in Antioch, I have learned to love the piping call of the lark. The birds also make Greece their home but here they are

more insistent. The inhabitants of this city call the lark their
own. They say that this land gave birth to the first of the birds.
They have a goddess who claims that name. Soon there will be
a festival to proclaim Her awakening. They will sacrifice beasts
for her and they will get drunk on wine. Joining hands, they
will weave and dance through the streets, imitating the bird's
song. Many of us who are pledged to the Saviour will hide. They
will drag us out into the streets, they will beat us, they will
tie rope around our necks and march us through the squares,
demanding that we sing. There are those who will still refuse to
sing. Whatever the punishment, they will refuse.

When I arrived in Antioch, I discovered that our cult had
many followers and many houses. But it distressed me to find
that these followers were divided. In one house bonded to the
Saviour, the followers live and worship as Judeans do. They do
not share their thanksgiving with Strangers and will choose
death rather than participate in the celebrations for the false
gods. In the ribaldry, drunkenness and singing, they see only
idolatry, and to them and to their house of worship idolatry is
death. The leader of this house is James, the Saviour's oldest
brother, and though they help the poor and offer charity to the
wretched, they will not accept those not born Jewish into their
house, and they will not share their worship with us.

In another house they are disciples of the Saviour but they
don't believe that he has risen. He died on the cross, they say,
but there was no resurrection: the meaning of his ministry is
in his life and suffering. 'The kingdom is here,' they proclaim.
'We live in it already; it came into being through the words and
example of the Saviour.' They do not marry. They do not bear

children. They share all possessions, they refuse to own land and declare against tithes and taxes. They accept both Jews and Strangers, and they will join any festivities—they love to drink and to celebrate. They say, 'Jesus danced, so we all must dance.' But their enthusiasm is such that it arouses suspicion—they dance in a frenzy and they sing in such ecstasy and abandonment that it gives rise to fear and to distrust. This house is pledged to the Saviour's twin, Thomas, and Paul says it cannot last.

There is still death, still misery, still suffering, still hunger. Caste still exists, and so does violence; there remains cruelty, punishment and prisons. In their wild abandonment they claim to be in the kingdom of the Saviour, but all around them is the truth of the evil world. How can they last? How can such teaching give any hope to those suffering that evil?

There is another house faithful to Mary, the Magdalena. And one of Peter, the Rock. There is the house of Judas and the house of John. They are all Jews and they made us welcome when we first arrived. They whispered, 'He is coming,' and I, in hushed tones, replied, 'Truly, he is returning.' They fed me and they fed my child and for that I will always be grateful. But I was exiled from their thanksgiving. I am a Stranger and cannot be taken into any of their houses.

I am bonded to the house of my teacher. I am of the house of Paul. And so our fate, that of my Salvation and me, our fate was written at the beginning of Creation and it was fulfilled in this eastern city of Antioch. Paul's is the true house of justice. For in our house it is not only Paul, it is not only myself, but it is also Salvation who has been made in the very likeness of the

Lord. In the coming kingdom that will be understood. Till then, we urge, let us sing and dance as a courtesy to our neighbours.

How my Salvation loved to dance, to the music of the Lord and the ancient King David, but also to the music of the Greek and Syrian gods. She released sounds that would mimic the songs, singing in the language of the Lord, and she would start dancing as soon as she heard the music, spinning and swaying to the rattle and jangle of the sistrums and tambourines, the pounding beat and echo of the drums, the teasing call of the flutes. When she was a child we would take her out into the alley, through the crowd, swinging her between us as we joined the procession. We were not singing to the goddess, we were singing to our Lord.

They shunned her. Of course they shunned her. The children called her names, the adults kicked at her if she came near them. Freak, cripple, imbecile. They were the kinder words. Outrage, abomination, abortion were more common. And always the whisper behind my back: 'You are her mother: how dare you let her live?' But she was a child and even the most ignorant and the misguided believe it a sin to harm a child. The kindest were full of pity. 'Poor imp,' they would say. 'Poor child—what a wickedness that your mother let you live.'

She grew taller. More awkward. A young woman and no longer a child. Then they didn't care if they hurt her. They spat at her in the streets. They set upon her with sticks. They set their dogs on her. They screamed in her face.

On the first day of spring season, the pipes and drums started at dawn to announce the return of the Daughter to the Mother and the arrival of the lark back into the world. But when I went to raise Salvation, she refused my hand. She refused to dance—she wouldn't leave our house. With grunts, with silent screams and violent kicks, she made her intent clear. She knew she was not welcome in this bitter world. And I knew then what I had to do.

My sisters and brothers in Paul's house tried to stop me. They said we couldn't survive on the wild mountain, we'd be prey to beasts, to hunger, at the mercy of storms. But I wanted the mountain over the city. The city had rejected my child. In truth, the city had also rejected me. I had learned its language but my Syrian was always clumsy. They knew me as a foreigner, an interloper, a Greek—promised to a faith they despised. Antioch is a city of foreigners: migrants have come here from all parts of the world. But our tongue always betrays us; every time we speak they hear our strangeness. So they push past us at the markets, demand that they as Antiochians are served first. They pretend not to understand my requests and questions. The meanest of them refuse to serve us. I try to do as the Saviour asked and turn the other cheek. That is the fate of the outsider: to always turn the other cheek.

So it was no hardship for me to leave that city and find refuge on the mountain. Our destiny was ordained at Creation and it has been fulfilled on this mountain top. All the children I have prayed for here, all the abandoned infants, they are my daughters and my sons.

From here the world below is as distinct as a sailor's map. I can see the winding avenue of the Roman road that leads to the western gate of the city. That was the road I took when I first came to Antioch, with Salvation still an infant. The first time I had seen a map was on the ship we'd taken; Perseverance had secured a berth for us. A brother in our fellowship was a sailor and he vowed to the captain that I was his widowed sister, heading to our family in Syria with my newborn. We hid the babe in a swathe of flax, so no one could see her face. I looked over the rail and watched Greece becoming smaller and smaller as the ship sailed. I was on the Aegean, I was on that mighty redemptive sea, the sea that had so transfixed me when I first came to Philippi, the sea that led me to the Jews and from the Jews to you, my Paul, and from you to our son, our brother, our Jesus. I had no fear on those waters, even as the craft lurched, as it plunged and rose in those titanic waves. I knew that sea, I trusted its waters. Our fate was ordained at the beginning.

The love of our fellowship amazed me. We are small in number but we are the spirit and the breath of the Lord. The ship landed in Rhodes and then sailed from Rhodes to Lycia. There we were fed and shown kindness by a house loyal to the Magdalena. A trader in leather took me down the long road, over mountains and coast, through plain and desert, fields and forests, and brought me to Antioch. We survived bandits, brutal soldiers, hostile villagers, wolves and wildcats, days without food and water. But always, somewhere, in a cottage perched on a crag overlooking the sea or from within a cluster of huts on a long and fertile plain, there was a house of refuge. Our fellowship fed us, housed us, protected us, until we came to Antioch.

I never saw my Paul again. I had no need to: I had his words. Those epistles he sent, those letters of love and hope that the brethren who could read would recite for all of us to hear. Always tender, sometimes admonishing, sometimes mournful, sometimes scolding and sometimes hard to understand. Often I would become lost in the words. But I was always sure of his love. And I always shared his hope. That there is a kingdom that is coming, that is truly coming, that is kinder and more merciful than our world.

I look down at Antioch, at the Roman road I once travelled and the Damascene road to the south, and beyond the winding river in the distance to the silver haze of the sea. I had no fear on my journey. Wild storms at sea, the crashing of the waves. Bandits and thieves on the road. The weariness and the hunger. Yet I never feared. I did as I was instructed by my teacher. I placed my trust in the Lord. And something more. On those waves, on those roads, I was never happier. I was the most despicable of wretches; I had abandoned my husband and sons and would have been condemned and tortured and killed if this had been known—as is right, according to all peoples and according to all laws. But I was never happier than when I was with my beloved daughter, on those waves and on those roads.

———

I find Salvation when I return from foraging in the day's first light. I know it even before I see her face. Death is a shade, a veil that divides the living from the taken. I walk through this veil, feel its cold touch on my face, and I know Salvation is dead.

I do not weep. I lift her in my arms. My life on the mountain has given me great strength. Bowed, straining, I take her to the stream where I baptised her. Gently I lay her on the ground.

Then I start to dig.

On those hard roads we travelled we always saw lines of crucifixes outside the walls of cities; we walked through the shadows of those gallows. Sometimes I saw them only from a distance, only realising their evil purpose because of the black cloud of the birds of prey that circled above them. Sometimes we passed directly beneath them on the road, the corpses bloated, bursting, stinking of death, the unholy birds pecking at the flesh. Sometimes the soul had not been extinguished, and we would hear the condemned man's desperate final sounds. I would force my eyes to look, not to turn away. By looking I thought I might finally truly understand the meaning of his death, the death of my son, my brother, my Jesus. And I might know why he was punished so cruelly, why he died so alone. But that understanding did not come. Compassion. Sadness. Sorrow. All that I felt, but not understanding.

And then I bury my child. I scrabble and scrape at the hard ground, my nails broken, my hands bleeding. I dig deep into the earth, not weeping, determined in my task, sure in my work. It is only when I am finished, when I drag the body of my daughter to the edge of the hole I have made, that I remember the words. Freak, cripple, imbecile. Outrage, abomination, abortion. Witch, dog, hag.

Then I break. I howl. For this child, for how she was exiled from this world.

Through the trees, a light pierces the forest. And I understand. The obscenity, the scandal, was not his death on the cross. That is not why the evil world despises him. I know from my journeys that such deaths are commonplace. So many have wept for those who have endured such punishment, so many have suffered such torment. What is outrageous, what the world cannot stand, is that these souls, these children, are to be reborn in a kingdom where the last will be first and the first will be last.

That promise, that truth, is what is scandalous.

And I push dirt onto my daughter, there where I had immersed her in running water and made her anew. And I am crying, but these are not tears of sorrow. The light is all around us; our mountain is luminous with light. If not tomorrow, the next day, and if not then, the next. One day soon. Soon he will come back. I am bathed in light. Soon he will return and my Salvation, my daughter, will awaken to a kinder world.

Saul II

37 ANNO DOMINI

'Become as passers-by.'

—THE GOSPEL OF THOMAS

The light, a piercing of the sky, the white of it a flame but without fire. He is racked by tremors, his bones as fragile as the empty shells of the sea. He lurches upright, reaching for the radiance, for heat and for succour, but as soon as he does the light is gone and all is darkness. He falls away from his body and from the world but not before he hears the voice ask, 'Saul, Saul, why are you pursuing me?'

Then blackness. Is it hours, is it days, is it eternity? All is black.

When he returns to the world a figure—is it a man?—is lifting a heavy cloth from his forehead. He sees all this in shadows; the light has returned and it is dazzling, its form and beams and brilliance have clarity, but within the whiteness and the trembling he recognises the clots of scarlet on the drenched cloth. Blood. His blood. He returns to oblivion.

———

He dreams of a road through a valley and parched barren cliffs. He sees yellow sand and burnished red brick. He should not be able to determine colour or shade for the sky is only stars and the moon is weak. Yet he sees beyond the night.

A date palm towers above their camp, the pods full and plump. He and Silas are at their fire, and the two Strangers, the escorts they have hired for the journey, are roasting a desert hare over their own flame. Saul is at prayer, to deflect the treacherous hunger arising from the forbidden scent. Yet with eyes closed, lost in his reciting of sacred words, he still can see Silas's tongue slide over his upper lip. That is how Saul knows that he is not in the world. That is how he knows he is dreaming.

The reek of the forbidden meat, the rough accents and sneering lewdness of the Strangers, the slush and grind of Silas's mouth as he chews on the stale dried figs, it is all Saul can do to force his attention to remain on his prayers. He lowers his brow till it rests on the cooling sands. *For they will bring war to you but they will not vanquish you, for I will deliver you*, said the Lord. And though his eyes are shut and though he is within the chamber of the Lord's words he sees Silas, his fellow trader in hides, a man of the north and not as devout or learned as Saul—but he is, is he not, a friend? Silas's face looms over him, troubled. Saul can feel himself being shaken, prodded, and he hears the larger of the Strangers ask, 'Is he ill?' And that's when the blinding light hurtles towards him and out of him and he feels the sand crunch and slither underneath him as he jerks and thrashes. He cannot see except for light but he can hear one man ask of Silas, 'Is he dead?' And he hears his friend—is he a friend?—answer, 'I think not.' And the other Stranger, who only grunts and curses, he says, 'He's dead alright.' And though there is only the dazzling light, Saul sees the man's foot rise and swing down and he hears it crack into his face. But there is no pain. This is how he knows he is still dreaming. He can feel hands all over him, stripping him of cloths, of his tunic, finding the hidden pockets, taking all he has.

Saul spasms and twitches and moans. He feels a man holding him down, sees a child bathing his face and hair. Saul falls back to peace and sleep.

But he sees the girl look up. Hears her say, 'He hunts us, don't he?'

The man lifts a hand to the girl's cheek. 'What did the prophet Yeshua tell us to do to those who hate us?'

'To offer my other cheek?'

The man smiles. 'That is right, little sister.'

The girl presses the damp cloth to the brow of the broken man.

He falls into further darkness.

———

Saul awakens and cannot tell if it is day or night. As yet he can only discern shadows. Then comes the wretched stink of shit and he feels the foul wetness around his buttocks and thighs. In shame he attempts to sit up and the blow of the pain is as if his spine is shattered. There is further shame when he recognises the howling of a beast as that of his own agony. A man's hands are carefully turning him over and softer hands are cleaning him up. He unleashes a thousand apologies.

'Hush,' a man's clear voice says in Greek.

And then, 'Can you hear me?'

Saul forces his mouth to work. 'I can hear you.'

'The Lord is great.'

There are stirrings and whispers. He hears a new voice, boyish but assured, and swiftly his body is being lifted. He sags limply across the bridge of four strong arms. A rustling. When he is placed back on solid ground the rough hide beneath him is dry. He hears the splashing of cloths being rinsed in water. A gentle hand is wiping him. Through parched lips he struggles to speak to the shade ministering to him.

'Are you a woman?'

'No.'

It is the voice of a boy. 'Do not be shamed, uncle, the women have gone.'

Saul's breath is pain, it tears from his chest as though it might split him asunder.

'Don't speak. You must rest.'

The man's voice. Saul reaches out into the dark for the shadow. His fingers alight on skin, the soft floss of a young man's beard. He cannot yet surrender to sleep and return to the blessed light. He must ask his question.

'Are you—' he almost chokes on the struggle '—are you a Stranger?' The effort of expelling the words breaks his body once more.

'I am of our people, friend. I am of Israel.'

Saul, relieved, falls back onto the bed. But he must ask one more question.

'And the boy?'

'He is one of us,' the man answers, then adds, 'but he is born a Stranger.'

Saul tries to summon the strength to smack the boy's hands

away from his body. But he cannot. He cannot even speak. He groans his distress and distaste.

The man addresses the boy in Syrian, and the boy's shadow and touch move away.

'Sleep,' the man pleads, 'you must sleep.'

Saul wants to fall back into the light. But he can't trust sleep. He is one of us but born a Stranger? Such insane words mean that he must be still possessed.

———

The next time, Saul wakes to day. A figure is sitting cross-legged next to him, his head fallen forward as he releases a long whistling snore. Saul stretches out his hand, his fingers search the wooden floor. The sound wakes the man.

Saul is urgent in his need and his pain. 'I have to piss!'

He feels the cool of the metal between his thighs, a fumbling at his groin, and then the ecstatic release as his waters hose the pot. Bladder empty, Saul rests back on his bed, marvelling at the glory of the colours he can see. The blanched blue of the sky against the red ochre of the opened shutters. The blushing skin of the man who has been ministering to him. And he feels something else, bringing a different but equal joy. Hunger and thirst—he has to eat and drink.

He finds the man's hand, clutches it in gratitude. 'Brother, I can never thank you for everything you have done. I am so grateful but I have one more thing to ask of you. Is there food?'

The man's smile is radiant, kind: it too is an elation.

The meal is brought to him by an old woman, her face pox-scarred and her manner brisk. Her hair is veiled, but from a corner of the linen shawl that is loose at her temple, Saul glimpses grey stubble. Before Saul touches the bread and the gruel that is being offered, his eyes wander to the man, who smiles and urges him to eat.

'She is born of Israel.'

'And awakened in the Anointed Son.'

The man has spoken in Greek but she has answered in Syrian.

Saul thanks her in her language and then, without shame, like a ravenous dog, he devours the offerings in four quick scoops of his hand. Just as quickly, he wipes the bread across the dish and dispatches it in one fierce swallow. The man and the old woman laugh with pleasure and relief at his appetite.

Saul dares to ask for more.

The old woman takes the dish from him. 'There will be more later,' she says gently, smiling down at him. 'I promise you, sir. But we daren't give you too much all at once.'

She turns to the man, her voice grave. 'Call me immediately if he can't keep it in.'

The man nods and the woman bows to Saul, then says quickly, again in her language, 'The Lord be thanked.'

Laying his hand over his full belly, Saul turns to the man. 'Is she bonded to you?'

'She is my sister.'

Saul frowns. The man's beard is a shiny black lustre and his hair is long and thick. He cannot be enslaved.

'What is your name, brother?'

'My name is Ananias, son of Nathaniel.'

The man places a cloth under Saul's head. He looks down at

him, the coal of his eyes as dark and unnerving as a well without bottom. 'And you, my brother, you are Saul.'

Confused, Saul asks, 'How do you know me?'

Ananias's smile is wry. 'I know you. You and your friends chased me out of the Damascene meeting house in David's city. You had a whip at my back—you said that if ever I returned to Jerusalem, you would turn my flesh to pulp with rocks.'

Saul immediately recalls the man, his false prophesying, his insane declarations of allegiance to a crucified Saviour, his blasphemous claims. But he also remembers the hands that nursed him and carried him into that startling and luminous light, the light that healed him. The man's hands and that light—Saul is certain they healed him.

Exhausted, wanting to sleep again and, if possible, if the Lord be willing, to be returned to the light, Saul rests his head back on the bed.

'May the Lord forgive you,' he says weakly. 'And may the Lord forgive me.'

———

He has been saved from death. He knows it from the way his limbs won't obey him, from the lack of vision in his throbbing left eye. In his delirium he cannot tell how long he has lain in this strange bed. And yet he is not in despair. He marvels at the solace of the light, the joy it brings him, and feels closest to a happiness he hasn't felt since he was still a student. Before that first flush of beard; the deepening of voice and sprouting of hair and the more sinister unwanted and dangerous stirrings of youth. Lusts and desires and shames that cannot be spoken. He had last known joy sitting in a circle of boys, listening to the recitations of their teacher. On becoming a man that had been stolen from him. He had to surrender to labour, and keep vigilant and futile watch over his disobedient body. Manhood had corrupted friendship and poisoned hope. Until this moment, with his body violated and broken, when joyfulness had returned. He has been searching a lifetime for such light.

Saul knows he has to pray and ask and seek. He has to understand why the Lord has brought him to this bed and to this house and to these people.

———

The house is always full. There is the man to whom he owes his life, Ananias, and the old woman, Bathsheba. The Stranger boy is called Pup, and there is another boy who sometimes peeks in through the curtains, and scampers back down the stairs as soon as Saul lifts his head. He hears activity and conversation, and often laughter and singing, coming from downstairs.

He discovers that Ananias doesn't like being referred to as the head of the household.

'No, sir,' he would counter, shaking his head, while feeding Saul soup or pieces of honeycomb. 'We have no head in this house—we are all, from the old to the very young, brothers and sisters.'

But not in blood. Some are slaves, like Bathsheba and the curious boy who spies on him. Some are Jews and others Strangers. But it isn't a divided house. Saul suspects that in the rooms below the household has their meals together. And that is forbidden, a violation. And he now knows that they are disciples of that despised teacher, that would-be prophet, that crucified Nazarene crank. Over the years Saul has heard of Yeshua's teachings and they never made any sense to him: sometimes he had preached as a devout Jew, but at others spoke as an apostate. He had some learning but no understanding, and he did not keep faith with the Lord's sacred words. That was why his followers had been led astray into blasphemy and perversion. That was why Saul spied on them, bore witness against them. But now he is in their house and they have saved him.

Yet, as he lies there in his bed, with a body that no longer obeys him, he feels neither fear nor rage, not even confusion, as he thinks about why he has been brought here, saved by the very people he has for years now persecuted. The light is no longer a dazzling source from which he is comforted and nourished. That blinding gift has faded and softened to become shimmering rays that dance through the open window, the gleam on a thread of a spider's web, and the magnificent luminance in Ananias's eyes. The astounding light that had first overwhelmed him had been a tempest that had cocooned him in its serene centre while all around was chaos and destruction. And the soft light in this room, on the faces and in the eyes of those who care for him, that is the forgiving breeze of the day after the storm. But whether in tempest or in calm, it is all one light and it is all the whisper of one Lord.

―――

Saul awakens to screaming from the street. Two boys—they must be boys, their voices are shrill—are accusing each other of theft. The argument is so heated and the abuse unfurled so obscene that Saul can only discern half of what they are saying. The argument is solved when he hears a crack and a man calling out, 'You dirty little she-dogs,' and then the whimpering and crying of the vanquished boy. Saul twists. And as he does so he senses his knee bend.

Carefully, fearfully, he attempts to bend the other, and that leg too gently moves.

He wrenches his body off the bed. The shock of movement, of being on his feet again, is such that he trips and stumbles after three ungainly steps, as if he were drunk. He smashes one side of his body against the wall. His innards heave outwards with the impact; forcing himself with a mighty will he falls to his knees in front of the chamber-pot and vomits. Emptied, his breathing steadying, he tests his legs again. He stands with greater care this time, balancing carefully, and walks to the door. His head roars with blood and for a moment he thinks the walls of the room are collapsing and that he too will drop with them through to earth. But he is standing. His hand moves to the heavy canvas nailed across the door. Then, aware of his neglect to the One he must never neglect, he falls to his knees and kisses the wooden floor as he gives his thanks to the Lord.

He is heavy with exhaustion, and cannot raise himself again. He crawls to the curtain and pushes it aside.

There is laughter, a chanting. He looks down to the room below.

A fire snaps in the open hearth. The household is seated in a circle around a rug on which are placed three loaves of bread and a long thin vessel. He can make out Ananias, the old woman, and Pup. Squinting, catching flashes of faces and bodies in the light of the darting flames, he sees that there are six others included in the circle. The room is small, squalid, and they are all touching shoulder to shoulder. Women and men, children and slaves. He stills his breath. He listens.

A veiled woman with her back to him begins a chant. He recognises it as a prayer of thanksgiving to the Lord. At first he thinks it is one of the songs of the blessed King David, but the words do not follow the decreed order. The Lord is blessed, as Protector and Creator, but the prayer also praises a son of man. When the woman finishes, she reaches for a loaf and tears a chunk out of it.

Ananias speaks. 'Our Saviour, Yeshua, anointed by the Lord, said that we must remember his teachings as we share this bread.'

The others speak as one.

'We remember your teachings, Yeshua.'

The woman tears more bread from the loaf and passes it around the circle. There is silence as they eat. Hunger stabs Saul. He forces himself to be quiet.

The woman takes the vessel and holds it aloft. 'Our Saviour, Yeshua, anointed by the Lord, said that we must remember his sacrifice as we share the wine.'

And then the chorus: 'We do not forget you, Yeshua. We drink this wine to remember the blood that you shed for us.'

The woman places her mouth over the narrow opening and sips at the wine. She passes it to the child sitting next to her. She too places her mouth over the lip of the jug but as she drinks drops of wine fall on her white tunic.

It looks like blood. Could it possibly be blood? Saul feels faint again; the walls sway as he looks at them. This is what they say of the followers of this Yeshua from Nazareth: they drink blood and eat human flesh and thus make themselves more deranged and despised than the Strangers. Saul himself has often whispered these rumours to anyone who would listen.

And his own heritage and faith return with almighty power to reawaken his anger. You corrupt the law of the Lord, you make a libel of the promise of the Saviour, and you return us to Baal, to the sins and calamities that destroyed Israel. Death is what this evil sect deserves.

And the anger is fire and might and, though fury will not return his damaged eye, nor make his broken body whole, his righteous anger will return him to the truth of the Lord. He will rise, he will declaim against them.

He struggles to his feet, ready to condemn the wicked circle below. But he suddenly realises that the light has gone.

He is upright but he cannot speak.

They hear him. Nine faces are looking up at him and they are smiling, women and men, children and slaves.

Pup jumps up, elated. 'Uncle, uncle,' he calls in his mangled Greek. 'Us join, us please join.'

Saul cannot move. He is looking at Ananias's composed, rueful face.

'Brother Saul may not wish to join us,' he says, placing a warning hand on the boy's shoulder.

He is speaking to the boy but his eyes don't move from Saul. 'You are welcome to join us, brother. But you need to know that some of us were born Strangers.'

Saul knows that if he chooses to join the circle, he will exile himself from his world as surely as death partitions the flesh from the soul. He trembles and a shudder runs through him. A flame shoots from the hearth, raining a thousand glimmering sparks. The faces below are lit up, made shining and incandescent. The light has returned.

'Boy,' Saul calls to Pup, 'come and help me climb down.'

———

There are salted acorns; there are boiled greens in oil; and all manner of Syrian fruits, dates and persimmons and stewed figs, pomegranates and olives. There are thick slices of goat cheese that Saul will not touch. A shyness has descended on him; he dares not ask how the food was cooked, what law guided the preparations of the women in the kitchen. There is no meat, and he wonders whether it is forbidden to them. He takes some wine but is careful. He must not get drunk in this company. His skin brushes against a slave and he forces himself not to flinch, not to betray his revulsion. Reaching for a date his hand knocks against the hand of a woman. It is as if he has touched fire, but again, he makes no sign of this. They think he is exhausted, lost within his sickness. But he can't speak now because he must not cease his silent prayers. He prays to be absolved of the sins he has committed by being here, by that unclean touching of skin. He does not know if he can be forgiven. But it is as if his body demands the warmth and comfort of the light. Is this illumination granted by the Lord or is it an evil conjured by sorcerers? He does not yet know. He *must* pray.

But though he prays, keeping faith with the words of the ancients and the prophets, his ears are sharp and catch every word, in both Syrian and Greek. Smell, touch, all is alive in him. This must be a gift of the light. They live as a family but they are not blood: their roots spread out of this crowded city, stretching across to the mountains of Anatolia, to the Phoenician sea and even into the wild sand ocean of Arabia. Their faces, the differing shapes of their noses and eyes, the varied shades of hair and skin, the markings on their palms and wrists; they are every tribe of the world.

Saul is startled to hear that part of their belief is that there will be no property and no one wealthier than another—that all that they earn is distributed in common, even to the slaves.

'It is one of Yeshua's commandments.' Ananias speaks as though he can read Saul's thoughts. He gestures around the tiny room. 'This is all we have and all we need. And all we have we share with one another. The Saviour said that the rich must give all they have to the poor. The kingdom of the Lord is all the treasure we need.'

Saul bites his lip, his head bursting with suspicion and spite. He finds he can't remember the words to a prayer he has recited a thousand times over his life. For the first time he feels he cannot trust this fool Ananias, this blasphemous Jew. Saul knows all about the ardour of the young and righteous, the rhetoric of fanatics and desert dwellers, how the Zealots think themselves better than he is. He has worked hard. His hands are torn and callused from the skins he has washed and dyed and stretched, from the canvases he has sewn. He is equal to any Zealot.

Having broken from his prayers he finally speaks. 'I have no money or possessions to share with you, sir. They were all stolen from me.'

The nine around him are momentarily silent, before giving in to laughter. He finds himself laughing with them.

Pup grins. 'Uncle,' he says, 'we will clothe you and feed you.' His eyes are blazing. 'Uncle, we are full of love for you.'

The roar in his ears is as loud as the world splitting asunder in the inferno of an earthquake. These Strangers, these disciples to insanity, they are full of love for him? For *him*? This weak flesh, this noxious heart, this conceited mind and despairing spirit? He searches every single one of their faces, but can find no cruelty or mockery in their laughter.

There is noise in the street. The day is ending and a mob of drunks is staggering home after squandering their day's earnings at the inns and brothels.

One of the young women gets up and finds her sandals by the door. She uncovers her hair and it springs forth long and thick, dyed scarlet with henna. 'I am sorry, sisters and brothers, I must return to the temple.'

The circle breaks up as they stand to hug the young woman and bid her farewell. Saul is still sitting. She offers a kiss to Bathsheba which the old woman returns. The girl hesitates, then crouches and places a tender kiss on Saul's bearded cheek. 'Welcome, brother.'

He watches her rush into the indigo of the coming night. The night that will cover drunkenness and brutality, the darkness that will hide lewdness and sin. This can't be the Lord's promised kingdom, he thinks. This is more madness.

The two slaves are also preparing to return to their owners. But Bathsheba urges them all back to the circle.

'Sit, sit,' she commands. 'Before you depart, let us pray for our sister, Ariadne. Let us pray that the Lord God, the only God, will give her courage to withstand the evil she has to endure as one betrothed to the temple of the idol Aphrodite the Cypriot Maiden.'

Comprehension does not come immediately; it is as if the words must find their way through the ruins of his mind left behind by his sickness. But when it does, he is stricken. He knows the temple and the debauched deity that is worshipped there. A shiver runs through him. Ananias's eyes are shut in prayer. Saul does not care. He attempts to rise, falls and crashes amongst the bowls and plates, upsetting the jug of wine. The rich red liquid flows over the rug like blood. As it might be. Blood of demons. Saul crawls over to Ananias and grabs the man's heavy coarse tunic. He will throttle the man, he will destroy him.

'She's a *whore*? You let me eat and drink with a whore?'

He remembers the fleeting kiss and claws at his cheek.

He will crawl to Jerusalem on hands and knees, he will neither sleep nor eat until he arrives at the Temple on bloodied limbs. He will wash himself in the baths for an eternity. But even then, would that be enough?

It is not Ananias who answers, it is Bathsheba. 'And you, sir, have you never sinned?'

Their insane vanity. The outrage of their insolence to the Lord. Everyone commits sins but not all do so wilfully, not all sit in judgement of others. He is right to hunt them, he is right to bring them to justice.

Blasphemers, whores, procurers and law-breakers. Stone the whole fucking lot of them.

He will not stay. This is not light, this is the emanations of Satan. He must escape. Pup tries to embrace him, his eyes an outpouring of grief. Saul musters his strength and shoves the boy away.

On the street, twilight and freedom. He stumbles, he lurches, and at one point bumps into a man who angrily pushes him against a wall. But his weakened limbs and unsteady feet do not betray him. As his rage quietens and night gathers, he becomes aware that this part of the city is unknown to him. However, being lost is preferable to being at the mercy of the profaners. Saul decides he will walk till he finds a landmark or a site he recognises. He will walk till daylight if he has to. He will collapse and die in a dingy alleyway if he must.

A young slave is making offerings to a stone idol. She hears his heavy tread and glances around. On seeing his face she screams and rushes back into a courtyard, banging shut the gate behind her, scattering the food offerings onto the ground. He must look like an ogre to have frightened her so. A mangy cat hisses from a wall, then leaps to the spilled food and feeds ravenously.

Saul becomes aware of steps echoing behind his. He turns to faces the potential threat.

A man emerges from the shadows.

Weariness floods through Saul. 'Leave me.'

'I will guide you to wherever you need to go,' Ananias replies. 'Just let me see that you are safe. I won't bother you.'

Ananias walks in step behind him. The silence of night is only broken by the barking of dogs, the whispers and curses of the wretched as they prepare to sleep on the streets, and the quiet directions offered to Saul by the man who saved his life.

When Saul reaches the meeting house gate, he turns back. There is only darkness and shadow.

———

The courtyard of the meeting house is strewn with sleeping bodies, travelling Jewish labourers from the mountains and from the endless desert plains of Syria. He knocks on the door to the house and the young man who answers grimaces at the sight of Saul's battered face.

Saul offers a greeting and a blessing.

The boy returns the greeting and repeats the blessing. Then he frowns. 'What do you want?'

'A room.'

'Have you coin?'

'I am Saul, son of Judah, born in Tarsus and now a resident of David's city.'

The young man sniffs, unmoved. 'I asked, have you coin? If not, you're welcome to find a bed in the yard.'

He thinks I'm a beggar or a madman, Saul thinks. He peers over the youth's shoulder into the long hall where men sit eating at long tables. Above the din and laughter he can hear the intonations of prayer.

'I'm a leatherworker and a tentmaker,' he says quickly. 'Is Joseph, son of Samuel, here, a brother from Antioch? He will vouch for me.'

The youth doesn't reply and slams shut the door.

Saul is grateful that the evening air is warm. He only has what he wears: the tunic given to him by the profaners. Of course the youth won't return—he thinks Saul is a lunatic, a beggar or a sick wretch. Saul determines to ask for mercy and a blanket. He can find a bed on the stone.

But the door opens and Joseph is standing there, his face flushed and his beard stained from wine. He recoils in shock, then grabs Saul in a rough hug. 'Brother,' he roars, 'what the devil happened to you?'

———

There is food, sanctified food, there are cheeses and yogurt, roasted turnips and salted meats, there is bread and date paste. With his mouth full and spitting crumbs, Saul tells his friend about the beating he'd been given, and how Silas stole everything and left him to die and rot on the desert road. Joseph listens intently, cutting slices of cheese and fruit for his friend and filling Saul's cup with wine as he speaks. Finally Saul finishes both story and meal, wiping the oil from his mouth and pushing his plate to one side.

Joseph raises his cup. 'The Lord is great, friend, the Lord has saved you.'

Saul too raises his cup. 'The Lord is great.' He looks across the crowded hall at the faces illuminated by the flickering lanterns.

Joseph shakes his head. 'No one has seen Silas—he hasn't been at the markets. We thought that bandits had got you both.'

He grabs Saul's hand, brings it to his own chest. 'I was going to send word to Jerusalem, friend, I swear. I was certain that you had been murdered.'

Saul can feel the heart beating within his friend's broad chest.

Joseph drops his hand and winks, leering. 'You were never pretty, Saul, not even as a boy. But now they have really made you a monster.' He guffaws and burps, gesturing for more wine.

Saul, his head already spinning, his stomach full, cautions his friend.

'I'm paying, Saul. Eat! Drink! You have come back from the dead, friend.'

Joseph slings his arm around Saul's shoulders, eyes narrowing. 'You were supposed to get here on Sabbath eve fourteen days ago and it's Sabbath again tomorrow.' He raises his chin, clicks his tongue, pulling at Saul's robe. 'Where were you all those days? Who nursed your wounds?'

Should he lie? Above their heads a torch illuminates the rough-hewn stones of the meeting hall. He reads on them in their ancient tongue the commandments received by Moses the Lawgiver, blessed into eternity.

'I was found by a fellow Jew. His name is Ananias, son of Nathaniel.'

'The stonemason?'

Saul feels ashamed. In all the time he spent in Ananias's care he had not once asked of his work, or of what his life was outside those small rooms filled with a family who were not blood.

Tables and benches are being moved in preparation for the last of the prayers. Already some are washing their faces and necks out of the water troughs that runs along the far wall of the hall.

Joseph takes a large swig and empties his cup. 'He is a good man. You are not the first he's rescued.'

Saul gets up. He needs to be cleansed, to kneel and pray.

Joseph is tracing a circle on the surface of the table, following the recess of the grain. 'Don't witness against him.'

Saul flinches. 'I don't bear false witness against anyone.'

Joseph nods, his finger still circling the groove. 'I dare say you don't, friend, but it is no secret you receive money for the information you give to the priests.'

Joseph raps loudly on the wood. His lips are against Saul's ear. 'Ananias is deluded. He believes in the atrocious lie that our Saviour was some poor bastard the Roman swine nailed to their crosses.' Even in here his friend has to whisper the last of those words. Then, more loudly and firmly: 'But he saved your life.'

———

Fatigue is sewn into his bones, into every part of him. But he cannot sleep. In the low-ceilinged room where he lies next to Joseph, amidst a large mob of sleeping men, he can't summon forgetfulness. He recalls the hands that tended the wounds and cleaned his filthy body. And as he remembers that tenderness, he stirs, his body rubbing against another man. Lust bursts within him, a flame that destroys sleep. The moon shines its beams through the window, the open shutters allowing the faintest hint of a breeze. But that light is not the light he is longing for. It neither warms nor comforts; it offers neither peace nor bliss.

———

Saul starts working for Joseph, slowly recovering to his previous proficiency and vigour in working and stitching the hides. He stinks of it, the labour and the fluids. His mind also becomes clear of the fog brought on by his beating and his illness, healing from the urgency and exhaustion of work but also through what it takes to barter in the marketplace. He works for Joseph and Gilead and for a Stranger named Anaxis who fears the Lord and allows his Judean workers to observe the Sabbath. Saul feels that he is a man again and that he has fully returned to himself. Until that morning when he stepped over a puddle and looked down to behold his reflection: the burst of purple and the crisscross of lesions over what was once an eye.

He sends a message to his family that he is alive and well and working to soon buy a new mule, to resume his trade and again be able to buy offerings for sacrifice to the Temple. In the same message he asks Ebron to send word to the Roman prefect in the Greek city of the crimes of Silas and the two men they hired. Tell them, he instructs, that a servant of Rome was violated near Damascus; remind them that my father's father was granted freedom and made a Roman by dispensation of the great Caesar Pompey. Urge them, beseech them, to see that justice is done and that Silas is never again to set foot in Jerusalem. And there is one thing that he does not dare say to the scribe he has hired, but he knows that Ebron will read his message and will understand: if Silas dares return, any one of our house has the right to draw a blade across his treacherous neck.

He has done what needs to be done. Soon he will have enough coin to rent a bed for himself and not rely on the cold planks and crowded rooms of the meeting house of the Damascan Jews. He is gaining strength and all is well. Thanks be to the Lord.

But he is not at peace. The merchants who employ him never stop complaining about their devious clients, all of whom are out to swindle and to thieve. They mistreat and hit the boys they pay to fetch and carry the skins and rugs. They resent every coin they have to pay and they demand subservience and unceasing loyalty in return for the meagre diet and stone floor they give to them. Have they always been like that? Had he been blind to their venality in the past? Saul has seen where the poor lads sleep: a stone slab at the back of the market stalls, a narrow trench overflowing with their shit and piss, the whole tiny cell beset by flies in the daylight and the pricking of mosquitoes by night.

The jokes and camaraderie of his fellow labourers also weary him. Endless boring stories, their pathetic fantasies about a slave girl's buttocks or a whore's mouth. He knows he comes across as surly, loathsomely pious in his constant prayer and his abstention from drunkenness and rutting. What they don't see is his blind terror that if he gives in to the slightest pleasure, he will not be able to stop—there is no abomination he will not surrender to. Such is the darkness to which he feels bound.

One night as he lies sleepless, in constant silent prayer to banish the demons that claw at him, he hears a cry of shattering distress. He rises, trips over the sleeping bodies, and makes his way out to the courtyard. The yard is strewn with bodies, as if after a calamitous battle. Saul peers into the tepid moonlight. A young lad, a travelling beggar boy, is crying in his sleep. Saul picks his way carefully across the sleeping bodies till he reaches the crying boy, his frame dreadfully thin, his limbs covered with the sores of a growing sickness. Saul takes the boy into his arms, softly kisses his damp forehead, whispers to him a song of David. The boy, lulled, grateful, begins nodding towards sleep, his small fingers unfurling, his sobs weakening. Saul keeps up his hushed singing until a man lurches upright and peers over the sleeping forms. He sees Saul embracing the boy. He scowls in disgust and laughs coarsely. 'If you want to pound that beggar boy's arse, do it outside.' He spits, then rolls over back into sleep.

Saul cannot control his fury. It is as if his anger has taken whatever good remained in him, whatever he'd retained of the light. He feels he will never be in light again. He lies next to the boy, stricken by his own shame, mortified by his animal hatred. He lies awake till dawn.

A third Sabbath passes and then another. With nightfall, the men feast. They only look up when they hear the rich tone of a kithara being strummed; the reverberating pounding of a drum; voices in beautiful harmony. Musicians have gathered in the courtyard.

The men stream out into the yard, amongst the beggars and amongst the poor, drawn by the sweetness of the singer's melodious voice and by the intoxicating savagery of the music. The men dance and Saul too is dancing, his arms aloft and his body swaying, his feet leaping within the circle, a circle within a circle that gathers speed and movement as their bodies twirl and shake and the men open their throats, a song of the sea and of nets and fish and of nights alone on a craft on still and calm waters. And even though Saul doesn't know the song, the song knows him and he too raises his head to the night and to the stars and he too is singing a song of the sea and of fishing and of nights on calm waters and within the circle of gathering strength and movement the light from the moon broadens and deepens and it is no longer the beam of that tender sphere but a light beyond, a light that has slashed the vault of the sky and spilled out of the heavens and Saul is in joy. Saul is dancing and singing and in joy. Next to him a giant, a tall man with an amber beard, raises his hands and claps. 'Keep singing, lads,' he urges. 'Keep singing your Galilean song.' And there, still part of the circle within the circle, mesmerised by the strength and movement of the dance, his hands still high in the air and his feet still stamping, Saul is filled by light and knowledge and understands what he has to do.

———

'He's not here.'

Bathsheba is bent over, sweeping the floor with a low broom. She rests on it, glaring at Saul. Then, as if reminded that her astonishing vows have made him her brother, her voice softens. 'Ananias will be home soon.' Then quickly: 'Will you stay and eat with us?'

He washes his hands and arms, his neck and his face.

Bathsheba is sitting in the street, chopping radishes and celery.

Saul squats beside her. 'Have you another blade?'

She clicks her tongue. 'On the hearthstone.'

He finds a sharp knife and sits down beside her. Silently they work.

There is a sound of running, a tumble of feet. Two young children are standing behind them.

The elder boy shyly places a hand on Saul's shoulder. 'Are you a brother?'

Bathsheba's stare is searing.

'Yes,' he answers.

The elder boy takes the youngest to play in the street. They throw off their tunics and wrestle naked. Saul sees that the older boy is circumcised, the younger not.

'They're not brothers?' He corrects himself. 'Not in blood?'

Bathsheba leans close. She whispers, 'Judah is the son of our sister Miriam, a widow left destitute by her married kin. The youngest is Peri, he's a good boy, though he has a terrible temper.'

And as if hearing her, Peri starts to howl, bashing his fists onto the belly of the other. 'Not fair, not fair,' he squeals.

'You know his mother,' continues the old woman. 'Our sister Ariadne, who you called a whore.'

And then, collecting the peeled vegetables, she rises.

'Come,' she orders the boys, 'enough of your silly games.'

———

'She was going to abandon him.'

Ananias points to the mountains that loom above the northern walls of the city.

'We visit there whenever we can, try to convince the mothers not to leave their children. We save the ones we can.' He shrugs, as if the cruelty of the world is beyond dispute. 'Too often they are already dead or irrevocably wounded by wild animals.'

Saul shudders at the cruelty of the Strangers.

He looks at his friend's hands, rough and scarred from a lifetime of work.

'Why have you come back to us, Saul?' asks Ananias softly.

Saul looks into his eyes. He asks a question he has never asked before. 'Why do you follow Yeshua?'

They are sitting on the steps. The two men are alone; the rest of the household has gone to bed.

'I am Galilean.' As he says this, Ananias smiles. 'Nothing good ever comes from Galilee. Isn't that what you southerners say?'

A blush colours Saul's face. He is glad the darkness hides it.

'I was a lad,' Ananias continues. 'So young. Yeshua, son of

Joseph, was already teaching—he was a follower of the prophet John.' He stops and turns to Saul. 'Do you condemn the Baptist as well?'

Saul is shocked. 'I do not condemn the prophets or the martyrs.'

Ananias laughs. 'I am teasing you, brother.' He sucks on the cardamom seed he is rolling around in his mouth. 'Yeshua's family was dirt poor so he must have been a very bright lad to be offered schooling. He was tutored by priests in Nazareth—he alone of his brothers was taught to read.'

'He was pious?'

'Pious, god-fearing, preaching the imminent coming of the Saviour.' Ananias's voice drops to a hush. 'And the destruction of Rome.'

His tone sharpens. 'He made no impression on me when I first heard him speak in a meeting house in Cana. You know: the world is ending because of our sins and wickedness, and the coming of the Saviour will bring us to right. There was nothing new in any of it.'

'What did he look like?'

Ananias spits the chewed seed into his hand, rubs it to fine grit between his fingers. 'Strong-shouldered. A long fine nose. Black eyes, deep set, very intense—they really drew you in. His hair was dark but receding. I thought his certainty and righteousness were so immature, almost arrogant. One of his fingers was ruined, the small finger on his right hand. His father, may his soul rest in peace, was a woodworker. All his sons were woodworkers or fishing men.'

'And he made no impression on you at all?'

Ananias shrugs. 'It's not just Jerusalem that has her Zealots. Every valley and every port and hillside in Galilee is crawling with young hotheads preaching the approaching end and the coming beginning.' Ananias shakes his head. 'No. I forgot all about him.'

'And now you follow him.'

'My father died, may his soul be in peace, and my eldest brother's leg was crushed by a landfall in the quarry.'

Saul touches his palm to his heart. He is about to speak but Ananias continues.

'Such calamities happen to stoneworkers all the time. I'm not asking for sympathy. It happens. But I was the next brother and I had two sisters to marry and a younger brother to school. It was my mother's wish. I bonded myself to a quarry owner in Capernaum and it was outside those city walls that I heard Yeshua preach again.'

The man's fingers grip his shoulder and Saul flinches. But Ananias does not relax his hold. 'Brother, I swear, it was as if he were a different man. The foolishness of youth had left him but so had the anger. He spoke against wickedness and against the lawbreakers, but his voice was as serene as a bright morning after heavy rain.' His voice is filled with wonder, as if he does not quite understand what he is saying. 'All of us there were filled with that voice.'

Ananias releases his grip. 'You don't know what it is to be a slave, Saul, and may you never have to.' His voice becomes hard. 'They do what they want to you. You are their dog, you don't have a soul. They do whatever the fuck they want to you and every night and every dawn you are on your knees, thanking the Lord they haven't killed you. That's what I learned being bonded to that quarry.'

Silence.

Ananias's voice lightens. 'On that hill outside Capernaum he preached that it was *us*—the enslaved, the poor, the beggars, the prisoners, the lepers, the fallen—it was *us* who were most loved by the Lord.'

Ananias grabs Saul's hand. 'A miracle happened, brother. When I returned to my master that night I was not angry, I wasn't filled with hate. But even more amazing, I was not filled with shame. I thought, let him beat me, whip me. Let him violate me. I am with the Lord and he is not.'

He raises Saul's hand to his mouth, he kisses it. 'In Capernaum I befriended Yeshua's twin. He believes that the Lord's promised kingdom is not awaiting us. He claims that it is already here.'

Ananias points to the ground. He touches his chest. 'We *are* the kingdom, Saul.'

'He had a twin?'

Ananias speaks quietly in the darkness, as if speaking only to himself. 'It was Thomas, his twin, who baptised me.'

Saul knows about the rite of baptism, said to be the way to the new world by all the crazed followers of this strange and disturbing cult.

A hound calls mournfully in the night. Deep in the darkness, where the wall of the street curves and descends, he sees shapes and shadows, beggars asleep on their stone beds. He hears hushed insistent voices: drunkards bartering for boys and whores.

'How can this be the kingdom promised to us?'

Ananias is defiant. 'He has come. Yeshua is Israel's Saviour, anointed so by the Lord. I believe that.'

Saul sneers. 'And was nailed to the gallows?'

'Is that not prophesied? I don't read and write, brother—you tell me.'

Saul is silent. Then, with a sigh from the depths of his being, he reaches for the knowledge he has loved since a boy, since he first prided himself on learning. He recites the words of the prophet Isaiah. 'But he will be pierced for our transgressions, he will be crushed for our sins; the punishment that brings us peace will be upon him, and by his wounds we will be healed.'

Ananias nods. 'That is what I believe, brother.'

Saul shakes his head. 'That cannot be the meaning.' His face floods with rage. 'On a cross? Nailed to a Roman cross? There is nothing more degrading.'

Ananias's face mirrors his rage. 'You think so? You've never been a fucking slave.'

But then the bitterness leaves him. His friend leans across and gently kisses Saul on the lips. The light is on his mouth: the light has returned and is in him.

'The first will be last and the last will be first—that is what Yeshua said and that is what I believe.'

There is a cry in the night, a terrified wail. The dangers and temptations of night never allow Damascus to sleep. But here, alongside his friend, Saul is in peace. 'What else did he preach to you that day?'

'Many things. I will tell you in time. But the three most important were that the Lord's kingdom belongs to the poor and cannot be entered by the rich, that we must be as passers-by and not seek influence in the world, and that the greatest commandment of our Lord is to love the stranger.'

Ananias looks over his shoulder, into the dark depths of the house. 'He was at that stage preaching to Jews and Samaritans, to Strangers and to slaves—to anyone who would listen. All the poor are brothers.'

He turns to Saul. 'No wonder the Zealots threw him out. They would have hated that.' He spits. 'Scratch a Zealot and you find a rich prick's son.'

Saul peers into night, trying to discern colour and shape in the shadows. 'And you believed he was the Saviour promised by the prophets? And you still believe that? Even after you heard what they did to him? How they violated him and broke him? And then crucified him?' Saul shakes his head in disbelief. 'May his soul rest in peace. But such a wretch is not our Saviour.'

Ananias brings his hand to his chest. 'Do you want to know my shames, Saul?'

His words promise an intimacy, but even in the night's shadows Ananias's eyes gleam with a fierce and engulfing anger. 'I will tell them to you, brother. Do you want to know them?'

And the fire in Saul's heart and in his lungs and in his head burns with such ferocity that he cannot move. For it is his own shames that erupt in the night sky, his calamitous transgressions parade before him on a demented and ever-shifting canvas: from youth to manhood, all his crimes are visible. To himself, to his Lord, to his world. The veiled girl-whores, their plump flesh. The henna-tattooed faces of the boys, their soft hands and mouths. The mortification he has craved in taverns and brothels and even in the courtyards of meeting houses, all the dishonour he has courted on the road, from Anatolia to Judea to Syria. The shames he has committed and the shames that he has allowed to be done to him. He is in Hell. He could pray for eternity but his Lord will never forgive him. How can Ananias bear to sit next to him? His touch, his breath, his words, they must corrupt everyone who comes near him.

'Saul! Saul! You are loved!'

Saul comes back to consciousness sprawled in the other man's arms. His tunic is wet. Is that the derisive laughter of a child he can hear? He comes slowly back to night.

Bathsheba is in the doorway. 'Is he ill?'

Ananias sends her back to her bed.

Carefully, the dark sky now blessedly free of visions, Saul releases himself from his friend's hold. 'Forgive me.'

Ananias places his hand on Saul's chest. 'I recognise that darkness, my friend.'

And something momentous has indeed been shared between them. How it can be, he cannot say, but he knows that Ananias has shared that terrible hallucination. It is as if they are as pure and naked children in front of each other.

Saul places his hand over Ananias's.

Ananias strokes it. 'Our Lord forbids us to take our own life.' His voice is halting, but strengthens as he speaks. 'But after I was released from slavery, all I wanted to do was cut my own throat. It could be the brightest of days, the sky clear and the horizon endless, but all I could see was darkness. I could not bear life. I could not bear to see and know how I had betrayed our Lord.'

And this, Saul understands it completely.

'I was feeling this despair, Saul, when I heard Yeshua preach again. He spoke about how our Lord loved the most wretched and debased of us. He told us about the Lord's love for the slave, the prisoner, the beggar, the prostitute, the diseased and deformed. No priest or Zealot or fucking rebel had ever spoken like that before. His words were a light. I was filled by it. I know now that that light was the Spirit of the Lord and that convinced me, even more than his words. I felt the darkness go. I shed shame, I shed cruelty, I shed bitterness, I shed hate. That light hasn't left me.'

He grabs Saul's hand. 'Who are the most wretched on the earth? Isn't it those damned to crucifixion? There is nothing more loathsome or debased than those poor souls. But that is why I believe him. It is because of what they did to him that I know he is the one that the Lord promised to us.'

It is night. But they are cradled and cleansed in light.

Saul hangs his head. 'I have committed terrible shames.'

'So have we all, brother.'

'I cannot resist.'

'The Lord forgives. Even while we are sinning, the Lord is with us. He is a shepherd, Saul, he guides us back to the light. That is what Yeshua teaches us.'

The Lord cannot want me. Saul knows that he will not be forgiven. He starts shaking, his head jerking back and forth. But Ananias is holding Saul's face, and he is forced to look into the other man's eyes. And in those eyes he sees no revulsion or fear.

'Saul, you are a stubborn cloth-eared fool. The Lord loves you. He will not abandon you.'

The brilliant light. This is my friend, thinks Saul in wonder. This man, an enemy only a moon ago, was now a friend. More than a friend—a brother, but closer to him than any brother in blood. Saul cannot comprehend the force of the light within. Or how much he loves this man.

'Baptise me.'

'They will despise you.'

'Baptise me.'

'They will hound you.'

'Baptise me.'

———

The river runs from the mountains sacred to the idolators. The two men walk alongside it, following its flow. Behind them are the city walls. Cloud storms are gathering over the mountain and, though the heat is rising, the day is grey and shadowless. Birds sing their curiosity from the cypress trees as a man leads another from the bank of the river and into the water, holding him steady in his arms as the other falls back into the burbling stream. 'Awaken,' calls out the first. Saul opens his eyes. He doesn't see cloud nor glade nor embankment; not man nor even river. All he sees is light, from the glimmering sheet of the heavens to the answering sparkle of water and gleam of the earth. He is not man. Saul has been reborn, as and into light.

Faith

VRASAS, ROME
63 A.D.

'Some French writer that I read when I was a boy, said that the desert went into the heart of the Jews in their wanderings and made them what they are. I cannot remember by what argument he proved them to be even yet the indestructible children of earth, but it may well be that the elements have their children. If we knew the Fire Worshippers better we might find that their centuries of pious observance have been rewarded, and that the fire has given them a little of its nature . . .'

—W.B. YEATS, 'EARTH, FIRE AND WATER'

We are drinking the blood that is pouring over us and it froths and spills from our mouths we are inhaling the valiant breath of a toilworn beast that refuses to surrender life we inhale and the blood fills our throats and tastes of the earth and of war and we can taste a heart beating as we hungrily feast on the blood and we tilt our heads back to take in more of it above us the bullock is still clamouring its hooves stamping the boards and the scaffold shakes and we do not move we are determined not to move though within this black hole the earth is splitting and above us the beast batters the wood it cannot bellow its windpipe has been severed so instead there is a wheeze of the last desperate gulps of life through the slats we see The God the sun is fire spears of burning light that explodes the darkness that marks with a blaze the dark earth the blood is in our mouths and in our nostrils and has made black masks of our faces and the beast has collapsed its life disappearing but returning in us the life extinguished is reborn in us as we stand underneath

the sun the light that is The God is also in us the sheaves of fire
that we also swallow and the light and the blood choke our
throats and fill us and the beast is dead but it is living in us now
and our engorged stomachs and our swollen bladders have
stretched to contain so much life and so much blood and we will
not allow ourselves to spit to waste even a drop of this life for it
would be ill-fortuned it would betray the sun the fire The God
and our three bodies press closer together and we are wet with
blood and sweat and our bodies are one as we were when we
were soldiers and I am no longer a cripple and he is no longer
impotent and he is no more being eaten away from the disease
that cannot be named and we are soldiers again and we are young
again and we are three warriors in the marshland of a desolate
and forsaken plain and we are crushing skulls and slitting throats
the blades of our daggers slice through flesh and bone as if man
is butter and we slaughter the longhaired foes and the blood that
spills from their bowels and from their throats and from their
eyes and from their guts it splatters upon us and it makes us
stronger and bolder and we are warriors under the sun we are
warriors for The God above us the sun illuminates the field of
battle to the horizon and beyond and The God is rapturous and
The God is with us and The God feeds on the blood we are
sacrificing to Him and we march and we storm and we burst
into song and we break through the woeful defences of our
enemy and we have kicked down walls and we are setting fire
to huts and to tents and to cellars and we are bursting into rooms
where women cradle their children in their arms and we are
nourished by their cries and lamentations for their men are dead
and their fathers are killed and their husbands are slain and

their sons are butchered and they now belong to us every woman and crone and every child and maiden and we pick our favourites and we enter the tight unsoiled cunts of the girls and we break open the tight buttocks of the boys and our spirits and our sex are guided by the hand of Venus and our hatred and our lust is enflamed by the mighty Mars and all is permitted to sanctify Venus and her escort the god of noble war and beyond the sibling gods we raise shouts and we chant songs to the gods The God who is the god of we soldiers and who is also the god of victories and the god of vengeance and as we spill our seed into the children and the maidens and the women and the crones we know we are continuing the justice of war and our bawlings are the songs of exertion and exhilaration and our cries are for victory and we know we are beloved of The God and in this sodden pit our sex is full and we smear our sex with blood and we spill into the earth as we once did as soldiers we raise our arms in gratitude to death and we raise our arms in gratitude to the sun and we raise our arms once more in thanksgiving to The God and the blood that still pours through the slats still flowing we cup it in our hands and we bathe our faces in the blood Oh fire let it be a son and we moisten our necks in blood we rub our chests and shoulders in blood Oh fire remove this curse from my loins and we smear our sex and arses in blood and we wash our thighs and calves and feet in blood Oh fire banish this canker until we are the colour of satisfied earth sodden with rain renewed in life and we are the colour of life and we are the colour of death and we are the colour of blood.

In blood. Only blood.

We kneel in the stinking wet earth and make our prayers.

In its dying, the slaughtered beast has unleashed its bladder and bowels and we smear the slippery dung and the warm piss over our skins over our lips we lick it with our tongues, we bring the taste of over-ripened fecund harvest for that is what blood tastes of, of life begetting death begetting life, and we bring it all to our mouths. We make our prayers.

I open my mouth once more, I let forth a lowing of pain and trembling, I have taken the dying beast into my own body and it has filled me up, it stretches my gut, my skin, and I birth it, I give birth to death and I am the living, I am its strength, its power, its courage. I drink the last of the spilling blood. I open my mouth, the paste of the blood is a thick honey coating my eyes and I am blind yet I see The God, I see fire dance its dance in spurts of warm red and shimmering orange and black night. The dry blood over my eyeballs cracks and I stare up through the shaft into the sun. I am blinded in white flame.

I make my prayer.

Oh fire, let it be a son this time.

————

The blood drips slowly now. The stench of my fellows brings the vomit to my throat and I know my stink sickens them as well. But we are at peace, we have sacrificed and been anointed in blood to The God. We are emptied of vanities, we have no rage and we have no hate. There is a circle of light, a circle of fire where the sun, The God, fills the pit. Looking up through the shaft, there is the blue of a virgin sky, the first sky of the first day of the first creation after the last destruction. Fire scorches my eyes. But I will not close them, I will let the sun, the fire,

The God have me. I howl once again, the sound soars up the pit and is flung to the sky.

We can hardly move but I force my hand to slide down into the moist earth. I grab a handful of dirt and bring it to my mouth to kiss and to make my prayer.

'O fire, O earth, O Mother, let it be a son this time.'

We call up through the well into the light.

'Drop the rope,' we bellow, still united. 'We are done.'

———

I am the last to heave myself up the rope. Filius, the unmanned, is first. Domius is too weakened by disease to climb the rope and can't even get up on my shoulders, so I lift him, and Filius leans down, extending a hand. With a grunt I push and Domius is pulled through the narrow opening of the chasm. I climb up the rope and through the opening to see Domius still collapsed on the ground, trying to catch his breath. His young son runs to his father's side and cradles the sick man's head on his lap. We do them the grace of ignoring their shame.

A priest is chanting, singing the prayers to fire. His two boy acolytes have put on their aprons and have started hacking at the dead bullock. The sounds of life are everywhere: the shrill cooing of doves, the frantic buzz of flies are swarming over the meat, the wet kiss of the stream in the valley below us. I have the fine senses of a newborn, and as I rise to my feet I can smell the malt tang of the boy acolytes, the sharp smoke of the incense rising from the fire at the priest's feet, the rotting dank floor of the beech forest behind us.

The priest ceases his song. I bow and kiss his hands and Filius follows me, doing the same. Pelius has been waiting for us. We have been soldiers together and so we are bonded in friendship for eternity. He steps forward, slipping the priest three coins; he too kisses the old man's hands. The priest makes one final blessing. In the new world of shining flame he seems ancient, his skin pock-marked and jaundiced. His trembling fingers have curled tightly around the copper. He disgusts me—his greed and his age are foul. I turn away from him but he calls me back. 'You can take some of the sacrifice.'

The boys step back from the kill. I grab the dagger from the younger one and squat next to the butchered animal. I can sense the old priest's eyes on me. I grab a hind leg, cut neatly below the bone joint, rip it from the flesh. I reach into the open belly of the animal and I pull out a kidney; it is a rich purple, healthy and strong. I offer a silent blessing. I search for the other kidney and twist and pull it out. This one is blackened, a skin of white pustules covering it. I take that one as well. The animal was a weak bullock, cheap, but it was all we three could afford. I glance around and see that my comrades are still at prayers. Quickly I take the well-omened kidney and bite into it, my teeth breaking the silken membrane, as my mouth fills with a rank ooze. I gag but I swallow it all and I make my gratitude known to The God. O fire, let it be a son.

I place the leg across my thigh and with all my strength I crack the bone. It snaps easily and I cut through the meat and hand the larger portion to Filius, for taking the kidney. I walk over to Domius and I give him the lesser kidney. He looks at it, his eyes question mine. I shrug and say, 'Both kidneys were identical.' His son is frowning. He has pluck and he returns my stare, but soon looks away. He is too young to challenge me. Domius nods then and, with a mighty effort, raises himself to his knees, salutes the priest and devours the raw meat. I can hear his prayer through his silence. Fire, make me whole, drive out this dishonourable disease. Grimacing, he forces down the last of the meat, but his weakness is such that he begins to retch. He vomits up a slimy slop and in desperation he then picks at the pieces of regurgitated meat and forces them back down his gullet. The boy claps a hand around his father's mouth as he chews for it is blasphemous to reject meat offered to the gods. No number of prayers will save Domius. The gods have abandoned him.

I counsel his son. 'Don't forget to make your share of payments to the priest.'

I walk to where I have abandoned my robe, tear off a fragment, wrap the meat in the rag.

The priest scatters dirt over the fire and incense. His acolytes begin to dismantle the scaffolding.

I offer to help the boy take his father to the river but my offer is declined. 'That is my duty,' he says firmly.

Domius is dying but he leaves behind a brave son. I am shocked by the violence of the jealousy I feel, and force down a curse. I know I was correct to keep the good kidney for myself; this time, the gods willing, I will have a son.

Pelius gathers my robe, I take my share of the sacrifice, and we begin our descent down the hill. The flies are swarming over me now, shattering all peace. I search for the deepest pool in the stream and I walk into it.

In the dying afternoon light Pelius washes me in the cold, clear water. It too lives, this water; it dances and shimmers with light, it too is a child of the gods. Pelius dunks my head under and I hold my breath as he washes the crust of drying blood off my scalp. I scrub at my face and my neck; I wipe my chest and belly as Pelius washes my back; the water churns as I stand upright. Pelius vigorously scrubs my thighs but his soldier's hands become womanlike and timid as they approach my ruined leg. A little further downstream the luckless Filius is also washing away blood and muck. We are no longer united—no longer warriors or victors, but a cripple, an impotent cuckold and a doomed man.

———

That night, the Goddess reigning in the sky now that her betrothed is asleep, we feast in the courtyard. Here are my neighbours, my brothers and their families, my mother in wedded kin and her sons and their broods. We men form a circle and the women sit in an outer ring behind us, our babes on their laps. The infants crawl around the edge of the carpets, the children play on the stairs and the bigger boys run and holler and kick stones in the alley outside. The night fills with excited talk. And then the food comes, earthenware laden with grain cakes, with aromatic beans and farro, with fire-scorched marrows and roots, and pitchers of wine. Bowed and covered, the girls step between us and lay the platters in the middle of our group. The talk abruptly ceases. Eyes shine, mouths swallow and noses twitch. It is a truth; we all become mere animals at the sight of food. A young nephew leaps off his mother, crawls over his uncles, lunging for a grain cake. The mother shamefacedly steps over the men and swoops on the boy, gathering him in her arms. She smacks him twice and he begins to howl.

I raise my arm and stop her from punishing him. 'Let him eat,' I say to her. 'Let him enjoy the feast.'

Ferros, my eldest brother-in-law, throws back his head and laughs, revealing blackened, toothless gums. 'You're feeling generous tonight, Vrasas.' He cups his hands together, shakes them five times in my direction. 'Bless you, bless you, brother.'

He pulls the child from his wife, breaking off a small piece of the grain cake, holding it over the boy's head as the little tyke twists and struggles to get it.

'He's a strong lad, this one, isn't he?'

The men murmur agreement but his unkind grey eyes are looking straight at me, taunting, ugly. He smiles down at his son. 'Your uncle is host, boy. Ask him if I may feed you.'

The boy's eyes are all greed. Hunger stretches the skin of his face, his chin points towards me but his eyes won't leave the cake dangling just out of his reach. Though he has recently begun to speak, his hunger is so desperate he cannot form words. I suppress a grin. I am sure that if I were to hesitate a moment longer the brat would reach out across the circle, reach for my face and scratch at it.

I quickly mutter a small blessing to The God, and Ferros drops the crumbs of cake straight into the boy's open mouth.

'Is it good?'

The boy ignores me. He yelps, like a pup, wanting more cake.

'Is it good?' I yell this time.

He turns to me, his face twisted in spite. He nods exaggeratedly, then grabs for more cake. His father throws him off roughly, returns him to the women. 'Enough. You'll eat when it's your turn.'

The boy is only an infant but he is already defiant, insistent; this is what a son must be. Compliant, always needing to please— that is what my daughters are.

My eldest brings out the largest platter. Carefully stepping around her uncles, she makes sure not to catch a man's eyes, not even mine, as she squats and places the dish of still-sizzling meat on the rug in front of us. Hunger now beats as a heart. All we are is hunger.

I raise my hands to the sky, palms open. The moon is ascendant, the Goddess keeping vigilant watch. And I dare it, to challenge her. I whisper it to myself, emboldened by the blood I have feasted on this morning: I will continue to honour you if I am granted a son. I close my eyes, my arms still raised to night. All are waiting, desperate and furious in their hunger. I am terrified from my wager but I must open my eyes. I do, and there, in the black, a star soars across the heavens.

I call out the name of the Goddess, I call out the name of the gods and The God, I cup my hands and shake them over the food five times—air, water, earth and fire, but above these all the sun, we are all servants to the sun. I remember and honour my dead—my father, my mother, my brothers, my comrades—and only then do I drop my arms to my sides.

With the food blessed, we men fall on it like dogs. In a breath, our lips, our chins, our fingers, our smocks are stained and glisten with fat and grease.

After we have had our fill, the mothers feed the boys, and then what remains is shared between the women and girls. The fragrance of charred meat has brought almsmen and beggar boys to the entrance of the yard. They start cackling in a mangle of languages and though most of it is noise and nonsense to our ears we know that they are begging for food.

Pelius gets up and kicks at one of the old cripples, slapping a few beggar boys, commanding them to leave. They scatter at his shouts, but as soon as he has taken his place back on the rug, they are there again, leprous, spindly, pleading.

I get up and grab a chamber-pot from under the stairs, go out to the street and throw the contents over the foul creatures. With threats and howls they scramble away like the dogs they are. But one of the boys spits and calls out, 'Up your arse, Clod Foot,' and they all laugh and start a hideous chant. Their insults ring through the alley. I limp back to my seat. Even my wife and daughters won't look at me.

Only Pelius doesn't turn away. Covertly, he salutes me. And I him. We are soldiers and we will die soldiers. We are of The God, of sun and of fire. We belong to Him.

Pelius raises his cup. 'Vrasas, we thank you.' He turns to my wife. 'Arté, to your son.'

The men also raise their cups and thank and salute us, drinking to our coming son. But the boy's jeers still ring in my ears. I can feel the power of the sacrifice seeping away, sinking into the rotting earth.

O, let this expense be of some use.

O, let it be a son, I pray.

The girls and women wash up and put the children to sleep, and the courtyard empties as the men finish their drinking and head to bed.

Pelius has stayed and comes and sits beside me. 'It will be a boy this time, friend, I am certain of it.'

I want to tell him about the soaring star, and how the Goddess has assured me that I will have a son. But I cannot tempt the fates, so I keep silent. He falls asleep leaning on my shoulder and I lay him carefully on the ground and cover him with a rug. I look up through the bannisters to our room, where behind the draped curtain my wife and daughters will be asleep on our bed, where the incense will be burning and the grains will be smouldering in offering to the Goddess. My youngest will be in the middle, her hand on her mother's taut protruding belly, feeling the beat of her brother's heart. My wife will be clutching the small wooden phallus she bought from a witch at the markets. At the foot of the bed her mother will be sleeping, the old hag belching and farting foully through the night. I will let them sleep. I strip off my smock and lie next to Pelius. He turns, still asleep, and he drapes an arm over me. All around is the sound of our neighbours in sleep. I feel exhausted but not fatigued, still nourished and exhilarated by the sacrifice. I fall into blessed sleep, in the arms of my beloved friend, as we slept when we were soldiers.

———

I have saved a strip of meat for the old prisoner. As I unlock the door and walk down the dark cramped passageway that smells of mouse shit and cat piss, I can hear him at his incessant praying, those never-ending supplications to his god.

I enter his cell and he abruptly ceases his dirge, rudely sniffing the air. 'You stink of blood.'

You decrepit worshipper of death, old defouler of gods. I am convinced he is a sorcerer. He possesses second sight.

I push open the shutter and light floods through the barred

window, the hands of The God reaching out to us both. But of course the dirty unbeliever turns his back to the sun.

'Uncle, I have brought you some food. That is the blood you smell.' I unwrap the cloth and place the morsel on the low table.

With an arrogant tilt of his head, imperious and effete at once, the old man spurns my offering.

An old woman, that is what he is, or a petulant child. He condescends to sit on the stool, he sniffs at the cold strip of cracked skin and cooked flesh; with disdain he wrinkles his nose as if my offering were rotting. As if he wasn't starving. My father's voice roars in my ears, the ghost of his hand is laid on my shoulder. *Arse-fuck the old cunt, place your prick so far up his Jew hole that he vomits shit from his mouth—break him!* The roar is a tide, it fills me as I wrench the foul old easterner off his seat.

'What right does vermin like you have to refuse a gift sanctified by The God!'

My father isn't there. There is just me and the prisoner. I feel ashamed. He is just a frail old man, bald, dressed in rags that are so torn I can see the faint scars on his hollow chest, shadows of past lashes all over his body.

He nods slowly and takes the meat. 'Your god is not my Lord.' He only speaks Greek with me.

With his toothless gums he starts suckling on the meat. I squat beside him and watch him eat.

He gnaws on the flesh for a small while and he is done. Gulping, forcing the last of the meat juice down, he pushes the chewed meat away. 'Bless you, son.'

I answer him in Latin. 'You are welcome, uncle.'

I pick up the sodden meat, now defiled, and I walk to the window. I stretch onto my toes; agony pierces the tendons in my crippled foot but I force myself to stand there, looking down at the small courtyard beneath. Goats and sheep are tethered there, fowl peck at the earth; in a pen a heavy sow and her brood are sucking at mud. An old woman sits on a stone stoop, peeling a squash. She clutches it close to her withered chest, as if terrified someone might rush past and steal it from her. She looks suspiciously at a beggar boy who is scratching in the dirt, forming a well. He finishes and then squats over it.

'Boy,' I call down to the lout, 'here's alms for you.'

I throw the ruined meat at his feet. Still shitting, he grabs at it and in one sure movement stuffs it into his mouth.

The old woman cackles then shades her eyes, frowning up towards me. She can't see me for the sun. 'Don't encourage him,' she calls up to the sky.

The boy cleans himself with a handful of earth and weeds, stands and wiggles his arse at the old woman. She throws a fist of vegetable peelings at him and though they fall short he runs for them, smacking away the competing fowl, and scoops them up. He chomps on them, swallows, then turns and wiggles his shit-stained arse at me.

'Want some of this, Clod Foot?'

I work my mouth, spit a gob through the window. But he has already run off, cursing me, cursing the old woman, cursing his fate.

Behind me, the old man is groaning, his eyes shut tightly, as he forces himself to his knees. He bends forward, kisses the floor, and begins his rocking back and forth. Setting my feet down flat

I wince from the pain. I sit in a corner of the cell, watching him, listening. He prays in a tongue that I don't know. I close my eyes.

A loud rapping brings me back to the world. The prisoner is still praying, still crouched in supplication to his vain and jealous god. I carefully rise and walk down the dark tunnel to the door. A rat darts by and I kick at it but my aim is not true and it burrows into the dirt. I unbolt the door.

Three figures are standing there, in thick cloths though it is high summer. The man bows; there are two women behind him, both pulling their veils over their faces. One of the women has a goatskin container perched on her head and is steadying it with one hand. The man, still bowing, blesses the First Amongst Men, the imperial family, blesses the city. I salute all he mentions but I also offer thanks to Rome's gods.

'You may speak.'

He thanks me and stands upright. His stare is confident and I sense he is an equal to senators and noblemen. He is barefoot, and clothed in rags not a toga, but his unblemished skin, his bearing and his confident manner mark his caste. I make sure to bow and lower my eyes.

'Sir,' he begins, and though he's speaking familiarly, as though an equal to me, his haughtiness and formality cannot help but creep in, 'we ask you to accompany us and the prisoner you are guarding, our brother Paul, to visit one of our fellowship. She is condemned to the arena and she has asked to receive a blessing from him before her death and the coming resurrection.'

He fumbles on this last word, as though it is unfamiliar to him, though most probably it is in anticipation of my reaction. He fears that I might jeer, or break into laughter.

The sun is high, the streets are filled with livestock and slaves. I want only to return to sleep. But he is a citizen, and whatever his shameful pretence at being an ordinary man, it is clear that he is highborn. The old Jew has been under house arrest and in my charge for over a year now. This gentleman is not his first noble visitor. It is a weakness of our highborn castes that they are bewitched by eastern cults. Being unfamiliar with war, work and struggle, their minds and bodies grow useless: how else to explain the outrageous fact that these aristocratic pricks venerate the insane deities of our slaves? The old Jew is fortunate to have been able to seduce such weak men. If I had my way I'd throw the old goat into a common prison, have him share a cot with murderers and rapists and the arse-fucked—that's what a blasphemer deserves. But he has plied his sorceror's tricks and is now protected. I can't refuse them.

'Very well. I will accompany you, sir.'

The gentleman turns to the women, and the one balancing the goat bladder, hands it over to him, her face still covered from my gaze. But as she does so her headscarf slips, revealing the shaved head of a slave. It's disgraceful that these bitches have their heads covered, but they are his slaves and what they do is his business. I let the gentleman through, slam the door on his women.

In the cell, the younger man places the water pouch on the floor, then rushes to embrace the prisoner. They kiss each other on brow and lips, stroke each other's cheeks, greet each other in their ugly eastern tongue. Once done, they break apart.

The stranger assists the old man to his stool and kneels before him. 'There is a maiden, brother,' he begins, 'a sister in the Lord.

She is to be sacrificed to the circus this day. She asks to see you, she wants your blessing.'

The old man looks up to me. I nod my assent. For the first time all morning, he smiles.

They continue to chatter in Greek as the prisoner sits atop his chamber-pot, urinates, farts, opens his bowels. He rises and the younger man then takes a rag from underneath his smock, and with no indication that this abominable servility is an indignity to him, he uncorks the goatskin, pours water onto his rag, and begins to wash the old man's face and neck, his scrawny arms, his knotty feet. A gurgle rises from deep inside my gut to my throat, and I force myself to swallow it. And then I am truly shocked: the younger man is about to wipe the old man's shitter. His dishonouring of himself forces the gurgle to my lips: I spit, not hiding my disgust.

But the old man—he at least is not insane—has taken the rag off him. 'No, no, brother Philip,' he chides, 'you don't have to do that.' He cleans himself and drops the soiled cloth into the chamber-pot.

In the yard, the gentleman named Philip hands the pot and the emptied skin to one of his slaves. She takes both and throws all, rag and shit and skin, into the pen. The swine squeal and battle to be the first to rub their snouts into the filth. The action of the slave is practised: she manages it all with her right hand still holding her shawl over her face. She doesn't loosen her grip on the empty chamber-pot but there is a moment when she dares a glance at me, and I see a streak of arrogance in the set of her mouth, as if she is going to hand the pot to me, for me to return it to the cell. What kind of creature is this: slave but proud? It is her master's fault—what happens when duty is ignored. This is what you get from being lenient to the gods of our foes. He should knock her to her feet. I could clobber the bitch for her insolence.

Seeing my fury, my prisoner grabs the pot from her. 'I'll return this,' he says quietly, 'and then we can go.'

———

We are walking through the blacksmith's district. The air is thick with the reek of sulphur and smoke from the furnaces. The stench clings to our skins, burns our throats and nostrils. Beneath it, a damp rotten stench rises from the river. We cross the square of Mars in Victory, where merchants squat next to their drays and stalls, and shrouded women tout for buyers of their fruit and seed, most of it fly-blown, dregs from the harvest's bitter end. A boy sits cradling a kid goat, stroking its hide, kissing its neck and face, as the voices of the priests rise as one in praise to the god of war, and metalworkers bang flat sheets of copper and tin, naked in the summer heat, their bodies tanned brown and black. Slaves haggle for the provisions they are purchasing for their masters' households; incense mingles with the stink of sewage; the rot of overripe fruit is overpowering. A butcher lops off the heads of chickens, his sons strip the feathers off the carcasses and his wife chops up the meat and throws it into a bubbling cauldron of oil.

As we walk through this chaos of smell and sound, we hear the blast of horns, then the strike of horses' hooves on ground, followed by marching feet, the steady jog of soldiers, so familiar that my own feet fall into rhythm and I stumble and fall against one of the slave girls, grabbing at her cloth to steady myself. As I do she screeches in fury but the retort on my lips is drowned out by the horns blaring above us as the first line of the guard advances into the square. There is the steady march of the soldiers, those who lead and those who follow and those who carry the imperial carriage on their shoulders, and all there shout out praise to the First Amongst Men and his family, we bless Rome and we bless her gods. We are exuberant in our cheering. It is only my charges who are silent. At the last salutation, as the sounds of the horns and marching fade and the thrum of the stallions' hooves make their last echo, the square fills again with the sounds of selling and buying. The slave girl turns to me once more and hisses in my face, 'How dare you touch me,' and I hiss back, 'I know you did not salute the gods,' and she shrinks back, afraid, and covers her head.

Just beyond the blacksmith's district, between the workshops and the river in which they purge their filth, there is a fallow field that is usually home to beggars, but today it is bustling with the activity of workmen and slaves. A fence has been placed around it, and through the gaps in the posts I can see them setting up tiers of makeshift benches. At the far end of the field, a squat wooden tower has been hastily assembled over the coops and pens of a livestock bazaar. A bronze-skinned boy is nimbly climbing the tower, cords of gathered hemp between his teeth, lashing together the posts. My prisoner stops to examine a roll of animal skins that will be pitched as a tent. He prods it with his cane, then squats and rubs at the vellum. I help him to his feet.

'It is a shoddy job,' he whispers to me. 'The stitching is already coming undone. Thank our Lord it won't rain.'

The game for the entertainments is corralled together in the cages: wild-eyed boys, beggars and thieves, mad witches and old imbecile sorcerors, delirious young girls, most of them with the mark of their crime of being runaway slaves carved in gashes across their foreheads. They are naked, squashed together in their filth. A youth keeps guard over them, his harelip a deep gouge that splits his scowl. Men are squatting or sitting at the back of the pens, forming a line that disappears into a gloomy alley.

I bow to the gentleman Philip. 'Is she with the prisoners?'

He nods.

I gesture to the squirming mass inside the cages. 'Which one is she, sir?'

He makes to walk into the bazaar but the sentry stops him and looks at me. I reach beneath my smock, take out my pouch and show the youth the imperial seal. He waves us through. The gentleman Philip goes up to a cage, searches the cluster of bodies inside, calls out a name. As he does so a young boy leaps onto the netting, wailing like a tortured cat. I grab the old man's cane, jabbing the end of it into the boy's face. He falls screaming into the muck and the other bodies fall over him. But at least my act has silenced the infernal scrum.

The gentleman Philip is beckoning to a figure in the huddle. A girl, barely maiden, pushes through the swarm. Blood has dried in runnels down her legs. One hand covers her breasts; they are full, and would excite me if it were not for the splashes of vomit across them. Her other hand protects her damaged sex.

The old man has moved to the gentleman's side. He pushes his hands through the netting and brings the girl into an embrace.

She looks at him with awe, as if he were a demigod. 'Are you the witness? Are you our brother Paul?'

He is stroking her dirt-encrusted hair. Her ravaged scalp is alive with lice.

'Sister, what can I do for you? What can I tell you?' says the old man.

'You have seen him?'

He nods.

'You really saw him?'

A crone pushes her face into the netting. 'Saw who?'

I slap her away. She makes to bite me and this time I bash her hard with the thick of my palm and she tumbles amongst the condemned. The cage stirs, a wave of bodies rocks back and forth.

Only the girl is unmoving, held in stillness by the old prisoner. 'Describe him to me,' she demands.

'He is light, he is tranquillity.'

She pulls back, resists his hold on her, clutching at the netting.

'I want to know what he looked like. What colour were his eyes, his hair? Was he tall, was he handsome?'

The old man sighs. The women behind the gentleman Philip have edged closer. They too are eager for his answer.

'His skin is coarse and dark.' The old man releases his hold on the girl, closes his eyes and touches his own face, as if calling memory to himself. 'On this cheek, there are the scars of the pox. He has thick lips, his hair is already receding. It is black, as are his eyes, the darkest eyes I have ever looked into. But for all their blackness, a light shone out of them. It was undeniable.'

As he continues his description, the girl has dropped her

hands to her side, sliding to her knees in the filthy earth. She is muttering to herself, 'Yes, yes, I see him.'

'His hands are larger than mine,' the old man continues, as if in a trance. 'They are strong hands. The smallest finger of his left hand was cut off and scarred at its end, severed in a work accident.'

'He was a woodworker, weren't he?'

The old man is kneeling in the filth and is again stroking her hair as he describes their god of death.

'Yes. He seemed very tall.' The old man pushes his face hard against the nets, kisses the top of the girl's head. 'But, then, I am short. Maybe he only seemed tall compared to me.'

The girl starts crying pathetically. 'I won't see him, I won't be here to see him return.'

The old man is transformed by a sudden rage. 'Whoever preaches that is wrong,' he declares. He seizes her shoulders. 'Do you believe that the Lord sent his son to us?'

The girl is lost in her tears and has stopped listening, but not those huddled against her—even the imbeciles and demented are quiet and listening.

The old man shakes the girl. 'Do you believe?'

'Yes.' It is a dull, listless reply.

'Do you believe he was crucified?'

'Yes.'

'Do you believe he was resurrected on the third day? In mind and body? Resurrected in body—not only in spirit?'

She turns her face to him again. 'You saw him?'

'I did.'

'You touched him?'

'Do you believe?' he demands. 'Do you believe he was resurrected?'

'I believe you're a stupid old cunt.'

I stifle my laughter. It's the boy I whipped with the cane. He's risen, is poking his tongue out at us, not daring to come close.

At the brat's words the girl has pulled away from the old man, has turned and faced the crush of naked bodies around her. She slumps. I have to look away. Her misery, her defeat, is clear. She is preparing for the world of ghosts.

But the old goat reaches through the netting, grabs her by the shoulder. With the other hand he is pointing to the vermin in the cage.

'Is this it?' There is severity in his voice now. 'Is this your end? Don't you want more than this life?'

You are cruel, you bastard. This is her fate. Don't rub it in the poor child's face.

I haven't spoken out loud. The gentleman Philip, his shameful servants, they are nodding at his words.

He releases her and she falls back amongst the others. 'Believe,' he says quietly, 'or this is your end.'

Her hands are clutching at him, her crying is pitiful, desperate. 'Don't go!' she screams. 'I believe! I believe!'

His arms reach through the gaps in the netting and he brings her close to him, her sobbing now muffled as her face rests against his hollow chest. 'Has she been baptised?'

One of the slave bitches behind the gentleman Philip dares to speak. 'I baptised her, brother.'

The old man pulls the girl in tighter and his lips hover over her scabbed shorn scalp. As if he wishes he were caged in with her, as if he has chosen condemnation over life. 'If you believe in the Lord, and you have been reborn to the light, then when the kingdom comes, you too will rise. In body, in spirit. You will be free.'

She can't be consoled. 'But I won't see him return,' she whimpers.

My charge, however, is made bold by her doubt. 'None of us should sleep soundly,' he says.

He has turned to look at me, trying to ensnare me with his sorceror's eye. I call on the shade of my father; he is behind me, his breath on my neck, giving me strength to resist any magic. I spit, then look away.

'You are condemned to die,' he continues, turning back to the girl. 'But we are all condemned to suffer. You must accept your fate, my child, but do it knowing that, very soon, all who you see around you—these guards, these prisoners, all these people—will be gone and forgotten. They will be ash and dust. But you will live forever.'

His hand has slipped through the net; it covers her eyes. 'Can you see him coming?' he asks softly.

And the terrorised child is now nodding. 'I see him, he is as you said.' His tricks are working. 'I am ready, sir,' she continues shakily. 'I am ready for death.' She bows her head.

I can't stomach it. I leave the bazaar, the reek of dung and beast, the filth and waste of humans, the terrible profanity that is life in love with death. He should be telling her to scream and curse and defy them—to be alive, as alive as that young boy I struck; he at least was not waiting meekly for his end, but living to his last moment. That is what the gods demand, ardour and fire and spirit, not this blasphemous desire for death. I take deep breaths, no longer caring that the sulphur scalds my lungs—at least I can feel my blood pounding, at least I can taste life.

There is a line of men near the cages, squatting and gambling as they wait. The line winds into the darkness of the alley, from where we hear the sounds of a child shouting. It is a girl, and she is insulting all of us men, begging the gods to make our wives barren, to make our sons devourers of cock, our daughters sluts. Her screams are full of life and fury.

A sentry notices me watching and winks. 'Do you want a go?' he asks. 'It's only a few pennies.'

I realise what is happening; this is prostitution for paupers. Since virgins cannot be sacrificed to the gods—that is abhorrent—the condemned girls are being broken before their slaughter. I shake my head. But I silently salute the violated child; she is facing death with defiance, with courage.

Did that simpering child listening to the old man's fairy tales curse and fight and condemn, or did she just lie there while they defiled her? Was she thinking of her raven-haired god who couldn't save himself, let alone a prisoner condemned to the arenas? The raped child's screams do not stop, her fight continues, as man after man drops his coin into the sentry's hand and takes his turn to fuck her. Is she a runaway, a thief? A murderer, a child-killer? Her crime does not matter. As a soldier I understand that the mark of who we truly are is only revealed in death's call. I salute her. And I condemn the cowards to the ignoble death they so desire.

When the death-seekers emerge, having sat in shit, having told their lies to the condemned, the old man is beaming, invigorated. It takes all my will not to punch him in the face.

My father's shade stands sentinel behind me, his breath is fierce and cold on my neck. I am the son and the grandson of warriors; I was born in the filth of a city but my ancestors breathed the clean air of mountains.

The old man takes my hand. The gentleman Philip and his women follow us to the gates.

The sun is at its zenith, eclipsing all. The gentleman Philip has secured our seats and guides us to the unsteady lower tiers of the stalls. We are blacksmiths and carpenters and labourers, we are former soldiers and travellers and freemen, but the noble-born Philip shows no distaste or disgust about being here with us, when by rights he should be sitting with the elite. Not that there are any princes or first citizens here today. This is a cheap affair, a grovelling attempt by some low-born merchant who has struck it rich to find favour with the First Amongst Men. I glance at the gentleman Philip. He appears serene, but his acceptance of such dishonour is lunacy. I whisper prayers to The God that I do not fall ill to his contagion.

With high noon the drums begin and in front of us a man lifts his son onto his shoulders, the boy moving with grace to the pounding of the drums. I am chewing on some spiced nuts I purchased from a stall outside—I offer some to the death-worshippers but they, of course, decline. Slaves run into the arena with flaming torches and set alight the posts that ring the theatre. The timbers have been stuccoed with crystal salts and they burst into coloured flames that leap up high into the skies. We cheer and clap. The drums now beat ferociously, the juice

from the nuts I have been chewing begins to take effect: I can
see where the fingers of The God reach down from the sky,
where He touches and calls the fire from the torches to Him.
Grant me a son this time, I pray. Do not let this one be stillborn.
I repeat my prayer three times and I am rewarded with a flame
that rises higher than any others.

Across from us in the newly built tower, a curtain is being
pulled across and all our eyes are drawn to it, as if by some
enchantment. It is made out of scarlet weave, like the screens
that shield the gods in the temples. A soldier marches across
the sand and flings the curtain open. The merchant who has
paid for the circus is sitting there in a sedan chair, holding the
hand of his wife. Behind him are his sons and daughters. First
his children stand, then his wife and finally the fat old crook,
their arms outstretched to us. We are not fools; we know that the
planks we are sitting on are rotting, we know that the musicians
are ill-practised and out of tune, we know that he has paid the
minimum he could in order to satisfy the First Amongst Men's
decrees. We know his contempt for us. And as one we rise and
turn our shitters to them, laughing and making farting sounds.
The merchant glowers but he is frightened of us and dares not
insult us. But he clenches his fist as a salute to the First Amongst
Gods and then to the First Amongst Men and we hush. He calls
out salutes to the Empress and the princes and we echo his words.
We are proud to do so. The merchant adjusts his skirt, takes his
seat and clasps his wife's hand. She leans into him and whispers,
her eyes sweeping across us, and he laughs scornfully. We know
they detest us as much as we loathe them.

The posts are still alight. It is cheap and shoddy but we lean forward eagerly, stamping our feet in anticipation.

A reed pipe plays a gentle note. An accompanying instrument answers in a deeper strident tone. We lean further forward: a favoured moment, our expectation keen and not yet disappointed. *Look!* We follow the cry from within the pack. A gate scrapes along the ground and two long boards are carried into the arena. The sea, crested sapphire waves with silver foam atop, is painted in glowing dyes across the boards. The heads of the waves are cut out in jagged silhouette. Shrouded black figures are on either end of each board: the first board swings left, the wood frieze behind it slings right; we also swing left, we swing right, we follow the motion of the water. From the sea a figure rises: the god Neptune holding his trident sheathed in silver leaf, a fisherman's net slung over his shoulder. The little boy in front is entranced and also frightened. He is now sitting beside his father, who puts his arm around him. The sight makes me pray: O Lord, O my God of the Sun, make the next one a boy.

A streak of fire shoots high above the arena. Our eyes follow its path, and then it explodes in a shower of colour and light. Lightning. And then there is the crack of a baton banging on a metal drum. Thunder. The glistening blue of the sea, the silver of the foam, shines and beams. The boy is jumping up and down—he has moved away from his father—and excitedly reaches out his tiny hands to the God. A slave, an old man but upright, with sinewy powerful arms, has come into the circle, dragging a huge canvas bag behind him. The sack bulges and writhes. He carefully empties it onto the ground. Pythons! We are thrilled but terrified. They are as thick as an oarman's arm, and as long as two men lying end to end—no, one must be as long as three men. The beasts uncoil, slithering across the sand, raising their glistening heads. We yell with excitement and some young ones shriek. We are mesmerised by the serpents. Neptune is climbing over the waves. He whistles and a young slave boy, naked except for a crossbow over his shoulder, runs through the gate and takes the god's trident. We scream with laughter! A huge thick cock has been strapped over his own boy-penis; it hangs below his knees. Delighted by our approval, the boy struts around, swinging the fake cock at us. Our loins are stirred: he is handsome, hairless, with skin so pale that it seems transluscent—he is of the savage north. An old drunk yowls: 'I want you between my legs, Hermes.' Another man shouts: 'He really wants you between his arse cheeks.' We laugh harder. A python darts towards the boy, and in terror he drops the trident. We roar. The old slave is the only one without fear. His hands dive and he lifts one of the serpents, holding the beast aloft as it writhes and bucks, its muscles stretching and bending. But the old slave is strong, and he keeps a firm grasp on the beast, even as the muscles on his neck seem close to bursting. Holding the serpent high, he parades up and down the stalls. Some of the younger children are crying. The boy in front of me is enraptured. He stands absolutely still. The god steps forward. We hush.

'Who has defied Poseidon?'

The god's face is a copperplate half-mask, eyebrows made from crushed shells, mouth painted a bloody scarlet.

'Answer me, you mortal shits. *Who has defied Poseidon?*' His voice booms around the arena.

A call springs from us. 'Odysseus!'

We repeat the Greek name, call it out in one voice. 'Odysseus, Odysseus, Odysseus!'

A shooting flame.

Lightning.

Thunder.

A naked youth, his wrists bound, is pulled into the arena, a Greek warrior's helmet perched clumsily on his shaved head. The runaway-slave gashes are visible across his brow. The boy is drugged; his eyes roll white, unseeing; he can hardly stand. The crowd mutters. The boy has been made imbecilic from opium— this will not be a fucking contest. The actor playing the God is backing away from us, sensing our anger. I can feel the push of the angry mob behind me; we are ready to destroy. But it is fortunate for the God that there is one amongst us who remains convinced. It is the little boy: he is calling out, pointing to the drugged slave.

'There, God,' he squeals in delight. 'There, can't you see him? There's Odysseus.'

We bellow and point as well. 'There, God, there—there is Odysseus!'

Except for the four sitting next to me. They have started their prayers, the two women with covered heads and faces, and the old man clutching the hand of the gentleman Philip, who both have their heads lowered.

I dare not touch the gentleman but I shake the old man's shoulder. 'Look!' I command.

But they will not cease their damned jabbering.

Neptune is pointing to Odysseus and the old slave has taken one of the pythons and wrapped it around the youth's neck. The feel of the scales on his skin rouse the boy. His pupils become visible. He is awakening, and we roar our approval. There is terror in those eyes now as the beast begins to tighten across the boy's shoulders. The old slave takes another serpent, which he wraps around the boy's waist. Neptune raises His torch and He stands before Odysseus. Hermes is kneeling next to the God; he takes his massive sex, strokes it lasciviously, placing it over a shoulder and then coiling it around his neck, mimicking the slow movements of the beasts. Neptune brings the torch close, the fire almost touching the serpents. Their muscles tighten. We push forward, holding our breath.

Except for the death-lovers, who will not look with us; they are lost in their chanting.

The old slave is holding the third serpent and the God reaches towards it, performing a dance to the beat of the drums. But as He gets near, the snake's head darts, as if to bite Neptune's hand. The God releases a cowardly screech. Will the actor shit himself? We are delirious with joy. The God orders the slave to put the beast on the ground but not to let it go. He lowers His torch to singe the scales of the serpent and the animal spasms in agony. The God keeps the flame against it and the rage of the animal is too much even for the tough old slave. It has escaped his grip as the fire feeds on its flesh. The arena fills with black smoke and the smell of burning meat.

The dying beast's terror has been communicated to his brothers. The first serpent has wound itself in three solid bands around the youth's neck and the second has slowly wrapped itself around the boy's frail body. We are completely silent. We hear the crack and breaking of the first rib, then the second, then the third. The boy is spewing bile and blood. There is incomprehension, the most bestial pain in his eyes, and then they once again roll white. The body tumbles to the earth, jerks, shakes, lies still. Odysseus is no more. The snakes realise it too. They uncoil themselves from the body.

We stand, we cheer, applauding as the god bows.

But the old man, the blasphemous fool, he is wailing. I turn in disgust from him.

———

There are several gladiator bouts, each more pitiful than the one before, with scrawny, frail slaves, prisoners of the British wars near comatose from torture and starvation. But we are intoxicated by it, we crush against each other, bathed in sweat from the relentless sun, stinking, delirious. The rich merchant's wife has fallen asleep and is snoring behind the mesh screen. A play is staged and we half listen to it, heckling loudly. The actor playing Jason is tuneless and his Medea wears rotund breasts, but the actor playing her hasn't even bothered to shave his chest and abdomen. We don't wait for them to finish; we insult them and throw whatever we can find at them: stones, mud, dried animal dung. The actors and musicians are scared and their fear spurs us on. 'Let's give them a whipping,' a drunkard shouts. But before we can riot, the virile old slave appears again, pulling a cage into the arena. Inside there is a lioness, hungry and emaciated; her skin is stretched over her jutting ribs but she is still terrifying—her roar silences us.

From underneath the tower the gate is pulled open and four slaves wheel out a chariot carrying the Greek Goddess Athena,

a model of an owl perched on Her shoulder. The slaves take Her
vehicle to the centre of the arena and Athena descends. It might be
because of the actor's regal and powerful bearing, or the chilling
swoop of his gaze as he surveys the crowd, but we find ourselves
making our salutations to the Virgin—we are bowing to Athena,
and those of us who can find space in the crowd fall to our knees.
The actor's chest is shaved bare, and there is no need for him to
don ridiculous appendages to suggest a woman's breasts: this actor
commands and conjures; we believe he is the Goddess.

A slave comes through the gate, dragging a naked young
girl. I recognise her immediately. She has been washed since
the afternoon, and her head has been shaved. Beside me the old
man stirs and begins to rise, but the gentleman Philip pulls him
back to his seat. The four of them resume their praying, as if the
outside world doesn't exist. I turn away from their ravings, I lean
forward, gripped by the drama in the arena. The slave pushes the
girl forward: her tits just formed, the rise of her shaved pubis.
She is made more beautiful by the gentle glow of the day turning
to twilight. Athena lifts Her slender arm and the most honeyed
of voices, the voice with which women first come to you when
you dream as a boy, She praises the First Amongst Men. Our
voices ring out as we too salute the Caesar. The condemned girl
also forms the words with her mouth but we cannot hear her
voice. The Goddess calls up to the sky, making obeisance to
the Imperial family. Our voices answer as one, the girl moves
her lips, and then the lioness roars auspiciously. All life, all the
world, honours the Imperial family. The Goddess walks up to
the girl and then around her, touching her nipple and sliding a

finger from her sex to her neck. She raises the girl's chin so they are looking at each other.

The Goddess's voice rings out again, true and clear, rising beyond the theatre to the very floor of Heaven. 'Honour me, slave. Fall to your knees and glorify me, your Goddess.'

We start to offer our prayers but our words become frozen in our mouths as the girl does not kneel, her lips do not praise.

The Goddess steps back, calling out to all of us, 'What would you have me do?'

Our rage is unfettered, it storms our veins and threatens to choke us. This is why the harvest did not come, this is why we are hungry. The catastrophes have come because of the blasphemies of the death-worshippers: those cults that deny the gods and those acolytes of an unhinged cult who drink blood and eat flesh to satisfy their perverse crucified god. We scream and we shout: let her jealous god drink our piss, let him gag on our shit. Kill her, we demand, absolve us of her blasphemies, rip her open, cut her into pieces.

The Goddess flings up Her arm.

We are silent.

The Goddess kisses the girl on the lips. As She does, She whips out a dagger from the folds of Her skirt and slashes the girl's cheek.

The girl does not wince from the cut. She has closed her eyes, her hands joined together; she is singing her prayers. The four beside me are whispering in unison.

The Goddess climbs back into Her chariot and the slaves wheel it back to the tower. As the gates start to slide shut, the old slave releases a rope from the cage and leaps with astonishing dexterity to hurl himself into the darkness beneath the tower before the gate is shut. Simultaneously the front bars of the cage clang to the earth.

The lioness sits on her haunches, as if she cannot believe the possibility of freedom. She sniffs the air, she smells blood, she growls. Slowly she emerges from the cave, sways languorously towards the girl.

The theatre is silent. No one breathes.

In an eye-blink, the beast leaps and, with one bite, has torn out the girl's throat.

As the lioness feeds, as her claws rip open the belly, as the intestines and guts spill over the corpse, it is as if my own seed has been spilled. We are sated. As one, we rise. As one, we cheer. As one we salute the First Amongst Men, our city and Her gods.

The gentleman Philip and his slave women are weeping. But the old man's eyes are dry. His back is straight. He notices my gaze and answers it in the Greek tongue. The words are not clear to me. What's needed has been done? What's needed is accomplished?

He stands without help. 'Come,' he orders, and I have never seen him so full of strength. He has abandoned the cloak of his death-loving, he has drunk blood, his eyes shine with life.

'Come,' he repeats impatiently. 'It is done.'

———

The booming rents apart the night and violates my dream. My mother in Hades, shorn as a slave, is reaching out to me, but she vanishes with the onset of the calamitous noise. I jolt awake, grab my dagger. But the earth has not opened; the stars are in their place and a cover of black cloud shields the Goddess moon.

From below I hear the old man. He is screaming, a terrible sound. A missile curves out of the darkness, it falls and skips across the tiles of the roof. I peer down into the courtyard below. In the thick summer night, families and beggar boys are sleeping in the dirt, lying between the goats and the sheep.

'Shut your swinish mouth!' The man screaming up at the prisoner's window is a lone-legged cripple balancing on his crutch. He has another rock in his free hand and is about to throw that too but I hang over the parapet and call down to him. He seems ready to spew more abuse at me but at that moment the Goddess intervenes: the clouds part and Her beams shine off my dagger's blade. He grumbles, but not loudly enough for me to discern his words.

Slowly, banging my fist against my corrupted leg to awaken it, I climb down the ladder. The prisoner's wailing fills the narrow corridor, a rage that makes the walls shake as the rats run back and forth across my feet. I storm to the door, unchain it and burst into the cell.

The insults die on my tongue, they cannot be released. The old man is in spasms, his body rocking forward and back in convulsions. It is not human and it is not animal: it is possession. He is on his knees, incessantly slamming the palms of his hands onto the stone, though he seems to feel no pain. He also pounds his head into the ground, and each time he does he shrieks out curses in a harsh language not known to me.

I draw back, aghast at the viciousness of the evil spirit devouring him. He bawls, screams and then wails in Greek, though with an effort that sees him spit bile across the dirt, as though his tongue is caught between earth and underworld. Through gritted teeth he growls, 'Why do you not come? Why don't you show yourself?'

I take a breath, call on The God and step forward. On seeing me, the old man hurls himself against me with a force that is not human and I am slammed against the wall. I try to get up but he is standing over me, spit and blood from his wounds spraying. He is looking straight at me but he doesn't see me. And he never stops that inhuman howling.

'Show yourself,' he screams. 'You lover of demons, you Nazarene peasant shit, you liar and traitor and blasphemer, you feckless enchanter—show yourself!'

I get to my feet and draw breath once again, then I lunge at him. I grab him and I keep holding him. I cannot comprehend how his old and feeble body can have such strength but I call on The God, and I hold him. His agitation is such that my own body is bucked by his frenzied movements, but I tighten my grip on him and slowly the night stills. His body is his own again; whatever shade had possessed him has fled. I call the names of The God—Helios, Apollo and Sol—and repeat them to myself. The old man's lips brush my neck, he shudders as he falls limp into my arms. First there is the warmth and then the wetness: his urine is running down my legs and splashing around my feet. Incensed, I push the demented old fool away from me and he falls to ground.

He is still shaking but there is no power in his limbs; he curls into himself, he weeps.

'Why do you not return?' His final lament is as anguished

as the grief of a soldier over his fallen comrade, of a mother over the corpse of her child.

My anger is gone. I crouch next to him, feeling his forehead. It is damp from blood, and his body burns with fever. 'You are ill, uncle.'

His eyes spring open. In the darkness the white of his eye shines fierce. A choked gurgle comes from his throat. I cradle his head and pull his tongue loose. But his shivering has resumed— malevolence has returned to the cell.

I order him to breathe.

He resists but I have his head in my palms. I order him again. 'Breathe.'

He inhales and exhales.

I too make the call to the sun.

We inhale, we exhale.

The God enters us, The God leaves us.

He is finally at rest.

I gently lay his head on the ground and search his small room. A rat scurries across his bed and I stamp it with my foot, grab it by its tail and fling it through the bars of the window. By the bed there is a vessel filled with water, mercifully unspilled.

He has not moved; he is curled as an infant. I wash his face, his bloody hands, I bring water to his parched lips. Then I splash the remaining water over my thighs and legs, wash off his stink.

His eyes recognise me now. 'Why are you here?'

'You were screaming like a demented madwoman in the markets. I came to quieten you.'

'But how come you were here?'

I sit next to him. The Goddess is nearing the end of Her reign, The God will be rising soon. I will not return to sleep.

'I couldn't bear the snores of my wife's mother,' I explain. 'And as it is a gentle, mild night I prefer to sleep on the roof. I'm a soldier, uncle; sometimes the world of women and children is unbearable to me.'

'You are married?'

He has never questioned me before.

'I am married. I have three daughters; we are awaiting a son.'

'And you don't enjoy lying next to your wife?'

'I don't enjoy lying next to her mother.'

This makes him laugh. And the laughing makes him cough. 'Is there more water?'

'With morning,' I answer. 'I'll bring you more with the morning.'

He has unfurled, he is lying on his back now. His tongue slides across his thick, cracked lips. His toothless grin sickens me and I turn away.

'I never married,' he tells me.

I scratch at the earthen floor and loosen a pebble. I prepare to listen. It always happens with those you guard: there comes the time when you must listen.

'I have never married, I have never raised children. I abandoned my family and I turned my back on my people. What do you think of that, Vrasas?'

He has never used my name before. I turn to look at him. His arms are folded across his chest. The bottom of his smock is still soaked. I place my palm flat on the earth and force myself to stand. I go to his bed and take his blanket.

'Get up,' I order.

He obeys. I grab hold of his smock to take it off and, as I do so, he raises his thin arms above his head, the way my youngest daughter does when her mother is undressing her for bathing. I take a dry corner of the cloth and wipe him clean, then place the blanket around his shoulders.

We sit cross-legged, facing one another.

'You are a soldier?' he asks.

'I was a soldier,' I reply sourly. 'I am now your guard.'

He points to the shadow of scar that runs from my thigh to below my knee. 'What happened to your leg?'

'War,' I snarl. 'War happened to my leg.'

'Do you miss it?'

Only one who has never soldiered could ask such a question. The answer is obvious to any soldier: with every breath. With every awakening and with each return to sleep. With every breath.

He reaches for me, puts his hand on my arm. 'I abandoned my family. I abandoned my people and I turned away from their laws. I asked you, what do you think of that?'

It is abominable, it is dishonour. It is right they condemn him. I do not know what crimes he is supposed to have committed—I do not know their nature for I have not been told. But if he speaks the truth, he speaks an outrage.

'I only know the ways of soldiers, uncle,' is what I say to him. 'It is my occupation to listen and to obey, not to speak or to question.' I take his hand and put it back on his lap.

'So you always obey the law?'

His Greek confuses me.

'I always obey my orders.'

A surge of anger flashes in his eyes. 'It is as I said, then: you always obey the law.'

He has dexterity with words. Is he mocking me?

'I obey my orders,' I answer carefully. 'The law belongs to senators and lords. The laws change from season to season. I obey my orders.'

'And the law of God, do you obey that? Do you obey Him?'

Oh, how I detest the sophistry of the Greeks. They have poisoned us all: we Romans, and he and his Judeans with their jealous desert God. We have all become men of the word rather than men of deed. That is how the Greeks poison us.

'A soldier requires discipline, uncle,' I say in a rush, 'not knowledge. I obey the gods, I must. But fuck knows what the gods want, what the gods think. Every witch and every sorcerer who pretends to speak for them is a liar. That's all I know.'

I thought this would infuriate him. But instead he laughs out loud, his mouth open so wide I can see the sores along his scarlet and black gums.

'I like your answer, Vrasas,' he chuckles. 'You are a wise man. Discipline is more useful than knowledge.'

He says something in Greek.

'I do not know that word, uncle.'

'Discipline,' he says. 'Discipline,' he repeats. 'And obedience.'

And it is as if I am no longer there. He looks beyond me and I half turn, convinced by his certainty that there is someone behind us.

'You came,' he whispers joyously, sounding as carefree as a child.

I tell him I am off to the barracks, to get him some water and some provisions. I speak to him but he does not hear.

I leave him sitting there, caressed by the sun, whispering in the voice of a child, over and over again, 'You came, my Redeemer, you came. You have returned.'

———

Ten fingers, ten toes, the clear grey eyes of his grandfather, his cries clear and strong, his skin smooth and ruddy, tiny spherical testes like those of a puppy, a little plump cock with a fine hook of skin. The God shines on us, we are in His embrace, blessed by Him and by His betrothed and all the gods of the celestial realm. They kiss us and cradle us in their arms and we are beloved and honoured by them. We have a son.

The labour was a long ordeal which my wife endured for a day and into the following night. Throughout it all, I sat in my neighbours' house. Or, rather, my neighbours sat. I could not. I paced the rooms, the courtyard, the streets outside, listening to my wife's animal whimpering and screaming as our son struggled to free himself from her womb. With the rising of the Goddess we heard the infant's cries, warm and full of blood and life. My eldest clambered down the steps and called for me. I ran over to the house, to where my mother-in-law was cooing over the infant in her arms. I grabbed him from her. We had fathered a son: I counted his fingers and his toes, I inspected his chest and his back, his limbs and his sex. Before I gave my son back to them, I silently spoke his names, like a prayer.

I will not yet tell my wife. I won't tempt fate by saying them aloud. The first name is mine, Vrasas, then Mellitus to honour the man who liberated my father, and finally I give my son *his* name, the name he will carry into the world. It is Lupus, a name from our mountains and what my father was called, denoting strength and cunning and patience—the name he is born to.

Finally, I have a son. My duty is done and my father can at last find rest.

———

I am barred from my home for a cycle of the Goddess. Pelius offers me his hearth but I cannot in good conscience accept his offer. He has five children of his own and is also the protector of his wedded kin. His house is always packed. The solstice has passed and though it is still winter and still cold, the days have started to lengthen, so I claim a space above the prisoner's dwelling. I pitch a tent on the roof and make my bed there. I don't care how cold it is—let it snow, let there be rain or hail—my son is born, my son is healthy. I will sleep naked and unsheltered, I will not complain. The prisoner too has welcomed the news; he chatters and gives thanks and fusses like a mother.

He counsels me, 'Do not sleep on the roof, brother Vrasas, it is bitterly cold. Sleep here with me; you can share my bedding.'

I laugh and reply, 'Thank you, uncle, but I prefer the biting winter air to your never-ending praying.'

He chides me and calls me ungrateful, but with a grin and with good humour. Have we become friends? I am a father, and spite and jealousy and suspicion have abandoned my heart.

Every morning, my first duty is to return to my house. I stand in the courtyard, greeted by the salutations of my neighbours. I call up to my family and I receive news of my son. He thrives, my wife strengthens, we are well. I return to the prisoner, I tend him all day, then fall asleep under the protection of the night sky and its gods; his prayers from below, no words comprehensible, just sound and song, lull me to sleep. The god of sleep embraces me. I have fathered a son and I can finally rest.

———

I have been dozing on the stoop in the noonday sun. My eyes are closed and The God teases me: He kisses my eyelids, I feel His breath across my lips. I am with The God and He is with me. I am asleep but I am also alert; that is one of the first skills a soldier must learn: to be at rest and to be ready at the same time. I doze but I can hear the women across the street mutter and gossip. They are berating some poor whore, some sister or niece whom they abhor. As a soldier I should call out to them, 'Cease your jealous gossip, women!' But I know they cackle about me as well—they could answer back, 'And who are you, cripple?' I ignore them, I am at peace with my God.

A shadow falls across me. I reach for my dagger before I can even flick open my eyes.

Incandescent gods are before me and I lurch forward to kneel before them. But then I stop myself, bring myself back to the day and to full wakefulness. These are mortals. One a boy and one a man, both of their faces beautiful and alluring; but they are of the earth. Their clothing is ragged and soiled. I collect the praise forming in my throat, swallow, and release a grunt instead.

'Good morning, uncle.'

His robes are those of the destitute but his manner is poised. He is not noble, but he is well spoken—his family must have some means.

I answer accordingly. 'Greetings, sir.'

I struggle to get up, and he shoots out his hand to assist me. It takes all my strength not to strike him. I shake my head, forbid his pity, and he steps back.

He has a beard, sparse and wispy bristles, but his glinting eyes are still those of a youth. So too his skin, tanned dark by travel and sun but retaining the softness of the young. He is a child and a youth and a man; all appear before me at once in the same body. I cannot tell his age. The sun is directly above us and I take the opportunity to shield my eyes from the glare. His beauty so startling that I am blushing.

The younger one is still a boy, soft down covering his upper lip. He keeps his face lowered. He has thick curls such that any vain maiden would covet. Aware of my eyes upon him, he lifts his head, trying to show me courage and pride but finding my scrutiny too intense. He flushes and bows. His large dark eyes are deep alluring pools, and must have been blessed by some sorcerer for I am convinced they would awaken the loins of a dead man. I can feel my own cock stir and I grasp the medallion attached to my belt, silently asking the gods to ward off enchantment. I make sure to sneer before I return my eyes to the older man.

'What can I do for you, sir?'

He takes a scroll from underneath his robe and hands it to me. The seal is one only permitted to the most superior of castes. I break it and glance at the characters.

'I am grateful,' he says quickly, kindly, 'to my patron for vouchsafing our request to meet with my friend and teacher.'

He stands patiently as my eyes follow the letters. He understands that I can't read and I am thankful that he has spoken the letter's contents so as not to shame me.

I return the letter to him and I unlock the door.

As soon as they enter the prisoner's cell, the old man and the older visitor fall upon each other. So tight is their embrace that they form one body; they stroke and kiss each other's cheeks, weeping and laughing. 'My Paul,' the younger calls, 'my teacher, my soul, my dearest friend.' And the old man sobs, 'My Timothy—you have returned, my love, you have returned.' Neither of them can step back, neither wants to be the first to break the hold. I lower my eyes, shocked and embarrassed by their display.

So is the boy beside me. We both stare down at the dirt floor.

When at last the two separate—but barely, as they sit on the old man's bedding, knees still interlocked, hands clasped, brows touching—they offer prayers to their god, and give thanks. Their words tumble and rush alongside each other, they join to form one tongue.

'The Saviour has risen. Truly, he has risen.'

'He lives, he lives.'

The force of the words seems too much for the old man—he chokes and returns to weeping.

The man called Timothy comforts him, gently holding the old man's face. 'My beloved,' he says, the Greek not Attic and long-vowelled but eastern and clipped. 'My beloved, I am always here with you.'

The old man raises his smock, stained with sweat and grime, and pats at his wet eyes. He turns to me and the boy, wiping his running nose with his hand.

Timothy waves for the boy to come over. 'Come, brother Able. This is our teacher, this is brother Paul.'

The boy won't move. I sense his fear. But I hesitate. I have kept guard over this blasphemer long enough to know that amongst his cult even the most noble wrap themselves in rags.

But it is not possible that this boy is high-born, that a noble's child could be so filled with fear and humility. I push him. 'Go,' I bark. 'Go to him.'

The boy walks over to the bed and shyly takes the old man's proffered hand.

'I have heard much about you, my son,' the old man says gently. 'I am a loyal friend of your . . .'

He stops. A poisonous spirit has suddenly dashed into this tiny cell; I can sense it in the alarm on Timothy's face, in the old man's abrupt stiffening, and in the boy's naked terror.

I brush my palm against my tunic, silently call on the gods, and the spirit has vanished.

'. . . a loyal friend of your father's,' the old man continues, his voice steady.

The boy's face crumples and he begins a monstrous wailing. The prisoner does not release his hold of the frightened lad; he brings him closer and wraps an arm around the boy's waist. My hand itches with the desire to strike the pitiable child. He is coming into manhood. If one of my daughters were to show such weakness, I would give them the lash. For a boy to do so is unthinkable. I pray to my God that my son is never so humble and weak.

Timothy is now standing by the window, looking out to the light. I understand that he too must be shocked by the young boy's diminishing misery. The child's wailing lessens; he is now on his knees, sobbing into the prisoner's lap.

I spit. The lecherous old goat is stroking the boy's thick curls, he kisses him there. It is unrighteous and unseemly and it takes all my resolve not to march across the cell and fling them off each other.

'Can I stay with you, teacher?' The boy is wiping his eyes. He is clasping the old man's knees, as if the old fool were a temple priest.

Timothy turns to them. His voice is firm. 'Tell him what he has to do, Paul. Please give him counsel.'

The old man makes no reply. His hands rest on the boy's head.

'Tell him, brother.' There is insistence in Timothy's voice, and annoyance too. I see it in a flash: he doesn't like the brat. I spit again, sickened by the childish jealousies of these three arse-fuckers.

The old man raises a warning hand to Timothy. With his other hand, he lifts the boy's chin, looks straight at him. 'Why do you want to stay with me, child?'

'I wish you were . . .' The boy hesitates, casting a rapid glance in my direction and an even quicker retreat from my gaze. But not before I glean something cunning in the boy. He is far from noble; far from it. I smell it, sense it—his servility.

He finally blurts out, 'I wish you were my father.'

An anger from deep in my gut rises to my throat and is released as a roar. I take a step towards the bed, my arm rising. There is no shame on this earth or in the world below or in the realm of the gods that is as repellent as that of a son dishonouring his father. If the old death-worshipper doesn't crush that little bastard's head against the wall, I will do it for him.

Timothy makes to stop me but shrinks back, comprehending he must not touch me in my rage. The old man has more daring.

He flings out his arm, his palm splayed to stop me. Before I can even register his warning, he strikes the boy across the cheek.

I'd have bashed the little bastard's head in but at least this appeases me.

The boy doesn't cry. He waits for another blow. But instead the old man is caressing the inflamed cheek.

'I am not your father, child,' he says. 'There is only one father and He is the Lord. Jesus the Saviour is coming, and when he returns there will be a kingdom of peace in which we will have no fathers and no masters. We will all be one, as sons and daughters of the Lord.'

I have to look away, disgusted by such absurdities.

He cares nothing for my agitation. He takes hold of the boy's shoulders, no longer affectionate but now stern.

'Be patient till that day, little brother,' he counsels. 'But until then you will return to your father and you will ask for his forgiveness. That is the law and that is right.'

I want to add: *And if your father decides to turn you over and push a pike right up your arse and up through your useless guts he has every right to do so.*

The boy knows it too, knows what is his due. 'He will flay me.'

'I promise you he will not.'

My hand searches for the talisman on my belt. That is not the prisoner's promise to make. The natural law of blood must be honoured. These blasphemers will not up-end the world. The father will destroy this son, that is the only righteous law.

The boy now stands. He no longer seems soft and effeminate. Finally, he has assumed dignity and manhood.

'I will do as you say, teacher.' He cups his hand into a fist and bangs it across his breast. 'Uncle,' he says to the old man, 'may I ask for a thanksgiving before my return?'

Joy transforms the prisoner's face. He grins and nods, turns to Timothy. 'Timos, bring wine and bread. We have much to thank the Lord for today.'

As Timothy goes to do his bidding, the boy and the prisoner sit next to each other on the bed. The old man starts speaking, charging him to remember every word of the story he is going to tell him so he can recite it faithfully to his father when he is home again—after he has fallen at his feet and begged for forgiveness.

'It is said,' he begins, 'that Jesus the Saviour spoke of a rich farmer who had two sons. The elder one was diligent and honourable but his younger was profligate and impatient. He'd asked his father for his half of his inheritance and then spent it all on wine and on women. Soon his share was exhausted.'

I listen to this ridiculous fable as he speaks, silently praying that my son will never be so disloyal. I'll cut his throat if he is, I swear it to The God and to all the gods. The boy listens silently.

'This son,' continues the prisoner, 'is now poor and destitute. He returns to his father and he says, "Father, I will be your slave, I will become your servant—I have squandered my inheritance."'

I cannot help myself, I speak my thoughts out loud. 'Such a son deserves nothing less than to be enslaved.'

The old goat beams at me. 'See?' he retorts gleefully. 'What Vrasas says is the truth of the world.'

Then he winks at the boy, as if my words are a joke. 'But the loving father was joyous on seeing his son return and he ordered that the fattest of their lambs be thrown onto the fire for a feast.'

I dare not say: *That is why that father bred a rubbish son:*

he indulged him and spoiled him. That was surely the meaning of such a fable, but the old fool does not stop there. He continues to tell how the eldest son asks his father: 'Is it just that you give our best offering for sacrifice to a dissolute and undeserving child?' That brother is correct—he speaks the truth. But so bizarre is the weak and death-loving god they follow, that is not the truth that is spoken.

'No,' says the prisoner. 'For the Lord is heartened and most pleased when one who is lost returns.'

He kisses the boy on the lips. 'These are the words of Jesus our Saviour, and these are the words you will repeat to your father when you greet him again.'

What travesty and what ugliness this cult believes—such madness and corruption! I will go to a temple, any temple, I will beg for forgiveness from Apollo or Minerva or Venus or even from Jupiter himself, I will scrub myself raw to wash away the dirt of such words.

The boy smiles and nods. This is a cult that inverts justice and denies punishment. Even the air in the cell is soiled.

I am relieved when Timothy returns with a small flask of wine and a portion of bread. The three form a circle, on their haunches, and the two watch with reverence as the old man tears at the crust.

I listen to their communion and I am appalled. 'This is the body that was sacrificed.' So is it true that they are indeed flesh-eaters? 'This is the blood that was spilled.' Are they ghouls?

The immensity of their sacrilege is overwhelming; I can hardly breathe. I push open the door, walk down the corridor, kick open the gate and am in the street. The sun is on my skin; my

God wraps His strong and conquering arms around me. I gulp, hungry for the warmth and light, stand there open-mouthed, face to the sky, basking in the rays from The God. With every breath I make a plea—'Let me raise my son honourably'—and make a vow—'I condemn those blasphemers'—and I am returned to peace. I lay a fist across my breast five times—one for my God and one for the gods and one for the First Amongst Men and one for my ancestors and one for my descendants—and I have protected myself against their worship of death.

I walk to the small fountain that feeds from the pipes below the streets. It is behind the dwelling I guard, in a small courtyard that is near empty. I squat before the fountain and wash my face, the pits under my arms, my hands and my neck. I can still hear them at their incantations and sorcery; the shutter is not drawn and their chanting escapes through the small cell window. I block my ears to expel their evil babble. I make further promises to The God.

I take my hands away from my ears. They are speaking as men now—I can just make out what they are saying. The boy is making a vow to the old man; I can hear him saying, 'I will return to my owner.'

All is clear. *To my owner.* Now I understand.

I do not fear their spells of death, the evil spirits they raise through sorcery. As I storm across the yard, it is as if I am defying the cruelty and shame of my rotten leg. It is as if I am again a young soldier at war, filled with only one urge: to cut the throat of an enemy. As I burst into the cell, I am an avenging fury, a righteous warrior.

The boy is in the old pederast's arms. Timothy is coming

towards me with his hands out—can that sweet womanish weakling think he can stop me? I push him and he falls to the floor. I tower above the bed and the shock I see in the craven face of the slave boy makes me more fierce as I grab his thick hair and pull back his head like a beast one is ready to slaughter and I raise my elbow and I bring it down hard as I call on The God and all the gods to do justice and the bone of my elbow smashes into the slave's eye, and he is screaming, thrashing as in a seizure, but I will not let go of him, nor let his hand reach for his burst eye. I am ready to tear off his face, to kill the animal, when the old man bellows with an authority that must be beyond him, must come from the savage, desert God he worships. It has none of his usual shrillness or weakness—it rings out in a fierce command.

'Vrasas! The boy belongs to a noble—kill him and you must pay. And if you cannot pay, you or your son will be bonded to the boy's master.'

I am a soldier. I call forth all my strength and I control the desire to kill. The old arse-fucker, the old death-lover, he counsels correctly. I release my grip on the slave and he shrieks and brings his trembling hands across his face as the blood gushes. I have damaged him—that eye will never heal. I have enacted some justice. I have killed his beauty.

There is one more thing I have to do. I unsheath my dagger. The old man jumps from his bed with an unnatural grace, but I push him back. I take the shivering slave and I grab a handful of his hair and scrape it from his scalp with the knife. I do it again and again, till the blade is wet and coated in blood and scraps of his skin. The dirt around our feet is covered by matted and bloodied clumps of his hair. I continue until he is completely shorn. Then I grab him by the throat, fill my mouth with phlegm and spit in his face, right into the bastard criminal's broken eye.

I am righteous and I am with the gods. I let him fall.

I walk to the prisoner's water jug, raise it and tip water over my arms and my hands. I make my prayers.

The slave is keening.

'My beloved,' the old man says to Timothy, 'you will take Able to Chloe's house. They will hand him over to a judge. But tell them to treat him as a brother.'

Brother? He calls this fugitive scum a brother? This is the madness and corruption of his raped and crucified god. I spit again, right into the old goat's water jug.

The prisoner walks over to the degenerate slave and crouches before him. 'Son, if I could, I would come with you. If I could, I'd bear your punishments. Your master Philemon is a brother.' He smiles at the distraught slave. 'He will be lenient.'

I turn away in revulsion. If the owner is any kind of man, he should show no mercy.

'Get up, boy, get up,' the old man says, shaking the slave, but his voice is tender and cajoling. 'You are going home.'

Still moaning, the boy is on hands and knees.

I step forward. I don't trust these vermin atheists to honour their word. To whom would they forswear honour?

'I will take him.' I kick the slave. 'Get up, you useless cock-muncher.'

He obeys immediately. He has been returned to grovelling obedience, to what and who he is. I have done right, by my God and the gods. I have served justice.

His eye seeps and bleeds and is already swelling. He will never be an object of lust again. That eye will never see and that brow will be forever ruined by the brand of the runaway. His crime and his dishonour will mark him till blessed death takes him. May his master deliver the fatal blow on the slave's return, so that justice be done. May he order that they crucify the cunt.

———

We deliver the criminal. The woman I hand him to is freeborn and dignified; I have to believe that she will deliver the slave to his deserved punishment. I leave that fool, Timothy, at the dwelling of the demented sect. I can hardly bring myself to farewell him. His tunic is soiled from the slave's blood and tears. May judgement soon be passed on the old atheist. Such a handsome young man should be giving himself over to everything that is potent and manly, he should be fucking a hundred slaves and whores and foolish peasant girls, he should be thinking towards marriage and to children. This cult the old man has bonded him to has destroyed all that is vital.

That night I do not return to sleep on the roof. Such are the dishonours I have been witness to this day that I fear pollution. Has my prisoner got enough provisions and water for the night? I don't care. Why do they keep him under house arrest? Why do our lords and senators protect vermin such as he? This is why they rebel against us in the north and the east—they smell our corruption and dissipation.

I have only one thought, one need, one will: to be with my wife tonight. As I climb into our bed, her mother starts complaining. I tell her to shut her cantankerous old mouth, and I take my wife.

It is not customary to be with her so soon after the birth, but I need to kiss her flesh, to feel her plump nipples in my mouth, to inhale her scent, to forget what I have seen. I suck and kiss and taste my wife, I fill my senses with her; and I fill her with my seed. I have to do it. I will ask the gods to grant me clemency. At the temple of Venus and the temple of Mars and the temple of the Great God and the temple of my God and the temple of the Augustan Mortal Made a God, I will kneel and make sacrifices at each altar. But first, tonight, I must embrace and release myself into the intoxicating tastes of my beloved wife. I must be a man tonight to erase all that I have witnessed today.

———

Everywhere there is talk of insurrection in the east. The Syrians and Judeans grow proud and violent and reckless; they defy our legions and they defy Rome. Everywhere there is talk of crushing them, once and for all. We have been too soft with them. We have allowed them to disregard our gods and thus they have no respect for us. We hear of a soldier murdered in their city, that whore Jersusalem. We respond by entering their meeting houses here in Rome on their slothful day, we run them out of their homes and march them through the street, we hurl abuse and curses at them. We beat them with righteous fury. We have made exceptions for them, but where is their gratitude? They mock our clemency and perceive it as weakness. We should crush them: march on their city, take it in siege, smash down those ancient walls; we should plunder their gold and bugger their sons and daughters. We should reduce their temple to rubble and banish forever their jealous and angry God. We should make them our slaves.

A fleet of ships carrying grain from Egypt is lost at sea. The gods are punishing us for indulging the death-worshippers—they will make sure our city goes hungry. To appease them, we root out the secret houses of their unhinged cult that feeds on flesh and drinks blood and worships a corpse nailed to a gallows. We march their acolytes through the streets, we flog them and beat them, we bash their heads against the stones. 'You worship death, do you, cock-munchers? Good, then you can have it!'

Hunger. Misfortune. Rebellion. All because of our weakness and leniency. Our indulgence of the death cults: Syrian, Judean and Egyptian. What are these kingdoms? They were once slaves. What should these kingdoms become? Slaves again. We soldiers whispered these things amongst ourselves but the whispers have become louder and now they are heard everywhere. We all demand: *Make them our slaves.*

I hold my son. Lupus has grown pudgy, and he has a loud, insistent cry. Thanks to The God and the gods that he is healthy. I hold him in my arms and tell him stories of his ancestors, of our mountain home and of the cold springs that erupt from the ground there. I tell him that he will be what I am and what his ancestors were—he will be a soldier. I leave him with Arté and his sisters; the girls are in thrall to him, fight each other for who will be next to hold him. My Arté is with child again. And I know it will be another son.

For we are doing The God's work on the streets—we storm the meeting houses and dwellings of the death cults, ordering them to kneel and to pray to our gods. When they refuse, we slit their throats. We offer their blood to our Emperor and to our city and to her gods. And those effete senators and nobles who have shielded the blasphemers and the Jews, they are terrified of us, terrified of our power. They won't let their sons walk around the streets of Rome at night. They know our strength, they know our rage, they know that we are blessed by the gods. They know we are right. And my God and the gods, they hear us: *Make them slaves!* The First Amongst Men hears our roar: *Make them slaves!* The world hears our promise: *We will make them all slaves!*

That is how I know I will have another son. We are taking back our city, we are returning it to the gods.

And my prisoner? His sorcery is spent; those who have shielded him have slunk away. At the barracks, collecting the old man's rations, I am ordered to keep a closer watch over him and to deny him any day leave. I understand my orders: the prisoner does not have long to live. He craves death, he calls for it, he holds out his arms for death's embrace. Death listens and the blade is sharpened. Death is answering his prayers.

———

Timothy comes to see him. He is the only one who braves the streets—he is the only friend left. On seeing him, the old man is almost senseless with joy. He grasps at Timothy, kisses his hands, his neck, his face, his hair. Their devotion to each other is so ferocious they are unable to speak. No father has loved a son more than this, I think, then swiftly touch the medallion on my belt, asking first my God for forgiveness and then begging mercy from the shade of my father. I remind myself that theirs is not an honourable affection. Their love corrupts.

'Beloved,' the old goat moans, 'you must leave.'

The young man will not let him go. 'I will not abandon you.' His voice muffled, his lips brushing the old man's ragged tunic.

'You do not abandon me, Timos. You have to go back to Greece and Anatolia and bring the world our good news.'

'I will not, I cannot.' He is as a child. His true father will be cast into shame in the underworld.

The prisoner takes the younger man's hand. 'Listen to me: is he not returning?'

This time those words do not act as a balm. Timothy shakes his head. 'I will not leave you here alone.'

The old man draws upright, fury lending power to his bones.

I lean forward eagerly, hoping he will hit the younger man.

'Do you understand nothing?' he says firmly. 'I'm not alone. I'm with the Lord and with the son and in fellowship with everyone who knows this truth. This is your duty: to spread our truth. I command you to leave.'

'No, brother, no. I have to stay in Rome.'

I swallow my rage: *as if Rome wants you.*

And the old man, for he understands, replies, 'Rome isn't safe.'

Timothy reaches for the old man's hand, but he is pushed away. He tries again, like a brazen infant desperate for his mother's tit. The old man crosses his arms and the boy collapses to the ground, defeated.

'If it isn't safe for me, then it isn't safe for you,' Timothy pleads.

'I don't matter. And you don't matter.' The prisoner points towards me. 'And the sullen Vrasas keeping guard doesn't matter. All that matters is the Lord and His promise. You will spread that promise. You have to: that is your duty and your test of loyalty.'

My medallion digs into my palm. My son matters and his son matters and my descendants matter. *Stand up, boy*, I want to roar at him. *Stand and be a man!*

The old prisoner's voice softens. 'We of the first generation will soon be gone. Your task now is to instruct the new generation. They will be the ones to witness the Saviour's return.'

Timothy shakes his head, his eyes beseeching. 'No, brother,' he insists, 'you will live to see his return.'

Gently the prisoner lifts the young man's hands. 'I am tired, Timothy. Your generation and the generation born now will continue our worship. You will build our faith.'

Again he points to me. 'This man's children, they will be as the Israelites were in the desert. I have led you to them. You will lead others.'

'I will not leave.'

The younger man is crouched into himself, denying the old man, refusing to listen. The prisoner is looking at me. Is that a nod? He is asking something of me.

I understand. He wants to die as a man. He is not father, not grandfather, not honoured—all that he has in the world is this companion, Timothy, and it is long past time for this silly young man to come to understanding.

I walk over to them. 'You cannot stay, sir.'

Timothy doesn't answer me.

He finally looks up as the old man continues. 'Don't you understand, Timos? I have chosen you to continue my work. Will you let our faith be stillborn? Go out to the world, tell them our good news!'

Timothy brushes away tears. He remains defiant. 'You are not yet dead, Paul. Brother Peter is not dead, James is not dead, Magdalena is living and so is the Twin. You will all see the Saviour return.'

The old goat's face is transformed. It twists with loathing. He spits out his next words. 'All of them illiterate, all of them deaf and blind to the truth. They know nothing about the prophets, nothing about our Lord's promises.' And now he is glaring at his companion. There is no adoration there, only ferocity. 'And the Twin? What use is he? Thomas doubts the resurrection and speaks against the son's return. You betray the Saviour every time you speak his name.'

Such venom. In all the time I've been guarding this prisoner I have never seen him release himself so wholeheartedly to the gods of wrath. This Thomas he speaks off, this Twin—he feels nothing but hatred for him.

Timothy is still. 'He was our Saviour's twin, Paul, dearly loved by our Saviour. Thomas will be with us in eternity.'

The old man looks murderous. 'We have no mothers and no fathers and no brothers and no kin.' His words are heavy. 'Being the Saviour's twin won't save Thomas. Thomas is dead and he will not rise. You know this—he says it himself. You have heard him. You will never see him again.'

He takes the younger man's head in his hands. 'Never. He will not rise. Thomas will not be born into the new world.' With that final curse, he releases his grip on the lad.

Timothy takes deep, shuddering breaths as he gives in to weeping.

Both of us, guard and prisoner, watch him till his wretched heaving subsides. He wipes his eyes. When he speaks again, it is as if the mantle of his youth has been lifted. His voice seems older—it is weighted and weary.

'You are hard, beloved—you are so unforgiving.' There is a distance in his eyes.

Timothy stands, drawing his woollen shawl over his shoulder. He leans forward to kiss the old man. At first the prisoner turns away, but then, as if the very scent of the man dispels his anger, he is returned to what he is, a wasted and corrupt old man. Their lips touch and the kiss is long and tender.

Timothy draws back. 'He is coming, brother.'

The old man smiles, relieved. 'Truly, he is returning.'

Timothy takes his satchel and walks past me to the door. He turns one final time.

'I will see you, Paul,' he says defiantly. 'I will see you when our Saviour returns. I will be with you and we will be there with our brother Thomas.'

The old man seems ready to argue, to be a man once more. Then, the smile diminishing but still visible, he raises his hand, places it over his chest and then holds it up to his friend, palm out.

Timothy returns the gesture.

When I return from letting Timothy out, the old man is seated on his bedding, his palm still outstretched. He looks up at me. 'I pray he will be safe,' he says sadly.

And though their ill-begotten yoke to one another revolts me and their mysteries and ways are corrupt and an insult to the gods, the grief in his eyes is brutal in its destitution. Before their love—though I know not what such devotion is, or even if it is proper—I cannot be cruel.

'Uncle,' I answer, 'I pray too that he is safe and soon far from Rome.'

———

Though my brother-in-law is as useless a barren ewe, and less honourable than a swine's arsehole, the idiot makes good wine. Bacchus has blessed his hands and the grape responds to his charmed touch. Past the most distant hill of the city, a nobleman of the equestrian class has a vineyard and this is where Ferros toils. I ask him to bring me some wine, and though he is a miser and a stranger to hospitality, he can steal like a beggar, and he brings me a half-flagon of blood-black wine. I dip my fingers into it, bring a drop to my tongue, and my mouth fills with the wine god's kiss.

'It is good, brother, is it not?'

I force myself to embrace him and thank him through unwilling lips. I pour most of the wine into three copper dishes I plundered long ago from an Illyrian farmhouse, and I offer libations to The God and to the gods for granting us a healthy son. I fill a skin with the remainder and bind it securely.

———

The prisoner is watching me as intently as a cormorant scanning the waters. I take the bloated skin and I carefully empty the wine into two cups.

'What is this, son?' he asks, his nostrils flaring at the scent of wine, his toothless grin widening. 'What are we celebrating?'

I make no answer. I kneel and pour a handful of water into each cup. The purple becomes crimson. I give him his feed and he divides the soggy meal in two. He offers me half.

'There is no need, uncle, I am sated.'

His good eye, the blood flecked white, watches me guardedly. 'Is this to be a last meal, Vrasas?'

He's a sorcerer—I swear he can see the future.

'It is our last meal together, uncle,' I answer gently. 'Tomorrow morning I am taking you to a new home.'

I am shocked to see him become jovial. His eyes widen, he sets his food down and grabs my hand. 'What great news, child! I will have my trial; I will be freed.'

The realisation comes to me like a blazing dawn: all his talk of death has only been words—the old man loves life and wants to live. Like all of us he is in denial of his fate. He is chattering now about the journeys he will take on his release, how he will secure passage on a ship, how he will take his teachings to Spain and all the way to Carthage.

There will be no trial. A decision must have already been made—I am sure of it. He is not a nobleman and he has not once recanted his allegiance to his odious and malicious corpse god. There will be no sea journey. The sword's blade will be his end. His fate has been ordained.

The meat of his palm is callused with scars—even there they have beaten him. Our clasped hands are wet with sweat. I let go.

'Don't think me a fool, Vrasas,' he says, his smile departed, his hand hovering over my cup, forbidding me to drink. 'I know I have no influence. I know you think that judgement has already been pronounced.'

His voice trembles now, not with fear but with spirit and defiance. 'And I know I am not a nobleman. But I belong to a kingdom that knows neither slave nor master.'

I allow him this sacrilege. I make no objection.

'Can you dream this, son?' he asks. 'Can you imagine such a kingdom?'

He has half risen, his hands are outstretched over my head, casting his spell.

I bang my fist on the earth. 'Uncle, this is the earth I know, this is my country and this is my city. Let's drink to the fortune that we are not slaves but let's not be fooled into believing we'll ever be the masters.'

'That is not what I asked.'

But my speech has quietened him; he grabs at his food, he lifts his cup of wine.

'Will you allow me a prayer?'

'Of course, uncle.'

He brings a finger of gruel to his mouth.

'When we eat this, we remember the Saviour as a man who feasted and was amongst us.'

He brings the cup to his lips. 'And when we drink this, we remember his sacrifice.' The wine spills on his chin, his bare gums mash on the meal.

I turn away, sickened, my loins clenched. This is the most depraved of sects, flesh-eaters and lovers of death.

He is blind to my revulsion. 'Son, eat with me,' he urges. 'Drink with me—share this mystery with me. Can't you see? He is with us now.'

I silently call on my God, the True God, to erase the evil he
has spoken. Released, I eat and I drink with him.

———

I embark on my journey deep in the heart of night and on the eve
of Martius. There are still some of the very old that claim this
the beginning of our new year. And leaving the city, entering the
bosom of dawn, it strikes me that our ancestors are right, that
the sky and the earth, the fields and woods are being reborn.
Young and fragile sprouts shoot from the ground, there are
pregnant buds on every tree, promising imminent, bursting spring.

I make my way carefully and slowly, as sheets of frost-hardened
ice cover the ground before me. But with the ascending of
The God the firm crust of the snow glistens, cracks and melts to
slush. The further I go from the city, the louder the song of the
returning birds. In the distance I can hear the rush of newly
filled creeks and springs from the distant hillsides.

It will take two days to reach the grove dedicated to the God
of war and, defying my accursed leg, I am determined to reach
the sacred site in the allotted time. I am a soldier: I have sworn
my allegiance to the Sun and with His assistance I will not fail.
Though the day is only young, the sun already blazes with an
intensity that blinds the eyes; I shade them and look towards
The God. His form rolls and coils, kicking against the skin of
his fiery husk. The snow has now melted, the bricks and stones
of the road glisten in the wet, and the colours of life and the
revitalised earth fill my lungs and eyes: the shimmering gold and
bronze of the meadows, the perfume of the woods and scrub, the
blue of sky and the silver haze of the horizon. With every step I

take, one sure and one clumsy, I breathe in the world and listen to my blood singing. With every breath I give thanks to The God.

As I turn a bend I see the long-limbed shadows of four scarecrows. But coming closer, the elongated black lines take shape and are revealed as crucified men nailed to their rough gallows. I spit, I touch my chest five times, I pray to life to ward off death.

With the sound of my steps, the sky blackens with crows, the day filling with their relentless cries. They come to rest in a field beyond and form a thick black carpet. They wait impatiently for me to pass so they can return to their unholy feasting on the corpses. The air is rank with death, and I gag, covering my mouth and nostrils; but even so, the rancid and fermenting slaughterhouse stink seeps into my very skin. I walk faster, glancing up at the contorted bodies as I do. A collapsed ribcage has broken through the flesh of the first; his eyes are empty black holes, pecked clean by the crows. The sound of flies is louder than an ocean of cicadas at evening: I fear I will be deafened by the sound. I spit, I beat my breast five times.

A low and desperate sound makes me stop. I wind my cloak more tightly around my nose and mouth, and I approach. The condemned man still has his eyes, the birds have not yet pecked them hollow. The raw and still-bleeding slashes across his brow makes his crime clear: he is a runaway slave. I spit, I paw my chest five times, I whisper against death.

But I go near. The man's body is slumped forward, his arms broken at wrist and shoulder, but there is the very slow rise and fall of his distended abdomen. He lives. The gallows are streaked with the dark stains of his emptied bowels, his sex has shrunk into its sheath, the black hairs there are damp with blood and sweat and piss.

The rise of The God is reaching its apex. By now my old prisoner will have been executed. I stare up at this abomination on the cross. I try to imagine a God flayed, raped, beaten, nailed and dying on such a gallows. I try, but the obscenity is a folly, an outrage: it mocks life itself but it also mocks valour and honour and city and country and caste. It defies life and blood and we who are the living. It violates my son and it violates my father and his father. It defies all that is sacred and calls for the end of time and the end of man. There is no honour in such a death. Only suffering. Only shame.

I prise loose a stone from the road. I take aim. The rock arcs, slams against the side of the condemned man's head. There is a last cry, a final shudder. The man is dead.

———

I walk with the sun, I walk in the brightness and life of day, I leave the dead to the crows and to the flies. With every breath my blood is nourished by life. Those who pray to death hate this: that we are alive, that we experience joy, that we also suffer and that we know pain; but all of it, the pleasure and the endurance, all of it is worth it, for it is life: all we have is life. Those who call on a new world, a world beyond this world, hate us for our loyalty and our pride, our lovemaking and our fecundity, they detest us for our laughter and our singing, our vitality, our joy, our connection to the very ground we walk on. They despise our love of life and our love of earth.

I spit, beat my chest five times, and send a prayer to the old prisoner's departed spirit. Foolish old man, living in death and forgoing the rapture of the fleeting moment. A foolish man with a foolish God. Yet, he was kind and he was loved: may the gods have mercy on his shade. I spit once more, I touch my heart and I make a final prayer.

I continue along the road, I walk day and night to reach my goal, my steps guided by the gods and The God of sun and light and valour. I offer the true gods my son, to make him strong, to make him fruitful, to make him love life.

I leave death to the carrion-eater, to the flies and the maggots and the worms.

I walk towards the sun.

Saul III

45 ANNO DOMINI

'There is neither Judean nor Greek, neither slave nor free, nor is there male and female, for you are all one in Christ Jesus.'

—THE LETTER TO THE GALATIANS

'He is wondrous, isn't he?'

At the sound of Saul's voice, Timothy turns around quickly, his face grimacing in shame.

'No, he's foul,' says the youth, 'a wicked idol.'

They are working in a secluded garden, perfumed by irises blooming along the terrace. The sickly odour of sap rises from budding myrtle trees. A vibrant mosaic decorates the bottom of a sunken pool, bringing to life a world of nymphs and their pursuers. A statue of a beautiful youth has been set into the pool, his slender marble arm reaching out as if to touch the enthralled Timothy who was gazing upon him. The statue is only small but the sculptor's artistry is faithful to life: the fine pointed fingers, the gentle contours of the nose and the jaw, the sinuous neck and the faint swell of belly; one can believe that the boy is about to step out of his bath and join the living.

Timothy still wears an abashed smile on his lips. In the glare of the morning heat, his tawny curls appear forged by the very sun itself, his slight flush of beard glowing russet.

You are so much more splendid than that idol of cold marble, Saul wants to say. He swallows his words.

'You think I'm an idolator,' Timothy ventures.

No, lad, I am the idolator, I am making an idol of you.

'No, no, of course not,' Saul says impatiently. 'I know you are faithful to the Lord.'

He is lying on a granite rock, its top levelled for a seat. The youth comes and squats beside the older man. He leans his chin against Saul's knee. Saul runs his fingers through the youth's curls. They are the only ones in the garden, blessedly alone. Saul knows that they will be like this, exactly as they are now, in the promised kingdom to come. They will be like this, pure, without sin, in an eternal garden.

It cannot be resisted: both pairs of eyes return to the boy climbing out of his bath.

In the years since his awakening by the Saviour, the power of such statues and images to disturb Saul has abated. Once he reviled such idols and was disgusted by them and their abominable challenge to the primacy of the Lord. And their very presence attested to the fact that first Greece, and now the Romans, had conquered the world. His revulsion was not gone completely—he could still feel it faintly stirring in his belly and in his heart—but it didn't explode as it used to. He has travelled far, into Arabia and to the foothills of Persia, and he has witnessed the monstrosities of four-winged demons and lascivious sphinxes, towering phalluses and many-breasted pregnant witches. All would soon be ground to dust. His hand rests on his beloved's head; Timos's hair warmed by the sun. This beautiful youth, the Lord's creation, this is what is truly wondrous.

'Shall we get back to work?' says Timothy.

Saul doesn't answer. All he wants is to stay there, lying next to each other in the lap of the sun. To believe in Creation renewed and reborn. But already the peace is receding. Beyond the line of pruned myrtle trees, beyond the wall, he can hear the frenzied sounds of Antioch. Sellers calling out in the markets, the clanging bell of a shepherd herding his flock down an alley. A mother is scolding a child. A beggar is cursing his fate. This is the world, the fallen world.

They return to their work. As always, Saul marvels at the sharpness and lucidity of his companion's memory. The older man listens as the youth faithfully repeats the words Saul had composed only that morning. The words flow from Saul's mouth and the boy listens and recites them back to him. In the evening, when they return to Astephania's house, where their kind sister has given them shelter, his Timos will kneel before the kitchen table, and the stylo he holds will fly across parchment as he transcribes every one of Saul's words. The letter will be written and his words will be unerringly copied there in the boy's careful calligraphy.

Timos never presumes to correct the older man's grammar, even though Saul encourages him to.

'You are a Greek, brother, you know it better than me. I know I sometimes make mud of your language.'

The boy always shakes his head and refuses to change a word. 'You are inspired by the Spirit,' he always answers.

And the union forged by their work is indeed sublime and astonishing. A bond wrought by the Lord.

Now, listening to the youth's recital, Saul becomes aware of a gentle tapping in his head. His back stiffens, his lip trembles. It is only faint now but he fears that it will become a fierce pounding, as it has done in the past. His shaking hand reaches for the goatskin and he brings the bag to his mouth, sucking desperately as water rushes down his chin.

'Are you ill, brother?' asks the young man, rushing to his side.

'Continue,' growls Saul. 'I did not tell you to stop.'

He is being unfair, he knows. This boy, this friend and brother, has been steadfast for over a year now. He closes his eyes and listens to Timothy's faithful recitation. Saul listens to his own words. Days and nights—the urge to make the words real and in making them real make them truth has made sleep impossible. Saul knows that his words do not belong to him, that the foundations of all that he has to communicate, all that he believes, have been ordained a long time ago, in the ancient truths of the prophets. And as every day passes and every night ends, it is this understanding that strengthens his conviction that he has been chosen by the Lord.

In those long and ugly years in the east, he had been lost to drunkenness and wrath. It was a rage that had come out of fear: why had the Lord chosen him; why had the Lord demanded his exile from his family and from his world; why had the light, the risen Saviour, appeared to him on the Damascene road? Those questions had tormented him and his confusion and fear had led him to surrender to the darkness, to committing all those acts of wickedness that were loathsome to the Lord.

But in desert villages, in mountain hamlets, in foreign cities forsaken by the Lord, he had always found a welcome at the hearths of those who had heard the words of the man Yeshua, and who had pledged allegiance to that most incomprehensible of miracles, a crucified Redeemer. That could not have been a mere accident, that absurdity the Greeks called fate. Wherever he strayed, he would find Jews and Strangers who feared the Lord and loved the son. Even though he reeked of wine and dissolution, they had still taken him in. Even though he had cursed and abused them, they had fed him and given him shelter. Though he reeked of the sins of the flesh, they had washed him and clothed him. And he came to understand that what Ananias had first offered him—the knowledge that even in sin the Lord was there, that He would not abandon Saul even at his most wretched—that was a truth he could in turn offer to others.

So he slowly let go of his doubt and distrust, and he accepted their food and their shelter and their kindness. He returned their love. He knew the commandments and the words of the prophets were inscribed across his heart. At first reluctantly, and then with gathering awe, he realised that this would be his gift to the coming kingdom. *He knew Israel.* He was schooled and trained in Israel, he was of Israel. The coming of the crucified Saviour was not an aberration. His suffering and death and arising, and the redemption to follow, had been willed at the dawn of Creation. The Saviour had been nailed to the Tree of the Knowledge of Good and Evil, and thus had the circle been completed.

So many of his brethren—poor and destitute, many of them slaves, unschooled and ignorant even if some had been born Jews—had heard the Anointed One's words but could not comprehend his meaning. Yeshua the Nazarene was the new covenant. That was the truth Saul had been chosen to reveal.

And with that revelation, his thirst for wine and hunger for flesh had fallen away. Not completely—that was impossible in a contaminated and debased world. But the Lord forgives. That was the thing about the Jews that the Greeks and Romans could never understand. Their gods despised men for not being gods. This was the greatest wickedness, the worst lunacy. The Lord was the only god that forgave men *as* men. This was the revelation that had saved him.

The very same light had saved this boy, this Timos: his scribe, his companion, his brother. His friend, his love: eternal and indestructible. When he had come across Timos in the Anatolian city of Lystra, that boy had been lost. He had surrendered to wine, to depravity, to lust. The boy had stunk of it.

Saul, his eyes closed, is back in Lystra. He is back in Labour's hut; they have just completed their thanksgiving. There is Labour, her daughter, Dawn, a slave named Giant, and a freedwoman, Virtue. All Strangers. Earlier, at the meeting house of the Lystrian Jews, Saul's words had fallen on hard and unwelcoming soil. They'd laughed at his story of a crucified Saviour. They'd howled in derision and cursed in fury: 'We want a new David, a hero who will slay Rome. We don't want a virgin boy nailed to a fucking cross.'

So to the Strangers he goes. It is in the penury and misery of Labour's poor dwelling that he finds those with ears to hear. The thanksgiving is done, they have shared their wine and bread, when they hear the whimpering. And then the baying—as though a beast is at the door. An animal crying out in pain and imminent death.

Giant moves the hide away from the door and Saul sees a boy, on his knees, scratching at the earth. Giant bends and takes the boy in his arms.

Dawn calls out, 'Bring him inside.'

'He's soaked,' the slave complains.

'Bring him in.' It isn't an order, but a plea.

Giant enters the hut carrying the boy.

The rancid stench of man. The boy stinks of it. It is wine, it is sweat, and it is something else: the fetid odours of decay and death. Saul recognises this terrible stink; it oozes from loins, from between thighs and armpits, from arses: the stink of flesh. The boy's head falls back, his eyes roll and then scarlet bile explodes from his mouth. Giant places the limp form on the floor. Dawn is at Giant's side, rag in hand, to wipe the vomit away. Saul marvels at the miracle of their fellowship: a freewoman cleaning a slave.

The boy's head is lolling in the dirt.

Saul asks, 'Is he a brother?'

Labour nods sadly. 'He wants to join us.' She doesn't bother whispering—the boy is in a state between sleep and death.

'His mother is a Jew, like yours, Saul,' she continues. 'And his father is Greek. They have banished him from their home.' Her next words are heavy and sour. 'His shames are known throughout the town. Ours is the only house that will welcome him.'

Her daughter has poured water over a cloth and gives it to Dawn, who squeezes it over the boy's mouth. At first he remains insensible, as if dead, his body unmoving and his eyes unnervingly rolled back, their yellow whites bisected by red veins. But then suddenly his mouth opens and his tongue strains towards the water, craving its touch. And with that, his eyes blink.

He looks up, searches the room. His gaze settles on Saul. His lips dry, his tongue heavy, he slurs, 'Is this a brother?'

'Yes,' Dawn answers, 'this is our brother Paul.'

The boy had spoken in the Lystrian dialect, but in deference to Saul their sister has answered in Greek. The older man and the youth lock eyes. As they do so, a crushing sadness overtakes Saul. This handsome lad is so young that a beard has not yet had a chance to grow. He is not yet a man, yet he reeks of a debauchery that Saul has only glimpsed in the most desiccated and destroyed of men, those who have dedicated a lifetime to wickedness and sin. He can see life leaking out of those eyes. Saul makes fists, hoping to stay the swell of misery that promises to break inside him. Misery at what the world is. At what the world can do.

The boy's deadened eyes will not leave Saul. With a ferocious struggle, the boy jolts forward, lifts himself up and then falls onto his knees before the older man.

'You saw him?' The question is almost a scream. 'They say that you saw him!' No longer a question, now a demand.

And as suddenly as it consumed Saul, the fierce grief within him is gone. It has melted away and been replaced with a feeling of lightness, as if Saul is one with air. Is one with spirit. For in the depths of the youth's despairing eyes he has perceived a shimmer. He has seen beyond rancid flesh.

Saul kneels in front the boy. 'Yes,' he says, 'I have seen him.'

He reaches out but the boy recoils.

'Don't touch me, sir,' he groans. 'There isn't one of the Lord's laws that my vile body hasn't broken.'

Saul grips the boy around his neck. He will not let him go.

'You are forgiven. I promise you, boy, if I am forgiven, you are forgiven.'

Saul realises he is taking what was once given to him by Ananias and offering it to the boy. And he knows that this too was ordained at Creation: that the boy's burdens will also be his.

Saul's eyes open, he looks at the handsome young man before him, the one who unerringly transcribes Saul's words. Timos's skin is clear of blemishes, his eyes are wide and shining, his body unbowed. There are bruises across his neck and left shoulder, delivered some days ago by Strangers who were outraged by their allegiance to the crucified and resurrected son. Saul recalls their curses as they rained punch after punch on him and Timothy: 'Fuck you and fuck your corpse God.' But the bruises and scars have not destroyed the boy, they have not felled Saul. They have only marked flesh. They cannot strike at the spirit or touch the light within. Both spirit and light had been all but extinguished when he'd first met the boy who'd slumped across Labour's dirt floor. Sin had nearly conquered him.

'Thank you, Lord,' Saul whispers in the garden. 'Thank you.'

Timothy has seen the tears welling in his friend's eyes and has come to comfort him.

'It is nothing, nothing at all,' Saul says, wiping his cheeks. 'I am recalling our first meeting and thanking the Lord.'

At these words, the young man's eyes too begin to brim and a half-smile forms on his tender lips. 'I was so broken.'

'I was broken too,' Saul reminds him. 'All of us have been broken, brother.'

Timothy sighs with such overwhelming sorrow that for a moment the youth in him disappears and Saul glimpses what he will be when he's an old man. A silver sweep of hair, a wrinkled and unsteady neck. It is a flash and it is gone. Youth stands before him once more.

Saul clasps his companion's hand. 'Passover is soon upon us, brother. I have taught you well. You know the sacred texts and, more importantly, you understand them as well as I do—I have no doubt about that. You will stay here with our brethren for a while, and when I return from Jerusalem, we will resume our travels.'

And again, a great happiness floods Saul. He can see the long Roman roads, the great caravans they will join, he can feel the sea winds whipping across his face and shoulders.

'We will go to Greece, Timos. We will bring the Lord to the world.'

But the lad's hand has slipped from his. His face has become a mask. And Saul knows how rare it is to see hardness or defiance in Timothy's face, and for that reason it is alarming when it does emerge.

'Take me with you to Jerusalem.'

The older man shakes his head. His joy is gone. 'I cannot.'

Petulant, the youth looks away. A group of young street children has entered the garden, five beggars. The oldest, thin as a reed but with the fully-formed muscles of a wrestler, is dividing up their illicit gains stolen from market stalls. The boy snarls and Timothy returns his gaze to Saul.

'Take me.'

When are you returning, Yeshua? When? And with that question, Saul fears he does not have the strength to continue. He has baptised Timothy himself, he has brought him to Israel, to the Lord. But Saul knows that his conviction, his love for Timothy, is not shared by their brothers and sisters in Jerusalem, the first disciples of their Saviour. A stab of resentment runs through him. Their ignorant, unlearned, illiterate and uncomprehending brethren in David's city. Fools and doubters—barriers to the kingdom. It is no wonder that Saul has been chosen by the Saviour.

Pride, his arrogant pride. Saul is ashamed by his own meanness of spirit.

'You must be patient, Timos,' he says finally. 'I will make our brothers understand.'

But the lad is shaking his head. 'Cut me. Make me circumcised.'

His words strike Saul to his soul. He is reminded of the great chasm of age that separates them. How can he counsel patience to this young man? The boy knows that the world will change and the world will end and a greater one will take its place. Saul shivers again. There are so many like his Timos, young and therefore impatient, pledged to the Saviour but in their impatience led astray. So many charlatans proclaiming that the kingdom has come. They must not take this boy from him.

As if seeing inside Saul's heart, the lad insists again: 'Cut me.'

Louder this time, so that the leader of the beggar boys lifts his head. He sniggers, says something, and the boys burst into laughter.

'He is coming, Timos.' And Saul forces sternness, not doubt, into his voice. 'He is returning and then we will all be in the kingdom together.'

'Saul, do you believe me to be of Israel already?'

'Yes.'

'Then cut me. My mother is a Jew—it is allowed. You can make me of Israel now.' And he adds once more: 'Cut me.'

'I will not.'

For a moment he believes that his firmness has prevailed, that the lad is accepting.

Timothy sits beside Saul. 'I'm coming to Jerusalem.'

'I will not take you.'

'I'm coming to Jerusalem, brother. I will be there for Passover.' As he speaks, Timothy has brought his fist up to his chest, as if to thump at his breast. He swiftly drops his hand.

'Cut me,' he pleads softly. 'Please, my brother. Don't let it be Peter or James. Let it be you that brings me to Israel.'

Saul's first thought, with sadness: I have already brought you to the Lord. Then, with spite: You are still a Stranger, look at you, wanting to bang your chest to appease the filthy Greek gods. And finally, the turmoil that renders all other emotion powerless—the jealousy that snakes around his heart so tightly that Saul believes it will crush him: not them, not Peter or James. I will not have it, I cannot allow it. He knows it is wickedness, knows that jealousy and pride are both awful sins. And that they blind him to the light, bind him to the earth. He doesn't have the breath, the strength to ask forgiveness from the Lord for his weakness.

'I will take you to Jerusalem,' he says, his voice cold. 'I will circumcise you.'

The youth falls on him, embraces him, kisses him fully on the lips. The beggar boys are open in their derision now. One of the boys grabs another, the smallest, and bends him over and pretends to rut him. Timothy is oblivious to their scorn. But Saul knows that he is committing a greater sin than such boys know is possible. It is his conviction, forged over years of aversion and confusion and finally enlightenment, that his Saviour has sent him out amongst the Strangers to preach that the Lord is truly the God of all. To the circumcised and to the uncircumcised. And now, in his cowardice, his reluctance to challenge James for fear of being excluded, is he betraying Yeshua?

He pushes his friend away, holds him at arm's length. 'Are you prepared, brother? Are you ready for great hardship?'

'You are my teacher,' Timothy answers. 'With you by my side, I can face any hardship.'

———

The long Roman road is thronged with pilgrims who are also making their way to the Sacred City for Passover. Saul and Timothy set off before first light, but even then a river of humanity is already on the march: ascetics and musicians deliriously chanting their praises to the Lord; women riding mules clutching infants on their laps and to their bosoms; men and older children balancing loads on their heads and shoulders; depleted old men, skeletal with hunger and clothed only in the thinnest of cloth, sacrificial ash smeared across their foreheads; eager youth in full sonorous chorus, arms linked as they recite the Lawgiver's sacred words.

Saul finds himself singing, calling forth the ancient songs of

King David. He could do so freely, as there is no danger on this journey, no fear that bandits or madmen will attack this great crowd, this glorious proof of the Lord's love for His first and most cherished of people. The calamities and the dishonour that had befallen the Jewish race were dispelled in the unity of their song and in their communal desire to make sacrifice at the altar of the Lord's Temple.

These are not the wealthy Judean nobles who have compromised their faith by coveting the luxuries of Greece and Rome. They are not the enervated priestly caste, grown fat and indolent on privilege, spewing forth words that have long ceased to touch their hearts. These are caravans of Alexandrians, Greeks, Anatolians and Phrygians, Galatians and Egyptians: they are the true source of Israel, these virile men, these stoic wives, these joyful children. Here, amongst these poor and labouring men, farmers and freedmen, here is the coming strength of the realm promised to Abraham and championed by the prophets. These souls are the light that will defeat Rome as they had defeated Assyria and Babylon, they are the vengeance that will topple the pretender kings of corrupt Jerusalem. These are the heirs of Elijah and of Moses the Lawgiver, of the houses of David and Solomon, and of the blood of the Maccabees. This is the kingdom that the Saviour had been sent to redeem and, in saving it, to return all of the world to unspoiled Creation.

Saul's voice cannot stop singing: these are his people and his kingdom and also the world to come. His voice rings out strong and bold. Let Rome listen and be afraid. The song has been forged in slavery, in the wanderings in the desert, in the mines and quarries of Babylon, in the choked streets and temples of the great Egyptian and Greek and Roman cities. Let them hear the ancient roar and recognise that the kingdom is coming. Rome will fall and Jerusalem will rule the world. The whole world will belong to Israel. It is promised and it is coming. Let them hear. Let them quake.

Saul grips his beloved's hand, raises it to his lips and kisses it. 'Thank you, Timos,' he says, breaking free for a moment from his song, 'for making me promise to bring you along.'

He surveys the sea of pilgrims.

'This is the kingdom promised by our Redeemer.'

———

They enter the desert that cleaves Syria from the Lord's northern kingdom. On a sun-bleached plain, a giant cloud of black flies descends, to attack and feed. The pilgrims light torches so their smoke will repel the insects, but the great swarm only rises then descends once more in fury. The air is filled with the sound of their thunderous buzzing, and with the wails of children, the curses of their fathers and the laments of their mothers. Lice also make their attack, burrowing under veils and robes, into beards and folds of flesh and hair. Lines of fresh blood stripe the exposed skin of the pilgrims, marks of the incessant scratching, and every person is in torment.

Saul too cannot bear the relentless assault of the insects, the relentless itching and biting, yet he does not want this journey to end. On this long road he is at one with his beloved and he is at one with his Lord and their people.

All decent accommodation—inns, taverns and meeting houses—along the way has been taken. Across the inhospitable hilltops, villagers are eager to rent out rooms and stables, even the most derelict outhouses. The tavern owners, as is their wont in this holy season, ask for double or even triple the usual amount to house the pilgrims. Those who can afford it pay, but most of the travellers refuse, saving their coin for the sacrifices of Passover. They look for any bed they can find in the yards of the meeting houses. But even they close their gates once their courtyards are full and will not open them again, no matter who comes calling, till the rising of the sun.

Saul and Timothy are happiest when sleeping out in the open and don't bother to secure lodgings. On a night of a diminished moon, along with a group of young men who have travelled from the Pontus, they make their bed in a cave, its mouth yawning from deep on the side of a steep mountain.

It is in that cave, in the dark, damp hollow, body lying against body, the relentless scratching and the rumble of snores broken by a narration of the Lawgiver's defiance of the enslaving Pharaoh, that Saul is first challenged on the road. As the chorus recites the words of Moses, a single high-pitched voice interjects with the warnings of the prophet Jeremiah. It is a youth lying next to Saul; his ardent denouncements of the sins and capitulations of Israel soon quiet those who are still awake: of Her betrayal of Her people and Her becoming a whore to the seductions of first Alexander and now the Caesars. 'Amen, brother,' he is answered solemnly. 'Amen,' calls another.

'The Saviour is coming,' the protesting youth announces defiantly. 'He is coming and will wipe away the filth that corrupts our lands.'

Saul fastens his stare onto a glimmer of wet stone glinting

above him on the low rock ceiling. The only light. The nails driven into the Saviour's feet, the wounds of his torture, the agonising death on the cross. Saul must find such courage. Breaking through the answering cries, he lifts himself up on his elbows and dares to speak.

'The Saviour that was promised has come. The one anointed by the Lord has come,' he proclaims.

Beside him in the dark, Timothy finds and grips Saul's hand. It is only then that Saul realises the danger of his having spoken. Not for himself—that he can bear—but for his beloved. The youth is of the kingdom that is coming, he is convinced of this: the boy is circumcised in spirit if not in flesh. But this truth is not known to the ignorant pilgrims all around them. Uncircumcised, the youth remains a loathed Stranger. He has put his Timos in danger. The boy should not be here with them.

A voice threatens in the darkness. 'Who is this Saviour who has come?'

Saul will do what he must to save the lad. 'The signs are being fulfilled with each passing of day,' Saul answers meekly. 'He must be coming.'

This time he is answered by a grunt. And from deep in the cavern, an answering call. 'He is coming.' And the chorus agrees.

Saul does not speak. The flesh on his neck, on his cheeks, it bursts into flame. Of shame. Of fear. Of exile.

Timothy squeezes his hand and then lets it go. He knows that the youth will have brought his hands over his sex, cupping his loins in fear and in shame.

Forgive me, Lord, Saul prays silently. *Forgive me.*

———

It is the open sky that first announces their proximity to the Lord's city. The sheet of endless blue above them starts shimmering at its edges as they turn their backs to the coast and ascend the rising path. The roads are clogged with the multitudes making their pilgrimage to Jerusalem.

After hours of negotiating the massive crowds along the way, they decide to find a place to rest for the night. They have to be ready for the icy night ahead.

Saul watches as Timothy gathers twigs and branches and builds a small pyre in a hollow on the ground. The youth strikes stone against rock, sending out sparks of silver and blue, and the twigs soon smoulder. On their knees the men blow into the smoke and glowing twigs. There is a crackle and the fire is lit.

As the day fades, fires are burning all along the slope that falls in gentle undulations to the far valley below. Around them are huddled groups and families, exhausted pilgrims knowing their grail is close. There are slender youths whose ragged clothing declares their zealous devotion. There are those with broken, twisted limbs and those disfigured by leprosy and other cruel diseases. There are children possessed by the evil spirits of madness or imbecility. All are preparing for their final night of sleep. By the next nightfall, under the gathering strength of the moon, they will all be—the Lord willing—in Jerusalem.

Saul beckons to Timothy. The youth reluctantly moves away from the fire and joins his companion on the peak of the hilltop. The darkness shrouds the landscape but through the broad cleft of the valley a thin white line glimmers as it plays and catches the light of the burgeoning moon before disappearing again behind the solid black of the next hill.

'Do you see it, brother? That is the Jordan River. That is where our Saviour was baptised by the prophet John.'

Saul traces the air as if it were a solid stretch of parchment, as if his fingers were pen and ink. 'This is the only point where we will see it,' he continues. 'Tomorrow we march south.'

His finger darts to the ghosts of the mountain face across the valley. 'And beyond there, you will see our city.'

Timothy stretches his hands out across the night, as if seeking to hold the whole of Judea: the distant river, the desolate peaks, the dark valleys and the bleak sky; as if he could step forth and leap into the lap of the land.

Saul laughs and ruffles the youth's hair. 'Day will come soon enough. But first you must sleep.'

Timothy starts down the narrow path back to their fire. He turns around. 'Aren't you coming, brother?'

'Soon,' Saul replies.

But he remains standing on the peak for an age, watching the moon travel almost halfway across the sky. He gazes into the dark, his heart and spirit contorted and restless, as if there were angels within him, wrestling for dominance. One is light, eager to enter the gates of the city and breathe once more the holy air. The other is night, choosing to stay on the hilltop, fearing those with whom he was once bonded, those he considered kin and friends. He knows that many in the Sacred City do not welcome him.

When he finally returns to their camp, the fire is all but extinguished. His arms around Timothy, shivering in the cruel night on the mountain, Saul finally finds sleep. He lets the angels continue their wrestling in his dreams.

———

They arrive mid-morning at a hut on the far side of Mount Scopus, a house belonging to Benjamin, son of Emmanuel, and to his wife, Agatha. They are devout Jews, poor but generous, and they too proclaim the resurrected son. Saul has been grateful for their kindness on his previous journeys to Jerusalem. But as he and Timothy make their way down the mountain, there is fear in his throat. Will they reject Timothy? Will they refuse him as a Stranger?

There is a tremor in his voice as he calls out from the yard. 'Friends! The Lord bless you. It is your brother, Saul.'

Agatha's shadow is at the door; and then she runs through the tiny yard as fowl scatter from her and a skinny dog starts madly barking. She embraces Saul, kissing him and greeting him joyously: 'The Lord bless, the Lord bless,' and then, 'He has risen,' and Saul answers, 'Truly, he is returning.'

He had nothing to fear. She welcomes Timothy with kisses and with an equal embrace. Timothy has pledged himself to the Saviour. That is all that matters. Tears come to Saul's eyes and will not cease. Fear is vanquished and he is in light.

Agatha feeds them a meagre meal, but it feels more like a banquet to Saul, so enraptured is he by her kindness and acceptance. The Judean sun is fierce but Timothy insists they eat in the yard so he can look onto Jerusalem, at the glorious sight of the towers of their Temple rising in the distance across the valleys and hills. Respectful as always, the boy had wanted to eat separately, away from Saul and Agatha, but she had refused and chided him gently, 'Didn't Yeshua eat with Strangers?' She was looking at Saul as she asked this and he had been unable to answer, overcome by gratitude. Here was an illiterate woman, an uneducated peasant to most eyes. But not vainglorious, not stupid, not deaf nor blind. The tears welled up again. Unable to speak, he'd nodded. They three eat their meal at the same table.

Saul is about to sip from a second pouring of wine when he hears Benjamin's voice. He turns around and his smile of welcome is frozen across his face. For there is his friend, a clutch of timber across one broad shoulder—but behind him is another man. Benjamin puts down the wood and rushes forward, his strong arms gathering Saul to him. But Saul feels neither his friend's embrace nor his kisses. His eyes are on the other.

He cannot speak. He cannot move.

It is Agatha who has to introduce Timothy to her husband and the other man.

'Brother Timothy,' she said, 'this is one of our Lord's disciples: this is Thomas, this is Yeshua's twin.'

Saul knows that when the coming kingdom is established, this moment will be impossible to forget or to deny. This moment will be with him forever. As if time has slowed, he sees Timothy on his knees, bowing to Thomas, having forsaken all that Saul has taught him. As if the Twin were an idol—as if blood were more important than spirit. He sees how the youth's downcast eyes shine with adoration for the man before him. Thomas is not handsome. His face is broad and scarred by sun and work and time, his neck is thick and lined, his grey hair thinning. But he is vital and strong. The jealousy is a punishment, it abrades beyond flesh and lashes at his soul. When all other defeats had been dispelled in eternity, this scouring could not be forgotten.

'Get on your fucking feet!'

That rough Galilean voice, the snarl of it.

'Don't you dare bow down to me, boy. Don't you dare bow down to anyone!'

Swiftly, Thomas turns to Agatha. 'Sorry, sister, I should cut out my filthy tongue.'

His hand reaches down and effortlessly pulls Timothy to his feet. 'Promise me, lad,' he bellows, 'promise me that you will never bow down to anyone again.'

And before the bewildered youth can answer, Thomas has kissed him hard on the mouth.

Only then does he turn to Saul. Letting go of the boy, his arms fold around Saul. The kiss he delivers is harsh. It burns.

Thomas pulls away. 'How are you, scholar?'

So much derision and anger in that final word.

Thomas smacks his belly. 'Have you left us any food?'

———

Thomas falls on the meal as if he has not eaten for days. He fills his mouth with bread and date paste, swallows, and reaches immediately for more. Saul can't stop watching his Timothy, how the youth's eyes do not waver from the Twin. The boy seems besotted, as if he has not ever seen anything as marvellous as this coarse and thick-limbed man. Thomas is sitting cross-legged on the warm stones of the yard, his fleshy thighs appearing shockingly naked, his dark skin covered by even darker flushes of hair. As if he were an animal, Saul thinks sourly. The delight he has taken from his time on the road, it has gone.

The boy's awed gaze reminds Saul that Timothy is a Stranger, that he is more his father's son than the child of a Jewish mother. As a Greek, Timothy sees gods and sprites everywhere: the unholy foolishness he was born to makes nymphs out of rivers and streams, and believes trees and sky and seas to be gods. Does he believe that Thomas being Yeshua's twin makes him equal to the Saviour? As if the Saviour was created through blood, not the Spirit—the breath of the Lord? Can the foolish boy really believe that the Lord gave birth to the Saviour, does he think the Lord has a womb? That He laboured and birthed the Saviour and his twin? Timothy looks at Thomas and believes that he is gazing upon a man that is near immortal. Saul must be deranged to have brought this Stranger to Jerusalem.

Thomas wipes at his grease-spattered chin, picking crumbs from between his teeth. 'Is this your first Passover in Jerusalem?' he barks at Timothy.

The boy, shamed, finally turns away. 'Yes,' he replies. And then, his face reddening with the humiliation, he blurts out, 'My teacher is to cut me.'

'What?'

Timothy's Syrian is crude. Thomas has not understood the lad.

'The boy's mother is a Jew,' Saul says, stuttering in his rush to explain, 'but he himself has never been circumcised.'

Thomas roars with laughter. He turns to Saul. 'Have you changed your mind, scholar? Are you now demanding circumcision of the brethren?'

Saul scowls. 'No. The boy demands it.'

Thomas leans forward, putting his hand on Timothy's knee. He playfully flicks a finger across the lad's cheek.

His voice now stern, he asks, 'Do you believe my brother Yeshua was a prophet, the man chosen by the Lord to be our Saviour?'

And Timothy, in ecstasy, his eyes now closed, is nodding. 'He has risen,' he says.

And the boy waits. But there is no answer. Thomas says nothing. And the boy still waits. Such, thinks Saul, will be the silence at the end of this wretched world.

Timothy opens his eyes, shocked by the lack of response from Thomas.

It is Agatha who answers, quietly yet firmly. 'Truly, he will return.' She starts gathering the empty bowls.

Thomas sits back and takes a swig of the wine. He then looks up at the sky, squinting, as if wanting the glare to burn away the sadness that has appeared on his face.

'Has the lad been baptised?' he asks.

'Paul baptised me.' In his confusion Timothy has answered in Greek.

'I baptised him, Twin,' Saul interrupts quickly, aware that Thomas knows little of Greek.

Thomas glares at Saul. 'Then you know there's no reason to cut the lad—he is of the kingdom.'

'To come,' adds Saul, with equal savagery. 'The kingdom to *come*.'

Timothy, perceiving an enmity he cannot fathom, babbles, 'I'm doing it to honour my mother, sir. She always spoke of the Lord's city, of our Temple. I am doing it for her, to honour her blood.'

Timothy's words banish Saul's distress. This is why he loves this boy, why he has chosen him for his companion: the lad is honourable, dutiful.

As for Thomas, he seems about to explode. But then the anger is gone. 'Suit yourself,' he says with a shrug. 'As long as you don't pretend you are doing it for my brother, Yeshua.'

His hand sweeps the ground for a twig. He splits it and starts picking at his teeth with a large splinter. A silence falls.

Saul knows he should get up and make his preparations for entering the Sacred City. Distress again begins to swirl in him, to burden his thoughts. He knows he has to go, but he is reluctant to leave this company. He doesn't want to leave his Timothy with this man.

And as if the man is indeed a demon, as if he can read minds, Thomas asks, 'Are you sure that my brother James will permit you to cut the lad? You know how stiff-necked he can be.'

'The boy is a Jew.'

'*I* know that.' Thomas laughs loudly. 'But you have to convince James. Have you a gift for him?'

'We have tithes from the brethren in Antioch,' Saul answers flatly.

'That's good.' Thomas is still chuckling. 'That's probably conviction enough for James.'

Abruptly he is stern. 'Do you know he has made us royalty?'

'Enough!' Benjamin is standing, looking down at Thomas. 'He is your oldest brother and you owe him your respect.'

But Thomas flings open his palms in plain disgust. 'He claims that we are of the house of David. He claims that Yeshua came from a royal line of kings.'

Benjamin's tongue clicks harshly, indicating his annoyance. 'I said enough, Twin.'

Saul's head is pounding. He is struggling to make sense of it.

Thomas won't be silent. 'He corrupts my brother's teachings; he is creating a dynasty in Jerusalem—wants to make his son a king. He makes poison of Yeshua's words. He declares Yeshua the Saviour, but he shits on his teachings.' And at this, Thomas spits. 'As if Yeshua cared for kings, as if Yeshua didn't damn for eternity all the rich and the kings! The last thing my brother would claim is kinship with the arse-rutting, corrupt descendants of King David.'

There is a gasp from Agatha, an outraged moan from Benjamin. Then there is silence.

Yes, thinks Saul, this appalled silence will be what is heard at the ending of the world.

And with the pounding now in his mouth, in his chest and lungs and loins, Saul stands abruptly, grabbing Thomas's ragged tunic. Saul's hand is raised, and though he knows he is weak he knows he must act to avenge such profanity. He gathers all his strength and strikes Thomas across the face.

He will tear my head off, thinks Saul, he will kill me.

Thomas leaps up and his hand does become fist.

Saul closes his eyes.

And then the kiss.

In the blackness, Saul thinks it is Agatha who is sobbing. But he opens his eyes to see that it is Timothy crying. Saul can feel the wetness that Thomas's lips have left against his cheek.

Thomas apologises, first to Benjamin, then to Agatha, and

finally to Saul. He points to the summit of the mountain. 'Lord forgive me,' he says meekly. 'I'm going up there to pray.'

His final words are to Timothy. 'Lad,' he says calmly, 'know that you are already loved by the Lord.'

———

Saul walks down the mountain, past the graveyard of ruined dwellings, the history of his people. His feet bash against thistles and rock; a snake slithers out of a collapsed wall then whips away from Saul. He doesn't see it: the world is invisible to him. The squall in his head will not cease; he wonders if he will collapse, fall to the earth and expire on this ancient ground.

Of course Timothy had wanted to come with him. 'Not yet, not yet,' Saul had roared. 'You are still a Stranger; I will collect you and take you there when I return.' He had thrown the boy off him, and he could not bear to look at his companion as he pushed him away. For what he remembered was much worse than the deranged Twin's blasphemy: it was the fact that the boy had not understood—that his terror was not caused by the Twin's vile insult, but by the violence between the men. For the boy was a Stranger; he could cut the boy, but he would always remain a Stranger, remain uncomprehending. King David, the history of their land, they mean nothing to him. He will never understand.

Saul cannot see the earth below him, the endless sky above, the immortal city ahead because the storm inside him will not abate. That tempest is doubt. He can bring a thousand souls to Israel but they will remain oblivious of what that means. It is not in their blood. Under the burning sun, Saul groans and says, 'It is not in Timothy's blood.' His brethren are right, all of them who mock or fear his mission amongst the Strangers—they are right. The Lord doesn't care about the rest of the world.

Suddenly he stops. He can now see the sky above him, the earth beneath his feet, the city rising. *Lord, please forgive me.* He will bring Timothy to Jerusalem because he cannot bear to be alone any longer. These last few years with Timothy have banished his loneliness: given him an opportunity for love, to take comfort in the embrace of another. This is why he must bring the boy to Jerusalem—not for the Lord, but for his own need, his own hunger. He cannot bear to leave this boy behind.

Saul falls to his knees on the stony ground. He is sin, he is evil. The storm inside him rages and scorns. He will never conquer the serpent that coils around his loins—its poison floods his heart and mind. What arrogance to believe he is loved by the Lord! How vain to think that he has been chosen by the Saviour. He is not chosen, he is outcast. Weeping, still on his knees, he looks beyond to the city. It is an abomination for someone as corrupted as he is even to dare approach that holy place. But as he peers across to the shimmering citadel, the sun falls gleaming on a barren outcrop of jagged rock outside the walls. The judgement ground. And as if in dream, Saul sees the shadow of the defiant girl, the one he condemned to death. He hears her voice: 'If you are without sin, then cast your stone.' And there, beyond the judgement ground, the abhorred and desolate place of execution. No poor souls hang from crosses on this day: the Romans would never dare such an outrage so close to Passover. But what cannot be erased is the sight of the collapsing frames of the gallows. Even from this distance, the broken planks are black shadow, the wood is soaked in blood.

Saul's eyes are dry. He rises, lifts his eyes into the open and forgiving and eternal sky.

'Thank you, Yeshua, for sharing this burden.'

And comprehending it all—his selfishness, his sin, his weakness—the storm has gone. He can see clearly and he can hear. The world is singing around him. Saul adds his voice to the song. 'Lord, forgive me, Lord, I thank you.' And with that understanding, wearily now but also humbly, Saul makes for the western gate of the city.

———

He turns into the dark narrow alley and she is there. Saul's chest tightens on seeing how Channah has aged. Her back against the stone wall, her skirts rucked up, her feet unshod, she is pounding grain. Her hair is covered but a damp grey lock is plastered to her cheek. Her naked arms are so thin he can see clearly the bones beneath.

A child, a boy, is squatting over the granite mortar, holding it still. Is it her grandchild? The boy grimaces as the dust from the pounding sprays his face. He rubs at it and then sees Saul down the lane.

'Grandmother,' he says, 'there's a man there.'

'Who is it?'

His sister half turns and Saul realises that she is blind.

He steps forward. 'Channi,' he softly, 'it's your brother, Saul.'

She grips tightly to the pestle. 'Hold it still,' she barks at the child, and then spits onto the ground. 'I have no brother called Saul.'

Because of his learning, and now because of his faith, he sees he has always been lost to her.

'Don't you come closer,' she warns.

But he dares her wrath and walks towards the grandmother and child.

Clearly fascinated, the boy holds firmly onto the bowl, but his eyes take in Saul's face, noting the scars and the bruises, the dead and useless eye.

Saul crouches next to the boy. 'I am your grand-uncle.'

He goes to pat the boy's hand, and the boy, still squatting, moves as elegantly as a cat away from him.

With a moan, Channah lets go of the pestle and it falls to the dirt. The boy rushes to grab it and give it back to his grandmother. But she smacks him away and lowers her veil over her face, rocking back and forth.

'Devil, devil,' she wails, 'why have you returned?'

He lifts a hand to raise the veil, to see her wizened and ancient face, then stops, fearing his touch will enrage her.

He chooses his words carefully, knows that for her, family is everything. 'Is this our Gabriel's son?'

The boy stands next to his grandmother, placing a protective hand on her shoulder. His young bright eyes are narrow with suspicion. 'I am Judah, son of Gabriel.'

'And where is your father?'

The boy tugs at his grandmother's dress. 'Should I tell him?'

But the old woman is hunched over, in tears. Saul goes pale. His beloved nephew is dead.

But as if hearing the ill-omened thought, the boy rushes to speak. 'He is at work. But he's coming back and he's going to beat you for making my grandmother cry.'

The defiant words of the child are the balm that is needed.

Brother and sister burst out laughing. The boy scowls, fearing they are laughing at him.

Channah's breathing settles. 'Judah, this is your grandfather Saul, your father's uncle. You must respect him.' She wipes her thin lips. 'Though he has no respect for us.'

Saul cannot let this stand. This time he dares to touch her, brushing a hand over her shoulder. She lets it stay.

'Channi, you cannot unmake me your brother.'

Her head searches for the boy. 'Judah,' she orders, 'help me up.'

Carefully the boy and the man assist the old woman to her feet.

'Are you hungry?' she askes her brother.

'I am famished,' he replies gratefully.

He helps his sister into the house.

———

Cross-legged and no longer fearful, the boy is giggling at how much food the stranger is stuffing into his mouth. Saul winks at him and burps loudly and that sends the boy into peals of laughter.

Saul pats his full belly and drinks from a cup of water. 'Where is Ebron?' he asks the child.

The boy's grin disappears. He looks anxiously towards his grandmother, who is seated on the first step of the doorway.

'He died,' she says quietly. 'May his soul rest in peace.'

Her head cocks; there are footsteps in the lane. A shadow falls over her.

Gabriel is standing in the doorway.

His nephew's happiness is not in doubt. He pushes past his

mother, ignores his son, and kneels before Saul, embracing him and kissing him again and again. And Saul can't break the embrace, can't release himself from this kindness and love, this unforced and precious welcome. Here, in this man's arms, he is not despised, nor feared, nor pitied. He weeps with joy and for what he has missed. On hearing Saul's sobs, Channah bursts into tears.

Releasing him but still gripping tight to his uncle's shoulders, Gabriel examines Saul's face, his scars, his ravaged skin. Saul has forgotten how handsome Gabriel is: the strength in his jaw and his neck, the honest intensity in his grave, wide eyes—the eyes that Judah has inherited—and he has to look away. He's ashamed of the unmanliness of his emotions. He rubs his eyes.

He steels himself; he has to ask. 'And your wife?'

Gabriel smiles. 'She is well. She is at her sister's—you will see her tonight.'

He calls out to his mother. 'Tonight we feast!'

'There is nothing prepared.'

Gabriel ignores Channah's reprimand. 'I'll scour the neighbourhood. We're going to have a banquet for my uncle.'

Saul cannot stop himself. 'The Saviour spoke of the prodigal son, of how he was welcomed back with great love and forgiveness. I am that son.'

But his words cause a darkness to fall over the crowded room, as if a shadow has settled over them.

Gabriel releases his hold on Saul. He turns to his son. 'Go, Judah, fetch your mother.'

The boy leaps to his feet. He stands close to his grandmother before departing, as if waiting for her permission to go. She nods, and he runs out into the street.

Once they can no longer hear his running steps, Channah turns to Saul. She spits, and speaks. 'That bastard is not our Saviour.' The curse holds all the hate of the world.

'Mother, watch your tongue.'

But even the support of his nephew cannot bring peace. Gabriel has become the man of the family, and Saul is reminded that this was a position he neither had the courage nor skill to command.

He knows he has to speak. He has to bring them towards the light. Only then can he lead them.

He speaks gently. 'He is the one who was promised by the Lord, Channah. He is our Saviour.'

The old woman spits again, as if there is an endless reservoir of bile within her.

'A criminal nailed to the cross? You say he is the one anointed by the Lord to save us?'

Saul steals a glance at his nephew. Gabriel can at least look at him, though it is clear he also can't countenance such blasphemy.

'I have seen him, sister,' says Saul.

She lets out a scornful and disdainful laugh. 'We all see ghosts, brother. I am blind and yet I see them all the time. You got duped by a ghost. That makes you the greater fool. Or in league with the devil.'

He must make her see. If he can make her understand then he can bring the whole world to that knowledge.

'Let me tell you his words,' he begins. 'Let me give you that understanding.'

'Don't you dare!' she screeches, blocking her ears. Then, bitten by the furies, she drops her hands and turns, as if seeking him through the fog of his fear and his shame.

She is blind but she is looking straight into him. 'I know his words, I know what his mad followers claim of him. That we must love our neighbour as we love our own children. That we are not kin in blood but kin in spirit.'

She inhales, taking in strength, and her next words are an explosion that tears through the room. 'What kind of insanity is it to claim such a kingdom? What kind of devil would want me to love another more than I love my son? What kind of evil is such talk? Who is capable of keeping such commandments?'

Her tone goes cold. 'Only one like you, brother, who doesn't know what it is to raise a child and to bury a child—only one like you could believe in such a Saviour.'

In her house—and though it is now led by Gabriel, this hovel will always be her house—it means nothing that he has been called by the Lord. He is unmanned—unwifed and childless. But a greater outrage is that he thought that he could bring her guidance. His coming here doesn't bring her closer to the Lord; it drives her further from Him.

In the oppressive darkness, Gabriel offers light. His nephew answers for him.

'You're a foolish woman, Mother. You know nothing about the Lord and the law. We are also commanded to love our neighbour.'

She releases another sneering laugh. 'Yes, son, I am unlearned, and I thank the Lord for that. I am a woman, yes, and I gave birth to you. I know the Lord and I know our ways. All that matters is land and blood. May the devil take the Strangers.'

Her head bobs, searching for her son. 'Will you sacrifice Judah to a Stranger? Will you let him marry any Syrian or Arab or Greek whore he wants?'

She has won. Her son has hung his head. To that, he can make no answer.

Saul sighs. 'Do you despise me that much, sister?'

There is a moan, an agonised sound from the back of her throat. He cannot tell if it is avowal or exasperation.

'I will leave,' he says simply.

Again the moan, but this time she also speaks. 'Saul, stay. Don't be a petulant child. That is the problem with all you men who remain unmarried.'

Her knuckles rap against the doorway. 'This is your home, Saul, even if you forgot about us for all those years. We are your family and this is your home.'

To abandon it all. To suck on wine and forget his mission. To grow old with Gabriel and his children. To die and have sacrifices made for him at the Temple. To be home and be free of wandering.

To never again be in light.

Knowing this, he has to speak. If he doesn't speak now, his faith cracks and shatters into doubt; if he doesn't speak now, he betrays the light.

'My family are now my brethren in Yeshua the Saviour. They are my brothers and they are my sisters. I cannot stay here.'

She says something he can't make out.

'I can't hear you, sister.'

'Go!' She roars it through her sobs. 'Go, pursue your madness. This whole deranged city is full of madmen like you pursuing their insanity.'

He embraces Gabriel. But Channah won't let him touch her.

He turns once, when he has reached the end of the alley. She is sitting on the step, her black shawl covering her head and her body. As if she wishes she weren't there. As if she no longer wants to be in the world.

———

James's house is a narrow two-storeyed stone dwelling, its whitewashed walls tarnished with age. Two young boys are in the lane, pretending to be soldiers at battle. At the sound of his footsteps, the oldest drops his imaginary sword and gathers the younger boy close. He looks up at Saul fiercely.

Quickly, Saul says in a hushed tone, 'He is returning.'

Relief sweeps across both the boys' faces. 'Truly,' the older answers, 'he is returning.'

And then he calls out with gusto, 'Papa, Papa, a friend is here!'

Warily, Saul waits.

James is at the door. His beard now greying and his body stout. A wicked thought: of course he's grown fat; he sits here while we march across the world proclaiming the Lord. But the older man's smile is kind and welcoming. Saul is immediately chastened.

'Brother Saul, welcome, welcome.'

James ushers him into the house. At first, walking into the interior darkness after the blinding glare of the Jerusalem sun, all that Saul can discern are moving forms and shadows. And

that hands are reaching for him, arms are enfolding him, lips are
brushing against his. The small rooms are filled with people, most
of them pilgrims like himself, recently arrived for the imminent
Passover. All of them, men and women, greeting him joyfully. He
returns their embraces and their warm welcomes. As those greetings ring around him, he feels himself lightening, unburdened
of his sister's censure. And of the Twin's obstinance. Channah
and Thomas are both veiled in ignorance and in fear—they do
not understand the wonder of what he has in this community
of friends. These are his true brothers, his only sisters. They are
his true family. Now he is home.

As he tells James of his journey, he unhooks the pockets inside
his tunic and delivers the tithes he has faithfully collected from
the Jews and the God-fearing Strangers of Antioch.

James takes what is offered with gratitude. 'These offerings
will help feed all these hungry mouths,' he says. And then, with
his arm around Saul's shoulders, he announces that a thanksgiving will begin.

There is the breaking of the bread, and its passing from hand
to hand around the circle, a morsel taken into every mouth,
reminding them of the broken and resurrected body of the
Saviour. Then the cup of wine is passed from hand to hand and
mouth to mouth around the circle, the wine that recalls to them
the spilled blood of their Redeemer. This is the miracle that is
their thanksgiving feast. Warm in the love they all feel, Saul
forgets that he is brother in blood to a woman called Channah
and uncle in blood to a man named Gabriel. Here, in this circle,
he is loved by truer brethren, and here in this circle he once
again is revealed to light.

In their joy and thanksgiving, in their song and their prayer, the light courses through him and he is on his feet, praising the Lord and praising the Redeemer promised by their Lord—and he knows, even though he cannot comprehend how it can be so, that he is singing the light in languages known and unknown to man. He sings for Israel, and he sings for the Strangers who are coming to Her.

Slowly, one by one, their ululations and singing fall away. Saul is overcome by a feeling of depletion, as when he had previously exhausted his seed in the wickedness of lust. But unlike then, in this ecstasy the body is not sickened and his flesh and mind are not corrupted. The doubt that had bored into his heart at the house of his nephew has been vanquished. This bliss he feels now, bliss uncontaminated by sin, this proves the truth of his faith.

And after the thanksgiving, their feast of love, then come the questions.

'Did you travel this long distance on your own?'

'No,' he answers Sara, James's wife, 'I came with our brother Timothy.'

'And where are you staying?'

'At Benjamin and Agatha's.'

Should he add that Thomas is there? He looks across at James. The old man is full of cheer, he has a grandchild on his lap. Saul decides to say nothing.

'You must stay with us.'

Saul looks around the crowded room and laughs. 'There is no room, sister.'

She raises her eyebrows in mock anger. 'There is always room for one of the apostles.'

He could kiss her, he could kiss her feet. For her faith in him, for the trust she shows that he was chosen by the Saviour.

'Then I will stay,' he affirms, and then adds timidly, 'I will return with our brother Timothy.'

James, overhearing, lifts his shaggy grey head and booms out over the feasting crowd, 'Timothy cannot stay.'

'He is of our way and he has been baptised,' Saul responds brusquely.

'Your friend Timothy is not one of us.'

'His mother was born a Jew.'

This does not satisfy James. 'Has he been circumcised?'

The light abruptly extinguishes as when the flame of a candle is exposed to harsh wind.

'Yes,' he answers firmly, 'he has been circumcised.'

James nods in satisfaction and peace, smiling widely at Saul. Vipers stir in Saul's chest. Blood does not matter: so spoke their Saviour. Saul is closer to the Lord and to the son than this illiterate peasant. What does James know about the law and the prophets and their faith? He looks at the boy bouncing on the old man's knee and recalls Thomas's slur against James. Is this scrawny boy—insipid, you can tell by looking at him, with a lazy mouth—is he to father a dynasty? Can a king of the Jews arise from such a wretched house, from such poverty and ignorance?

Pride, arrogance, envy: they are the weaknesses of his spirit, equal to the illicit cravings of his flesh—Saul knows this, understands this of himself. The Saviour came from such a house, and so that must have been part of the Lord's purpose at Creation.

'Friend,' says Saul, and as he takes James's hand and kisses it he is convinced he speaks truth, indeed he knows it to be true, 'our brother Timothy is one of us.'

———

As he climbs the path that winds to the summit of Mount Scopus, the blade in his hand feels as heavy as virgin quarry rock. He can hardly breathe from the exertion of carrying it. He follows the well-worn track to Benjamin's house. The villagers he passes eye him with cold suspicion. They are either mistrustful of the bizarre sect that their neighbours have bonded themselves to, or weary of the proclamations of yet another Saviour. He should feel glad to be amongst his own, not a stranger amongst the Strangers, the burden that has been his for so very long now—but the knife he carries seems a heavier weight.

As he turns into a narrow lane, nearing the house, he can hear laughter. It is both raucous and harsh and he knows it comes from Thomas. He enters the courtyard to see the man stripped to his waist, a fold of cloth all that shields him from base nakedness. And then Saul feels that his heart might have stopped: his beloved, his Timothy, is lying on the ground. Has the mad Twin felled him? Saul tightens his grip on the knife: he will murder him. But then he sees that the lad, equally and shamelessly nude, can't get off the ground because he is laughing so much. Thomas is standing above him in the mocking stance of a victor—as if they were children, as if they were play-acting at being gladiator and prey. Arms still raised in victory, Thomas sees Saul and nods. There is a thick flush of hair in his pits, a grey pelt of fur all over his chest and belly and his shoulders. A beast, thinks Saul, the man is an animal. No wonder they mock us and doubt us. *This* man is a twin to our Saviour?

Still giggling, the boy rises. His slender limbs are smeared with dirt and sweat. 'I'm no match for him,' he says to Saul. He's proud, shameless.

Saul wonders how he can believe it's possible to bring these childlike Strangers to the Lord, raised since birth as they have been with fairy tales of woodland spirits and lascivious gods? He could say that James has not given him his permission, that he is unable to cut Timothy. He could throw the blade into the dirt. That would end the foolish child's happiness.

'Wash yourself, make your prayers,' he barks to the boy. 'What I am about to do is sacred.'

On hearing him, the oafish Twin comes to stand between Saul and Timothy. 'Don't do this, Saul—you know it's not necessary.'

He will pledge himself to James; he will give up his mission to the Strangers. Let there be nothing of agreement between himself and Thomas.

'Prepare yourself for the ceremony,' he orders the youth.

Timothy runs to him. The boy's kiss, his long embrace, the heady sting of his sweat and his youth, even these cannot diminish Saul's rage.

———

Saul goes to prepare himself for what is to come, reciting his prayers as he washes himself thoroughly. He doesn't know why his hand is so unsteady; he has performed this rite countless times. He has circumcised all his nephews, and so many of his neighbours' and brethren's children. But this time his hand shakes; it will not be still.

Benjamin has washed the boy and has also made him drink cup after cup of the sweet and potent newly fermented wine— Timothy is drunk to the point of nearly passing out. As Saul enters the tiny bedchamber he sees that Benjamin is trying to get the lad to smear a wild-nettle balm over his sex. But Timothy is so drunk that he can't make sense of Benjamin's urging. He is sprawled on a coarse rug, mumbling in Greek, the words so slurred they are incomprehensible. Saul grabs the bowl of paste and rubs it over the boy's loins, hoping it will numb him.

He then holds the blade over a flickering flame until its edge glows red. Benjamin is there to assist him; Thomas is nowhere to be seen. Satisfied the knife is clean, Saul takes several tremulous breaths and takes hold of the hood of skin that covers the youth's sex. With his other hand he flicks the blade and cuts where the thick skin meets the silken head. Even in his drunken oblivion, the boy heaves and screams as his blood spurts. Benjamin has to push down on Timothy's chest with all his strength to restrain him. Still the youth twists and convulses and the blood will not stop spraying. His screams are a torment. Thomas bursts into the room, stares in horror. The blood will not cease. The shock of its scarlet gush has turned Saul to stone. Never has he been witness to such an eruption. And the screaming, it is unbearable—the boy's suffering is unending.

Thomas, now enraged, takes the blade from Saul and pushes him away. With one hand Thomas pushes down on the boy's wound, and with the other he holds the knife over the fluttering flame. In the wan candlelight, Thomas's hand is black from the surging blood. And at this sight, will returns to Saul. He snatches back the blade, and it is he now bending over the lad, it is his hand stemming the flow of the blood. He must save Timothy. All that matters is that it is he—not the Twin, not Benjamin, no, not even the Saviour—it is he, Saul, who must save this boy. He lifts his hand and swiftly and firmly presses the heated blade across the boy's wound. Timothy releases a howl, bestial and eternal. The room shudders from the violence, and all around is the gamy stench of seared flesh. Thomas and Benjamin, in dutiful attendance now, grimly hold the boy down. And as Saul glances at his own blood-soaked hand, feels the warm seeping damp, a revelation comes to him. It is only blood. It is only of flesh. With this thought, the light descends and the Spirit fills Saul with its warm radiance. This is love, this light; this is love. This is the knowledge that the Saviour brought. That blood does not matter. For blood comes from flesh. And flesh does not matter.

The screaming has abated; the boy has fallen listless—and the blood has stopped flowing.

Saul lifts the still-glowing blade.

The boy mumbles, groans, words splutter from his mouth. *Beloved?* Is that what he is saying?

'Beloved,' whimpers Timothy: to Saul, to Thomas? 'Thank you. You have brought me to Israel.'

And Saul answers, in a hush that only his Lord can hear: 'Forgive me, my son—for you were already of Israel.'

From this moment on, Saul will attest that to be in the light of the Saviour is to be drained of the blood of kin and of loyalty to land—of all that has gone before. Channah is right to hate him. To know this love is to be reborn as a stranger to the womb that carried you, the seed that formed you, the family that raised you and the kingdom that claimed you.

Saul sits beside exhausted Timothy as he sleeps, clutching his hand, soothing his fevered brow. If Benjamin and Thomas are still there, he cannot tell. The light and his beloved are all that there is—all that exists in the world. Saul prays to the light and begs to always be in this calm and in this love and in this grace. He now understands perfectly this most ruthless of commandments, this once unspeakable but now unbreakable new covenant of the Lord. Finally, in his anguish and remorse for his beloved, Saul knows it. Blood no longer matters.

Love

TIMOTHY, EPHESUS
87 A.D.

'Suffering turns us into egotists, for it absorbs us completely: it is later, in the form of memory, that it teaches us compassion.'

—MARGUERITE YOURCENAR, *ALEXIS*

Such luminance, such clarity. It is as if the very source of light itself comes from this great inland sea. The blue of sky was never so blazing and it is as if in this light I am endowed with immortal gifts: that I can see to the end of the world.

Along its shore are spread fishermen and their craft—they are mending nets, or bringing in their hauls or setting sail. Across the expanse of water, boats gently rise and fall to the eternal music of the receding and returning waves. But none of that exists, we are invisible to men and we cannot see them; the world only consists of this Galilean Sea, my Thomas and me. His smock and sandals are abandoned on the rocks and he is running into the water. He turns, naked and unashamed, and calls out, 'Come, lad, come be replenished in this splendid sea. This, my friend, is the Lord's sea!' I am made speechless by the wonder of my beloved. He is an old man, his hair as grey as winter, but his vitality is born of a heroic and ancient grace. Age doesn't diminish such strength; it perfects it. This is what the first man must have looked like, our first father Adam, made in the glory of the Lord's very image. 'Come,' Thomas roars one more time, and then plunges under the water. Fear of him vanishing releases me. I strip off my garments, stepping gingerly across the stones as the sharp rocks bite into my heels and the cold water laps at my feet. The fear grows, it battles the light: I do not trust the spirits and creatures that live below the waves. And just as I am about to scream, to implore the Lord to return Thomas to me, his head and shoulders break the surface. He turns, finds me, and laughs, a boom that rings along the shore and reaches the sky. His reappearance reminds me that I too am now naked. A bashful reticence overcomes me. I look down and I am young, I am handsome again. And then the shock, my horror, as my sex is revealed whole—the bond made with my Lord has been undone. My beloved, understanding my shame, roars again: not only the fishermen but the whole of the world must be able to hear him: 'Are you obsessed by your cock, boy? Why do you stare at it so?' I am bewildered, befuddled: I have returned to Galilee, I am in Israel, yet I am as I was when a Stranger. I find my voice. 'Brother,' I call out to him, 'I was a Jew and now I am a Stranger again. How can that be?' At this, he abandons his paddling and turns to me, incredulous. I hear him speak even though his lips do not move. 'Circumcision is nothing and to be uncut is nothing—it is only our faith in the Lord that matters.' It is Thomas's voice, but he is speaking the words of Paul, my teacher. Shame flares through my body. I feel the tongues of the fire even though I am immersed in cold water. In my exhilaration and happiness I have forgotten my Paul. Thomas has dived back into the water, and when he comes out again it is as if the sun has been suddenly vanquished by night; I cannot discern his features. Is it Thomas, is it Paul? A curious sensation cuts my breath and stops my heart; it is equal terror and wonder and all violence. Is it possible that I am to be granted the vision that has eluded me? Can it be that Jesus the Saviour is with me? Then the shadow's voice breaks through, the sun pours illumination across the world and it is my Thomas speaking. It is his voice, his laughter. 'I don't know what you're talking about, Timos, you were made perfect already by our Father the Lord.' Those words quell my shame, return my joy, and I plunge into the water. And there the miracle occurs, for even though I cannot swim I find that my body has become as joyous and reckless as that of a porpoise. I dance, I dive, I tumble and turn in the water, breathing in it as freely as I breathe on land, and my brother is beside me and around me and we circle and leap and play, and he tells me, 'This is where my twin and I learned to swim, in this very water. This is where we fished and played and laughed as children.' His hand ducks under the waves and he flicks a finger at my sex; he floats on the water and says, 'It's only your piss-rod, Timos, nothing but a piss-rod. My twin would always show his off, just because it was a little bigger than mine—just a little bigger, mind, I promise you that.' And with his laugh, I am no longer fish, I am now a bird of the sky, and not only can I ride these waters but I am flying across this sea and my strength outstrips that of my brother's skill and I am being carried by the Lord and I am across the waters and I know that I could easily reach the distant shore. I stop, the warm sun kisses my face, the great lake is a bed that I am lying on, and though I know I could sleep here, I could fall to eternal rest here, I know that my brother is no longer with me, that I have left Thomas far behind. I am looking up to the sun, the water lifts me towards the sun, and all that is evil is undone. This is the kingdom to come. But as I face the burning orb a thick cloud gathers weight and speed and it blackens the world, and when I turn my gaze back to shore there is nothing. The fishermen, their craft, Thomas: all are gone. And I scramble and my strokes are useless and the water is no longer air, the water is now death and I must use all of my will and strength to return to this empty shore. And as I do, finally, exhausted, near collapse, as my feet touch earth, I see Paul, I see my teacher, he is coming towards me, he is calling me but I cannot hear his words, and he shouts, his chest heaves and rolls, he must be bellowing, and as I break free of the water and I stand on land, I see him point to my nakedness and I hear his words—'I was wrong, Timos, I was wrong'—and when I look down to my body, below the blood-soaked pelt of my loins, where there was once my sex there is now only a gash, raw and violently purple meat; flyblown, host to crawling, feasting maggots. And I look back to my teacher and it is the horror in his eyes as much as that grotesque sight which makes me scream.

———

I awake. It is still night. I am mortified to find that my hand has reached down to my loins. I cup the slug that is my sex, I feel for my sacs. I am whole. All that remains of the ill-omened dream is the stink of my sweat. I am drenched in it. I rise, crouch over the chamber-pot, and release my urine. In the quiet of night it sounds shockingly loud, and I am not surprised to hear a knock on the door. I call out to wait and I hurriedly dress and open the door.

'I heard you scream, teacher. Are you not well?'

Brother Impetuous is my favourite. We are not meant to favour one over another—we are all equal in the eyes of our Lord. But I have never been able to master such a virtuous equilibrium. Impetuous is still a youth. Even in the faint light from the moon, the wispy beard that he is attempting to grow is comical. I resist the urge to tickle him under his chin.

'It was a wicked dream that awoke me, brother,' I answer him. 'There is nothing to fear.'

'Was it also ominous?'

'Not at all. I suspect I overindulged at our table.'

He nods. I know the rumours that circulate amongst the younger brothers: Uncle Timothy is fond of his wine. He places a palm over his chest as he says, 'He is coming, brother.' I do the same as I answer, 'Truly, brother, he is returning.'

I don't go back to bed; it will be impossible to sleep now. I struggle to get to my knees and groan as a jolt of pain shoots up my left side. The younger brothers encourage me to use a cushion, or at least a rug, but I have always refused. The first amongst us, those such as my beloved Paul, they prayed with their knees on rocky ground or on wooden planks. I refuse to do otherwise.

I speak my prayers, the words come easily, but I cannot find peace. Snatches of the dream return to me.

My dearest Paul, you came to me tonight. Surely that must be an omen.

I force my will to turn away from the nightmare; I intone the words that Paul taught me in my youth. 'The Lord God is with me and I will not be afraid. What can man do to me?'

There is an affliction that comes with age. It is not what the young think it is—a loss of memory. It is rather the blurring of time with memory. This ailment can strike at any moment, from full wakefulness to fitful sleep. As I try to lose myself in the sacred words, the face of my teacher vanishes and instead I see the Twin. He also came for me tonight. It feels as if he is here beside me: I inhale his smell, I sense his fury, his impatience. And I hear his laughter, the infectious sound that collects one up as does the great north wind and takes you soaring with it to the heavens. I see him, I hear his laugh and his voice, and I am overwhelmed by the need to abandon this world and return to the lull of sleep.

My brothers, my teachers Paul and Thomas, are more real to me than this room I am in. I am drugged by the power of the dream: I cannot make order of my prayers, I cannot remember the ancient words.

I bow, kiss the rough floorboards, beg mercy from my God.

What is required is work. In activity I lose myself to the Lord as fervently as I do in prayer. But it is still night and I dare not leave the room; it would be selfish to awaken the others. Fortunately the moon is nearly full and I take my desk and move it so that it catches the beams shafting through the window. I kneel before the table, take my quill and dip the tip in the thick ink. I let it drip to a point and on the rough-skinned and virgin parchment I begin to write.

For the last year I have been recording the words of our Saviour. It is a task that I have been urged to do by the new generation. At first I resisted such requests, believing that they betrayed the promise of our Redeemer and mocked our first vow that is also our first prayer: *Truly, he is returning.* But if youth is impatient and ruthless, it can also perceive the necessity for change that we, the elderly, resist in our resignation and our adherence to the old ways. Our family grows: we are three generations now. And another just born that will need to be instructed in the teachings of our prophet.

But this disjointed morning, words do not come, and all that I have been taught and all that I believe sacred becomes chaos in my mind. Seeking stillness I rest my stylo and I search the four corners of my small chamber. There is a mouse that shares this room with me. It has gleaming black eyes and its nose quivers with frantic glee whenever I pull crumbs from my bread to feed it or dip my finger in whey and let the drops fall to the floor. Through care and patience all of the last winter, I have earned the creature's trust. It will now walk up my fingers and sit quietly in my cupped palm. As my eyes try to find my tiny friend in the darkness, I find that my mind is becoming still. I cannot see him; the little one must still be asleep. How I envy his unbroken dreams.

I was wrong.

How, my beloved, how could you, chosen by the Saviour, speak falsely?

With effort I rise. I put away my pen and parchment. I straighten the pelts across my bed and, taking a ladle of water from the night jug, I wash my face, the back of my neck, my hands and feet. Clean before the Lord, I stretch my body across the cold wooden floor and I force myself to pray. I pray for those around me who have placed their loyalty and trust in us. I pray to be freed from the profanity that is the body. I pray to be liberated in the coming kingdom from the bonds that are greed and lust and need. I praise the Lord, I sing his prayer. I pray so I will not hear the treacherous rumbling that threatens to spill forth from deep within me. I pray, I sing louder, so those words will not escape. I do not say them but I feel them as violence: *Saviour, why have you not returned?*

———

It is wise to tread cautiously every time I leave my room. I step over children coiled tight around each other in their slumber. The morning that glowed softly as I finished my prayers has yet to illuminate the darkness of the courtyard below. My foot slides carefully along the planks till it finds the first step. I descend, my hand firm against the damp wall that always smells of mould, as do all the surfaces of our dwelling. But as I cross the third step that distasteful odour is replaced by a reek much more foul.

Is it the stink that first assaults my senses or is it the rumbling sound of the scores asleep on the ground? It is impossible to tell. The smell and the sound are as one; each intensifies the other. I stall on the final step as tremulous light ventures like a mist across the yard and I place my hand over nose and mouth. The frank odours arise from the bodies of the refugees, all of these asleep on the ground. The air thunders with their snores and the awakening cries of the infants. Some, carrying diseases from the lands they have fled, have been up all night, purging themselves of their poison. One child's cries are piercing. A young mother grabs the babe and raises it to her breast. She has hollow cheeks, hunger has fed mercilessly on her body, and on seeing me she raises a hand to her mouth in supplication and need. 'Food,' she mouths in the Syrian tongue. I pick my way carefully across the bodies. 'Soon, sister,' I answer in her language. 'They will feed you soon.' One hand fastens her child to her useless teat, the other hand rises higher, imploring me again to find a morsel for her to eat. 'Soon,' I repeat, this time with more force. I step around her to cross into the yard; in my haste I kick against bodies that stir and answer me with curses and threats. I push open the gate.

In the street I can breathe again.

We welcome them, we take them in, we tell them of the kingdom to come and we immerse them in our river and in our sea. Every day we bring new souls to the Lord. But each soul has a body and each body has a stomach that demands to be filled. Each day brings us more of them to feed. The masses that pour into our city from the fallen east are incomprehensible; it is impossible to fathom that Judea housed such a multitude. Each starving and beaten fugitive has a tale to divulge about the Roman sacking of Jerusalem. Those who survived the siege are the ones who speak the least. Their bewildered silence indicates the unspeakable horrors they have witnessed. We hear that hundreds of thousands have been sold as slaves, and the evidence is all around us in our city. Ephesus's servants, her gravediggers and masons, her field hands and dock workers, her prostitutes—they all seem to speak Syrian. And still they come. We ration and we beg, we implore the brethren who have means and who are patrons of the city to give us more food, more hides and garments to clothe the migrants. There is never enough. Every day they come and every day they die, their hunger endured for so long now that no meal can satisfy it.

And every day, each of them ask: 'Where is the raised son, the one who promised to return? When is he coming?'

———

As I walk slowly past the market square, the sun starts to warm me. It is early and only the slaves have risen. The shorn women on their way to the wells balance jugs on their heads. Strong young men are marching to the quarries. They bow as they pass me, and those of our way covertly greet me: 'Truly, he has risen.' I answer them back in a whisper: 'Truly, he is returning.' I enter the Imperial Road, and as I pass by the temple of the accursed goddess the sun takes this moment to shine his rays on her statue. The gold leaf of her skin glistens and shines, her painted emerald eyes flash and the myriad silver teats that hang from her neck seem alive, a writhing string of engorged asps. Even after all this time, even though I am brother to the first of the apostles, and though I have spent my adult life a follower of the true Lord and of His anointed son, there is some semblance of the heritage that goes all the way back to the seed that begat me, to the rituals my infant eyes witnessed, some of this I have yet to overcome, even now. Every time I am in the shadow of the accursed idol, every time I walk past her temple, I have to resist the urge to bow, to honour her. I avert my eyes.

'Timothy!' a voice screeches from above. 'Another sleepless night, eh? It is the curse of our old age, brother.'

For a moment I can almost believe that the work of gold-leaf and marble, of clay and stone, that Artemis has spoken. But such folly passes.

The old priestess Denisia limps down the wide marble steps of the temple, clasping a wooden staff with the head of a serpent, and comes to greet me. She stands on the bottom step, but she is so short that we are now eye to eye.

'Morning, brother, the goddess welcomes you.'

'Morning, sister,' I answer. 'And the supreme Lord, the one God, He awaits you.'

We hold each other's stares, and she is the first to smile. I answer with a benign laugh. For how many years have I been leader of our assembly here in Ephesus? How many mornings have we greeted each other with the same mischievous dare? The crone is a constant of my mornings. Unless celebrations keep her inside the temple, unless the Sabbath forbids my wandering, our mutual greeting heralds the start of the day for both of us. Denisia, idol-worshipper though she is, slave to a false god though she might be, is the closest soul to a wife that I have.

'Sister, is there some food you can offer us?'

She is kind—she doesn't hate us even though we refute her gods. And she often sends baskets of food to our house; the food is blessed to the goddess, but the starving don't have scruples. Even the most pious Jews fall ravenously on her gifts: the calamitous siege of the Romans didn't only annihilate the Lord's city—it also swept away His laws.

But today she scowls and shakes her head. 'I've been up half the night, Timos. Your degenerate followers threw shit at our goddess, they covered her in their foulness. I have been scrubbing her clean for hours.'

She steps to the ground, not daring to defile the temple steps, and she spits in front of my feet. 'Is there no sacrilege your vile death cult won't commit?'

An icy arrow spears my heart. I steady my voice, knowing how crucial it is that I seem calm. 'How do you know he was one of ours?'

She makes a derisory motion with her hand, whipping it across her lips then shaking it over the ground. 'I heard him—he was so stupid. He yelled out, "I do this in the name of Jesus the Saviour."' She laughs without mirth. 'That's your god, isn't it?'

My heart stops: are we already condemned? 'Have you reported it to the governor?'

A flood of relief; she is shaking her head.

It would be wisest to not speak of it anymore, to trust in a friendship that has crept up on us both over time, just as a slow-growing vine remains stunted and fragile for a generation until the morning one is astonished to find that it has attached itself resolutely to a stone wall.

The sacrilege she has described is one that no authority can pardon. My hope rests in the fact that she alone cleaned the idol. She must have kept it secret, otherwise the mobs would have already burned down our house and embarked upon their massacre.

Two emotions battle to undo the composed face I present to her. One is blind rage that some foolish brother has endangered all of us by such idiocy. The other is the awe I feel at this test of her loyalty. Loyalty towards me? An enemy of her gods? I am so moved a tear escapes from my eye.

Her face softens. 'I exaggerate, Brother Timothy,' she concedes. 'It was only one turd they flung at her and only at her plinth. It was easy to clean but the night and dawn were wasted in the ablutions I had to make.'

It is all I can do not to clutch her hand, but that would be an abomination for a priestess promised to the virgin goddess.

'Thank you, sister. We are in your debt.'

Her eyes are sharp once more. 'The outrage must be avenged, sir. Promise me that.'

'I do, I promise you.'

'Friend, your young disciples, those desert savages, they are insane in their piety and the way they worship.'

There is no rebuke I can make, no way I can refute her. She is right. My head is heavy with the thought of the arguments to come, how the young brothers will resist any plea I might make for justice. Their hatred of the Greeks is greater than their love of the Lord.

'Cut them loose. Is there no abomination they will not perform to satisfy the spite of your hateful god?'

I cannot allow this slight. 'My Lord is not one of hate, sister; He is the Lord of grace, of love.'

She snorts in disbelief. 'I know your rites and I know your lore,' she says with a grimace. 'I have been listening to you for years, Timothy. I am speaking about your god, not his son.'

'The will of the Father and the will of His son are one.'

She smiles now, deepening the wrinkles at the edges of her mouth and under her eyes. 'The children of our gods are like the

children of men. They defy their fathers, they are thoughtless
and believe the world began at their birth.'

I am shaking my head at her ignorance. 'He wasn't born in
the way the sons and daughters of your gods were born,' I answer
curtly. 'Our Lord doesn't steal maidens and our Lord doesn't
have mistresses and concubines.'

Her smile turns sly. 'We too have gods born of virgins.'

I start at her words. I have never spoken to her about this
superstitious invention, this peasant mischief. This is another
madness, another falsity that comes here from the east.

'Our Saviour was not born of a virgin,' I explain. 'He didn't
spring from his father's head nor from his father's thigh. He was
born and lived a man.'

She waves her hand in irked dismissal. 'That may be. But
the one you call Jesus Resurrected is a young god. It is his
father, the angry and vengeful god, that commands respect.'

We have rehearsed this argument over many years now. We
know that neither of us will concede. I am about to say the words
to contradict her, but the vision from last night's ill-omened dream
returns: the anguished face of my teacher saying, *I was wrong.*

Believing my silence to be acquiescence, she continues her
argument. 'Only very few men, brother, can become gods. Kings
and emperors maybe—but for ordinary men, that was only
possible in the heroic age.'

I find my voice. 'He was born a son of man, he was crucified
and died and was resurrected by our Lord on the third day. This
I believe.'

As always, on the release of that word—*crucified*—she cannot
hide her distaste. She snaps her fingers before my face. 'You will

not listen, friend, I know that. Pray to your god, love him and honour him and obey him. But do not seek to be like him—do not seek to be immortal as gods. That is the insanity we deplore.'

'Sister,' I answer, my eyes locked on hers, 'don't you want that too? To be raised in body and spirit for all eternity?'

She doesn't answer. This question is where I come closest to tempting her, it is what most intrigues her, though she won't admit it. But finally she raises a finger, runs it from her mouth to her breast to her belly. And it is always at this point, in that gesture which returns her to her body, when I lose my advantage. I don't even have to hear her words—I know her reply: 'A lump grows here, Timos, I feel the tumour in my belly. My back can't straighten, it is agony to walk. I cannot wait to leave this body, brother—I don't want to wander the earth forever.'

But today she responds another way. 'It is lovely, that promise.' Her voice is quiet, wistful. But then it hardens. 'Even I, with this sickening failed body, even I love life enough to be seduced by your words. But I don't believe you, Timos. I have been made curious by your dedication and your faith, I grant you that.' Her smile is no longer mocking or cruel; now it becomes sad. 'But your followers, those desert madmen, they are more honest than you are. Your brethren despise the body that the gods have given us. They hate that our bodies give birth to children, that they excrete blood and life, and they hate the sex that the gods have given to be the very essence of our bodies. I don't believe that they want to be resurrected to their old human bodies. I think they want to come back as gods.'

I look at her face, lined and withered. But I do not see age; I see a young maiden, dedicated to her god. 'Your goddess is a virgin,' I declare. 'You too are unsoiled, sister. And I am celibate. We both know there is a greater duty than that to the body. You too believe the soul is greater.'

At this she spits and waves two fingers across her breast. My words are pollution for her. 'Careful, Brother Timos. My temple is full of virgins and it is all I can do to guide them in their frustration and insanity. My goddess's dwelling also houses prostitutes and my work here has taught me that it is they whom the goddess loves and honours most. The whores marry and become mothers and fathers and they beget sons and daughters. They live a life that honours the gods.'

She comes as close to me as her worship allows. I can smell her stale vinegary breath, see her blackened gums and the surprising vibrant pink of her tongue.

'You are upright, as am I,' she states. 'All through my maidenhood my devotion was a burden—I was assailed by lust all the time. You understand that, brother, don't you?'

I don't have to answer. She knows me.

'But the one gift of age,' she continues, 'is that our lusts weaken over time. I love the goddess and I do not resent the vow that my father made to her. Your love of your god satisfies you, Timos. I believe that.'

She winks. Her breath is hoarse, a flush across my face. 'It must be harder for you, being a man. An old goat, certainly, but still a man. The vow of abstinence that you made for your god doesn't diminish or poison you, but you must know that it is an unnatural and cruel command for young men.' She glares at me now. 'Let your young brethren loose, friend. Let the boys prowl the brothels at night, let the girls dream of husbands and children, not of everlasting life.'

I answer gravely. 'He is coming, truly, he is returning.'

At this she sighs and turns her back, lifting her staff. I watch as she painfully climbs the temple steps.

On the last one she turns around and calls down at me, 'You promise that you will bring the defiler to me?'

'You have my word.'

———

Morning now is sovereign, and the city is noise and movement. The municipal servants have finished their dawn work; they have sprinkled the main avenue with river water to settle the dust from the tumultuous, unceasing activity. Many call greetings to me as I stroll, but I answer abruptly and absent-mindedly. I can't stop thinking about the old priestess's words. Her demand that someone be handed over for punishment is reasonable and justified; my mood sours as I think of the battle ahead.

It must have been one of the young fools, one of the refugees in our care, who has dared to insult the temple. It is devastating that someone has taken advantage of our hospitality in such a way. The young are always impetuous no matter where they are from. It is my role to temper their hot-headedness, to counsel restraint and to remind them that soon, very soon, this world will be destroyed. Yet this morning I feel overwhelmed by the immensity of that task. I don't know how to transform their hate, nor how to enhance their patience.

Many of the refugees are Jews whose families were annihilated by Rome's brutal, inexorable conquest. The older ones survived the siege and destruction of Jerusalem and the cities of Judea, and the younger ones have been raised to wreak revenge. They have found their way to us, even though they know we are pledged to Paul and are committed to welcoming Strangers to our community. In a previous generation, even if they had believed that Jesus was the Saviour promised by the Lord, they would never have countenanced living with Strangers. Their Messiah had been Jewish and only Jewish. But the Roman holocaust destroyed Temple and city and kingdom and kings. In that obliteration we lost James and Peter and the Magdalena. So many friends are now gone. That obliteration also created desperation and need—and hunger and exile have no time for old ways and old laws. In desperation and in need and in hunger, the refugees come to us. We feed them, we shelter them, we teach them, but their hatred of Rome is understandable and inescapable. And to them, Rome is not only Rome: it is also Greece and her gods and her rites and her people—how do I even dare counsel them to love the Stranger? I have lived too long and all my friends are gone. I am not capable of shouldering this burden that the Lord has placed on me. I must pray for Him to forgive me. Saviour, we are four generations—surely now you must return?

———

It is the smarting nip of cold that releases me from my anxious thoughts. I wrap my threadbare robe more tightly around my shivering body. I suddenly become aware that a silence has fallen over my city. Fear overtakes me. Activity has stopped and everyone is staring up at a swirling dark whirlpool of cloud that is rolling ominously over the library and the amphitheatre.

Shadow has covered the earth. All is quiet save for the bleat of goats, the anxious barking of dogs and the squawking of gulls. A lone billow of cloud breaks free from its mother and re-forms as a titan's finger—a sliver of grey stretching out its long dark nail. The cloud finger points down from the heavens to Artemis's temple. And in the next moment, as I exhale, the silence becomes a whisper becomes a shout becomes a cacophony.

'An omen,' they cry, and run to the temple. Prayers cascade from my lips. I give silent thanks for Denisia's friendship and loyalty. I know my city—I have lived here long enough to be an adopted son. If the priestess had revealed last night's desecration, if that had become known, the inhabitants of this city would have fallen on us as rabid beasts. The Ephesians would have slit all our throats.

I hear a voice. 'Father Timothy, the Lord be praised—I have found you.'

Brother Heracles is a dwarf. He stoops more than I do and his hair is whiter than mine, even though he is not yet half my age. A former owner thought it a great joke to name his misshapen servant after the ancient colossus. When he tired of him, the owner sold Heracles to a travelling circus troupe. But the wife of the circus owner had been baptised into our way and championed the dwarf's release. She'd been appalled by the cruel jokes made at his expense and the savagery of the beatings he'd had to endure to satisfy the audience. Out of gratitude, he too accepted our faith and has been a steadfast servant to the Lord ever since. Born on the northern shores of the Hospitable Sea, his tribulations and sufferings have not once shaken the code of respect that is shared by his people. As I am an elder, he will only address me as Father.

He spies a clearing in the mob marching to the temple and runs across the square to me.

'What is it, Brother Heracles?'

He takes a moment to recover his breath. 'Father,' he finally splutters, 'we are graced with a visitor. Father Able has come from Colossae.'

The little man then takes my hand, seeking to guide me back home. The generosity rooted in the soil of his homeland will not countenance keeping a guest waiting.

I have a darker heart. I would gladly evade that scoundrel Able.

I am untethered, reduced by such an ungenerous thought. It is me who is half a man, not Brother Heracles. He is the proof of the righteousness of our faith: it is the lowly, the despised and the broken who best comprehend the words of the resurrected son.

'Lead the way, brother,' I command. 'We must of course welcome our guest.'

Heracles and I have long practised an ungainly but by now harmonious step. He makes rapid leaps to compensate for his short steps but they perfectly match my elderly shuffle as we lock step, hand in hand. Our grip tightens as we pass the long shadow of Artemis. The crowd gathering before the temple steps is dense and unyielding; we have to squeeze our way through the crush. The omen has long dissolved and slashes of blue sky are visible through the shifting cumulus. The aged priestess is standing on the top step, haranguing the mob for its impiety and the meanness of its offerings. The flower-sellers are all smiling as the admonished crowd push and fight to be the first to buy garlands of petals and fruit for the goddess.

As we make our escape on the other side of the crowd I hear her call out, 'Brother Timothy, I expect you to keep your promise.'

The crowd is too busy proving themselves most devout and find no sinister meaning in her words. But I turn to her and nod. Her eyes are closed, her hands are cupped and raised above her head as she implores her goddess to show leniency to her adorers.

We turn into our alley. Smoke from the burning hearths and cooking fires obscures the sloping frames of the precarious dwellings. At the end of the teeming dank lane is our home.

The adults and children are out scrounging for work, scavenging for food, or begging. Only the very ill and the nursing mothers have been left behind. The women are at their domestic tasks: cleaning or pounding grain or kneading bread. They greet us: 'He has risen, he is returning.' And we answer them: 'Truly, he has risen. Truly, he is returning.' They go back to their work.

Heracles drops my hand. His voice low, his apology clear in his mumbling, he says, 'The esteemed father is in your room.'

We have no property—all is shared as the anointed son has commanded. It is only our community's respect for my venerable age that grants me the favour of a bed of my own and a room to myself. These are gifts, not possessions. But today my emotions are not worthy of my belief. My mood is foul as I climb the swaying planks. I knock sharply and do not wait for a reply as I enter my room.

My antipathy only increases when I see him stooped over my small desk, one hand laid over the papyrus parchment. But as I storm over to him, I remember that Able cannot read. My anger dissipates. Those frail shoulders, those tremulous hands and those thin, unsteady legs. We have both lived too long.

He stands, peers confusedly towards me, even though the shutter is open and the room is bathed in clear light. His shattered eye, destroyed long ago by a brutish gaoler in Rome, is an unsightly carapace. But his other eye too is now dead, sunk in a milky pool. He is nearly blind. I announce myself and we embrace. The breath that wheezes through his toothless mouth is surprisingly redolent. He exists on a frugal diet of vegetables and fruit, and forbids himself meat and milk. I fancy that my own breath is unpleasant to him for he sucks in his lips. A little of my ire returns. But I quell it and say cordially, 'He has risen, brother.'

He pecks my cheek and responds, 'Truly, he has risen.'

I return the kiss. 'He is coming, brother.'

'Truly, he is returning.'

Our greeting over, we are strangely tongue-tied. To break the silence I offer him the stool. He refuses and I offer it again. Only on my third bidding does he sit himself down while I arrange myself warily and painfully on the low bed. His sightless gaze follows the rustling of the bed straw and he turns to face me. But his blindness is such that he stares high above my head.

He clears his throat. 'I hope you don't mind, brother, but while I was waiting for you I examined your room. It is a large one.'

He is swallowing his spit, the knuckle on his throat rising and falling like a buoy at sea. The motion disgusts me. And his words are an affront.

'It's not that large. I have continually asked the brethren to let me sleep in the dormitory. But they refuse.'

He grins as he nods. 'Of course, of course, you are the super-
visor and head of the assembly in Ephesus. It is a small luxury
and undoubtedly deserved.'

I take the advantage of my still-functioning eyes and examine
him carefully. He is unbearably thin. The trek from his home
to here is long and must have been arduous—the skin on his
face and on his arms is blistered, on his nose it has peeled and
become scabrous. Still faintly visible are the three Latin letters
carved on his brow so long ago: the F and the G and V, the
fugitivus of the runaway slave. It is a reminder that should lead
me to sympathy. But in recalling his beauty as a youth, I find
the old man before me even more repugnant to behold. How is it
that we have become so hideous? He is younger than I but looks
older. His puckered mouth that he constantly chews and licks as
he sucks in air with the desperate terror of a fish caught in the
nets; the gnarled fingers and bony wrists, skin marked by pox
and scabs; the tufts of hair that protrude from his sunburned
ears studded by thick yellow wax. He is vile—so much worse
than me. I glance down at his naked feet. One foot is engorged,
adorned by red pustules close to bursting. My pride is chastened.

'What happened to your foot?'

'It is nothing—an adder bit me while I walked. But the Lord
protected me and the poison was expelled in a night's fever.'

Amid the swelling and bruises, the two crimson slashes of
the bite are visible.

I am wicked. Able is my brother, and one beloved by the
apostle, our teacher, Paul. 'I have some nettle balm. Let me rub
it into your foot; it will be soothing.'

He makes protestations but I must atone for my vanity and

pride. I find the salve and then, kneeling before him, start rubbing it into the diseased foot. As I do he slurps and kneads his gums in contentment. The enormous blisters crackle as I rub them, then burst, releasing their poison across my hands. I swallow my nausea.

'You should have sent us warning of your arrival—we are not prepared for you.'

He lifts his chin and tilts his head, as if to survey a room he cannot see. 'All I need, Timothy, is a cot and some bread. We are not used to comfort in Colossae. I will sleep with the brethren.'

My anger returns. Sanctimonious, overweening in his servility—Able has not changed. I finish my chore, get up with a groan and walk to the water jug. I wash my hands. Thoroughly.

Able clears his throat. 'Timothy, I was sent for. I received a message from your brethren asking me to come to Ephesus.'

My flesh turns cold. I feel ill at the treachery. Then it is as if I am emptied: all that is solid within me is replaced by weariness.

'Are you angry?'

I set down the water jug but I do not turn to face him. I can't bear the sight of him. 'Who sent for you?'

'Does it matter?'

I walk to the window and look up at the Lord's sky. I close my eyes, willing the screen of the heavens to split, for this to be the moment of the Saviour's return. I am too old and too tired and I have no strength for this.

Able's sightless eyes are searching for me. 'Brother,' he says cheerfully, 'you are the overseer of Ephesus and I am overseer to the assembly of Colossae. We are chosen and we are equal.'

I detest that word: *overseer*. The Saviour has not yet returned and these old donkeys, many of them not long freed men, are jostling for lordships in the coming kingdom.

The heat of the sun warms my face. I open my eyes and the punch of the glare is a reminder of my Lord's power. I am sickened by my ungenerous heart. I am not equal to my teacher. None of us are masters and none of us are slaves.

'Why did they send for you?'

He shuffles on his seat, guided by my voice. 'People are distressed that you give shelter to temple prostitutes and share your feast and your thanksgiving with them.'

The petty hatreds from the east—they come loaded with them on their broken backs, along with their destitution and their hunger.

'They are also our brethren,' I answer. 'They too have been baptised and born anew to the Lord.'

'They are whores.'

I know how to answer him. 'And the Saviour will ask us, "Are *we* without sin?" Only the Lord can judge.'

'Only the Lord can judge, Brother Timos.' His answer is swift and infuriating. 'But the Saviour did not mean the adultress to continue in her wickedness. Do you shelter whores that continue to sin?'

Their vengeful hatred extends even to children. Barius and Apollodoros, bonded to the brothels, are not yet men; Goldenhair and Verga are just shy of maidenhood. It is these children whom his words condemn.

As I struggle for a response, my tongue silenced by his unctuous piety, I look again to the sun and my eyes are slammed by an iridescent light: the force of it is so strong it becomes a gust that enters my mouth and nose and eyes and fills my body.

I was wrong.

My beloved, my teacher, my Paul. The sky is not empty and his voice is that rending of Heaven that I was longing for. Emboldened by the force of the sun within me, I am not the old spent man in his cell, I am young and full of vigour: I am sitting next to my beloved as the frightened, beautiful slave kneels before us and the sour reek of the crippled Roman guard fills my nostrils.

My back to Able, I answer him with Paul's words. 'Till the kingdom comes, brother, each man will remain in the condition in which he was called.'

I turn to the old man who was once a beguiling youth. 'Weren't you a slave when you were called?'

This time my words shake him. His responding rage is of such intensity I feel its flutter against my skin.

He points to the brand on his brow. 'I obeyed. *Brother.*' He makes spit of that last word. 'I obeyed and went back to my owner. I returned to the place I was called, as Paul requested, to await the advent of the Saviour.'

Having unsettled him, I can afford charity. 'And the brethren you condemn are also in the place they were when they were called.'

His strength is equal to mine—I fear it may be greater. He has collected his will, and his fury is evident in the straightening of his back.

'I returned to my owner as Paul commanded, but I returned as a child of the Lord. I did not foul my body or my spirit. I became his slave again but not his whore. I told him, "Slice my throat—I prefer death to your dishonouring me."'

I must trust that compassion begets compassion. I step away from the window, kneel before him, the crack of my hipbone so loud it makes him start. I touch his thigh, bring him back from fear.

'Able, your master Philemon belonged to our way, he believed what we believe. These lads and girls you condemn have been promised to the false gods. If they relinquish their servitude in the temples they will be killed.'

It is as if he can see me. The pearly cloud of his intact eye stares right into mine. 'Then they will be righteous and pure when they are risen to the Lord.'

The blood of my father, Greek, ancient, honourable and proud, swirls and engulfs my body. I am my father's blood, I can hear his insults: 'You chaste and dickless charlatans! You are fanatics to a death cult!'

'They are children,' I insist.

'I was a child too!'

And suddenly he jolts, his mouth twisting into a hideous grin. 'You are the overseer of Ephesus, Timos, the supervision of this assembly is yours. I won't interfere.'

'Thank you.'

But my concession is premature. The grin does not leave his mouth. 'That is not the only concern the brethren have, however.'

'What else?'

'They are unhappy that you will not immerse their children.'

Again, the sting of betrayal. The fierce blood of my father and the wise words of my teacher seep from me and take my strength with them.

'I do not baptise infants,' I answer weakly.

'These men and women, these poor souls who have suffered so much, they want their children to be with them in the raised kingdom. Your heart cannot be unmoved by this.'

We are as the psalmists: *How long, Lord, how long must we wait?*

'Able,' I say carefully, 'you and I are disciples to the apostles. We know that only those who repent of this world are able to enter the coming kingdom. I can only baptise those who can make such a vow.'

I am astonished: he has reached for my face, his touch is gentle and full of care.

'I am glad I cannot see you, Timos. I can trace your wrinkles, I can feel your age, but within the blank canvas of my eyes I imagine you as I first met you in Rome.'

Closing my eyes, I too reach for his face, his shrunken and weathered skin. I force memory to return to me the image of his youth.

We abandon our touch at the same moment.

'Is it a gospel you are writing?'

'Yes,' I answer. 'The younger brethren have demanded it of me for years. I have succumbed.'

'The life and death and the resurrection of the Lord?' There is a harsh click to his tongue as he asks the question.

'The life and death and the resurrection of the son.'

He works his mouth, his tongue darts across his gums. 'And are you writing of our teacher Paul?'

'Of him as well.'

'Of his vision?'

'Of his encounter with Yeshua the Saviour.'

He sniffs, his mouth contorts and he puckers greedily; as he does so comets of red and black disturb my sight, they burst into dazzling white light; my cell seems at a tilt, a stab of ferocious pain is at my hip and I put my hand on the wall to steady myself. It is as if he were sucking the living air from the room.

'The young are curious,' he says, 'as they should be. They are also easily swayed by rumours and lies. It is good that you, beloved of our teacher, are writing a gospel.' He puts a halt to his slurping. A tremor of reticence creeps into his voice. 'I too am writing one.'

You cannot write—you are an illiterate. At once, I am appalled by my Greek pride.

'I will be glad to read it,' I answer. 'We will share it with the brethren here in Ephesus.'

He waves a hand up and down, acknowledging my civility. Then he springs a question. 'What did the apostle Paul tell you of his encounter with the Saviour?'

A shadow falls across the room. In the endless void of open sky a cloud has suddenly appeared to mask the sun. I resist my first impulse, born from my father's blood, to discern in it a warning.

I keep my voice even and unhurried. 'That for three days he was enclosed in light, with Jesus our Saviour by his side.'

He nods in contented agreement to this. 'The resurrected Lord was the light that blinded him. Is that not so?'

My knees tremble, my head feels heavy and a swooning rocks the room. 'Excuse me, brother.'

Cautiously, that I might not faint, I walk over to my bed and fall on it. I mean no dishonour to him. I want to stop the shifting of light in my eyes, to still my nausea. I lie across my bed, concentrating on the rise and fall of my chest.

'Are you unwell, brother?'

I am old. I make no answer.

He reaches out his hand, searching for me.

'We too will share your gospel at our assemblies and at our thanksgiving feasts. I trust in your faith, Timos. You will not bear false witness.'

My response is harsh. 'And who is it who does?'

Locating my voice, he lowers his gaze to me. 'Those who are seduced by the sophistry of the Greeks.' He swallows. 'Those who are rich and who have never worked and who want to remake our Saviour into their own image. Those who would make Jesus a womanish philosopher.'

He wipes his mouth, as if that last word is an obscenity. His next words are the weapon he brandishes and he lets it fall. 'And I have forbidden the delusions that come from the forsaken Twin. I will not have them read at Colossae.'

I hate him. He is my brother in Jesus the Saviour and yet I hate him. I muster my strength; now I am not defending myself but defending *him* whom I love.

I make my voice my sword and I deliver a warning. 'Careful! You are declaring against an apostle.'

'It was also an apostle who betrayed our Saviour.' His voice is strong and defiant. 'And to preach against the resurrection is also a betrayal. Thomas is lost to the Lord.'

It is this disgusting former slave who is the false witness.

'He was the most beloved of them all—all the apostles vouched to that.' My righteousness lends me courage. I sit up from the bed. 'To say otherwise is a wicked falsehood.'

The devil dares to laugh. He cackles, he grunts, spittle sprays from his mouth. He wipes his lips, sucks and chews, and finds his voice. 'Calm yourself, brother. We all know the love you bore the Twin. But we must be loyal to our first martyrs. It was his own brother, the apostle James, who declared against him.'

He will not even speak his name.

I declare, 'I still love Brother Thomas. As we all should.'

His mirth has gone. Only the unkindness remains. 'Thomas is dead.' And then, reluctantly, after a silence. 'May the Lord have mercy on his soul.'

I cannot give an answer. My beloved must surely be dead. I close my eyes again, to remember him, to bring him to me.

Able will grant me no peace. 'You are greater than I am, Timothy, and are right to correct me. It is not the beloved Twin who corrupts our faith but those who preach in his name.'

A low chuckle erupts from his throat once more. 'After all, he was unschooled, just like me. You must think me ludicrous to even dare attempt a gospel!'

I answer, without thought, out of civility and habit. 'No master and no slave, we are all children before our Father, the Lord.'

A sneering laugh escapes from him again. I hear him rising, and then the sound of his staff on the floor. He stands above me. 'Rest, good brother.'

I stir, prepare to rise.

But he will not allow it. 'No, with the Lord's mercy I made it here. I promise you, He won't let me tumble down the stairs.

Rest, Timos. Your good flock have promised me a thanksgiving feast today.'

My first thought is bitter: I have not been told. And then I remember Denisia's benevolence and my promise to her. I dread what I must reveal. Quickly, I tell Able of the desecration of the idol.

He listens and for a long while he is silent. 'And you are convinced this—' he pauses, his next word hard and unforgiving '—sorceress hasn't revealed this to the authorities?'

The imputation is clear: I'm a fool to trust her.

'I am convinced.'

I force myself to rise from the bed.

Again he brings up his hand, says, 'No, brother, rest. All this can wait.'

Even with the open window, the air is viscid. My neck and shoulders ache, as though my head is a weight they can no longer bear.

I give in and lie back on my bed.

An evil jealousy fills me as I hear his staff search the stairs. Let him fall.

Such ugliness—to fling a curse—and such wickedness—to wish a hurt—spur me where body and spirit have failed: I get up off the bed and am on my knees. I bring my forehead to the cool plank of the floor and pray for forgiveness, pray for charity and for filial love.

Even as I do I swear that I can hear his reedy voice from below. I pray, but rather than being soothed by the balm of selflessness and duty, my heart is struck by the poison dart of envy. I can hear the women respond to him in cheerful greeting. I can't make out their words but I am convinced they are sharing gossip, at ease with a former slave in a way they can never be with me. Or I with them. The blood of my father flows through me. Even after years in one fellowship, I am still wary of the taint of their skin and the old laws pertaining to their caste. And they also fear my touch and are suspicious of where I came from. They know that I wasn't born noble and that we were never wealthy, but they suspect and they are right that my father owned and tenanted land. It is vouched for; the anointed son declared that only those without property will inherit the kingdom. I have nothing now. All that we have we share. But they know whose son I am, that a Greek landowner's blood flows through me.

I keep my brow to the floor, though the arc it makes spears agonising pain into my back. But I accept it as a punishment and will not move.

My trance is broken by a call at my door. How long have I been lost in my meditation? As I straighten my back to rise, my knees buckle and I collapse, my body slamming onto the floor.

'Are you alright, sir?' Her voice is as urgent as her knuckles rapping on the door. I call on my Lord, I call Him to grant me strength. I am on my knees once more.

'Come in, Sister Ephemia,' I answer. 'I am done with my prayers.'

'Good brother,' she squeaks as she pushes aside the screen curtain, 'all is ready for the thanksgiving.'

As she pours water over my hands to wash them, I ask after her husband and children, but she responds as though I were a revered and distant lord, and I am quickly silent. I don't want to torment her by compelling her to speak to me. She respects me but she cannot love me.

———

The long hall is packed and filled with joyful noise, and the assembly extends out into the yard. There is a hush as I make my way through the throng. In one voice they call: 'He has risen, brother.' I answer: 'Truly, he has risen.' They respond: 'He is returning.' Walking amongst them, patting children on the head as I go, I reply: 'Truly, he is returning.' And in doing so I realise that time has made a habit of those words, that I have uttered them with neither love nor testament. Time has robbed them of meaning and portent. I quicken my stride, as though a show of purpose can remind me of my duty and calling.

As I gingerly take my seat my hip burns, and I stifle a groan as I cross my legs. Able is already seated at my side before them. He acknowledges me by searching for and finding my hand, kissing it. I return the courtesy. We face our family.

Words do not come. I look down at the two rugs spread out in front of us; they form a barrier that separate Able and me from the faithful. The women have been busy and have spread dishes and jugs on each rug. But the offerings are sparse: unleavened bread, onions and garlic pickled in brine. One shallow plate is half filled with cooked fowl livers, a meal I know was scavenged from a butcher's trash. The jugs are more water than wine.

My silence causes the assembly to stir and to whisper. I clap my hands, beckoning to Heracles, and to the two others I have chosen for my assistants, Sister Silver and Brother Emmaus. They each take a platter of bread and share it amongst the brethren.

At the same time, Brother Cheerful, a tall and sinewy youth, rises and begins to sing our thanksgiving prayer.

The divine need not speak in tongues nor in prophecy; the clarity and harmony of this former slave boy's voice is a gift from the Lord.

The lad's exalted song soothes my agitation, the sense I've had since awakening that the world has been dislodged from its moorings, as if the day has been caught between night's end and dawn's stirring.

Able taps lightly on my knee, subtly urging me to speak. The prayer has ended. Heracles is holding a small crust of bread to my lips.

I begin. 'Jesus our Saviour, on the night he was betrayed, took bread and, when he had given thanks to the Lord, he broke it and said, "When you share in this bread, remember my teachings."' I eat the piece of bread that Heracles is offering. 'He then took his wine after the meal and said, "This cup is a new covenant of my blood, the preordained sacrifice that I must endure. Drink this and as often as you drink, remember: I am with you."'

Heracles fills my cup and that of Able.

'We remember Jesus our Saviour.' I raise my wine and drink.

They call as one. 'We remember you, Saviour Jesus.'

'He is risen.'

They shout, a diaphony that shakes the haphazard foundations of our dwelling.

'Truly, he is risen!'

'He is returning.'

And I do as we all do. I close my eyes and shudder at the exquisite promise.

'Truly, he is returning!'

Once, at this point, I would have felt a sacred light descending upon us: the Spirit and breath of the Lord. That brilliance was as tender as a mother's soothing touch and as comforting as a father's protective aegis. It is a long time since I have felt that peace. That radiant silence is now shattered by the impatience and the fidgeting, the murmurings and gossip, that bedevil our communion. We are now a family that stretches into a fourth generation. I preferred the circle of thanksgiving when we were few, each of us shoulder to shoulder with our brothers.

I call for two more brothers to assist the others in distributing the wine. They each take a jug and a cup and move amongst the brethren as they each take their sip.

I know it will take an age for each of us to partake in this feast of our love; I beckon to Cheerful, and he rises to sing again. He chooses wisely, one of the ancient psalms that I have taught him.

I look over to my brother. Able sits there patiently. His sight is nearly gone but he is alert to every tongue that takes bread, to every lip that sips the wine. I see again the white scars on his brow, feel that violent disfiguring. I can smell the burning flesh as the iron seal is stamped on his forehead, I can hear the young child's abominable suffering. Pity rises in me and I lean across to him and kiss him devoutly on the lips.

'He has risen,' I call into his mouth.

He kisses me in turn. 'Truly, he has risen.'

Cheerful's song comes to an end. The brethren are all quiet, every eye upon us.

Able looks out onto the assembly as if he can see them all,

as if in the mystery of our thanksgiving the Lord has returned his sight.

He turns to me. 'We are ready.'

My throat is parched, my lips dry and my tongue heavy. I swallow with difficulty and remind myself that we have feasted on love, on the bread and the wine, and that the spirit of the Lord is with us now. I look over the faces of the crowd. The very young to the very old. Widows from Judea who have lost fathers and sons, daughters who have buried mothers and infants, so many of them children of famine, siege and war. I swallow, and I breathe. I must have trust in the Lord and in His son. I must have faith.

I was wrong.

I begin. 'We welcome our beloved brother Able who has journeyed far.'

And a chorus of voices answers: 'Welcome, brother.'

My voice rings out. 'Why hasn't Jesus the Saviour returned?'

Able, who was smiling and nodding at my greeting, flinches at my words.

'My teacher was one of the chosen apostles. I am speaking of our brother Paul, may the Lord have mercy on his soul.'

The assembled murmur and whisper, a few call out: 'May the Lord have mercy on his soul.'

'He was a Jew, as are many of you. He was a proud Israelite and a defender of the law, so much so that he was entrusted with spying on and arresting those of our way who had proclaimed the coming and death and resurrection of Israel's saviour. Paul could not believe that a man whipped and scourged, hung and nailed to the Roman gallows could be the promised Saviour of prophecy—he was outraged by the very thought of that. For this is a scandal, a stumbling block to Jews and a folly to those who are Strangers.'

The silence in the room is absolute.

'Who here has witnessed a crucifixion?'

I sense their caution, their confusion. So I lift my hand and then press it to my heart. Slowly a few raise their hands, then more, and then it is a wave: all those before me, beginning with my brother seated next to me, then all the men and all the women and even the youngest children, we lift our palms and bring them over our hearts. From deep within the assembled there come cries and weeping.

'Our brother Bartholomew—' and here my voice cracks '—he was the first I saw crucified.'

And one by one they begin to stand. A man calls out the name of his brother, a father that of a son, another father moans and declares: 'My son and his son.' An old woman, her eyes white, her frailty such that she wavers and totters on her feet but she stands because she must stand, hollers in a voice that is not weak: 'My husband and my two sons.' The air is thick with the memory of blood and suffering, and the chamber fills with names. They are Judean and Greek, Syrian and African, names of the east and the west and the south and the north. The crying now is at a pitch that deafens the mind and scours the heart.

I raise both my arms. 'In the kingdom to come, they will be raised and they will be first.'

A voice from the courtyard yells out, 'We can't hear you, Brother Timos!'

I make my voice boom. 'In the kingdom to come, they will be first!'

I pause and wait for the sorrow to be spent. My voice is now as firm and clear as that of a young man.

'How do I know this?'

They are returned to silence.

'It was vouched for by the resurrected son.'

And next to me the whipped and beaten and branded fugitive, my brother Able, declares, 'Amen, amen, it is the truth.'

That word, which is Syrian and Judean and now also Roman and Greek, that word resounds amongst the brethren. *Amen. Amen.* A lightning bolt has been pitched into my heart and its fiery point emerges as my voice. I am speaking with the voice of the Spirit of the Lord and though my eyes gleam with that light and though my voice and my bearing are those of a youth at the height of his potency, what astonishes me most is my lucidity. I require no intoxicant, I do not rely on the holy text. My words come freely and with the power of the Spirit.

My hungry eyes search the assembled brethren, alighting on each one of them, bringing them to the light.

'The first shall be last and the last shall be first,' I insist. 'We are poor, we are destitute, we are hungry, we are ill and we scramble for shelter. But together we are rich and together we are wealthy and together we are sated and together we are healthy and together we are blessed. We do not declare against the orphan and the widow and we do not shun the beggar and the prisoner and we do not abandon infants and we do not deny anyone entry to our family.'

'When is he coming, uncle? When will we see the risen

Lord?' The interjection is shot from deep within the heart of the assembled. A man's voice, clear and lean.

The fervour that has given conviction to my voice fades away from me, just as water cupped from a stream slips through our fingers. They do not understand and they cannot see.

I raise my wine cup. 'He is amongst us now.'

Before me is a raven-haired youth, his sharp features savaged by war and famine, his eyes filled with doubt and mistrust.

I have to convince them of my faith. 'He is coming,' I continue. 'Truly, he is coming. That promise grounds our loyalty and our trust and love for one another. But he is also here now—that is the point of this thanksgiving, for it is also a test of your faith and your love. Stay your impatience. Whoever has ears to hear, they will hear: thus spoke the anointed son.'

I have lost them. I look at them and all I see is confusion and doubt. They want me to give them an answer that I do not have.

Able's hand clutches mine. 'My brother is a wise man and a good man. He has knowledge and he is correct: let those who have ears hear.'

He is not made anxious by their qualms. His voice, as he continues, rises and resounds across the hall, with its hastily raised rafters and cheap walls.

'Why has Jesus the Saviour not returned? Why is the promise unfulfilled?'

He leans forward. When I asked, it was in wonderment and sadness. He asks in wrath.

'Do not ask that of the resurrected son,' he commands, his voice gathering power and volume. 'He died for us. He was nailed to the damnable Roman cross for us! Do not dare ask anything else of him.'

Able has dropped my hand, he is pointing into the crowd. 'You, and you. And you there!'

It is as if his finger is his sight, each stab allots a target: this brother recoils, that sister hides her face in her veil.

'This one commits adultery,' thunders Able. 'And this one steals food from a neighbour. This one over there sells her body to those who would deny the Lord and this one over there is fevered with perverse lust for his sister or his brother. And you ask, "Why has he not returned?"'

Silence.

'He has not come because we are not deserving. He has not come because we are not righteous. He has not come because we are not worthy!'

First one, then another, they are on their feet, swaying, their eyes closed, their hands outstretched to the beams, imploring the heavens.

'Pardon us, Lord; forgive us, Father.' Able speaks in a hush that I can barely hear, so it is inconceivable that it was heard by anyone else. But they hear. They are all on their feet now, swaying in one movement as they pray: 'Pardon us, Lord; forgive us, Father.'

The pleas for atonement gather strength, the words repeated again and again, called forth from my brother next to me and echoed by the brethren before us. Without my bidding, Cheerful is on his feet and he sings the phrase, at first quietly and then proudly, and as it circles and casts itself into the gathering its munificent song cannot be separated from the chorus of voices. 'Pardon us, Lord; forgive us, Father.'

Able has offered them righteousness, which is certainty. I step back from him, I mouth the words but I cannot give myself to them. I am struck by what I am not when I look into this crowd. The words of my teacher are seemingly fulfilled: not slave nor master, not man nor woman, not Stranger and not Jew, they gaze upon me with one face and they shout in one voice. But I am as removed from them as the most revered noble who would not allow the gaze of a commoner to fall on him. My lips move but it is fear that drives my acquiescence, not love. Am I only my father's blood? Will I never be one with them?

The song is broken by a terrible cry as a youth flings himself before our feet, spewing forth vomit and bile, his body jerking in cruel torment. 'Uncle,' he screams, his mouth frothing, 'the demons of lust are eating my flesh, they will not leave me alone.'

I betray the boy. As he falls I recoil, make evident my disgust. It is Able who kneels before the youth and holds the boy's head. He shakes him and commands: 'Demons be gone! In the name of the resurrected son, in the name of Jesus the Saviour, be gone.'

The young man twists with the strength of a cornered beast in the arena, and I see his face. It is the face not of man but death—his teeth are fangs and his eyes are only white. In his writhing and desperation to escape, he scratches at the old man's face. But Able will not let go. He keeps a tight grip on the youth; he is without fear.

'In the name of Jesus the Saviour,' he declares again, 'demons be gone.'

The boy slumps. He lies in my brother's arms. Still on his knees, the old man raises his head.

'Can demons possess the kingdom to come?'

The hush seems concrete, eternal, and impossible to shift. But a voice calls shyly: 'No, brother.' And one more confident: 'They will not, brother.' It is followed by a clapping of hands and a joyous confirmation: 'No, brother, no, brother, they will not!' There is jubilation.

I have not moved. I am standing back. This spectacle sickens me; I have seen it feigned in temples from east to west. But I force myself to smile, and I give a quiet nod to Able. And he, assured by my agreement, allows two of the men to carry the child into the crowd. There, awakened, he is greeted with a multitude of kisses, hands reach out to touch him, to be part of the small miracle that has occurred.

Able offers them certainty.

He is at my side again, using a sleeve to wipe away the boy's vomit. His cheap actor's tricks bring revulsion from my belly to my throat. I do not dare speak. He's a freed man now, but born a slave. My thoughts are ungodly: he was born to the gutter; how can someone like that grasp the mysteries and meaning of the Lord?

He is breathing heavily; the struggle has revealed his age and his fragility. Now, it is now that I should step forward and speak. But it is as if with my spite all light has abandoned me and I am filled with darkness.

He finds his voice. 'Our brother Timothy told me this morning that one of the city's idols was desecrated in the night. It is said that the culprit claimed his crime in the name of the only God. Who amongst you committed this act? Declare yourself.'

He awaits, his head cocked, in patience and silence. Some dare not look at us, others glance at their neighbour then quickly lower their gaze. There are those, the hungriest and the most ravaged of the refugees, who raise their chins proudly, as if they are staring directly into my eyes, their scowls announcing their defiance. I labour with what remains of my will to return their belligerent stares but it is impossible to move these men.

But Able surprises us all, the bold and the meek. Our brother laughs. 'The idol, like all idols, is dung. It is not a sin to visit shit on shit, is it?'

The mutinous, the impatient, the pious and the hungry all burst into thunderous laughter at this obscenity. I cannot laugh. If there is just one among us working for the governors, that blasphemy condemns us all. I have to intercede, regardless of the rage that will follow.

But I hesitate too long; my fear has made me timid.

Able has stepped forward and is declaiming, 'You would be mistaken!'

The dazed silence is the monumental quiet of the morning after the great Deluge.

'It was a sin, it was an outrage,' he continues, 'not because of the insult to the impotent goddess but because it insults our neighbours and the First Amongst Men.'

There is a bellicose stirring from the refugees at the mention of their subjugator. Able does not care. 'We are all, regardless of origin and regardless of caste, loyal subjects to Rome.'

Dark mutiny flashes across the faces of the most zealous.

Able stumbles over the rugs, scattering the plates and cups. He throws himself into the crowd; he is amongst the most bitter of the refugees. He grabs at a man, one who fled Jerusalem on the last days and had one of his eyes torn from its socket; his vivid purple scar is as terrifying as the face of a Cyclops.

Shaking the man's shoulders, Able intones, 'Carthage and Athens are conquered and Damascus and Alexandria are conquered. And do not be mistaken, Jerusalem is conquered. Israel is no more.'

Able's voice drops to a hush again, a whisper that is heard by all of us, and taken up by all and repeated from brother to brother and from sister to sister.

'Nazareth is not conquered, Nazareth conquers. He has risen, he is returning and he will conquer.'

I cannot bring my mouth to speak or even muster the strength to raise my hand. I am shocked by the affront of his words. No apostle claimed this. This is not the teaching of our Saviour. But the brethren neither know that nor care. They are now shouting in fury: 'He has risen, he is returning and he will conquer.'

Able has offered them vengeance.

He raises his arms, calling for silence. The uproar subsides.

'I ask you once again: who was it desecrated the idol?'

Not one eye moves from him; not even the infants cry; yet no one admits to the offence.

'What did our Lord, our Redeemer, say? Let he who has ears hear.' He adds with fury, 'But you lot are as deaf as you are blind!'

A murmur, almost a wail, rises from the crowd, but he is oblivious to the disturbance

'Who *doesn't* hate us? Who *doesn't* want to destroy us? The

Romans scorn us, the Greeks despise us, the righteous Jews shun us, and all of the unbaptised laugh at us. There is no tribe that doesn't slander us with the ugliest gossip and there is no authority that doesn't want us eliminated!'

Even I can't resist this passionate eloquence; I too have been seduced by that adamant, exalting voice.

'They kill us, they crucify us, they throw us to beasts in the arena, they sew our lips together and watch us starve. They bugger children in front of their mothers and violate men in front of their wives. The temple priests flay us openly in the streets. We are hunted everywhere and we are hunted by everyone.'

In his fever he has returned amongst them, touching shoulders, heads, the fingers and hands that reach out to him.

'Look around you, brothers and sisters—we are still alive! We are despised, yet we grow. We are tortured and crucified and yet we flourish. We are hated and still we multiply. Why is that? You have to wonder, how is it that we not only survive but we grow stronger?'

I am transfixed, as eager as the most desperate of my brethren to hear his words.

As if awoken to my enchantment he finds his way back to me, sits beside me and takes my hand. 'Do you not ask yourself why they hate us so, Brother Timothy?'

The first urge is to best him, to win the brethren for myself. Then I am ashamed of my pettiness, as if I am a silly boy competing for a tutor's favour. I resist, I resist vengeance. I remember the words of Paul. I will cast my anchor on faith.

'They hate us because we speak the truth,' I respond. 'That there is only one God, only one just and righteous Lord, and He sent a Saviour to redeem us, who was born as a man and lived as man and died as a man to be born again as a son to the Lord. As we all will be.'

I have spoken simply. The words hit their mark. The calls thunder—'Amen! Amen!'—and the youngest and strongest brothers stamp their feet in thundering chorus.

Able nods at my words as the pandemonium of the stampeding feet eclipses all other noise and becomes the only sound on earth.

He turns back to the crowd. His eyes are raised to the sky and his arms are outspread. The calls and the shouts die away.

'You are a fortunate assembly,' he begins. 'Possibly the greatest one we have. I doubt the assemblies in Rome herself are guided by anyone as noble or as right with the Lord and His anointed son as is our beloved brother Timos. He speaks wisdom. Always trust this man's voice; he speaks directly from the apostles.'

Then he shatters that goodwill. 'And you do not deserve him! Because you are filthy cowards.'

He stoops, fumbles for the thanksgiving cup, lifts it and brings it to his lips, as if to drink the last drop from it. Instead, he spits into it.

'It is just copper,' he says quietly and drops it with a clang.

That sound resounds with a ferocity that will echo till the defeat of time. None of us speak. None of us dares to challenge him. None of us dare move.

'Copper doesn't matter, brothers, metal doesn't matter.'

He pinches the loose skin on his arms. '*This* doesn't matter, brothers. Neither flesh nor copper nor stone nor marble nor gold nor silver. None of it matters. We survive, we flourish, because we have the word of the Lord. No sword, no stone and no flame can compete with that word. Our weapon is the word of the Lord. That is our lance and that is also our shield. That is how we multiply and that is how we conquer.'

A voice calls from amongst us. 'Tell us, uncle, what is the word? What is the word that conquers?'

His eyes are shut, his arms are once more outstretched, as if calling forth a light. We await the word.

'Jesus the Saviour said, "Do not resist the wicked foe. If the evil-doer strikes you on the cheek, then turn the other to him. Those who do so are beloved of our Father, the Lord of us all."'

Sincerely I follow, 'Truly, it was spoken.'

But the divisions of our fellowship can be seen in the response to my brother's words. The literate and the citizen, those born Greek, those born in Ephesus, they assent with a nod of their bowed heads. This is the wisdom and profound compassion that has brought them to the Lord. But the refugees, those fleeing death and war, they abhor these words.

My brother has no fear. He speaks directly to the newcomers themselves, to those who have lost everything: land, kin and sons. They who hunger for revenge.

'He is Jesus the Saviour and he is Jesus the Judge and Lord of not only Israel but of the world. These are his words. Would you deny your king?'

As a violent shudder of the earth can carve a perpetual gorge between neighbours, so does Brother Able's question tear apart our congregation. The success of our grand initiative is marked by how our brother's demand fortifies one group, frightens the other, and is of no consequence to many more.

I don't look for the answer amongst the hungry and the homeless, I know what they want—a king to rise again in the east. For
them, Jesus is the anointed son. I want to see how the youngest
of our generations respond: boys coming to manhood and
sisters reaching maidenhood. They have only known emperors
and have only known Rome. Yet they too are fervent in their
agreement. For them, the Sacred City of Jerusalem is as distant
as the splendour of Persepolis and the wretched villages of the
wild Britons. What they desire is a Saviour who is to be the First
Amongst Men and a Lord who is the First Amongst Gods.

I finally comprehend: we are now more Strangers than we
are Jews. I suck in my breath, awestruck by what I have not
understood before. We are into our fourth generation and in their
veins flows a blood that has not been named before. *Christian*,
the derisive slur from those who detest us and want us destroyed,
this cruel and scornful word, it no longer stings. Theses people are
not Greek and they are not Romans and they are not Jews. They
are no longer even Strangers. They are Christians. The Saviour
is their inheritance. Theirs is not a king of cities or kingdoms
or empires; theirs is a king of all the world.

My brother, gifted with preternatural talents, he claims this
now. 'He died as Yeshua the Jew and he arose as Jesus, the Lord
of us all.'

As if guided by the Spirit itself, he lunges once more towards
the refugees. He searches faces, settles on a strong youth with
fierce, rebellious eyes that now lower.

'Which of your false saviours survived the siege and onslaught
of Jerusalem?'

He takes a handful of the boy's long black hair. 'Answer me!

Which of those Zealots armed with bows and slings and swords and knives, which of them survived? Who didn't starve? Who didn't get sliced and gutted like a pig by a Roman soldier's sword?'

The young man's eyes brim with tears.

Able releases his clutch on the boy's hair, and strokes and kisses his face. 'What is your name, son?'

The youth's will returns his strength. 'I am Adam, son of Simon,' he declares proudly.

'We can turn our cheeks, Brother Adam, for we have the greater weapon in our arsenal. I promise you, son, we will conquer. We will remake the world. That is the meaning of our Lord's words.'

I stumble forward, as if a punch has been delivered to the back of my head. This is an obscene perversion of our faith. Our Redeemer has asked us to be as passers-by—they are his very words and his instruction to us. We must turn from the world because the world is of no importance. Let the world hate us as it did him. We have to turn away, to offer our cheek for another blow, because it is not this world that matters, but the world to come.

But even as my mouth starts forming the words, the elation of the brethren snatches them from me. They want only to change this world—to seize it and conquer it. They are impatient with waiting. The words of my dream ring in my ears: *I was wrong.* The youth embraces the old man, there is a stamping of feet and resounding applause, as if this were a wedding or a dance. And maybe it is—in this certainty of victory, in the here and in the now as much as in the next world to come, the Jew and the

Stranger, the Ephesian and the refugee, the first generation and the fourth, we are united and we are one. In victory, we are one.

I was wrong.

A voice pierces the jubilation of our crowd. 'I, uncle, I insult the stone goddess.'

It is a boy, one of the refugees, his voice squeaking in fear, and though he struggles with the Greek tongue, his meaning is clear.

The crowd shifts till an open path snakes from him to the feet of brother Able. The boy, shaking but purposeful, walks unsteadily towards the old man.

Able welcomes him with an embrace. 'You are a brave lad. What is your name?'

'Jacob, son of Abraham.'

'Is your father amongst us?'

'My father is dead. He must rest, he must in peace.'

Adam pushes his way forward. 'He is my cousin. He has honour.'

With his thin arm still clutching the boy's shoulder, Able turns, his sightless eye seeking me. 'Beloved Timothy, we are one family in the Lord and the Saviour. Here is a son that we must all be proud of.'

A hushed assent grows into a roar of approval. The boy's bright eyes strike me to my soul. I can see, I am granted vision. The lashes and the clubs in the arena, his flesh torn by wildcats, a dismembering, a crucifixion—this boy will not see manhood.

I embrace him with tears that my brethren mistake for sanction. I whisper into his ear, 'Be ready for me at dawn.' He shivers, trying to be brave. 'Of course, uncle.'

I release him and he returns to his place, grinning as older men slap his back and embrace him, declaring him to be beloved of our Saviour and of our Lord.

Exhausted, dying for sleep, I know that there is one last thing I have to do. I raise my hands and command silence.

'Brothers, sisters, sons and daughters, it has been a long day. We have been honoured by the wisdom and loyalty of our dear brother Able. We have much to discuss but that can wait till our next thanksgiving.'

I cross my arms. I know my expression is stern, my eyes cold, but I resent the words I must now speak and I can't pretend the opposite. I search for a face, a young girl, a mother.

'I know there are those amongst you who would wish to baptise your infants. You understand that I cannot do so, for I have pledged otherwise to my teacher.'

And yes, the young mothers, their bodies bend eagerly towards me, anxious for my words.

'I see no reason, however, why our brother Able cannot immerse your children.'

I turn to him and bow. 'If you are in agreement, brother.'

His smile is indulgent; he knows he has won.

———

The boy, Jacob, is waiting for me in the burst of fresh morning. He only has a dirty cloth around his waist and his torso is bare. The first thing I do is scrub his face and neck and chest. There are no clothes left for him to wear—what we had has already been claimed by the latest arrival of refugees. But I cannot allow him to walk to the temple in near nakedness.

I strip off my vest but, though the wool is frayed and

moth-eaten, he shies away from accepting the garment. 'Is yours,' he says in his broken Greek.

I reprimand him in Syrian, remind him I am an elder, and he takes it and puts it on.

As we walk he turns chatty, with no premonition of the cruelty of his fate. He tells me about the mountain village he comes from, how the cracked desert stretched out from there in every direction but in the far distance one could see the silver waters of the Reed Sea.

But then he becomes silent and lets go of my hand, walking stern-faced beside me, as though ashamed of his moment of childish chatter. He is striding like a soldier now, wanting to prove that he is a man. He has survived war, violation and expulsion, so how indeed could he still be a child?

When we near the temple, suppliants have already prostrated themselves over the marble steps, their cupped hands filled with garlands, cracked wheat and ground nut-meal for the goddess. We step over them. The servants of the nobility carry squawking fowls under their arms; one young man leads a skittish goat up the steps and another clasps a struggling lamb under her arm. They announce the name of their house and master, cover their shaved heads, and the temple guards allow them to step through the arched gate of the antechamber. The poor and the beggars are praying on the bottom steps, they call out to their caste cousins, to the slaves, imploring them to whisper their names to the priestess so that she in turn can reveal them to the goddess, for Artemis to heal them, or to save a son from gaol or a sister from whoredom.

I see that Jacob's nostrils flare and his mouth waters as

hungrily as a dog's at the odours from the sacrifices wafting down through the temple colonnades. The air is thick with the smoke and the smell of grease and charred meat. Our empty bellies rumble, mine and the boy's, but also those of the believers banging on the stone and asking for mercy from their cold and false idol. Our hunger is the loudest sound in the world.

As we wait for the temple guards to glance our way, the boy begins to show fear. I respect the old witch, I trust that she is not given to malice, but in her eyes and the eyes of her goddess and the world, his crime is enormous. I pull him close to me, hoping that in this unity we can both find courage.

A guard takes pity on us and beckons us over. I bow, and as I do so I strengthen my hold on the boy, indicating he too must make obeisance. I feel him resisting, but he bows. The guard then allows me to speak and I ask for the priestess Denisia. I keep the pressure against the boy's neck, fearing that he might raise his head before she appears.

We hear her coming down the stairs, her silver anklets jingling. I lift my head.

Her eyebrows and her hair have been shaved off. A line of thick amethyst kohl is smeared around both eyes and across the bridge of her nose.

'Welcome,' she says, 'in the name of the First Amongst Us and in the name of the goddess.'

I discern the scent of the poppies on her breath. Her eyes swim lazily; she is intoxicated from inhaling their sap.

'Greetings,' I answer, 'in the name of the First Amongst Us and in the name of the true Lord.'

Her eyes are inebriated but her voice is sharp. 'Is this the culprit?'

Before I can answer the child steps forward. He knocks his breast, in loud and confident mimicry of a warrior. 'Me,' he says in his graceless Greek. 'Me do it.'

She brings her hand from underneath her shawl and swings it with speed and force across the boy's face. Surprised by the strength of this old harridan, he stumbles and steadies himself.

I clutch at his arm, fearful that in his humiliation and his fury he will strike her back. 'Careful,' I say to him in his language. 'Remember you have promised to accept your punishment.'

My words do caution him. But the memory of the previous evening's thanksgiving emboldens him. He even bows as he faces the priestess. 'Punish me. Kill me.' And with this declaration he again beats his chest. 'I die for the Lord.'

She seizes the boy by the shoulder and prods him up the stairs—he is gone from my care.

'When can I collect him?'

She has turned away but her hand shoots up to the sky. 'When our goddess the moon rises from her sleep,' she says, 'he will be yours again.'

Please, Lord—and here, on the very steps of this heinous temple, under the shadow of the terrible idol herself, I am praying—*please, Lord, return the boy alive to us.*

———

For the rest of the day I do not leave my cell. I ignore the calls at my door, I decline all food. I have no will even for prayer, let alone for returning to my writings. I sit on my stool, and I cannot move.

My thoughts hurtle me away from Ephesus, as if my recollections have wings. They return me to my youth, to my wanderings with my teacher, my beloved Paul. Our hunger, our poverty, the violence meted out to us by storms and by men, none of that mattered because we knew that the Lord had taken pity on His Creation and had re-entered the world to save us. He is returning, Truly, he is returning.

I was wrong.

He is not returning.

I am ashamed of this blasphemy. The past vanishes and I awaken to see that I am alone in my meagre chamber. The day has darkened and grown bitterly cold. The sun is leaving us. I find a shawl, wrap it around my shoulders, and descend the stairs, ignoring all those who call after me in greeting.

I abandon my household. I am glad to be in the godless streets of Ephesus.

The scuttling that announces night is of a different order to the confusion of the streets in the morning. Those who have shelter, they don't stop to chat; their bones and spirits are exhausted from labour, they are impatient and rush home. There are those who have drunk wine all day and their sloth and depravity is visible everywhere in the wet of the road stones, in the foulness they dump on the city's streets. One drunken fool, evidently a butcher by his bloodied and soiled apron, slips on a turd and falls flat on his nose. On his hands and knees he screeches, 'Who did it? Which whore's child did it?' A beggar boy takes the opportunity to grab a lone sausage from the drunk's belt and though the butcher scrambles to his feet and lunges after the thief, the boy is too fast and evades capture. I recognise the thieving child. He arrived in Ephesus last season, a Judean and a refugee. His ears were deaf to the promise of our Redeemer. He preferred the streets and homelessness; he would risk the violence of thieves and rapists rather than submit to the impossibility of a crucified and humble Saviour.

I tell my old feet to hurry. I cross the near empty agora.

Devotees are still crowding the steps of the temple. A cloud of incense rises above the columns guarding the goddess's chambers, shielding her from the stench of the city. I must be patient. I would be mad to interrupt the evening rites. As I wait it is as if my brother, my beloved, my Paul is beside me, whispering in my ear: 'The real stench, my Timos, is the goddess herself. She stinks of rutting, of dishonour and waste. She reeks of death.'

A young boy-girl, her head shaved, a minion—and, by the marks on her back, the poverty of her clothing and the rude scarlet paint and black kohl outlining her features, a slave of the lowest and most depraved order—hears my laugh and turns to me in delight. In her cupped hand she holds a lock of hair; she must have snatched it at her shearing and kept it hidden from the eyes of sorcerers and magic makers—it is all she has to offer to her goddess. She opens her mouth, black and toothless, revealing suppurating gums, and intones: 'Artemis, you were there at my birth.' She waits, her eyes flashing in hope, for me to return the expected fealty: 'You will be there at my end.' And I am close to answering, close to offering her this small and puny gift, some comfort to this abandoned boy-girl who has lived in poverty and destitution and sin, and who is deaf to eternity and the promise of it. I am close to answering. But I cannot and I will not. I turn away from her—yes, to defy her goddess, but also not to witness her disappointment.

How loud their eunuch priests shriek and how shrilly comes the response from their deranged priestess. With the setting sun, believing that their deity will soon awake, they are calling out prayers to rouse the goddess. The mob on the steps, stretched across the stone and marble, they too begin to wail and plead to their dumb god. In Greek and Phrygian; I also hear the quick guttural clicks of an older tongue: the coarse pleas of Alexandrian sailors and the pitiable lament of Egyptian whores. The calls of her devotees, from inside the temple and from its steps, reaches the ecstasy of completion. But all I hear is an empty rejoicing, one incapable of bringing forth renewal or light. It is self-pleasure, not love. She does not hear nor see nor comprehend.

Amidst the clamour, I whisper, 'Thank you, Lord, for my mother's blood.'

Finally, the screen is lifted and the bedchamber of the deity is revealed. The jubilant screams of her devotees are raised to the darkened heavens. And then, just as swiftly, after a glimpse of the reclined and bejewelled doll, the screen is drawn.

With the retreat of the idol, the extinguishing of the incense and the departure of the idolaters, I approach the guard and ask for Denisia. As I wait for her, I look at the moon arching into night. It is full and rosy, as if it has gorged on blood.

Denisia comes down the stairs and she has the dignity and respect not to gloat, nor delight in my agony.

The boy she is leading is taking slow, clumsy steps, as if he were an infant testing its gait. He is nearly naked except for a cloth that has been tied around his loins to stem the bleeding from both his rape and his castration. It is wet and dark with blood. He sees me and stumbles as I reach for him, taking him in my arms. His tears stream and his mouth gapes as if to howl but the sound that emerges is a terrible bleating. His breath smells of rot. His mouth is filled with blood; they have torn out his tongue.

They have drugged him. He is incapable of standing and I have to steady myself to take his full weight. His face turns to me, and even in the trance of narcosis I can see the unspeakable misery in the depths of his eyes. Bestial growls are coming from his throat.

'I am sorry, brother.' Denisia's voice is calm, subdued. 'He boasted to the High Priestess of his deed. He told her that he will never stop trying to dishonour Artemis. Well, he can't do that anymore. He will never disgrace her again, he will never insult her. His punishment is just.'

And now I cannot speak, for if I were to find my voice, I would unleash a thousand insults to that stone whore, abuse her, curse her, promise the destruction that the Lord will visit on her and her accursed disciples. And I would gladly hurl my hate at the priestess herself, knock her down with my fist, for her temerity in poisoning the word *justice* by bringing it to her lips. Their foul gods know lust and greed and torture and death but they do not know justice. No covenant can ever be made with such gods, for they have no loyalty to us and no love for us. Our God gives us truth: an eye for an eye and a tooth for a tooth—a truth that holds for everyone, whether they be master or slave, rich or poor, man or woman, Stranger or Jew. That is fairness, that is justice. I cannot speak. If I open my mouth, my path will emulate that of my Redeemer: my words will crucify me.

I summon my Lord to bring down vengeance, to unseal the covenant with our Saviour and bring down fire. I am my mother's blood.

'This is not just.' I say these words and only these words.

And I carefully guide the boy down the last step. The atrocities done to him cannot be lulled by the sap of poppies. No drug can soothe his suffering.

Here at the steps of the many-breasted goddess, that abomination, I am ready to tear off my clothes to cover the boy. I cannot bring myself to ask for kindness from the sorceress; better to disgrace myself than take anything from her. But she understands my quandary. She holds out a swathe of black-dyed flax, part of a temple slave's dress. I take it, I have to take it: the child is shivering violently.

I do not bid her farewell. We are no longer companions. We can never again be friends.

The streets are dark and empty. In an alcove near a small shrine to the god Priapus, I command the boy to grab tight to the obscene wooden appendage. He is terrified but trusts me. Carefully I unwind his drenched loincloth. The boy's testes have been ripped away. His sex is shrivelled and caked in dry blood. A thick paste has been applied across the incisions—underneath it the flesh is burned and charred from the flames used to seal the wound. I drop the cloth to the ground, tear a long piece from the linen the witch has given us, and tenderly wrap it once more around the boy. But even being as gentle as I can, he is still rigid from the excruciating pain, capable only of a defeated animal whimpering. When done, I wipe the filth of blood and muck off my hand onto the disgusting phallus of that most obscene of gods.

Can their foulness be measured? Is Priapus worse than their tyrant Zeus? All that are not of the Lord are evil. My mother's shade is before us. All who are not us are evil. I am my mother's blood.

A strength runs through me now, a power willed through myself but granted by our Lord. That strength lifts the boy to cradle him. This weak old man feels no strain as he carries this boy down the dark streets, returning to our home. I am nourished by my mother's blood. This blood that is consecrated to the Lord, that comes from Him and belongs to Him, this blood has wet and fed the earth for generation upon generation. This child in my arms, he is of this blood. Bring me a sword, place it in my hand so I can slice in two any child of a Stranger, that I can slash the throats of the sons of Greece and Rome. Their pride, their vanity, their wisdom, their knowledge, their enlightenment, their art, their laws, their idols, their temples, their towns and cities, all will be razed, all will be extinguished, all will be turned to ash when the flames engulf this world. Her nobles will have nothing left to call a kingdom and all the princes will vanish. None of their names will remain.

As the Lord grants me strength and renews the muscles of my arms, He raises a cloud of wind to ennoble my legs and my feet. I do not walk, it is as if I am a tempest in the very streets, I shove and I push and I ignore the curses that land on me. Everyone is foul and everything is corrupt. I thunder through the streets and alleys and only awaken to the world before me when my foot catches on a raised block in the square dedicated to the Awakened Apollo. I look down; the face of the victorious emperor has been stamped onto the face of the brick, it is newly fired. With the boy still in my arms I bring my heel down on the wicked face of he who dares call himself the First Amongst Men when he defames our brothers and he insults our Lord and curses our Redeemer. He who dares to imprison us, to sacrifice us to his blood-drenched revelries and orgies. He will be last, as will all who were before him and all who will come after him: generation after foul generation. All will be lost. Adulterers and violators of children, assassins, father-murderers and mother-killers, pornographers and whores; from the first of them, from the most august of them, to his depraved grandchild who dared raze the Temple, the dwelling of the one and true Lord. The blood of that whore Rome reeks of incest and perversion. And the day is coming—truly, it is coming—when no more will you be called beautiful and precious, where you will be forced to labour and to serve, where the veil will be ripped from your face to reveal your wickedness and you will lift your skirts and bare your legs and you will wade through streams of shit, the shit that you have vomited up, and all the world will witness your nakedness and your shame will be revealed, for the Lord will take vengeance and spare no one.

I am proclaiming this out loud, openly and fearlessly in the streets. I recite the very words of the prophet Isaiah that were taught to me by my beloved, my brother Paul. *You were not wrong!* I see the prophet's words as if the darkness of the night is the parchment of a sacred scroll. I throw my head back; let them hear my abuses, let them listen to the truth: I am ready to roar.

But as I pause to draw breath I sense the weakening heartbeat of the boy against my chest. His eyes are open wide in dread and incomprehension. And as when a fire engulfs a forest and the wind sucks all that is living into the centre of its blaze, the Lord reaches down and lifts the strength off my shoulders. I struggle, I clench my teeth and I dare not drop my charge. My rage is futile bluster and insanity.

I whisper to the boy, 'Don't be frightened, Jacob. Our prophet Isaiah promised us that a child will be born, we will be given a son and the world will rest on his shoulders.'

Fear has not left him but he no longer struggles in my arms.

'That promised child was Jesus the Saviour. He was broken as you are broken, he was violated as you have been. He died and was reborn on the golden morning of the third day, as you will be. Whereas those who did this to you will be forever condemned.'

I kiss the boy's hot and feverish brow. 'This I promise you.'

He cannot smile, but his dread has gone. As I struggle to carry him, solely through exertion and will now, my knees buckling and the sweat pouring from me, the boy lays his head against my chest, if not at rest and not at peace—for how can he any longer achieve either?—at least in faith. I feel his trust. I carry him home.

———

The refugee women fall to their knees, smashing their palms on the dirt floor, gnashing their teeth, beating their breasts, weeping and screaming. It is impossible to not be moved by their distress and the child once again becomes agitated. They try to wrest him from my arms, but he will not give himself to them. He struggles and breaks free, landing on his knees on the ground, his body and movements imitating those of a moon-drunk hound, a mountain wolf—his eyes and face searching the beams and beyond for light, for the Lord, but his useless mouth can only bark piteous coughs and snarls.

A voice commands, in Syrian, 'Stop! Are you not a man?' It is one of the leaders of the Judeans, the brother Adam who had vouched for the courage of the boy. He storms into the mob, pushing aside the women, oblivious to propriety or law.

The child, still on all fours, falls silent before his older cousin. Adam picks him up by the shoulders as one might a newly born cur, ignoring the boy's gargled whimpers. Adam inspects the damage done to him. He then clasps him in his arms, says quietly to the boy, 'Let us go.'

This, finally, gives me voice. 'Where are you taking him?'

The man will not face me. He keeps his tears hidden. 'He is ours.'

I will not accept this. 'We are not divided,' I insist. 'We are one.'

Adam sighs deeply. Age is a shadow that has suddenly descended on him. When he does turn to me—the jaw clenched, the lines of pain etched—he is no longer a youth.

'Uncle Timos, I mean no disrespect,' he says, his voice dutiful now, 'but we are Jews from Galilee. I believe in our Saviour but I also believe in the traditions of our ancestors. Jacob is the son of my cousin Abraham, may he rest in eternal peace. I need to do my duty.'

The boy is limp in the man's arms. Life is seeping from him, the light is vanishing.

'Treat his fever,' I implore. 'Seek assistance from the brothers who have knowledge of medicine. I can go out into the city—there are men of learning I can ask.'

Adam is shaking his head. 'Uncle, I promise you, what I do I will do honourably.'

A hand is at my wrist. Able is beside me. 'Come, Timos,' he says gently, with profound kindness, 'you can hardly stand. Come with me.'

And then he does something that shocks with the cataclysm of a bolt from the sky. He brings his fingers to a point and, over the child but not touching him, he brings the fingers down the body, and then across over the chest of the boy. This is a rupture of the world; the veil is torn and there is a new dawning, whether terrifying or blessed we do not know. All we can understand is that something new has been born to this world. I have never before been witness to the sign he makes but I know it as if it had been there with me since my own awakening: he outlines the shape of the abominable gallows. He makes the shape of a cross over the boy.

I am stripped of speech, even of memory and vision, as Able leads me up the stairs to my cell, one arm draped across my stooping back. I am bathed in light, I am in the Spirit. When he sits me on the stool, when I can gather breath and speak, I clutch his hand, I kiss his wrist. I say, 'You have healed him.'

It is as if I know this already: the sign he made is the very manifestation of the Lord's promise. The boy will not die. The boy will live forever.

———

I pass the night not sleeping but in attendance to visitations. True, there is my brother in my bed, he mops my brow, squeezes water from a cloth to wet my cracked and feverish lips. There is only me there in my tiny room and my last brother, my Able. But we are not alone. Throughout the night my beloved brothers are on either side of me: my Paul whispering in one ear; and my life, my glory, my eternity, the Twin kissing the other. Each takes their turn to speak but they both speak in the one voice: 'The boy will be saved.'

The day banishes the night. Able is kissing my damp brow.

I grab at his hand. 'Did you see them? They were with us, our brothers Paul and Thomas.'

The old man attempts a smile. I let my grasp slip. He did not see them but I did. They were there. And I know that the child will be safe.

When we go downstairs, the women at their tasks will not look at me. I ask for Adam and I am told that he has left to look for work. I demand to know where Jacob is but no one answers. It is only when I threaten to climb to the very rafters to search for him, and do not care if I fall and crush my skull, that a young girl, a refugee maiden, draws back her veil.

'Uncle, the boy is dead.'

Doubt. I am swept up again into the maelstrom that is doubt. As I make sense of her words, I am close to a faint. A cold, wet hand is at my throat, covering my face, the voice of Satan is in my ear: 'What good is his crucifixion and reawakening—can he not even save one boy? Why do you follow such an impotent and useless god?'

Fate. I will drown in the unconquerable waves of fate. I am the first generation and the boy is the fourth. Between us lie three generations, three generations in which I have not spoken to my father, my mother, my brothers, my cousins, my kin. We are human and the gods play with us, for the gods despise us. It is not the voice of the Lord's adversary in my ear. It is the voice of my father.

Faith. I am pulled from the tempest by faith. I believe. I have sacrificed all and I have done this willingly. I will not let the furies come and tear my flesh. I will not and cannot and must not succumb to doubt. I have only found peace in love; I have only found strength when I love. When I held the ruined boy in my arms, a madman flying through the cruel and ignorant streets of Ephesus, I loved that boy as a father loves his child and in that love I am father and brother and son. I bring my fingers together, I recall the sign that Able's fingers followed. I press my lips, my heart, my right breast, my left. And as if God's words are written across my chest, I am freed of hesitancy and uncertainty.

I turn to the girl. 'Did Jacob die in the night?'

'Yes, uncle.' She places a hand over her breasts. 'May his soul rest in peace.'

'Where is he buried?'

I notice the hurried glance she throws to an older woman. 'I do not know, uncle.'

I have to use all my will not to hit her.

My brother steps forward. 'In the name of the Lord, sister,' says Able, 'in the name of the risen son, is it true that you don't know where the boy is buried?'

The girls slips to her knees, kisses the hand of my brother. 'Uncle, he is outside the walls. He is beyond the world.'

As soon as I hear these words I turn and march out of our house. Able calls for me to wait but I ignore him. I damn my feet, I curse them, demand from them speed and agility. I know the meaning of our sister's words; she's referring to an escarpment, a narrow and desolate field just outside the southern wall of the city, barren except for stones and weeds, bordered on one edge by the fallen rubble of the ancient wall that marked the first city built on this land, its name and its people lost to those of us who came after the heroic age. In this evil wasteland live beggers and villains, the diseased and the criminal. The destitute take shelter there at night, though reality makes a nonsense of that word: what shelter is possible in a snakepit of rape and murder? It is indeed beyond the world. It does not lie far from our dwelling, but it is accursed and I have forbidden our brethren to go there. One fine youth had his throat slit there; a sister's maidenhood was taken there even as she convulsed into death. We did not dare to report those crimes, knowing that the wicked inhabitants of that godless place would have no qualms about accusing us of atheism and treason. But this morning I have no fear. It is to this Hades I go.

Though it is only the dawn of the day, they have already begun to drink and to fornicate. A girl, still a child, her naked body without hair, is slurping from a small urn, the firewater spilling onto her lips and chin. A cheering gang of boys is encouraging her to drink more. A nearby crone watches and shouts insults and obscenities. She is mad and she is diseased; half of her face has rotted away. With one breath, she damns the boys to the cruellest of punishments in the underworld; and then in the next voice she gives licentious instruction on how best to pleasure the girl. As I storm past, she spits in my direction and calls out, 'You have to pay if you want a go.'

At the far end of the field is where our city throws its scraps, the waste that even the starving beggars don't want. I stop before a mound of raised earth. A piece of material is visible in the dirt and shit. I scrape away the soil and reveal a body bound in cloth. I dig further, maddened now myself. I unwind the flimsy, filthy shroud.

It is a boy's body. A dagger has sliced through artery and throat, so violently that the head is nearly severed. I lift a hand of the corpse. The fingers are stiff and unbending. It is Jacob. In the mud and slime, I kneel beside the boy and take him in my arms. Behind me, the world has fallen silent. Even the rapist boys, the insensible girl, the insane crone and the drunken lepers, even they are brought to stunned pause by my offence in touching the dead. I kiss and embrace the corpse.

'Brother, this is not wise.' Able is behind me. At the edge of the broken wall, Heracles keeps an anxious lookout.

'Those who have done this will pay.' My voice is iron. 'I will banish them from our fellowship.'

With great effort, his face puckered, Able squats before me. 'Timothy, you must find understanding. They are a proud and upright tribe. What was done to the boy cannot be undone on earth. He would not have wanted to live.'

I lash him with callous words. 'What was done to him was done to you, scores if not a hundred times. Why do *you* live?'

My envy and my jealousy, my arrogance and my pride, their

hollowness is now revealed. There is no anger in him—his face is peaceful and serene. I cannot wound him.

He answers gently. 'I was born a slave, brother, and I was born a Stranger. There was no one who granted me any honour and so I had no honour to lose. Only one man showed me respect and charity, and that was our beloved Paul. He came into my master's house and he spoke to me. He honoured me, because the resurrected son had entreated him to honour those who are shit like me.'

Even now, so many years later, his voice conveys the astonishment wrought by such a bizarre act of kindness.

And then his voice steels. 'But trust me, brother, there were many times before I heard the words of the Saviour that I wished I could bring a blade to my own throat.'

His hands dart, search, he dares pollution and touches the body still in my arms.

'Let him rest,' he counsels. 'He was a Jew and what those ungodly priests did to him nullifies the Lord's first commandment to his people. He could never be a father—he could never truly be a man now.'

His voice is hard, hard as flint. 'Trust me, he would not have wanted to live marked by such dishonour.'

That is true. There can be no denying that truth.

'I will not let him be buried here.'

That is also true and nor can that truth be denied. Those who abandoned him here thought him polluted and beyond the care of the Lord. They remain ignorant. When this boy rises again he will be the first among men.

I carry Jacob back, as I carried him home the day before.

I carry him on my own. The beggars and villains and diseased scatter from my path, sickened by my derangement, making pleas to their wicked gods, beating their chests and spitting as we pass.

The foul odours of that pestilent field still cling to us but I am no longer nauseous. The boy has been violated and disgraced, he has been castrated and defiled, but his scent is a miracle— the closest I have come to sensing the true Lord. The boy smells of the foaming sea and of the morning dew. Amidst all that is monstrous, this broken body cradled in my arms smells of the Lord.

———

A carriage is sent for and two deathworkers are called. I insist that only Able travel with me.

I urge the deathworkers to drive till there is no more land, till the sea beloved by my teacher stretches below us. It is placid tonight. A small path curves and drops sharply down to the beach. But just before the steepest descent there is a cliff face of granite, flecked with quartz so that reflected light of the stars and moon sparkle there. Throughout, a network of tunnels goes deep into the mountain. In there is where we lay Jacob's body to rest. We have brought him to the Lord.

And then I bathe and cleanse my old and dying skin in the waters of the blessed sea. The first sea, the Great Sea that my Lord, the God of the Israelites, created. And then my Lord wedded His son to the world and took ownership of every land and of every country and of every ocean. But this, this sea loved by the heroes, this first sea, this water remains the most beloved of our Lord.

I emerge naked from the gentle waves.

Able takes my hand. He places a fleece over my frail and shivering body.

'Let us go home,' he says.

———

On returning to Ephesus, Able announces his departure. It is right that he should do so. He has baptised the infants. His own family, his assembly, are waiting for him—they have been denied him too long.

Of course, I insist on our doing what is dutiful and right for our brother. The thanksgiving and the feast of love on the eve of his departure is long and generous; throughout our house, from the cellar to the yard, there is the sound of laughter and of cheer. As I have done so often, I remark on the loyalty and affection that my brother commands, from Ephesians and from Greeks, from the most lawful of Israelites and from the most superstitious of Strangers: they all make clear their care and devotion for him.

This must be our final parting—for what else can it be? We are ancients now, and destined never to see one another on this earth again. Knowing that, I feel wonder and joy that I experience no envy nor any sign of pride. I say all that I must to show our gratitude to our brother, and I perform all of the rites that I must to honour his work—even to bringing my joined fingers from brow to heart to breast, a sign that delights the brethren and which I know will be rehearsed and copied and taught to the very youngest amongst us. And I do not mind. I do not find reason to admonish the unlearned for their reliance on ritual, nor to berate the superstitious for their attachment to signs. If there are further generations to come before the advent of the promised kingdom, those who come after me will need to patiently teach and convince our growing family that we don't need any signs or symbols—no liturgy, no mysteries, no temples, no priests, no sacrifices, no pomp and no idols. All we need is the word of the Lord.

———

The day after Able's departure, I scribble notes to the two wisest and most learned of our assembly, Silver and Emmaus. She was born a slave and a Greek, and since being granted her freedom from her master in Galatia, she has come to a thorough and compassionate understanding of the meanings and deeds of our Saviour. He is a proud Jew, upright and grateful to walk in the light cast by the Redeemer. I hope that they will be the ones to steer our family, for in their dual care they unite what is best of my father's and of my mother's blood. But I can only make my suggestions. It is the strength and miracle of our fellowship that such a decision must be made in one voice. I farewell my brethren in the words of the resurrected son: *Let him who has ears hear.*

On the second morning I refuse breakfast. I have no need for food, for my body is sustained by light. I decide to begin a new letter. A sister knocks, dares to shift the screen, and I voice my disapproval of the interruption. The poor girl was only bringing me fresh water. I call her back, offer apology after apology, and drink even though I am liberated from thirst. When she leaves I kneel by my desk to commence my writing.

I struggle to find the words. I am stricken by all that I do not know and all that I cannot comprehend and all that I must make amends for. I am burning with shame, of my ignorance and my sins. Of my fear of death.

You have no courage, Timothy, I curse myself. I dip the nib of my pen in the dye, stretch out the reed parchment, and I write.

I write to my nephew. I haven't seen him since he was a plump-cheeked infant. What great joy had greeted his arrival. My brother and my father slaughtered three of the finest of our herd, shared the offering to the gods with all our neighbours. My mother sent prayers and offerings for a sacrifice to be made in the great Temple in Jerusalem. Knowing my attachment to her faith, she said to me, her youngest, 'One day soon you will know this joy, my Timos. One day you too will honour the greatest commandment of our Lord—to be a father.'

My tears fall as I write.

Is my nephew still alive? And how many others have been born to my brothers and sisters? My parents must be long dead and so probably are my brothers. In renouncing them and choosing the Saviour—choosing Paul and the road—I have not dared to return to my ancestral home. I did not have the courage to face their fury, their contempt, to acknowledge my shame.

Yet I write to my nephew. And if he is dead, then I hope he he might have a son to read my words. Surely one of his sons will have been educated and coddled, just as I was. This thought brings a wry and tender smile to my face. Maybe none will have been schooled. It may be that my wasted example warns against such an extravagant indulgence.

I wipe away my useless tears. I write. I confess my arrogance and admit to my disgrace. I am a son who failed to mourn his parents. I never married and I never fathered a child. For such transgressions my nephew owes me no loyalty and I assure him I understand this. I declare that I am without means and without property. Anything I had has long been distributed amongst my true family, my brethren in the holy breath of the Lord. What I do ask of him is that he conducts, in my name, the rights and the honours to my father that I should have performed myself. In the folly of zealous youth I refused to do so. But my abandonment of my father is a wound that has not healed and I implore my nephew to make whatever sacrifices and say whatever prayers are required for my father to finally pass over the river Styx and rest in peace.

Dear nephew, I who have no rights over you and no bond with you, I ask that you do this one thing in my name. To honour the blood of your grandfather.

How do I end such a letter? I stare at the scratches my pen has made. How to amend for the bitterness and sadness I have sown?

I take the pen and I write: *Peace.* I write that word and I hesitate. I was to write: *Peace, nephew.* But we are no longer kin. Instead I finish: *Peace, brother.*

I do not eat, I do not move from my desk. I have a gospel to finish: that of my teacher, my friend, my beloved, my Paul.

I write of his understanding that the meaning of our Saviour is to be found in his death. Morning becomes day and turns into night and I am no longer aware of the changes across the sky or of the light's depletion in my chamber. I write of how Paul was transfigured by light on the road to Damascus, of the heavy burden demanded by the Saviour, that the promise of eternal life requires a terrible renunciation: that to be with the Lord requires us to turn from all that binds us to this world. Be it blood, be it parents, be it kin, be it children, be it creed, be it emperor, be it law or be it our very ancestors—all these bonds must be broken if we are to be reborn as new. To the Lord and only to the Lord through the terrible sacrifice of the crucifixion. To understand the hatefulness and cruelty and injustice and arrogance of man, that is why the Lord entered human form and for the first time experienced all that is endured by His Creation. The Lord came to know fear and the terror of death, which is the source of all despair and all calamity. And the Lord had to bear witness to the depths of our misery, to the body broken and slaughtered on the gallows, the body humiliated and violated, flogged, disowned and defiled. And through that knowledge the Lord saw that there stood above justice a greater law: a law of love. In our faith it is not the gods that chain Prometheus to the rocks, it is man who leads the Lord to understand suffering.

I am no greater than the most despised and ill-treated of slaves. Paul came to understand this and in this understanding his blindness was lifted. He took his staff and prepared to journey to the ends of the world, to proclaim that if we do not have faith that the Lord truly knows our suffering, we cannot believe in a better world to come. And without this hope in a better world to come, then we are doomed to selfishness and greed and fear. Without faith there is no hope and without hope we cannot love our neighbour or love the stranger. Without faith and hope we cannot love.

This is the gospel of Paul.

I slump across the desk, I upset the ink, it flows onto my robe. My knees crack and cannot support me. On the cold wooden floor, I sleep.

I arise again to the third morning.

I do not eat, I do not let my sister bring in food.

I write. I write the gospel of my lover, my friend, the beloved disciple. I write the gospel of Thomas.

I write of his understanding that the meaning of our Saviour is to be found in his life. Of how he was born coarse and rough, born to labour and to work, but that the spark of truth was in him from childhood and he was apprenticed to the priests. Of how in youth that truth within him was tethered to hate, to his abhorrence of injustice, be it the injustice of Rome or the debauchery and hypocrisy of Israel's kings. Of how the fire of the Zealots was in him. But the truth is not only fire, it is also light. The Zealot pledges to justice but in the violence of that pledge he is stripped of compassion and understanding. In the Zealot's declaration against the world, he is also declaring against the beauty of the Lord's Creation. That beauty is found in the faces of those most stricken by poverty and disease, in the face of a prostitute and in the face of the thief. That beauty is found in the face of both Stranger and Israelite. And Yeshua, son of Joseph, became the Saviour when he was transfigured by this very comprehension: that to change the world is to alter nothing for the world has been changed again and again and always, after every alteration, suffering and poverty and slavery and hatred and war return. The kingdom to come cannot be wrought by man but is born of the Lord and that kingdom to come is here whenever we greet our violator with forgiveness and meet our foe with sympathy and submit to our enemy with acceptance. But we must not forget that the Saviour is not a god, the Saviour is a man and he understood the great exhaustion of feeling that comes with such love and the terrible sacrifice of such submission. To be a passer-by to affliction is the greatest burden demanded of us by the Lord. Jesus understood this as he suffered and died on the cross. There, his fury soared and he shouted, not with strength from the gods or from the worlds beyond, but the gathering and shrieking of living, grieving, human will: the Promethean scream, 'Father, Father, why are you demanding this of me? Why have you abandoned me?' But at the end, as his body slumped into death, he laughed. Jesus laughed. His beloved Twin attests to this. Because he had an understanding truer than death: that he was not greater than any other man. That the Saviour is no greater than man. When we reach that understanding, then the kingdom has come.

They are my final words to this gospel. *Jesus the Saviour, he laughed.*

And as I write these final words I laugh as well. I release an eruption of joy that I have not experienced since I was the young lad following my teacher Paul across Anatolia and Greece, or when I was rambling beside my beloved Thomas and he was showing me the shore of Galilee where he and his brothers fished. Is the path to the Lord to be found in the meaning of the Saviour's life or in the violence of his death? I am only a man and I will die without knowing this. It has taken the whole of my long life to come to this understanding, and the peace it brings makes me into a child again. I am a son of the Lord. I have known joy and I have known love. I will die in gratitude, and when I am raised, I will sing the song of thanksgiving to my God.

I roll up all that I have written in my days of blessed delirium, seal the scrolls with wax and place them in the cedar box that even after so many years still carries the perfume of my home. I leave them for my brothers and sisters to find. I take a small carnelian token out of the box. Latin letters are carved onto its surface. Andromenos, a nobleman of Ephesus, gave it after I'd baptised him. I had initially refused the gift but he had insisted I keep it, making an argument that still holds strength: 'You may require its protection, brother; there are many who condemn our faith.' I rub the dust away from the token and put it in the pocket sewn inside the sleeve of my tunic.

My work done, I kneel and close my eyes. There are no visions and no apparitions. I fall straight to sleep.

———

It is late in the morning when I awake. I dress quickly. At the doorway, as I push aside the curtain, I glance back at the room that has been home in my middle years and my old age. I offer a small prayer to the guardian spirits of my abode, who have looked after me so gently and so benevolently over those decades. I ask the Lord's indulgence for my childish whim in wanting to appease these phantoms. It is as if today it is my father's blood that is running through my veins.

The women are busy at their tasks and, though they greet me and offer blessings, they pay scant attention to me. I step outside to find that the wind is almost a gale. The streets are clogged with people and animals: beggars and merchants; dogs and fowl and goats; children playing as the wind sends swirls of sand around them.

I head towards the centre of our town and stop outside the gate to the bathhouse.

I have diligently avoided such Greek pleasures for years. It is past noon and there are no peasants, no workers and no merchants. Only the rich and idle use the pools at such an hour. I slip my fingers into the pocket of my tunic and present the chalcedony seal to the attendant at the door. He studies it, then bows and welcomes me.

It has been a long, long time since I have indulged in such luxury. Inside, the attendant shows me through to the ante-chamber of the baths and I suddenly feel faint.

'Are you alright, sir?' the attendant asks as he guides me to a stool.

'Yes. Thank you, brother.'

At that word—*brother*—he jumps back as if I have struck him. As well I might have. He has seen the Roman seal and taken me for a gentleman. He turns his face away from me now to hide his distress at my vulgarity.

Gather yourself, old man, I scold myself. I have chosen this day and its progression and now I must obey its intent.

'Boy,' I call out impatiently, 'bring me some water.'

He smiles now and, with another bow, dashes off to obey.

The water is scented with apple and the air in these chambers is suffused with frankincense. As I step into the first pool and sink beneath the surface, it is as if the water brings youth to my limbs and to my bones. I come up for air and flick my eyes open. There are only two other gentlemen reclining in the water. They pay me no attention. I too fall back and float. The ceiling above is the night sky as inferno, smooth bronze plates studded with flecks of lapis lazuli, and slivers of red crystal and gold-gilt stars. At the centre of this rounded canvas is a mural of a glorious long-limbed Narcissus gazing down at us, his handsome face aglow with adoration at his own image reflected back to him in the still waters of our pool; the lovelorn nymph Echo is a wisp of silver behind his shoulder. In this idyllic vault there is the constant trickling of water entering the bath, there is the incense, the glowing daphne leaves burning before the statue of Hera Ascendant. I am not ashamed to be naked before these idols. Today, I am indeed of my father's blood.

This luxury is a sin, I know it is, but I am hoping that the judgement of our Lord, our true Father and the only God, will be tempered by the forgiveness of our Redeemer, his anointed son. The demands of my faith are brutal but I have surrendered to them willingly. I was not present at the hour of my father's death. I hope that he did not die in suffering and pain but that he chose the hour of his leaving. Did my mother outlive him? Did my brothers bury her as a Jew? I do not know how my teacher Paul died, nor how my beloved Thomas ended his life. We never spoke of death except of it as a force to be vanquished.

I was wrong.

In this warm and luxuriant pool, I understand. We were not wrong about the truth: we will find abiding life in the Lord. But we were mistaken to think that our mortal eyes would bear witness to the end of the world. Like all men, I cannot imagine a world without myself in it. Even my teacher, the best of men, a man chosen by the Lord, could not escape that most human of failings: vainglory. He believed he would witness that cataclysm. The destruction of this world as prophesied and as demanded by truth and by justice; truly, it is coming. But only the Lord knows the hour of its commencement. I will not live to see that day. But this generation just born will see it, and if not this generation then the next or the one to come. But we must die to be reborn. As all men do, I must die.

The air of the bathhouse is thick with heat and the sound of fires spitting and crackling in the basement below. One of the bathhouse slaves asks if I would prefer the attentions of a boy or a maiden. It has been the longest time since I have felt the soft caress of a woman. I ask for a girl, and the slave they bring me is tall and startlingly pale; her skin is as marble and her shorn hair has the tint of burnished gold: she is a child of the savage western lands. She lays a linen sheet across the slab and I lie on my back upon it. Now I am blushing from the shame of my nakedness. She takes a tiny amphora, tips some liquid into her palms and begins massaging the oil into my neck and shoulders. Her gentle and thorough ministrations have me sighing as if I were an infant being pampered by a doting mother. Her hands knead my hollow chest, my belly, they press into the slack folds of my crotch.

Then her actions cease and I open my eyes. She is staring at my sex, at the mark of the ancient covenant. I shift her hand to my thighs and she continues her task. I am not seeking any more gratification than that which she is giving me: the delight all men of my long age must feel from the touch of youth.

She then takes an ivory comb and runs it across the thin hair on my scalp. She finds the lice, pulls them off the comb, and crushes them between her fingernails. Done, her hands move down to my crotch. Carefully parting the sparse grey tufts cradling my sex and testes, she plucks out the lice and crushes them.

She asks me to turn over and her hands whip across my back, my buttocks, down the other side of my weary limbs. With my eyes closed, I see a vision of myself. It must be the heat and steam of the chamber, the rich perfume of the incense: I am transported and I am no longer this old man but I am returned to my birthplace of Lystra. I am seated at the doorway of my ancestral home and in the yard my children are feasting, for it is the end of harvest and my wife who has grown fat is smiling at me as she offers me bread. I can smell the yeasty pungence of the freshly baked loaf and I can hear the sounds of my grandchildren and I can see our bondsgirl standing at attention at the end of the table and in the field beyond is our bondsman, he too is a beautiful youth, and I know that I have possessed him as I have possessed her, have lost myself over countless nights in the glory of their bodies and in the tenderness of their kisses, and I know that this is a life that would have been mine if I had followed my father and I had not received the Lord. And I know that if it were only this world that was our due, then all of this pleasure and duty, all of this husbandry and mastery, all of this that is desired by men, would have been satisfaction enough. But I clench my eyes shut more tightly and the house of my father has fallen to ruin and the fields are overrun with wildflowers and instead of the sound of children there is only the desolate shriek of the wind and all that was mine is gone, dead and vanished. And beautiful as this first vision was, I know it cannot satisfy. I wanted to understand what accrues to us, the advantage and the cost, to have been created in the image of our Lord.

A voice calls through the chambers of the bathhouse: 'I was not wrong!'

The girl, startled, recoils from my shouting.

I grab the edge of the cloth, raise myself, and cover my nakedness. I thank the girl, then wash off the oil in the chilled water of the cleansing tub. An attendant returns my garments and dresses me. I thank him but as I am about to take my leave he glares at me. I have not paid obeisance to the seated idol at the door of the baths. These children have been gracious to me. I take Andromenos's gift and leave it at the feet of the garish bronze idol. But as I do I speak in my mother's ancient tongue, in the Lord's first language. I utter the words that my beloved Paul taught me.

'You are formed by man and as man returns to dust and oblivion, so will you; for you are nothing but the shadow of death.'

I turn and bow to the young slave. He returns my bow; he returns it three times.

———

At the eastern gate of the city, I look back to my adopted home. The wind still chops and rushes and the fall of dust is as a mist; the city is a hive of movement, of soldiers and slaves, taxmen and labourers, priests and beggars, shopkeepers and prostitutes. Even under a dull sky, the grandeur of Ephesus is thrilling. The gleaming marble temples of the acropolis are an island that floats serene over the unending chaos of the human city. The painted head of the goddess, adorned with garlands, looks up to her brother and husband, the sun.

The fading twilight illuminates the ravaged face of the hilltop we call Despair. As I climb the steep rise, I grab at shrubs and the limbs of trees to keep me steady. I find the first ledge, pause to regain breath and strength, and I enter the cave. The smell has the force of a blow, the reek of the abandoned infants. Ants swarm over the body of a recently left child; maggots are feasting. Vile waters rise to my mouth and run down my chin.

I tear at my tunic, wrap the cloth tight around my nose and mouth, but even so the stink of death and rot burns my eyes. As I venture further into the cavern I hear the susurration of the serpents and I steel my fear. My feet crush the tiny bones that form a carpet in this lair. I find a shelf, push aside the bundle left there. The sheet falls away and the skeleton of an infant is revealed. Death: this world cannot conquer death. I take a seat, and as I do I feel the weight of a serpent gliding across my foot. But I am beyond fear, just as I am beyond death.

I don't know how long I sit in my own silence. Long enough that when I come to after my prayers—the recitation of all the words of the Saviour that my beloved Thomas taught to me, all the instructions and preparations for the world to come that my teacher, my Paul, gave to me—when I open my eyes again the dark is absolute and the cold has me shivering. I am in night.

Hidden in the pocket I have sewn to my tunic I take out the blade. I ask the Lord's forgiveness. My mother's blood declares against the sin I am about to commit. But I turn away from the justice of her unyielding God and trust in the revelation that the Lord's son gave us through his death and his resurrection: I ask to be forgiven.

I bring the blade twice across one wrist, slicing through flesh and sinew, and then I do the same to the other. There is pain, stinging but brief. With the outpouring of my blood, there is balm and there is composure. I slide to the ground, bones scattering and breaking as I drop.

Lord, I am tired. I have done your bidding for three generations and I am exhausted by this gift of life. Forgive me my evil doing, the perversity of my lusts and covetousness, my envy and my pride. This death I am undertaking, I do so to privilege that which is best in my father's tribe, the understanding that man is nothing without dignity and self-honour, and that is why I choose this end. This blood that now flows out of me is his. But it is also my mother's, and from her tribe I have been granted the knowledge of compassion and of justice. From her tribe arose the Redeemer who will guide my passage in the world to come. From her tribe I learned that I am brother to the lowest of men, and that in poverty and in renunciation there is glory.

Where was I happiest, Lord? In a prison cell in Antioch, lying next to my brother Paul, him cradling me in his arms and imparting through his kisses the knowledge of truth and fidelity, of faith and hope. For without hope there is only despair: and this world I am leaving, it moans with the suffering of helplessness which is true misery. Even in a prison cell, my body marked with lashes and wounds, stripped of clothes and lying there in excrement and filth, I knew and was in love. In abjection I still had hope—and that is why our faith grows even into the fourth generation. We are granted hope: slave and master, maiden and youth, woman and man; we are not defined by our poverty and lack but are fortified and strengthened by the bond of faith which is greater than blood and land and tradition and which is a communion that will envelop the earth and unite us in the world that is coming. Truly, it is coming.

In faith, in knowing faith and having lived in this hope, we are more fortunate than the richest men and the most powerful kings. In prayer, we receive a solace that is unknown to the most privileged. I expire in joy, my Lord. I have lived in poverty and hunger and in suffering, but I count myself amongst the most blessed of men.

I don't know if my eyes are open or closed, if it is night or morning. I am no longer cold. I am loved. Here in this cave, surrounded by proof of the desolation of the world when it knows not or denies or refutes God, in this cave I am loved. I leave the world held in love. When next I see, when next I rise, I know that I will awaken to love.

Saul IV

57 ANNO DOMINI

'If the world hates you, know that it has hated me before it hated you. If you were of the world, the world would love its own; but because you are not of the world, but I chose you out of the world, therefore the world hates you.'

—The Gospel of John

The world has contracted to the limits of his prison walls, to the rough, chafing straw that is his bedding and to the announcement of dawn and nightfall by his guards. His world has become smaller but he is content. He has endured greater deprivations in other prisons. His present gaolers are brutish but not cruel and though the food is meagre it is all that he requires. He is accompanied to his toilet once in the morning and once in the afternoon, and those mean sojourns are his only chance to see the sun. Every noon, he is visited by Gabriel, who continues to petition the governor to clear his extradition to the First City—to Rome.

A fury burns in Jerusalem, a wrath so untameable that it threatens to engulf kingdoms and empires. No one is safe. Saul had returned to the Sacred City, as always relieved and grateful to find himself in the city of his Lord; and as always anxious and suspicious of the reception that awaited him there.

Even on that first day, he had witnessed how the Temple's priests were now shadowed on the streets by bodyguards, so fearful were they of the Zealot's dagger. In those first few hours he had been told about Ethan, whom Saul remembers as the arrogant and unfriendly young lad who would treat him with such contempt when paying him for his work in hunting the followers of Yeshua. Ethan's throat had been slashed by a young rebel furious that the priest was being employed by the royal house. The assassin had shouted, 'Roman dog,' as he hacked at the priest.

Rage burned everywhere. It was only on turning into the narrow lane to James's house that Saul started, realising that he had not crossed the path of one rich man on the way—the noble and wealthy now also feared Jerusalem's streets. 'Roman dogs!' was the favoured term of abuse. As he entered James's house hand in hand with Timos, Saul understood that even his own brethren now lived in fear. Their thanksgiving that first night was hushed, their proclamations muted so that their neighbours wouldn't hear. 'Be careful, Saul,' James had warned him. 'We are not safe.' But Saul could not resolve to silence, it was an impossibility. After all that he'd forsaken and all that he'd been granted in the light of his new conviction, to be silent would be a betrayal of it all.

To return to Jerusalem, he and Timothy had travelled from Ephesus through the mountains of Anatolia down to Antioch, where they had been taken to the forlorn and desolate mountain-side on which the Strangers left their unwanted infants. There they had kneeled in the cave where Lydia was buried, and prayed for her soul. She had been the first Stranger he had brought to the Lord; how he had wept at the sacrifice she'd made for her faith, for her daughter. 'You will be first, Lydia,' he had vowed.

'When we see each other again, you will be greater than I, greater than Timothy, greater than us all. You will be first.' They had trekked the desert valleys and traversed the severe peaks of the east, in mourning for a friend now gone, but also in constant joy because of their certainty of an eternal reconciliation with her. The light had bestowed on him that gift of joy, expressed daily in singing and laughing and sleeping on rough rocks and going hungry and ravenously scoffing wild berries and finding pools and streams to wash in. How glad his heart had been on the road; what joy to be sharing it with his Timothy.

How then can Saul be silent? Not that he was a fool—he hadn't been reckless. But he had been drunk, an old weakness of his, the wine, so rare now and therefore so welcome. He and Timothy had settled in a tavern and there no one had spoken of dogs, Roman or Jewish—Zealots and rebels had no time for taverns. They hadn't taken foolish risks, they had been laughing and singing, as if the small dark room they were in was an extension of the glorious road. They had been singing and laughing—what harm could that possibly have done to the world? Saul had no memory of getting back to James's house, no recollection of crashing into bed, no sense of his arms folding around his Timos—no memory at all. And then he'd felt the violent shaking, his nephew's face above him, dousing them both with water, Gabriel urging: 'Wake up, Uncle, they are coming for you.'

Then everything had been a blur: James giving them clothes, a sister preparing food for their journey, being taken into the cold night, his throat parched, his stomach roaring, making their way through the deserted streets, bribing the Roman sentry to let them pass. Still feeling drunk, stumbling through valley and up mountain, to their sister Agatha and their brother Benjamin, their mules tethered and waiting, of their ride through bitter night into cold morning and warm day, his head pounding and his heart leaping, following the sun's arc along mountain ridge and desert plain, through another night and into a new day, Gabriel with them, Timothy riding beside him, until they reached the summit of a small hillock and there before them lay the impossible breadth of Creation's first ocean. The sea breeze kissed their burnt faces. There before them lay Caesarea, the Stranger's city. When they reached the gates, Gabriel gave him over to the Roman guards, vouching that his uncle was a Roman citizen—'Roman dog, Roman dog!'—and that a fair trial was not possible in Jerusalem and pledging his own freedom as surety if his uncle were to escape.

It wasn't until a bored and weak-chinned young Roman soldier escorted them to the giant stone walls of the prison that Saul had fallen on his knees and given in to tears, knowing what his nephew had risked in bringing him there. Another bribe had again been paid. Out of the tithes that he and Timothy had brought from Ephesus and Antioch? Saul had been too ashamed to ask. And finally he had heard the nature of his crime. Sedition. Saul had proclaimed that Yeshua was king, anointed so by the Lord—a crime to Rome and a blasphemy in Jerusalem. He had wept and raged trying to explain: 'In the kingdom to come, in the Kingdom to *come*,' he'd insisted—but Timothy had kneeled and whispered: 'They do not understand your meaning.' And they hadn't—the Roman guards had thrown him into his cell. Timothy, ever loyal, ever loving, had said he would not leave him, and Gabriel had declared that he would never forsake their blood bond.

As always, reflecting on his nephew's kindness, deep in his subterranean cell with no day and no night, Saul's tears well again and will not cease. I am blessed, he thinks. Truly, the Lord is good.

Here, in the Stranger's capital in Judea, in this city built to Rome and named for the eternal emperor, he is safe.

———

He hears a rustling, the sound of a body shifting on the straw.

His eyes have become attuned to the black void of the cell. The other man's form is faintly discernible as a shape denoted by thin, phosphorous light—but was that his mind seeing things? Saul listens to the harsh rasp of the man's breathing; a sickness is there, clinging to the man's lungs.

'Are you awake?'

The form does not answer. But the breathing stops, as though in fear at Saul's question. Then an onslaught of coughing racks the night. Carefully, finding his balance in the darkness, Saul rises and makes his way to the man's bed. His fingers quickly search the dirt floor, brushing aside the rat droppings that litter their cell. Saul finds the cup—blessedly there is still water in it—and groping first chest then neck, finds the man's lips and brings the cup to them. The man's tongue laps at the water, makes a last feeble cough, and slumps back on his bedding.

'Thank you, brother.'

At first, Saul had kept faithful to the vow he'd made to the brethren in Jerusalem and had not spoken to the man. 'He is no longer our brother,' James had told him in a terrible rage. 'No longer my brother in blood, but he is also not brother of our fellowship. He is more repugnant to us now than the most cursed and ignorant of Strangers.' Saul and the others had agreed to uphold the condemnation. The man was to be disowned.

On the shocking realisation that he was to share a cell with the pariah, Saul determinedly ignored the man and pretended he wasn't there. Though the span of their cell was barely five paces, they had wordlessly divided it into two, each taking their allotted half for prayers and ablutions, for sleep and for meals. The outcast had initially attempted to initiate conversation, pleading for charity, listing their mutual amities and their shared persecutions, but Saul had strictly honoured his vow. Soon, the man bowed to his wishes and succumbed to the inexorable silence. Saul had made his intent clear: no reconciliation, no fellowship, no communication was possible with a soul so corrupted and damned.

Then the rat had bitten Saul. The vermin overran the prison and their scuttling and gnawing competed with the muted steps of their guards above and the scraping of the gaolhouse doors opening and closing. The rat must have been burrowing in the straw bed when Saul's foot had moved against it in his sleep. He had awoken with a scream, the rat's razor-sharp teeth sinking deep into his heel. The pain had been immediately unbearable, as if burning needles had been thrust into his flesh.

The condemned man had woken and called out; it had been a shock to hear that voice, deep and hoarse, that resonant blunt burr, a voice of the earth and of unstinting toil. With his peasant's wisdom, the man had pissed into his chamber-pot and sluiced Saul's foot with the urine. He'd then cleaned the wound with the remains of the water, and had then put his mouth over the punctures to suck out the poison, spitting it out and again rinsing the wound in urine. A delirium had overtaken Saul and he had felt himself slipping in and out of the world, beset by dreams and visions, awakening to the agony of the pain flaring in his foot. Through all of it, the man had not once relinquished his hold on Saul. With the arrival of the guard, who always carried a lantern—had he himself called out for wine to dull the torment or had the apostate persuaded their gaoler to bring it?—his fellow prisoner had poured the intoxicant down Saul's throat. And when Saul was close to stupefaction, the man had taken the flame and held it against Saul's foot. He had screamed, and then came the bliss of oblivion. When he had awoken, the blasphemer was still cradling him; a strip of cloth torn from the man's ragged tunic was tied around the wound.

Saul had made a promise with his brethren in Jerusalem, had sworn a vow to banish the condemned man from the Lord and from their faith and family and from their way and from the world. 'He is he who does not exist. He has no name and his life is worth less than death'—that had been their shared oath. But on coming to, the pain now little more than an irritating throbbing, Saul could only feel gratitude to the man and his kindness. And his heart could not stay closed.

'Thank you, Thomas.'

The man had been about to lean forward to kiss Saul, but had drawn back realising the iniquity of his apostate's touch. But now that Saul, in his fever, had broken his pledge to silence, dialogue was possible between them.

He dips his hands into the now-empty cup, his fingers touching the chalky ceramic bottom, where some moisture remains. He brings his fingers to Thomas's lips and places the drops of water on them.

'Thank you, brother.'

Saul binds his heart again. 'We are not brothers.'

He returns to his bed, his back to the fellow. He kneels, then prostrates himself to the invisible Lord, making prayers and thanksgiving. From the next bed comes another violent racking, the wretched clearing of the lungs, the sound raw and ugly, the splat of phlegm on the dirt. Then barely discernible murmuring; the other man is also praying. They pray together but apart, as if now they belong not only to separate sects but even to separate gods; they pray till they hear the bolt being wrenched from the lock, till they see the flickering lamplight.

'Get up,' the guard orders.

The other man continues to pray on his knees. Saul rises, wincing and rubbing where the straw has become embedded in his palms. He takes his chamber-pot and bows before the guard. But the guard is looking at the man at prayer.

'Hey,' the guard calls out again, 'you too—get off your fucking knees.'

Saul and Thomas glance warily at each other. Since they have shared a cell, the protocol has always been the same. Saul, who is younger but looks the elder, is the first to be taken to throw out his waste and to glimpse some sun. Then the guard returns for Thomas. So why is he demanding that Thomas rise now? Saul's blood chills. Are they being taken for execution? He finds his feet are frozen, that he has lost the ability to command his limbs. As ink disperses when spilled in water, so the panic flares. He can't move, he can't speak and a shadow descends on his vision. This is indeed death calling. He will fall, his bowels will release.

Until a hand is placed against his back.

'Careful, scholar.' Thomas has taken his weight.

He won't allow himself to fear death more than Thomas, he won't be bested by someone who denies the resurrection of the Saviour, who is possessed by demons that have bored into his heart and into his head—for how else could anyone account for the illiterate fool's wrong claims? That the kingdom has come? What absurdity. That the kingdom is this *shithole*? That this fallen and brutal world was the Lord's intended Creation? It is an abomination beyond abomination.

Saul must not show fear. Rage is stronger than terror. He roars, 'Do not touch me!'

Separately, apart, they follow the guard.

They are led past the cells down a corridor of the prison, and then ordered to climb rickety, dangerous ladders; their step is painstaking and careful. They are led to the first antechamber. That too is dark, but this time the guard doesn't herd them in their usual direction. Instead they are led into a second antechamber. Stooping under the low ceiling, they emerge into an unfamiliar room and are blinded by the light of the sun, harsh and terrible. Saul covers his eyes in order to block the glare and regain his balance. He can smell the sweet exhilarating scent of wild fennel. He warily opens his eyes to see a profusion of life: plants bloom in pots studded across the light-coloured wall, and there is a blaze of wild poppies growing among the colonnades, their vermilion colour so intense that it too sears his vision. Red—how long has it been since he's seen the colour red? Behind him, Thomas must be experiencing the same awe, for his hands are skimming the flowers until the guard barks out another order and takes them through an arch into the next room.

Both prisoners fall to their knees. They have walked into the most intense of deliriums. They are assailed by colour, sensation, the whorls and rapid shifts of motion; it is as if the world is spinning. Saul has to close his eyes tight, to bring them to pain by that squeezing, in order to escape the ferocity on the walls and gain peace in the blackness. He hears nothing but his breath, and only guided by its gradual slowing, by the calming of the clamour of his heart, does he dare to open his eyes once again.

This must be how the world looks to a newborn infant.

The chamber is flooded with light that streams from an opening in the ceiling. A fountain, a statue of Hermes, stands majestically in a pool, one hand on his bow and the other hand, palm open, lifted in honour to the sun. Spread over the four walls, across the ceiling and along the tiled floor is the demon universe of the Strangers. The kneeling prisoners are looking straight into a massive depiction of Apollo, the sun god, raging from his chariot and rampant stallions. The cloak and tunic of the Strangers' god glistens with gold leaf; from his hair sunbeams shine up to the heavens in alternating flashes of silver and gold. The god's left hand holds the reins of his horses but the other hand reaches across the wall—across mosaics of polished amethyst, of crushed cerulean-inked stone, of agate and amber—to where the First Amongst Men, the first of the emperors, the revered and feared and adored conqueror, the great Augustus reclines naked, holding a jewelled staff and wearing a shimmering crown atop his noble head. The false goddess Roma, shrouded as a priestess, stands above him, her hands open in supplication and adoration. Above the mortal emperor made god and the goddess of the city two Latin words are inscribed into the wall. *Divi Filius*: The Son of God.

This despicable and most absurd of all the Strangers' lies returns Saul to himself and to the truth of his faith and to the righteousness of the Lord. He has seen this falsehood proclaimed from the most eastern reaches of Syria, through the breadth of Anatolia and within the very heart of the Hellenic lands. He is not moved nor cowed nor fearful. He is safe in the nobility of his truth. There is the Lord. There is only the Lord. There is nothing above or approximate to the Lord. He knows truth and the world sees only deception.

The guards order that the prisoners prostrate themselves facing the entrance and touching their brows to the stone floor. Saul and Thomas obey; and then the guards too salute and kneel.

Saul hears approaching footsteps but doesn't dare look up until a voice, light and gentle as a morning songbird, commands them to rise. Even so, he is careful to keep one knee on the ground. Before them is a lady of the highest caste, evidenced by her artfully arranged plaited coiffure, the nobility of her stance, and the cloak of Phoenician purple covering her slender frame.

She looks first at Saul, then at the other. They both lower their gaze.

'Which one of you is Thomas, son of Joseph?' she asks. 'Which one of you is the twin of the Saviour?'

Thomas is silent.

'He is, my lady. But he doesn't speak Greek.' As he answers, Saul's eyes stay resolutely fixed on the tiled floor.

'Rise, sir,' she commands him. 'I am the Lady Drusilla and I welcome you.'

For the first time he looks into her eyes. They are peaceful, unblinking, but he senses a piercing sadness within their depths.

'And you are Paul, the great teacher?'

He smiles, lowers his eyes once more. 'I am Paul of Tarsus. But I am not great. It is the Lord who is great, as is His chosen Redeemer.' He hesitates. Then submits. He will give the anointed son the Greek name. 'Jesus the Saviour.'

He senses that he is under careful scrutiny. He is aware of the disgrace of his appearance, that he is before her unwashed and ungroomed.

She calls out to the guards, not looking at them as she does so: authoritative, dismissive. 'Leave us.'

The two young guards are uncertain, afraid of offending her but also of being in danger of abandoning their duty.

She is cold. 'I will not repeat my command. Your lord, the governor, is aware that I wish to speak to these prisoners in private. I have my husband's consent.'

At these words, the boys beat their chests, bow and retreat, walking backwards, still bowing.

The lady walks across the chamber and sits on a marble bench against the wall. She carefully folds the drapes of her robes over her ankles and feet. She beckons the men over. They stand before her and Saul is reminded of schoolboys nervously approaching a tutor. He almost laughs.

'Teacher,' she says, 'you have seen the Saviour?'

'I have.'

She looks at the other man. 'And does he look like his twin?'

Saul shakes his head. 'No, my lady, he is light.'

Does she have knowledge of their ancient faith? Of how the presence of the Lord burned Moses the Lawgiver's face? She lives in Judea but Saul is aware that this newly raised city faces west and breathes the winds coming off the Great Sea—belongs to Greece and to Rome, not to Israel.

Her brow has creased at his words. They are not to her liking. Instead, she turns to the other man. 'Do you resemble your twin?'

And quickly, without shifting her gaze, she demands of Saul, 'You will translate for me.'

He must look at the man, he must do as he is asked. He turns to Thomas and speaks in Syrian. 'She asks if you resemble your twin, if you are of similar countenance and shape to the Saviour.'

The man's first response surprises both Saul and the lady. He lets out a great burst of laughter. And again is racked by a bout of coughing. He sweeps the back of his hand across his mouth, and wipes it on the front of his ragged tunic.

He turns to Saul. 'I will answer, brother, but first you will give me my name.'

Saul is furious. The obstinate goat knows that it is forbidden for Saul to speak his name.

Saul glances at the lady. Her frown has deepened, her suspicions raised by their conversation.

Saul turns to the man. Is it indeed a resemblance to light that he sees? Or is it that, despite the old man's tough skin and silver-flecked hair, in the dark, challenging eyes looking straight at him out of that determined face, he sees a likeness to that young girl who'd declared so long before: 'If you are without sin, then cast your stone'?

Pride and envy; they are Saul's great burdens. With humble grace and gratitude he asks, 'Thomas, do you resemble your twin?'

Thomas raises his hand, as if examining it in the stark morning sunlight. 'Tell her that my hands are larger and rougher. That my nose is broad and his is fine. But yes, we are unmistakably brothers.'

Saul is about to speak when Thomas interrupts him.

'I am a peasant and he was a teacher. Our different work has made of us different men. If he were standing next to me she would know him immediately. By his light.'

'They are brothers,' Saul explains to the lady, 'but this man before you is rougher and of the land. Our Saviour is a teacher and he is bathed in light. It is the light, the breath of the Lord that matters, not his human form.'

Her next movement stuns them. She drops from the bench and wraps her arms around Thomas's feet. Now Saul knows why she banished the guards. Such abandonment and shamelessness can only be considered madness.

'He was raised from the dead. That is what they say. Is that the truth?'

'Yes,' Saul answers, 'that is the great and singular truth.'

Her hands have raised the mud-stained hem of Thomas's smock and she is rubbing her face in the filthy rag. She does not care; she kisses it, speaking as she does so, but her words are muffled by the material.

As if aware of her recklessness, she lets go of the man's feet. But she stays kneeling on the stone.

'Ask him. I want to hear it from him. Did he see his brother resurrected? Did he see him die nailed to the gallows and then did he see him rise from his grave?'

He cannot look at Thomas. Saul speaks as if into a void. 'She asks if Yeshua was resurrected. She asks if you were witness to this great reawakening.'

At this, Thomas falls to a crouch before her and, risking great punishment, he touches her face. She doesn't recoil. He holds her gaze.

'Tell her, brother, that the rising from death is not what matters. It's his teachings that matter. There are brothers that claim they saw him resurrected. I have not.'

He turns his face to Saul now, and though there is exultation, Saul also sees the greater anguish.

'But those who say they saw him rise did not see him die. They fled. I was there and I watched him die. And his suffering brought the Spirit into the world. That I can swear. Tell her that, Saul.'

Saul swallows, firms his resolve. This world, this evil world, is not enough. He has staked his faith to a greater truth.

'My lady,' he answers, 'he says that Jesus the Saviour suffered and died on the crucifix and then was awoken on the third day. In body and in spirit. He attests to this. We all attest to this.'

He senses the perturbations of the man next to him, the tensing of his body. Saul has to be careful to convince the matron before him of their truth: it is her husband who holds their lives in his hands. Or is Thomas wincing because he has heard that dreadful Greek word that he must know by now, that obscene word now made sacred: *crucifixion*?

The lady is breathing heavily but her eyes are sharp. The meditation she clearly is drawing from his words keeps Saul silent.

Finally, she nods, as if having fully comprehended his words.

'I have three sons. If I immerse them in water as it is said your cult insists on, will they live forever?'

Saul's heart is thrilled. They are bringing the world to the Lord. 'Yes,' he answers gladly, his eyes, his mouth, his very form, smiling, 'they will indeed be with the Lord in eternity.'

'Will he do this for me?'

Saul's calm is upturned and the spark of jealousy—that tinder that ignites another sin, pride—burns within his chest. It is unworthy.

He turns to Thomas. 'She wishes you to baptise her sons.'

'Are they of age?'

He translates this to the lady. She nods again.

'Then I will do so,' Thomas replies.

The Lady Drusilla carefully, elegantly, rises to her feet. Saul fights the desire to help her. She has touched Thomas but he cannot assume such liberty, cannot risk anger by laying hands upon her.

'I have lost a son, my beautiful boy, my Julius.'

She speaks to Thomas, as if the strength of her emotion will be enough for him to understand her words. 'If we are initiated into your cult,' she continues, her eyes filling with tears, 'will he too find salvation? Will he too be—' she pauses, struggles to release the strange and perplexing words '—resurrected?'

It is as if a fever has erupted, ruthless and all-consuming, taking Saul's strength. The immoral and godless murals have come alive, the false gods surging like waves. He knows that he is in rigor, the fever seeps from his mouth and he cannot speak. He feels arms around him. And then there is blackness.

Saul comes to, once again being held by Thomas. The walls are again solid. The lady is seated on the stone bench and is looking away from them, as if embarrassed by his loss of dignity and control.

One of the guards has returned with a goblet, the gold-leaf surface intricately sketched with images of satyrs and maidens. Ignoring the hideous relief, Saul drinks gratefully from the wine.

When he has emptied the cup, she dismisses the lad and points to the place beside her. 'You may sit.'

With profuse thanks and apologies, he sits beside her. She and Saul are both careful not to touch.

'Paul—' she says his name firmly, in Greek '—please answer my question. Will your god raise my child?'

His doubt reawakens. How can he be worthy of the burden his Saviour has placed upon him—of bringing Rome to Israel? Saul knows the law and the prophets, the traditions and the hopes of his people. He knows that this break in the world was inaugurated at Creation and it is the promise that a Son of Man who was nailed to wood would be awoken on the third day. And with this rupture, as in the previous miracle of the parting of the sea that led Israel from slavery to the Promised Land, the Strangers were now also being led to Israel. But the dead idolators are lost. They are only promised to death, outcasts of both the old covenants and the new. Saul cannot speak.

The lady has dared shame. She has grasped his hand. 'Ask him,' she pleads, her eyes on the uncomprehending Thomas. 'Ask him.'

And Saul is once more in the light—his doubt and fear have taken flight. He understands now why he has been bonded to this man, who was once the most beloved of disciples and is now the most accursed. Saul marvels again at the magnitude of the Lord's order, and the wisdom of His justice.

He turns to Thomas. 'She had a son, his name was Julius. He has died and she is desperate to know if he too will be raised in the kingdom to come.'

Thomas doesn't know scripture and he doesn't have learning. He has been driven first from family and then from home. All out of loyalty to a brother whose meaning, in his suffering and in his death and in his reawakening, Thomas is too clod-headed, too wild, too stubborn to comprehend and too doubting to believe. But this Thomas is beaming.

'Tell her that her son is already there,' he urges Saul. 'Tell her that our Lord is kind and loves the world. Tell her that our Lord is a shepherd who cares for every single one of His flock. Tell her that we are each and every one of us saviours if we proclaim this truth. Tell her that was the meaning of my twin's teachings.'

And Saul, translating, tells Thomas's truth and denies his own. 'Yes,' he says to the lady, 'he says that your son too will be awoken to the Lord.'

The lady is sobbing, on her knees, kissing first Thomas's and then Saul's feet. Her tears flow without end. But finally the tears stop. She is exhausted but unshackled—the sadness that he first saw in her eyes has taken flight.

'Thank you,' she says. 'I will guarantee your release.'

—

They are not returned to their prison cell. Instead, they are moved to an outdoor area where one of the guards, with bad grace, brings a cauldron of heated water, places it at their feet and gruffly orders them to wash. Saul and Thomas strip off their ragged and soiled tunics and greedily scoop the warm water over their bodies, washing away the grime, the filthy layers of crusted dirt and sweat, the husks of crushed lice and fleas. As Saul scrubs at his face he glances at the other man. He had once thought Thomas invincible, and indeed, for a long time, the Twin had seemed defiant of age; the power of his chest and his back had not weakened, the sturdiness of his jaw, the lion-like strength held within him had not depleted—it was said of him by the other apostles that he was so beloved by Yeshua that he would never grow old. But in the soul-crushing ever-darkness of the prison, old age had stealthily pursued him, and old age has won.

Saul has no idea for how many moons Thomas had been secluded in the cell before his arrival. And in the grim gloom of their gaol it is impossible to calculate the passing of time: their incarceration together feels like an age. No wonder the man's lungs burn and weaken. Such misery will be carved and written on a body. It is visible in the white clutches of hair over Thomas's chest and loins, in the sharp lines that scar his face. This, of course, would not be enough to weaken him. It is hunger that has been his most ruthless foe. The man's frame is pitifully slumped, his arms and limbs unbearably thin. Skin hangs loose over his bones. Saul knows that he must also appear more ravaged and older. But even so, such was Thomas's vitality that he feels a great and resounding pity for the man. The shadow of death covers him, even in the fierce sunlight where they stand.

Sensing Saul's eyes upon him, Thomas looks up from where he is washing his feet and he smiles.

Remembering the oath taken against this blasphemer, Saul forces his heart to harden. He looks away.

Clean, each dressed in goat-hair tunics, they sit again in the vast room in which the Lady Drusilla received them. This time Saul isn't disturbed by the paintings and friezes, the statues, the ornate decorations, the jewels and the gold. Cross-legged on the stone floor, he looks directly across at the naked form of the great and most respected of Caesars, the revered Augustus. He silently mouths the words of the prophets and in doing so begins to chuckle at the great foolishness of the Strangers. Assyria made its kings gods and Babylon made its kings gods and Persia made its kings gods and Greece made its kings gods and now they were all vanquished and gone, replaced by the Roman kings who believed themselves gods. And in that chuckle, in the breath between its emergence and its passing, a miracle occurs. A shadow falls across the wall, then another, and both intersect over the face of the Caesar as if to blind him. The shadows take the form of the Roman gallows, they make a giant cross against the wall, and all that was colour and sparkle is gone and all that remains is just the white of the light and the shadow of the cross.

In his elation, Saul dares to touch Thomas's knee, to draw the man's attention to the promise of the Lord written across the vainglory of the idols. Saul starts weeping at the immensity of what has just been given to him: as if he were Noah at the foot of the first rainbow or Abraham in the dazzling light of Mount Moriah. This gift, this grace, emboldens him and justifies everything—every shame, every rebuke, every insult and every curse, every lashing, every stoning and, even more powerfully, it assuages and vindicates his exile. He is too stunned to speak, but he insistently pushes Thomas's knee to make him see.

'What is it, scholar?'

With the other's words, the light dissipates and the painted faces and garish idols return. But though it lessens it is not gone for it cannot ever be extinguished. It is all that will be left when the world falls.

'Truly,' he answers Thomas, 'he is returning.'

The other man's breath is patient and long. 'He has come,' he says quietly.

And this time Saul is not angered by the man's mulishness. Again, as it was when they were stripped naked for their washing, in the tragic poverty of their flesh, he experiences only mercy for the other. This hollow world that Thomas believes in is the only world that he will know.

'Brother,' says Saul, 'I forgive you.'

There is no reply, only the deep, congested wheezing of the old man next to him. Thomas, cross-legged like Saul, has his palms open and is staring at them as if seeking revelation.

Thomas abruptly slaps both palms against the tiled floor. The booming echoes around the chamber; a swallow drinking at the fountain quivers at the sound and flees to the apex of the ceiling, searching and finding the light and disappearing towards the sun.

'We should be grandfathers.' Thomas's voice is hushed but the tone is low and rumbling, as if a great anger is being contained. 'We should be with our ageing wives, bouncing a grandchild on our laps. We should be proud of having lived in this world and having provided for our children and their children—that we have done everything in our power to bring good to this world.'

He turns and looks at Saul, and the haunting in his eyes makes Saul look away.

'What have we accomplished, brother?'

The peace and grace and forgiveness that Saul was feeling only a few moments before is seeping and vanishing, as wine leaks inexorably out of a punctured skin. He knows he has to try to bring this condemned man back to the light. This must also be part of the Lord's purpose. Why else have such bitter combatants been placed together? He must try.

'We are preparing for the kingdom to come. We are witnessing the birth of something greater than ourselves.' Saul hesitates, inhales, and forces the next words out. 'Do you know how much I hated your brother? I was glad to hunt down anyone who followed him. I didn't want a feeble saviour nailed to a cross.' And Saul finds himself whispering, and in doing so he recalls the ancient humiliation. 'I detested him,' he hisses. 'I wanted a hero, I wanted a leader, I wanted a saviour who would set us free!'

Thomas's face is implacable. With a jerk of his chin—is it scorn? curiosity?—he indicates that Saul should continue.

'Thomas, your brother appeared to me after his death. To teach me that he did indeed set us free. I cannot remake the world and I cannot renounce truth. You deny James, you deny Peter, you deny the Magdalena and John, you deny me.'

A surge of anger overwhelms Saul. He makes his hands fists not to submit to it.

'He loved you, you were his beloved disciple, the first to follow him. All I've heard is how much he loved you, Thomas. How can it be that the one he loved the most is the one who most doubts him?'

The man opposite him releases a moan of such agony it could shake the foundations of the earth. 'If what you speak is truth, then why doesn't he show himself to me? Why has he abandoned me?'

And this time it is Thomas who seems driven to convince Saul, it is Thomas on his knees, taking his companion's face between his rough hands, forcing Saul to look at him as he speaks, his words tumbling and rushing in agitation and purpose. 'You weren't there, Saul, I was—and you didn't know him as the arrogant prick who snubbed us because he was learned and we were still peasants and he was righteous and we were sinners.'

Softly, with a loving smile, Thomas slaps Saul's face. 'I wager you too, eh, that you too were a vain little shit? I can imagine your family got sick of *your* book reading, of your proselytising.'

Thomas has closed his eyes. Saul knows that he is conjuring the Saviour as a boy, shaping and rebuilding memory.

'I didn't care at all for his sanctimonious preaching. But my father and my mother, may they rest in eternal peace, they were alarmed when he returned from the priests and the teachers. They were scared he'd go over to the rebels, or to the Zealots.'

Thomas has his eyes closed, still under the enchantment of memory; but he too is aware enough to speak quietly now. They are in a Roman fortress, and as all conquered peoples say of the Romans, their walls have ears.

'Yeshua was full of talk, of the end of Rome and the rebirth of Israel. "The Saviour is coming, the Saviour is coming"—that's all we ever heard. My father ordered me to go with him, and our mother also begged me to look after him, to make sure he was protected. So I followed him—that's how I became the first disciple. I didn't believe a word of it. All during our long summers, Nazareth was a rank stench from the rotting of the crucified. From childhood I had witnessed what the Romans could do. I knew the words of our prophets didn't fucking scare them.'

With that obscenity, Thomas drops his hold of Saul.

'I followed him through Galilee. And he preached and some listened and a few joined us. He rattled off prophecies and commandments everywhere we went. He kept telling me, "I'm bringing the words of the Lord and of the judges and the prophets to our people, brother, that is my purpose."'

Thomas has his head back and is laughing. 'All bullshit. It was the road he really loved. It was being on the road and away from work and responsibility and family and village gossip.'

Thomas winks. 'Me too. I'd been working since I was a boy, I was happy to be travelling. You too, Saul, I know that you love the road, no matter what punishments it has brought you. That's what really unites us—we are a friendship of the road.'

Saul takes Thomas's hand. 'But you believe that he is the true Saviour; that you don't deny. When did you come to understand that?'

Thomas grips tight to the proffered hand, then releases it. His voice is a snarl. 'We were peasants, Saul, we didn't know anyone who owned slaves. It was on the road that Yeshua saw the evil that man can do to fellow man.' Thomas spits on the tiled floor. 'And it was on the road that he realised, Roman, Jewish, Samaritan, Arab, Greek, none of that mattered. It's how you treat your neighbour, the stranger, the exile—only that matters.'

But for Saul, this is no answer. 'When though?' urges Saul. 'When did you know he was the promised Saviour?'

Thomas turns to Saul and Saul is witness. To light. To Spirit. The man's eyes are the fire of the sun. 'You don't comprehend, do you, scholar? It doesn't matter. It doesn't matter if my twin is or isn't the Saviour.'

His hand is again at Saul's cheek, a smack meant to be playful, but delivered with some force. 'Maybe you're the Saviour, Saul? Maybe that's why Yeshua came to you?'

Saul pushes Thomas away, gritting his teeth in fury. 'I forsook everything, you wretch, I gave up everything. And yet you make a joke of your twin's meaning and teaching, of his suffering and death. You are worse than his friend who denounced him, you are even worse than the Romans who nailed him to the cross. You are his worst betrayer.'

Thomas's next words are equally hard, carrying a warning. 'Careful, Saul, you were not there.' Thomas raises his hands. 'These hands lifted his body off the gallows, Saul. These hands were wet and stinking from his blood and his spilling guts.'

The two old men, eyes unyielding, face each other. Saul sees it, the fall of Thomas's shoulders, a peace that scatters passion. Thomas reaches for Saul's cheek again, he strokes it tenderly.

'On our travels, Saul, on the road, that's where I understood. We were without work or family or coin, we had no property or children or belongings, and yet we were all happy. And we were generous and we were fulfilled. That's why I think Yeshua is my Saviour, Saul: with him we were in Eden. We were walking in the garden of the Lord.'

He turns to Saul, he grips Saul's hand once more, puts one arm around Saul's shoulders, drawing him in. 'That I saw, brother,' he whispers into Saul's ear. 'That I witnessed, that miracle occurred. I was in the beauty of the world, I knew it as the Lord knows it. The colours of it, friend, the creatures in it, the light within it, the sky that is endless and the sea that rolls to the end of Creation. I gave thanks for the friendship and the love and the sympathy contained within it. This world can be the kingdom, can't you see that?'

Even weakened, his strength is such that Saul knows this man could snap his neck if he wanted to. Saul marshals all his will, and shrugs Thomas's arm from his shoulders.

'How can this be the kingdom?' he asks incredulously. 'How can we live content in this world amidst such misery? To say that is to betray your brother again.'

Thomas is unshaken. 'Be as a passer-by to this world, Saul. You cannot undo Creation. That is what Yeshua realised and that is why the Zealots rejected him.'

Thomas bangs his fist on the stone, as if to break it. 'Underneath these damned tiles, below this vanity and wealth, there is earth. It dies in winter and is reborn in spring. That is the meaning of resurrection.'

The terror seizes and wrings Saul's heart; he fights for breath. Doubt, that many-headed demon, is inside him and is strangling his heart, which is love, and squeezing his lungs, which are hope, and crushing his head, which is faith.

Saul looks up at the brazen reliefs and paintings that adorn the walls: the false goddess and her lost daughter, six pomegranate seeds in the girl's hand that reaches out to the one the Strangers call the Mother; and behind her, dragging her daughter away, the god of the underworld. The unlearned, rooted to the earth, to the world: they cannot be broken away from those ties. Thomas is such a man and cannot be unshackled from those chains.

And Saul understands that this is why he is in this chamber and why he is with this tormented man. Doubt unclenches, loses its hold and falls away.

When he speaks, it is with severity. 'The kingdom is to come. Without that promise, not only your twin—his agony and suffering and violation and death—not only is his life without purpose, but so is the life of Israel.'

He must try once more to bring Thomas back to fellowship. 'This world is not enough, brother; we can't offer hope if this world is all there is. This world is beautiful, and yes, on my travels I too have been in the garden. But the world is not just. My Lord cannot be a bystander to a perverted Creation. This world is not enough.'

Saul hesitates, begs his Lord for guidance. 'Don't you want to see your twin again?' he asks finally. 'You must want that.'

The great light that shone in the Twin's eyes has been cupped and extinguished. They well with tears. 'My twin is dead. I buried him. I was the one who washed the hands and feet that had been pierced by nails. I was the one who wrapped him in his shroud and who placed him in his pariah's tomb. My brother is dead. But his words live.'

Thomas's body is upright, he calls on strength and he summons certainty. Yet all *is* false, as perishable as the forms and colours of the idols that surround them. Saul sees that Thomas's face is not skin or flesh but it has the contours and shape and horror of the skull. This is what doubt is: the face of death—that is its only promise.

And with that knowledge his blood flows and he can exhale and his head is released from the grip of torment.

Saul sits back on the tiled floor. 'You are lost, brother. That is why the Saviour does not come to you. You doubt and so all you have is this world. May it be enough for you.'

And with that he turns his back to Thomas. To combat doubt he must make his heart stone. Saul turns his back on the man's weeping.

———

Blessedly, not long after, the guards bring with them his nephew Gabriel and his beloved Timos. How faithful, how loving and how true they have been. How many days and nights have they spent petitioning for Saul's release? But as his nephew's arms wrap around him, as their tears fall on each other's shoulders, Saul perceives that Timothy has rushed to the other man, is clutching Thomas as though he will never release him. That ferocious love, that adoration fired by blood and heat as much as by faith and loyalty, how it pains Saul.

Gabriel releases his uncle and shudders at the sight of the naked and blasphemous idols that adorn the walls. Timothy, raised as a Greek, does not experience shock at such immorality. But Gabriel only knows Judea and Galilee, the desert borders of Syria; in his time in Tarsus and Antioch he was apprenticed to a faithful Jew—he has never entered even a humble home of a Stranger. He knows little of Greek worship and of Roman splendour.

'Are we free to go?'

At Saul's question, Timothy finally turns towards him, stretches out his hand to him. But Saul winces, seeing how the boy's other hand still clasps that of Thomas. It is forbidden for him to extend such friendship to the outcast.

Saul has spoken in Syrian, to include Gabriel, but Timothy, aware of the guards, answers in Greek.

'Yes, you are free to leave Israel. The brethren at Rufus's house await us, we have prepared a thanksgiving.' He nods towards Gabriel. 'Your nephew has vouched security for your release. We are committed to take you to Rome—you will stand trial there.'

Again, he glances at the guard. 'Governor Felix has been kind, as has his wife, Drusilla. He will not return you to Jerusalem. He cannot release you from the charge of sedition, but he agrees that no fair trial is possible here in Judea. He has agreed that you will be allowed to petition the First Amongst Men himself.'

Timothy's happiness seems infinite. 'We will travel together, brothers, we will go to Rome. We have arranged passage on a ship that leaves tomorrow. Beloved, you are taking the words of the Lord and of the Saviour to Rome.'

Only then does he speak in their language. 'As it was written and as it was foretold. Let them who have ears hear.' And then he almost bellows, 'Brothers, we are going to Rome!'

Thomas releases Timothy's hand. 'I'm not coming with you.'

Gratitude floods Saul's heart.

But his Timos is distressed, uncomprehending. 'You have to.'

Thomas, ignoring Timothy, addresses Gabriel. 'Am I to stand trial?'

'No,' says Gabriel, shaking his head. 'You are free to roam.' He hesitates, as if afraid to say his next words. 'But you can't stay in Judea. You are not safe even in Galilee. If you stay, you are a condemned man. They've declared you apostate. The governor can do nothing about that.' Gabriel's voice hardens and becomes stern. 'We sin for even having communication with you, sir. You are no longer of Israel.'

Thomas nods soberly at this censure. He forces a smile and turns to the distraught Timothy. 'You see, lad, I'm not welcome on your travels.'

And pretending enthusiasm, Thomas waves his hand around the chamber, indicating the day and the city and the world beyond the entrance. 'Leave me. I have a promise to fulfil for the highborn lady, Drusilla. This, my Timos, must be our farewell.'

'No!' Timothy has fallen on Thomas, is clutching the man's arms, his tunic, is beating his fists against the man's chest. 'No,' he repeats, and then gulping for air he pleads, 'or I am coming with you.'

Saul notices the leer on the guard's face, the Stranger's pleasure in witnessing this dishonourable abandonment. And it is shameful. Timothy's childish distress, his unmanly craving. This is not love. This is perversion.

This is the evil that doubt creates. It contaminates anyone who comes in contact with it; it is a tincture that floods and spreads from body to body, from soul to soul. *You have poisoned the lad.* But Saul cannot open his mouth, he cannot release those words. To release them is to concede. He closes his eyes. He will not faint, he will not stumble. He calls on the light. And the light comes but not with warmth this time; it comes in cold and severe conviction. His love of the Lord is greater than any love for man.

Saul opens his eyes.

Thomas's hands have gripped the younger man's shoulders, he is shaking him, his eyes narrow and his mouth clenched. 'I don't want you with me. I don't want to be reminded of what we have become, of how we have spurned and polluted my twin's example. You are weak, Timothy, you make me sick with your weakness.'

The younger man cannot hear, or refuses to hear. He is still struggling to be with Thomas, as if by force or will or magic they might conjoin in flesh and become one. He will not let go.

'Friend, friend,' cries Timothy, 'I am yours. Whatever you believe, I believe—whatever you are, I am.'

Thomas's hands push against the writhing, desperate boy, they reach for Timothy's shoulders. Saul wonders in terror if he will break the boy's neck.

Their mouths are almost touching.

'Your lord is not my Lord. Your god is not my God.'

Thomas releases one hand and his extended finger takes in the four corners of the room. 'The god that sits in the Temple is as false as the gods on these walls. He is not the Lord.'

The guard has been pulling at Timothy, to prise him from the old man. But there is now no need. Thomas's words are as sudden and final as the thrust of a sharpened sword into flesh. That blasphemy is truly the silence that will be found at the end of the world: the staggering utterance has separated Thomas from Timothy, from Saul, from Gabriel, from Galilee, from Israel. From his twin, from the Saviour.

He has called death upon himself, Saul marvels, he has cleaved himself from the very Lord. He is humbled and shaken by the glorious sacrifice. To allow Timothy to live, Thomas has forfeited eternity.

Gabriel, his face raging with disgust and loathing, turns to his uncle. 'We must go. Now. If I remain here any longer, I will kill this animal.'

Timothy is ashen, his lips moving but making no sound, his body shuddering, collapsing. Gently, Saul takes his beloved and gives him over to the care of his nephew. 'Take him,' he says. 'I will follow.'

The two old men watch Gabriel escort the almost benumbed Timothy out of the chamber.

Saul knows that he must not and that he cannot, but he places his arms around Thomas and brings him close to him. Their mouths touch.

'Thank you,' he whispers.

Thomas's laugh booms. But his eyes are wet and hold no light. 'Take care of him.' And then, his voice breaking, 'I love him. He's the only son I've ever known. But I can't bring him into my exile.'

His fingers playfully squeeze Saul's chin; and again Saul senses the hale force of the man, how he is of the earth. And he will return to dirt and dust, like all men who will not reawaken to the kingdom.

'He doesn't have your strength,' Thomas says, and then adds, 'Do not betray him to zealotry, promise me that.'

This Saul can do. 'I promise you that. I will counsel restraint.'

'Good. Be as my brother instructed.' And he laughs. Abrupt and curtailed. 'Be as a passer-by.' Thomas releases Saul.

I was wrong, thinks Saul, this is not death I see on him; it is the likeness of our Saviour.

Thomas shrugs, as if finally free to reveal his exhaustion. 'But you can't do that, can you, brother?' he says. 'You need to change the world.'

And with another shrug. 'Go, man, take your leave from this wretched sinner—go preach your fine bookish words to the world. The world's your home now.'

And now his smile is mischievous, and his smile is a dance. 'Let those who have ears hear.'

Saul has just stepped into the antechamber when he hears Thomas shout and looks back at him.

The man is standing in the middle of the glittering chamber, his hands clasped together as if in prayer. He calls out, 'And I forgive *you*, brother.'

———

Saul's arms rest on the salt-encrusted deck rail. The lacquered wood still hints of the forest that gave birth to it. But the tantalising promise of that scent is overcome by the stench of the ocean weeds knocking gently against the dock and lapping against the hull of the ship, and the smell of brine, and the sharp rankness of gutted and scaled fish. Cats slink along the pier to the very edge of the docks, scavenging and fighting for scraps of fish gut.

Across the length of the port, altars to the Strangers' gods have been lit, the incense barely discernible above the calamity of odours. Only the wisps of smoke spiralling to the false heavens indicate the presence of the altars. Sailors and their kin are the most devout of the false worshippers—Saul has always found it so, from the very beginnings of his travels amongst the Strangers. That is because death is promised in every tempest and by the invisible mountains beneath the seas. He will pray as well, of course he will, but to the living Lord, the Lord who has no need for incense and statues, a Lord who has abjured even sacrifices. The Lord has sacrificed His son. The old world is done for.

Saul can see the myriad forms of the gods along the port, on the prows of the ships and on the steps to the temples and forming the very columns that support the houses of worship. He believes he can see beyond; shielding his eyes from the still rising sun: there lies Egypt, Phoenicia, Judea and Syria; there begins Arabia and Persia. Generations of ruined temples and generations of statues disappearing under the earth.

The ship sways as the waves push it against the dock. But Saul has become master of the journey over time, on land and by sea, and his stride is assured as he walks over and leans across the railing on the starboard side. Facing west now, there is only the open sea. The men are still loading the ship and Saul is growing impatient, eager for his travels to begin.

His Timos is below deck. The poor lad has never got used to voyaging by sea. So he retreats below, alone with his tightly woven basket; if he is to be ill, only the Lord will be witness.

Gabriel is not with them. The lad has a wife and children, and a mother to care for in Jerusalem. These bonds, made to the Lord, cannot be unmade and Saul would never insist he do so. He gave his nephew a thousand kisses and set him on his way. Even though that was surely their final parting, for none of them know what Rome will bring, Saul's heart is glad. On the final evening, in the modest home of the freedman Rufus, his wife Clemency, his daughter, and two slaves of their acquaintance—the only brethren of their fellowship in Caesarea—Gabriel partook of their feast of love and even drank their wine and ate their bread. Saul, exultant, wanted to take him that very night and immerse him in the creek that feeds the Roman aqueducts. 'No,' the younger man had replied, 'I will be baptised when I return to Jerusalem.'

Jealousy flares and pricks at Saul. What a joy it would have been to bring Gabriel to the Saviour rather than that pompous untaught James. Saul quells the thought and acknowledges his pride. James is their brother, all are equal as brothers in their fellowship, and what matters is that Gabriel will be there in the kingdom to come.

If he is indeed baptised. Saul thinks about his sister, his brothers, and how they will rant against such a commitment. It is possible the lad won't have the strength to overcome such opposition. For they are his family and the bonds that tie Gabriel are those of blood and flesh. The sea breeze whips at his face and Saul wonders anew at his terrifying faith. That is what the coming of the Saviour has inaugurated: the almost intolerable rupture that is the forsaking of blood. Can he remember himself as a young man? Can he recall that man possessed by the sins of lust and greed? How could he have wed his poisonous body to another, to a wife, or to the children they would have brought into the world? The yearnings of his flesh were like a disease: he would have infected all. But his affliction was scoured and overcome by the outpouring of light brought by his Saviour.

'Let him be baptised,' Saul mouths to the open sea, 'so that I can see Gabriel again.'

The light has not abandoned him, even at this great age. It has vanquished flesh, and it has conquered doubt.

And now he doesn't see the lapping water or the endless sky. He is returned to the gilded chamber of Governor Felix, he is returned to Thomas. How can the world be both evil and the kingdom to come? But as age sloughs off temptation and wickedness, it also sheds animosity and hatred. A delight twitches and blossoms deep within Saul. Dare he pray, ask from the Lord through the intercession of the Saviour, that the Twin be forgiven? He wishes that it could be possible—that in the coming kingdom, Thomas will be there. To see his beloved Timos fall once more into the older man's arms and for them to find completeness together in eternity. Could it be that jealousy, that most ancient and deeply buried of Saul's sins, has been vanquished?

I forgive you, brother. They were Thomas's final words.

Forgiving me for my jealousy, for my pride, for my spite. For my doubt and for my failings. For my deceit and for my hypocrisy. Thomas has forgiven him but will the Lord do so? Saul laughs at his own vanity—yet one more sin to be forgiven.

The sea wind on his face; and he knows the question is unanswerable. The light, the Spirit, is too vast to be contained within one soul; it belongs to the Lord and it is foolish to think that a man can fully comprehend it. Saul doesn't know whether Thomas will be there with him in the life to come any more than he knows if his Timos will be there. Or Gabriel. Or the loyal Lydia, the first Stranger he brought to Israel. Or Peter or James or the Magdalena or even himself.

They all grasp for the light, trying to snatch parts of it, to hold it in their hands; but the light is as water, it runs through their fingers—but unlike water, it doesn't drain and vanish, it grows and amplifies: it is all around but can never be grasped. It is everywhere.

He does not know. Knowing is not what matters. We are mortal and we will fail. In our pettiness and in our vanity. In our temptation and in our sinning. And in our hatred and our misbegotten righteousness. We will fail and hope to be forgiven. We cup our hands and catch the available light.

Saul's eyes flash open. The anchor cranks and the captain calls the last of his men on board. The sea is calm and of such blue that it meets and becomes the open sky. The journey is beginning and this is the moment of the greatest thrill. What is ahead is not known but that is of no importance.

He stretches out his hands, his damaged and callused hands, and with his palms open he collects the light. The light of the sun and the light of the sky and the light of the sea. He does not know but he welcomes all that is to come. All that is good and all that is grace passes through his hands and slips through his fingers. No matter. He has held it once and he will hold it again. Light, not blood; light, not flesh; light, not the earth: that is all that matters.

The ship is setting sail and Saul calls out to the void, which has been made whole with light. The sailors around him are also offering their prayers. His is loudest for his is true.

Author's note

I first encountered the writing of Saul of Tarsus, better known by his Greek name, Paul, when I was an adolescent. At that time, I was estranged by the famous strictures against homosexuality in Paul's first letter to the Corinthians. I could not reconcile my Christian faith with the imperative to honour my own sexuality and independence, and so I became a non-believer. It was only in my late twenties that I returned to his letters during a period of personal confusion and despair, and this time I found solace, compassion and understanding in his words. It might well be that the seeds of this novel were planted back then. Since that time I have wrestled with Paul, wanting both to honour the great universal truths that I find compelling in his interpretation of Jesus's words and life, but also to question the oppression and hypocrisy of the Churches that claim to be founded on these very same words. Who was Paul? And is it possible to reconcile what is revelatory and crucial in Christian ethics with the fraught history of Christianity itself? That questioning is what led me to writing this book. I wanted to comprehend this man, who took the teachings of the Jewish prophet, Jesus of Nazareth, and proclaimed that they had meaning for the whole world.

It has been five years since I began work on *Damascus*, and in that time Paul has dominated my dreams, my imagination, my curiosity and, yes, my doubt. As always with a novel, the point of departure—*who was Paul?*—altered and shifted as I undertook my research, and then my writing. I had, of course, returned to the canonical gospels of the New Testament but my readings also took me, for the first time, to the apocryphal writings that had been excised from the canonical Bibles. Of central importance was my exploration of the collection of early Christian and Gnostic writings that were discovered in 1945, near Nag Hammadi in Upper Egypt. In particular, I was startled to read the Gospel of Thomas. This gospel is a collection of the sayings of Jesus, and though an exact historical dating of the text is impossible, it is clearly a very early Christian work, possibly contemporary to the Gospel of John. In Orthodoxy, Catholicism and Protestantism, our main knowledge of the apostle Thomas is that he was famously the one who doubted Jesus's resurrection. What is astonishing in the Gospel is that there is no reference to Jesus's crucifixion and resurrection. The Nag Hammadi texts reveal that there were myriad currents to early Christianity, including an understanding of Jesus as a prophet rather than an incarnation of the godhead itself.

There were many false starts and much confusion as I struggled with the early drafts of this novel. It seemed that

I wanted to do the impossible: to be faithful to both Paul and Thomas. In Aramaic, Thomas means the Twin, and there is an apocryphal legend that Thomas was indeed the twin brother of Jesus. (If the fact that Jesus had a sibling strikes a reader as disturbing or bizarre, I would direct that reader to the New Testament itself, to where the Book of Acts refers to Jesus's brothers and sisters and, in particular, to his brother James, who became the head of the Jerusalem sect after the death on the cross of his brother.)

There is no way of writing the story of Paul without coming to a reckoning with the man that Paul and Thomas both loved and followed, Jesus of Nazareth. And even though I am no longer a believer in the Christian myths, I discovered I am still committed to and challenged by the injunctions of this prophet. To love one's neighbour, to turn the other cheek, and to understand that none of us have the right to throw the first stone all remain fundamental to my beliefs. When I appreciated this, I knew how to shape the novel. Whatever the difference between Paul and Thomas, I believe that they too were moved and challenged and changed by these instructions.

As he declares in his letters, Paul was born a proud and observant Jew. He came to believe in the miracle of Jesus's resurrection after an encounter with the reawakened Saviour on the road to Damascus. He was convinced that he was chosen by the Lord to bring all of the nations of humanity to God. He made it his work to travel the Greek-speaking Roman Empire, and to bring the God of Israel to the Strangers.

I have used that term—*Strangers*—to identify all those he encountered who were not Jewish. In the Book of Acts we are told that one of the first Strangers he brought to Israel was a Greek woman called Lydia. She too has become a character in this novel. We can never be sure of how Paul died, or even where he died, but I have created a character, Vrasas, a proud pagan Roman and former soldier, who I have made Paul's gaoler while he is under house-arrest in the Eternal City. If indeed Paul did end up in Rome, as is suggested in the New Testament, it is highly probable that he was murdered in the catastrophic riots against Jews and Christians that erupted during the reign of Emperor Nero.

The character of Able is based on references in Paul's letter to Philemon, part of the canonical New Testament. Paul writes of Onesimus, a runaway slave who belonged to Philemon. The Greek name translates as Beneficial, or Able, and that is the name I have given him in *Damascus*.

If Judea had not fallen to Roman occupation and siege, if the temple in Jerusalem had not been destroyed, it is possible that Christians would have remained a forgotten Jewish sect. Such speculation is tantalising for an historian, but as a storyteller what I want to convey is the catastrophic consequences of that war and occupation on the refugees who survived the annihilation of their homelands. The penultimate part of the book takes place a couple of decades after Paul's death, and is narrated by Timothy, who was his companion, his friend, his amanuensis. In orthodox Christianity, Timothy is also a saint. I wanted to imagine Timothy as a man, as someone whose faith is the only bedrock he has in a world that has collapsed and which he believes is about to face destruction.

If it is tantalising to wonder what would have happened to Christianity if Jerusalem had not fallen, it is equally tempting to consider what Christianity would be if so many of the Gnostic texts unearthed at Nag Hammadi had been incorporated into the New Testament. It is the allure of this imaginative speculation that makes Thomas an increasingly prominent character in this novel. Yet if the non-believer in me is sympathetic to the notion of understanding Jesus as only human, I also know that it is Paul's powerful conviction that Jesus did indeed reawaken to life on the third day that offered the sweet promise of eternal life for all of us. If, in a secular age, we might scoff at such an understanding, we must also acknowledge how it was a promise that gave hope to the most destitute and despised in an often cruel and unforgiving world. The Gospel of Thomas counsels that we be as passers-by in the world. Paul's letters contain the seeds of revolution. The last few centuries have shown us that it is not only the religious who wish to found Heaven on earth. I hear Paul's whisper in every contemporary ideology that wishes to change the world. And I hear Thomas's echo in every dissident who doubts that the ends justify the means.

I began this work with a hunger to understand Paul, and that initial impulse has never left me. I am grateful that his mission gave us the great insights into justice and compassion that were forged over millennia by the prophets of Judaism. That is one of the great blessings that this ancient and still living religion has bequeathed to us. And I am so very grateful that his travels and teachings—and most importantly his letters—made it possible that the sublime and deeply humane teachings of the Jewish prophet, Jesus, were also offered to the world. I don't think that it is fair that Paul is blamed for the subsequent corruption of these teachings. I wanted to forget two thousand years of history in my struggle to understand Paul. I wanted to be guided by the solace, compassion and understanding that I found there when I returned to his letters. Of course history can't be forgotten and its ghosts have also made their way into this novel. But I am not wrestling with Paul any longer. I am walking beside him. With gratitude.

Acknowledgements

It is Paul's letters, which form a major component of the Christian New Testament, that have been that have steered me in writing this novel. It is through these letters that we can hear his voice. But I have also been guided by excellent works of scholarship that I read while researching the story of *Damascus*. Diarmaid MacCulluch's *A History of Christianity: The First 3000 Years* was pivotal in making me better understand the rich ferment of ideas and arguments that were being debated in the genesis of the early Church. Erudite and beautifully written, MacCulluch's is a magnificent book, and a wonderful introduction to Christian history.

There are many books about St Paul. One that inspired me greatly is *Paul: The Mind of the Apostle* by A.N. Wilson. I owe a debt to Wilson for bringing me closer to the flesh and blood Paul. I also highly recommend Karen Armstrong's *The First Christian: St. Paul's Impact on Christianity*. As in all her work, Armstrong offers great insights into both theology and history.

Elaine Pagel's *Beyond Belief: The Secret Gospel of Thomas* was instructive in making me understand the importance of this lost gospel. Pagel's *The Gnostic Gospels* is an excellent introduction to the apocryphal texts, and to the early Gnostic tradition in Christianity. I am also indebted to the insights gleaned from reading the historian E.P. Sanders, in particular *The Historical Figure of Jesus*. Martin Goodman's *Rome and Jerusalem: The Clash of Ancient Civilizations* brought the first century AD to vivid life. James Davidson's *The Greeks and Greek Love* was a highly entertaining but also immensely useful study of attitudes to sex and love in antiquity. Luke Timothy Johnson's *Among the Gentiles: Greco-Roman Religion and Christianity* and Timothy Michael Law's *When God Spoke Greek: The Septuagint and the Making of the Christian Bible* were also bracing reads on the relationships between pagans, Jews and early Christians in the ancient Mediterranean world.

Dale B. Martin's Yale University podcast, *An Introduction to New Testament History and Literature* was of terrific assistance in guiding me through the scholarship of the early Church.

I first read John Boswell's *Christianity, Social Tolerance, and Homosexuality* when it was published in the early 1980s. I returned to it in writing *Damascus* and I was reminded of the power of Boswell's compassion, and the breadth of his understanding of Christian ethics.

I am also deeply appreciative of historians in Rome, Athens, Ephesus and Jerusalem who were so sympathetic to my questions and enquiries.

My partner, Wayne van der Stelt, drew the map for *Damascus*. His patience and faith and love have also steered this novel. My friend, Catherine Woodfield, has provided succour and challenge in thinking about Christianity for decades now. Jane Palfreyman is my publisher and editor. Without her guidance and her questioning, and without her meticulous editing, this novel would not have been possible. I am so very lucky to be published by her and even luckier to be her friend. I want to thank Ali Lavau for her editorial wisdom and diligence, and to thank Christa Munns for her good humour and her editorial care and patience. Thank you indeed to everyone at Allen & Unwin for their support. I have also been fortunate in having Fiona Inglis, Angela Savage, Jane Gleeson-White and Chris Brophy read drafts of this work. Their comments and criticisms made me work harder, and for that I am deeply appreciative.

If it wasn't for Malcolm Knox's generous encouragement, I might have given up wrestling with St Paul. You pushed me, mate, you saw this was a novel even before I did, and though I take complete responsibility for the world and the words of *Damascus*, without you being in my corner, I wouldn't have had the courage to keep going. This is why it is dedicated to you: in deepest gratitude.

Christos Tsiolkas
July 2019